THIS RED EARTH

ALSO BY KIM KELLY

Black Diamonds
The Blue Mile
Paper Daisies
Wild Chicory
Jewel Sea

'colourful, evocative and energetic' – *Sydney Morning Herald*

'impressive research' – *Daily Telegraph*

'Why can't more people write like this?' – *Canberra Times*

KIM KELLY

THIS RED EARTH

First published 2013 by Pan Macmillan Australia
This edition published by Jazz Monkey Publications

Copyright © Kim Kelly 2013

The moral right of the author has been asserted.

All rights reserved. No part of this publication may be reproduced, stored in a retrieval system, or transmitted in any form or by any means, electronic, mechanical, photocopying, recording or otherwise without the prior permission of the author.

The characters in this book are fictitious and any resemblance to real persons, living or dead, is purely coincidental.

A CIP record for this book is available at the National Library of Australia.

Design: Alissa Dinallo
Cover image: Central West landscape, Kim Kelly; birds, Shutterstock
Author photograph: Dean Brownlee
Printing: IngramSpark

Publishing services provided by Critical Mass
www.critmassconsulting.com

For my parents

An opal-hearted country,
A wilful, lavish land –
Ah, you who have not loved her
You cannot understand …

Dorothea Mackellar, 'Core of My Heart', 1908

No doubt it suits them very well
To say it's worse than Hay or Hell,
But don't you heed their talk at all;
Of course there's heat – no one denies –
And sand and dust and stacks of flies,
And rabbits too, at Booligal.

AB Paterson, 'Hay and Hell and Booligal', 1896

Out West, where the stars are brightest,
Where the scorching north wind blows,
And the bones of the dead seem whitest,
And the sun on a desert glows –
Out back in the hungry distance
That brave hearts dare in vain –
Where beggars tramp for existence –
There lies the Great Grey Plain.

Henry Lawson, 'The Great Grey Plain', 1896

ONE

NOVEMBER 1939 – JANUARY 1940

BERNIE

I'm squinting out at the surf, out to the white spray shooting up off Wedding Cake Island, not looking at the Rock beside me, lying face-down on the sand, his shoulder so close by my hip I can almost feel him there anyway. See without looking the colour he's got to him, like the red earth after rain, promising … nothing I've ever seen. I've never been further west than Parramatta, on a school excursion I don't remember, don't know a thing about the wide brown land except for what you read in a six-penny romance, and he's going back out there tomorrow, home to Nyngan, going shearing, just as he did last year, and the year before that, and the year before that.

Shearin' – the way he drops his g's you wouldn't know he's just finished his final exams at the University of Sydney, that he's going to be a geologist. This is why I call him Rock. Rock Boy. You only get more than ten words out of him at a time if he's talking about rocks, Gordon Brock, who lives above the rocks of Gordon Bay, which I found funny when he started boarding next door with Mrs Zoc, almost four years ago now, and he looked like a boy, so skinny, such a long piece of string, he looked like the next southerly would blow him back over the ranges.

He's filled out a bit this year. Shearer's shoulders, like his father, my dad says, and he'd know. Our dads know each other, from the army, not that I've ever met Mr Brock. And not that Dad ever says more than ten words at a time about it, but while he reckons he had what he calls a 'good war' for himself, one where he got home in one piece to become a qualified mechanic, set up shop, get married and build a nice little Californian bungalow up from this beach – things he never would've been able to do if he'd stayed a bushie in Gilgandra – Mr Brock didn't have such a good war. He got invalided home at the start, from Gallipoli, then got a soldier's settlement on the edge of the desert that turned to dust with drought in time for the depression to put him in debt to the bank for nothing forever, and that was after his wife died, leaving him to raise Gordon on his own. *Bleeding misery,* Dad says, of both the circumstances and the man. But he would never say such a thing to Rock's face. *A fine job that father of yours did with you, son,* Dad tells Rock often and with conviction. *A degree from the university,* Dad says, shaking his head with the miracle of it, as they tinker over the rusty old Triumph motorcycle Dad's let Rock sort of adopt as his own. *Keep out of this war now, son,* Dad tells him too, *There's better things around the corner for you,* having sort of adopted him. He doesn't have a boy of his own; only me.

Me and Rock.

Rock and me.

Stop going on and on about it, Bernie. Rock this, Rock that and what he had for breakfast. Stop it.

Can't.

Dad loves him. Rock got his call-up letter on Wednesday, for this compulsory national service thing that's been brought in for everyone's twenty-first birthday, and Dad put it straight in the incinerator. *You've got essential national service to be getting on with in the woolsheds, son, and you can do it with clear conscience. Where was this Menzies in the last fight, eh? All mouth and no trousers, that one.* Dad doesn't think much of this new prime minister, or anyone that didn't serve, and he's not alone. *WHERE'S OUR SPIRIT OF EMPIRE?* is the question hanging outside the newsagent up at the Spot, looking right at the repat hospital across the road, and someone has stuck a note behind the wire answering, *Lost in Flanders.* But Dad needn't worry, not for Rock: he's safe. Shearers aren't allowed to enlist, essential industry, and at any rate he'll soon enough be getting a letter to trump the call-up one.

He's applied for a field position with the Geological Survey, and the recommendation he's got from his professor says he's already got the job. A government job; the army will leave him alone then. And the government will send him straight back out bush, looking for essential rocks. In his element. One day he'll find a rock that no one's ever found before, they'll call it Brockite, and it will change the world, cure the common cold, win him a Nobel Prize …

That makes me stare with some more determination past Wedding Cake Island. I don't know what's round the corner for me, but it's not Rock, not any boy. It's … What do I want if it's not Rock?

Certainly not my job in Chalmers department store. Personal assistant to the advertising manager sounds glamorous, but beyond the three T's – tea, telephone and telepathy – my job is practically only to make Mr Heany's catalogue copy a little less of a hideosity without him noticing, to make sympathetic noises when the illustrators call to complain about his rudeness and, come summer, to be swimsuit ring-in for mannequin parades, on account of my pins, which I agree to do mostly just to horrify Mum. I want to go somewhere beyond this, here, Coogee, a million lazy bathing Sundays and otherwise spending my time thinking up ways for Mr Heany to make the women of New South Wales desperate to want more and more things they don't really need.

I want things myself, all right – I want to see things, learn things. I want to *do* things. I want a purpose. I want a career. Awful as the thought is vague, maybe this war might let me find one. Maybe the world is going to change this time; people are fed up with history repeating like greasy pork chops, fed up with Alexander the Krauts going mad for a conquest of Europe and being asked to offer up their sons for it while at the same time being told that on-the-knee hemlines are the greater scandal. Maybe there's something for me in all this. An opportunity of some kind. Something beyond the girl next door marrying the golden-haired boy. Something coming round the corner I can't even imagine yet. Maybe. Maybe I just want to get to the end of maybe and *know*. Know I had a go. At … who knows? I'll be twenty-one myself next September, officially on the shelf, and *maybe* by then the army will be desperate enough to want *me*.

The laugh that bursts out of me startles a gull into the air and Rock says into his towel: 'Share the joke?'

I glance away north towards the flags, the beach filling up. 'I was just wondering, do you reckon Mr Menzies would give me a rifle?'

'No.' He snorts. 'He's not that stupid.'

'You're right – if armed, I might quickly become a public menace.' Or go AWL right now from the pitch of your voice alone: not high, not low, just perfect, just Rock. Just stop it, Bernie; and keep things light, keep the jokes coming. 'The government'll probably ban retail for the war effort next and put me out of a job altogether.'

'Now that *could* be a risky move,' he laughs, muffled, into his armpit. Don't look at him.

'Is that so?' I ask the ocean. 'I'd be a risk without a job to go to at all?' What's that supposed to mean? I'm not even worth marrying? Not worth the risk?

'Not you,' he laughs some more. 'I mean … banning retail … could make the Japs a menace to the public. Probably quickly.'

'Oh.' That takes my breath away. The *way* he speaks. His bits of sentences strung together with long-distance pauses as vast as his brain. He means of course that banning retail would prevent the Japs from continuing to sell us vast quantities of cheap imitation rubbish, which might then be excuse enough for the Yellow Peril to invade – turn all that iron ore we've sold them into bullets and bombs. I could reply with the expected quip about Mr Menzies here, otherwise known as Pig Iron Bob for selling this precious ore to the Japs in the first place, but I can't. My breath remains taken, and inside the crashing of the surf I am remembering the first time Gordon Brock took it.

It was at the end of last summer, he'd just come back from Nyngan and he was standing inside the scoop of honeycombed sandstone under Bare Island, out at La Perouse; we'd gone fishing, caught nothing; it was raining and blowing a gale, and I'd been blithering on about if or when another war was coming and whether or not politicians took a special oath not to talk straight about anything, when he told me that the only truth worth knowing is in the earth, if only rocks could speak. He ran his hand over the swirling caramels of the rock above his head and said: *Truth is like gold, not got by its growth, but by washing away from it all that isn't gold. Tolstoy said that – well, according to* Scientific Mind *monthly, he did.* I wouldn't know Tolstoy if I fell over him in the street, but I could have fallen for Rock then. His smile: hopeful, truthful. Wonderful. I could have kissed him then. But I didn't. I got him talking about iron ore instead – he was about to start writing a paper on some type of the stuff for his final year. Paper that has got him the job on the survey, that will take him away from me soon enough anyway. Just let that happen, gently.

I let myself look at him now, and breathe out as I tell the vast expanse of his back: 'I'm going to miss you.' That catches in my throat, because it's true.

He rolls onto his side and opens his eyes. His eyes are grey, cool but warm, a fine overcast, promising … perfect weather for anything. His hair streaked with caramel sunshine, needs clipping.

He says: 'Want to go fishing this arvo?'

No. Never mind gentle. I start lying for all I'm worth. 'No, better not.' I can't tell him the truth: that I can't go fishing with you because I don't want to kiss you, because if I do, that'll be the end of me. I'll disappear. Fall into the department-store catalogue of marriage, children, and worrying over whether the spuds will crisp while waiting for the postman to bring the next catalogue. Look away. Never mind the kiss. If I hop on the back of the bike with Rock this afternoon, soon as I put my arms around his waist, I'll have rendered myself unemployable for everything except being his wife. And at the very least I will then get the sack from Chalmers, that's an irrefutable law, and I will have no shelf to speak of at all.

So I tell him the worst lie I can think of: 'I've got a date. The club social, at the Aquarium.'

To put him right off. He doesn't think much of the surf club crowd, not that he's ever outright critical of anyone – he just becomes absent whenever there's a bunch of posers about.

'Oh.' He gives out a sound that stops short of a sigh with a sharp frown. I may as well have punched him in the stomach. A look that makes me want to reply, *Well, you shouldn't have followed me down here this morning*, as if this is an unusual event. As if we didn't discover three summers ago that we share a liking for Sunday morning pre-crowd quiet, right here, at the south end, not too close to the club and not too far from the Niagara for an after-surf, pre-roast dinner sneaky tub of butterscotch whirl. His frown deepens with hurt, and now I want him to say: *No, Bernie, you'll be coming fishing with me.* I want him to declare it, put his foot down, so that I have no choice. So that I will say yes, and he will stop looking so terribly hurt, and, most importantly, I won't be responsible for what happens next.

Instead he says: 'I'll take off then.'

Throws his towel over those bronzed Chesty Bond shoulders and he's gone at a jog, up and into the changing sheds, into the shadows of the line of concrete blocks below the prom, and I'm thinking: Gordon Brock, you really are perfect in every conceivable way, except that you could sulk for Australia. Doesn't he know by now I wouldn't go to a club social if you paid me? Tonight's is for the start of the water polo comp too, opening match between Coogee and Bondi – you won't be able to move for all the swelled-up blockheads and doubtless there'll be a fight. For an enormously intelligent man, Gordon can be as thick as all that lot. Come back and call me out on the lie; come back and tell me I'm wrong to let you go. I keep staring at the sheds, wanting to see the shape of him, the way he walks, always going somewhere, always with a purpose. But the glare off the concrete blurs my vision and I don't see him come out.

By the time I start walking back home, via a long Rock-avoiding vanilla malt at the Niagara, I've tried and failed a hundred times to find the words to explain, apologise, tell him the truth, that maybe in a year, or five, or wherever. Maybe might end, I ... go around and around until I've infuriated myself. Then, all the way up the steps of Heartbreak Hill, which has never seemed so aptly named or formed, I wrestle with my envy of his certainty, his doing, his knowing, and my knowing that the distractions that go on and on inside his mind are doubtless certain ones, important ones, about minerals and metals and maths and all sorts of things important to other people, to industry, maybe even to humanity. What am

I important to? *Baaa*. I've almost worked myself into a steam of resentment enough to blame him for my not knowing, when I round the corner of our street and find Mrs Zoc at her gate next door, hankie in hand.

'Oh Bernadetta, what will I do without my good boy?' she's crying, as she does every time he goes back home. 'He did not even eat his dinner before he is gone.'

What? He's *gone* gone? He's not supposed to be gone until tomorrow. I look up the side path for the motorbike, where it's always leaning against the fence. Gone. Well, that's not just sulking for Australia, that's world championship sulking, isn't it. Incredible. And not: I once laughed at him for knowing what type of granite the pylons of the Harbour Bridge are made out of and he didn't speak to me for a fortnight.

I put my hand over Mrs Zoc's on the rail. 'You know he'll be back. And he'll come back skinny, and desperate for your spaghetti.' I could fall in a great heap myself right now. I look away, out to the ocean, over the cliffs of Gordon Bay. Oh, Rock. What have I done? The right thing. For me. This is good. Of course it is. This is what I wanted, so I can stop going on and on about it now, put my own mind to something more constructive.

Dad pops his head out from under the latest eyesore, the utility truck he's been working on, out on the street in front of the house. 'You two didn't have a falling-out, did you?'

But before I can lie about that, Mum's barrelling down the footpath from mass. 'Who's had a falling-out?'

Dad says, getting up off the ground: 'Gordon's just choofed, in a sudden hurry to be home.'

'Oh.' I might as well have hit Mum with a brick. Speechless: not a common state for her. I think the last time I saw her face like this was when Dad told her the lad coming up from Nyngan was Presbyterian, and for which Mum gave him immediate dispensation after the opening *Pleased to meet you, Mrs Cooper.* She drops a string bag full of cumquats on the footpath now; obviously she was going to make him his favourite marmalade to take, visited Mrs Cronin's tree especially on her way back from St Brigid's, and I won't be getting dispensation for a while.

The three of them stand there gawking at me, cumquats rolling into the gutter and disappearing down the stormwater drain. Dad's big brown eyes are round with disappointment, eyes that have seen more of the world than I will ever know.

I send myself to my room. If you want me, you can find me in the catalogue under D for dill. And you can all start saying it now: Gordon Brock, my one that got away.

GORDON

'Going far today?' the bloke at this Penrith servo asks me. He's screwing the cap back on my fuel tin, too slowly, wanting to chat.

'Nyngan,' I answer him, not wanting to chat.

'Nyngan? Where's that then?' He looks behind him at the mountains that divide Sydney from the rest of the country.

'Between Dubbo and Bourke,' I answer him, about three hundred and fifty miles away from this stretch of nowhere, if you'd let me keep on.

'That's a fair way.' He sleeves the sweat off his forehead and looks at the bike again, looking doubtful she'll make it. But she will. It's only a bit of rust on her. She's still a Ricky Triumph that goes seventy flat out, and at the moment the only woman making any sense to me. 'How long will that take you?' he asks.

'Should get there tomorrow. Evening.' Probably. Probably would be more sensible to have got the train, but I've been looking forward to this ride for weeks. Or I was. A cow complains, bored and lonely, from behind the workshop and, yeah, that's about the strength of it.

'Where you stopping tonight?' this servo bloke is asking me now.

He's getting annoying. Or making me more annoyed than I already am. But then I suppose I'd be wanting company too if I was stuck manning a servo in Penrith on a Sunday. I tell him: 'Bathurst, probably.'

'Camping out?' he asks, looking at my swag on the rack. Rack that Bernie should be sitting on, holding on to me, only the tackle box between us.

'Probably.' I have my hand in my pocket to pay him now but I'm not quick enough before he asks: 'Going out there for work?'

'Yeah.' To make some money to buy Bernadette Cooper a ring. I've calculated how many sheep it will cost me to get her the one I've just put a deposit on at Prouds. It's a Bingara diamond. It's got a speck of graphite right in the centre, like a pinhole view into the universe. Alternatively, I could turn around now and be back in Coogee in time to clout whoever is taking her to this club social. If that was the way I did things. And I don't. It's Bernie I'm angry at anyway. She knows how close I am to asking her; she must do. She's giving me the shove, isn't she. Either that or she's a flip, doesn't know what she wants, and either way, I should leave it alone. I only feel as I do because she looks like Merle Oberon. The only straight lines on her belong to her nose and her teeth, and you don't need science to explain the effect of that. I'm only stuck on the look of her. And that's worse bull than her going to a surf club social.

I've been stuck on her like phenolic adhesive since the day I first saw her. The tight waist of her suit. She'd just got her first pay from Chalmers, only sixteen and she'd bought her parents a bottle of champagne, and they invited Mrs Zoc and me round to share it. *Here's to our Bernie,* Mr Cooper raised his glass, and then he said to me out the side of his mouth: *Don't let on to her it tastes like –*

'Warm today, eh sport?'

'Yeah.' And it'll be a lot warmer in Nyngan. I will make up my mind what to do while I'm there. Four years I've waited to ask her; another couple of months won't kill me, will it.

*

I don't stop again till Blackheath, at the top of the mountains, and I haven't been sensible on the way up. It's only half-past two. Good that it's Sunday and the wallopers must still be at dinner. I consider begging a traveller's beer at the pub on the highway, but turn off to Govetts Leap instead, to the lookout over the Grose Valley.

It's the best view; the best place to see that these mountains are not mountains at all but a series of escarpments. A massive plateau cut through with gorges.

This view always settles something in me, making me feel small, but in a good way. This giant block of ocean floor forced up from the bottom of another world makes me and whatever's bothering me seem like just grains of nothing on a scale of time that's unimaginable. I close my eyes, smell the eucalyptus oil coming up off the forest below, let the noise of the cicadas get above the engine buzz in me. I stretch out the cramp in my knuckles from gripping the handlebars and I'm not thinking about anything.

Till I hear a woman laugh.

'Oh, hello,' she waves through the banksia scrub, dragging her man out from a trail behind her. She's missed doing up the second button on her dress, and the hem of her petticoat's hanging down. Honeymooners. Surprised to find they're not the only people on earth. I don't think I even manage to smile at them. It should be me and Bernie up here.

I want to turn around again, be with her now, and ask her, right now. Bugger waiting till I can afford the ring. Tell her: *Marry me, now*. Promise her: *I'm not going to keep you in a box in the suburbs afterwards*. Tell her: *Come on the survey with me, I'll show you the world*. But I can't do that. I'd look like a halfwit now. Tearing off the way I did. Man with the shits – if it was a form of energy, I'd have saved myself a few bob in fuel.

I go back up to the pub to cool down with a beer, and when the first taste hits my head, I realise I haven't eaten anything since breakfast, so I order a pie. One that tastes like wet gravel as I realise that I am a bloody halfwit altogether: come on the survey? As if Bernie would want to begin her married life living in a tent while I map out bauxite deposits across the long paddocks of the Northern Tablelands. Show her the world: the one from Gunnedah to Inverell. As if they'd let a girl come out on the survey at all. And as if I'll be anywhere but living in a tent while this war is on: it's suddenly important for the government to know what we've got, and New South Wales is a big place. War or not, I could be waltzing Matilda for years.

*

Back on the Great Western Highway, Victoria Pass is good for clearing my mind with the concentration it takes to negotiate it: a gradient that should probably be illegal if it wasn't so grouse flying down it. Then after that, the road through the hills towards Lithgow is easy, and it's a pretty ride. This is what I came for, and I do enjoy it. I enjoy it so much I keep on going past Bathurst. The road is smooth and new, on this Mitchell Highway. It was a dusty stock road the last time I was here, and now it's been surfaced all the way to Narromine. Amazing. Civilisation has always stopped at Bathurst, according to those east of the ranges that decide where public money will be spent, but this Mitchell Highway, it looks freshly painted on. Not a pothole in it, though that's probably because it hasn't rained since it was laid.

There is, however, a kangaroo standing in the middle of it, about a hundred yards ahead. Roos, they make sheep look smart. There's no reason for it to stop in the middle of the road like that. It's just stopped there because it has, and it will take off again because it does. You can't read a roo. Last year I was kicked in the chest by a male, a grey just like this one apparently not noticing the motorbike coming towards it right now. I was coming out of the sheds at Mullengudgery, knackered after the rams, and there it was, as if it had been waiting precisely to quilt me, for no reason. Unless it liked the sound of Dad's laughter. That was pretty good really. A rare enough thing, Dad's laugh, but I don't think I'd get one from him if I chose to start an argument with a roo here. It's heading on for dusk, when they get up and about from spending all day just as pointlessly sleeping, so I'd better slow down, find a place to stop, get off the road. The roo continues to ignore me as I veer round it, and it's tiredness that hits me now, with a sudden shot of thankfulness for every drop Dad's sweated to get me here. All these years. Even with the scholarships, it's taken everything he had to give, and I'm half a whisker from handing it back to him framed. It can't end here in a collision with a roo.

Not five minutes on, a gully appears off to the right, a stretch of willows and green weeds between the gold of the hills saying there's a creek down there, coming off the Macquarie, and probably the spot to camp. It is. It's a beautiful spot, and it would be yabbies for tea tonight if, in my hurry to get away this morning and show the world how angry I was, I hadn't forgotten to bring anything to catch yabbies with. No meat. Except the bedourie oven full of spaghetti and mince Mrs Zoc made me take, a small lorryload, but that won't do. You need a piece of meat that can be tied to the end of some string. But then I remember I do have some meat, of a sort, shoved in the bottom of my swag: the tin of sausages I've kept meaning to toss out because they are not food. I work quickly, setting three stick-and-string traps on the edge of the water and getting the fire going.

And then I wait. The sky turns piccaninny pink, not a cloud in it. Blue dragonflies are darting over the surface of the water, too quick for yabbies. I look behind me over the hills. With the sunset, they're glowing now as if they really are made of gold, and that would be beautiful too if this colour wasn't caused by this country not having had a drop of spring rain. The grass is paper dry. Who'd be a farmer? Not me. My father would have shot me himself if I'd ever got an inclination that way. Good then that a fascination with rocks has taken me a long way elsewhere. Dad wouldn't let on he was proud of that under torture – not too proud for anything, he picked peas one whole long summer to pay for my senior school blazer, only work he could get at the time – but he is proud, of me. I can't wait to see him.

Dad won't know what it means for me to have impressed the Surveyor General with that paper on haematite, proposing that there might be a lot more high-grade iron ore than the estimated two hundred and sixty megatons we think we have in the ground, that if in fact this ground of ours did once spend a considerable amount of eternity under a muddy puddle we might have an entire continent of haematite, enough to sell to the whole world – a mineral jackpot. Dad won't care that Professor Richardson thinks it's the most exciting undergraduate paper he's come across for years, that even if it's a bit wild of accepted wisdom, it's imagination that drives science, and that will secure me the Geology prize. *A given*, Professor Richardson said. *That's good,* Dad'll nod, and then he'll add a smile to the nod: proud.

It would be good if Bernie was impressed, even just a bit. She finds my fascination with rocks either funny or boring. She either laughs or says 'hm' a lot. I don't blame her. How many famous geologists can you name? How many would know that Mitchell, whose highway I've got here on, was a surveyor, and Govett too? Most people, if they have heard of Govett at all, think he was a bushranger who leapt off the waterfall at Blackheath after being cornered by troopers. The reason why most people think this is because it's written in the *Junior Australian History Reader* which we all learned by rote in first form. Even the Department of Education thinks surveyors are too boring. This continent rides on the sheep's back, not a bulldozer, and that is an actual fact. I can still hear Mr Farris, the Science master, asking me, for the last time: *Are you* sure *you don't want to apply for the School of Medicine, Brock?* Not for the first time I wonder if I should have. I'd be just as boring, but I'd be a doctor, wishing I'd gone into geology. Would she be more keen on me then?

What's she doing now? Down at the Aquarium, having a dance, roller-skating? Laughing, at some other bloke. She can't really have gone to this surf club social. Can she? No. Hang on, isn't it the start of the water polo at the Aquarium tonight? She wouldn't go to that: the girls who go around with the water polo – Ah, I see. She has lied, hasn't she. She just doesn't want me, that's what she's doing. Putting me off. Too bloody boring, and I can't change a thing about that.

Before I can get too far along this dismal line again, I catch sight of one of the yabby sticks twitching. I've got one on the string, a big one, about five inches long, and he thinks tinned sausage is pretty good stuff. I grab him fast behind the claws and throw him straight in the billy. And when I taste him, muddy and sweet, it tastes like home. I eat half the spaghetti then and have another yabby for pudding and I'm nearly asleep as darkness falls and I crawl into my swag, already dreaming of her. She's wiping her chin, beside me close to the fire, saying: *These yabbies would be good in a cheese sauce, don't you reckon, Rock?* Hm, I do reckon. I want to listen to her talk forever; she's never got a wireless voice on, always just herself. Natural. She smiles, and that seems more like home than anything.

*

I've been walking for miles, days or weeks. Or years my legs are that sore. But I've found a sapphire, a huge fist-sized sapphire, and we're both holding it, between us. Her thick dark hair touches my neck and she's kissing me. Finally. The fact that she is kissing me is a lot more exciting than the sapphire. But she pulls away, holds it up to the light, like a hunk of frozen sea, and she asks me: *What's this type of rock again, Rock?* I tell her, *It's a type of corundum.* She laughs: *Conundrum! That's right.* I want to pull her back, to kiss her again, but instead, I say: *No, corundum – the crystalline form of aluminium oxide.*

I try to force myself to wake up, so I can't spoil it further with an explanation of corundum's atomic structural similarities to haematite. A whipbird is calling it dawn, so I should wake up anyway. But she's kissing my neck now, and now she's kissing my face. I don't want to wake up ever. But I become aware of an odd smell, which doesn't smell like her White Lilac scent, not at all.

I open one eye, and see it's a dog.

A red kelpie bitch standing over me. Wagging her tail. Her slobber on my left ear.

She's pretty keen for something. I open both eyes, get up on my elbows, and she jumps away, over to the bike, pushing her snout against the pannier with last night's leftovers in it, pawing at the buckle of the strap. She's a working dog, fallen on hard times, or maybe lost. She's also pregnant. Sorry Mrs Zoc, I'm going to have to sacrifice the spaghetti. This poor girl is so hungry she just about licks a hole through the bottom of the bedourie when I give it to her. As I'm packing up I wonder if I could get her into town somehow, into Orange, if she'd sit on top of the swag on the rack, she obviously belongs to someone, but when I look to see where she is, she's taken off. I whistle for her a couple of times, but she doesn't come back. Nothing here but me and a fine streaky mist hanging over the creek. If it wasn't for the evidence, I'd wonder if that happened at all.

The evidence of the drought extends almost all the way to Orange, where some decent rain has fallen, I can see on the hills ahead.

I wouldn't have the nerve for farming, I know just looking at the land, someone half an hour up the road getting good rain while you got none. A small heap of freshly shot ewes stacked on the brown grass against a fence here outside Lucknow is a temporary memorial to the sentiment. The grazier'll have a good year next year, he'd be hoping, and there'll be guaranteed prices for even the mangiest fleece, for army uniforms across an empire, and he'll be shouting the bar. That's what they live on, hope over logic, the smallholders at least, with nothing to fall back on but the mercy of the bank, that has nothing to fall back on but the sale of the clip, and round it goes. Dad reckons the big droughts come in roughly fifteen to twenty year cycles and we're due another now, but he would say that: he lost his hope altogether in 1919, apart from me.

I cross the tracks into Orange, its main street lined with roses and shop windows full of wealth, Mount Canobolas rising up behind, rich with volcanic soil, and it's always odd to think that Dad passed up an offer of a settlement holding here. A decision he stands by. This town is all church spires and orchards and pansified squattocracy – not his country. Too easy. I go for breakfast at the Hotel Canobolas, the place as brand new as the bitumen outside, and the couple of old rough heads already at the bar tell you of the season, swaggies tramping through with the stone fruit harvest and whatever piece work they can get, drinking their pay as they go, heading south and away from the heat.

I'm heading northwest, lucky me, with a full engagement card, nine weeks on twenty-five shillings a hundred head, and probably for the last time. That's sort of sad to consider, sad as the reason wages are so good this year, until I consider the hundred and thirty pounds minimum I'm banking on, half of which I hope will go to Prouds. When she sees that ring, when she sees how much I think of her, surely … Yes. She'll have to say yes. I bolt my plate of sausage and egg the quicker to be into it.

Into the heat. As the sun rises higher the air gets hotter and drier and the engine becomes a small furnace between my knees. The hills disappear into the plains, past Wellington, past Dubbo, and as the bitumen disappears into the dirt there's only one thing on my mind: only ninety miles to go and it's not yet three o'clock – I'll be home for tea. The road is as straight as the land is flat here. But it does contain a few cracks you could lose a dog in after Trangie, so I slow down a bit. Enjoy the scenery, of my country.

There's been decent rain here too, I can see from the extent of the grasses, the saltbush and the bluebush. There's wildflowers along the verges as well, lots of them, these little purple ones with yellow centres. I don't know what they're called, but they are the happiest things to come across, purple against the red lateritic soil. The rusted roof of the Nevertire Hotel says only fifty miles to go, but I don't stop in to say hello. A way off a big mob is being driven across the highway. The dust they're kicking up looks like smoke in the heat haze, a wall of smoke against sky that's so blue it almost hurts. A pair of emus watch me buzz pass, curious. I wave to them.

I am happy as a boy. Riding into the sun.

BERNIE

'This is wrong.' Mr Heany stabs the stack of catalogue proof pages with a finger, bad smell under his nose. 'What is this *slinky and svelte for summer*, Miss Cooper? *Slinky* is not a Chalmers word. It is not a word at all.'

'Ah, slinky …' I cast my mind back through my shorthand notes for Lingerie, to these slips he'd been told to push beyond the Young Miss market, because we've got half a warehouse full of them, and remember his original *comfy and cool*. I don't think the mothers of this State want *comfy and cool* if they're going to spend 15/6 on cheap and nasty Jap satin rayon that will stop up the airholes in your perfolastic girdle and broil you before you've stepped out the front door. I tell him: 'Yes, I think I recall Foy's used something similar last month for theirs, the taffeta rayon, so you came up with "slinky" – which suggests comfy, in a graceful sort of way, and er, cool, too, like a cat.' I am so full of it.

'Oh yes, of course, that's right,' he smiles, not at me, but at his own evil genius, and when he smiles like that he looks like Bela Lugosi's Count Dracula. I want to add: *Yes, Master, soon, soon you will be Supreme Overlord of Department Stores and every Australian lady's housekeeping will be yours!* And just as I'm thinking that, an almighty clap of thunder shakes the whole building, southerly buster belting into Sydney, flickering lights and all.

I squeak out an, 'Excuse me please, Mr Heany,' and make a dash for the ladies' down the hall, lock myself in and exhale with my back to the door. I've been in this job nearly five months now and I hate it, hate it, hate it. Hate that I seem to be very good at doing things I don't like – pointless, useless things – and doing them very well. I should be grateful, it's such a good job, half the girls here would kill for any three T's position in the offices of the top floor, Monday to Friday only, perfect job to have while you're awaiting promotion to matrimony: no typing, can't even break a nail. It could be a foot in to working in advertising properly too. A career. If I wanted to do that. And I couldn't think of anything more shameful at the moment, other than announcing to Mum and Dad: 'I'm not ready for marriage right now because I'd like to try my hand at prostitution for a while.' Whoring against my own sex. If you don't buy this vanishing cream or have an agitating spin wringer, you're not a proper wife, mother, woman. And woe betide you let anyone see your *flabby, disfiguring fat* stuffed beneath that perfolastically *fragile, stem-like waist.* Giving you problems you don't have but that only a department store can fix, while no catalogue even acknowledges that you wear underpants – everyone else in the family does, except you. You wear thirty-seven different types of euphemism.

I step across to the sink and press my forehead to the coolness of the mirror above it, don't know where I fit in to the picture. But I do know I can't keep going on and on with this dithering, blithering whingeing that's threatening to overrun me. Be realistic: I'm an ordinary girl with no specific talents or ambitions. Apart from a demonstrated aptitude for advanced blarney, I have certificates in level one accounting and stenography, as well as a diploma in dressmaking abandoned halfway through because I lost interest in it. Maybe I should go back to business college to try for university matriculation, see what it's like, see what I might do, and I said as much in the face of Mum's ear-bashing over *poor Gordon* last night. *Matriculate!* she squawked. *What on earth for?* Perfectly valid question, to which I have no answer but *maybe* ... Dad wasn't interested in the discussion, if you could call it that; he was out of sorts all day, went to bed before 'Singapore Spy' at eight, and he never misses his serials of a Sunday after tea. Barely said goodnight. That's punishment; his disappointment is a ten-ton load, even if he is a little bit to blame for it, for thinking I'm God's gift. And who can blame him for that? Not even Mum does, for all her carry-on. Because, whatever it is I do, he knows too well that there's a lot worse things can be done to upset Hughie, on first name terms with God as he is.

It's also not a reason to get married, to make Dad happy, or to give Mum something to stick in the beaks of the Catholic Daily gossip-mongers. I wouldn't do that to Rock, much less to myself. Because … Because … Because I miss him already and he's only been gone a day. I run the tap and splash my face. Better get used to missing him, hadn't I. He's not going to last long on the Young Miss market, is he. Saying I'm not ready now is saying no for all time.

Fat raindrops are splattering the window next to the mirror, and I look down through them onto the chaos of Pitt Street, people running through the traffic, taken by surprise, umbrella-less. Tears taking me by surprise. Oh Hughie, what have I done?

'Bernie, you in there?' Tap, tap, tap on the door of the lav. It's Yoohoo, otherwise known as Edie Peterson. 'Yoohoo,' she chirps with another tap to make that clear. One of the chirpiest people I've ever met, but I don't want to open the door to her. She's twenty-seven, the oldest of us top-floorers, and the idea of possibly still being here when I'm twenty-seven makes me want to jump out the window. But she is also one of the loveliest sorts you'd ever meet, and as it possibly wouldn't be a bad idea for me to spill my beans to a sympathetic ear at this minute, I unlock the door and swing it back.

'Yes, I'm in here.'

'Oh dear,' she frowns to match mine. 'Cattle dog strife?' she asks, supposing I've had trouble with Mr Heany over the catalogue. I wave vaguely, not sure what strife to begin with. Then she throws a pair of bathers at me. 'This'll cheer you up.'

I hold them up by the shoulder straps. A white Jantzen, skirted. It's a lovely cut, and I am a little bit cheered. The Jantzens are always a lovely cossie, you could be built like a brick and look great in one. Twenty-five shillings and you get what you pay for: style and functionality wrapped in Lastex, *the miracle yarn*. It is too: *Nothing swims like Lastex.* No moral quandary about that claim. Maybe I could go and work for Jantzen, or Lastex … In America …

'Bernie?' I am aware that Yoohoo has been chirping away, no doubt about where and when I am to parade this – that's her job, organising the parades, and balls, dinners, bridge club, all the public events. It was she who spotted the form of these pins during a staff tennis social when I first started in accounts. But she says: 'Did you hear me? You'll have to get yourself to Broadway by eight am sharp.'

'Beg pardon? Am? What for?'

Yoohoo rolls her eyes. 'The photograph – for the Summer Sensations programme.'

'What! Me?'

'No, the little purple fairy standing behind you. Of course you.' Then she frowns again, concerned: 'You look a bit pale – that time of the month, is it?'

I shake my head. 'No.' Sigh and spill: 'I think I've only let a wonderful man walk out of my life – ride a motorbike out of it, actually, at speed.'

'Oh, sweetheart,' Yoohoo wraps an arm around my waist, gives me a squeeze. 'Tell me all about it tomorrow? No time for a natter now. Will you be all right for the photo?'

'Yes.' I suppose so. Mum will be so pleased to see these pins sensationally programmed, scattered across the city in a thousand handbags. That might just give Dad cause to smile.

Yoohoo gives me the address, and a final chirp: 'Plenty more fish in the sea, Bernie – plenty.'

*

There are one million of them in Sydney and they're all on Pitt Street, bang on five, and it's still raining. The throng is so chock it's either barely moving or I'm fighting against the tide rushing for Central. I only have to get halfway round the block into Elizabeth Street, but at this rate I'm going to miss my tram.

I do miss my tram, watch the Coogee Bay disappear around the corner of Hyde Park from the wrong side of Liverpool Street. Poo. Fifteen minutes till the next one, and I'm not going to wait in the rain, so I pop down into Museum Station, under the park, to browse the paperback stand of the magazine man there. 'Evening, Miss. Nice weather for ducks,' he recognises me, and nods at the stand to his left: 'Some new books just in today, American.' He uses the term 'books' loosely and the term 'American' as if they might be a bit suspect, and I know what he means: if we're going to read rubbish let it be Australian rubbish, not more *ma'ams* on cowboy ranches in *She Braved the Wilderness*. These Yank ones here are all crime stories, though, and I never go for them anyway. I give the magazine man a smile: 'Well, at least they're not Japanese.' And he chuckles, 'Very good, Miss,' as I do my patriotic duty choosing *The Stockman's Daughter,* not wondering how many times that title's been rehashed as I hand over my sixpence, or if I've read it before. Wouldn't matter if I had: they're all the same.

Back up on the corner of the park, I'm faced with a far tougher decision: whether to turn right to the stop on Elizabeth, where I will be sure to get a seat on the tram; or left, the shorter distance up to Oxford, where I can wait in the shelter. I choose left: I want that seat; I want to give my heart and mind up to the stockman's daughter for the whole trip. I run through the rain, cold rain in the warm air, glorious, and only just make it, *ding ding ding,* sliding into the middle of this soggy toast rack on tracks. But I don't get further than *Jane Willoughby gazed out across the –* when I'm interrupted.

'Hey, Bernie!'

Stuff Jane back in my handbag, automatic reflex, can't be caught reading this sort of thing by anyone I know. But it's only Colin Quinn pushing through the sardine pack; I'm doubtful he can even read. He once put a handful of slobbery mandarin pips down the back of my school blouse in primary, last seen pouring a bottle of beer over his own head after his squad won the junior surf boat champs. Boys will be boys and surf club boaties will always be especially mental. But this one is wearing a suit, and a tie, in town. I'm intrigued.

'Hello, Colin, you're a long way from home.'

'Yep,' he says, very pleased with himself. 'I got a new job today.'

'Oh?' That makes me soften a little. Colin lost his job with Howard's Automotive a couple of weeks ago, for his twenty-first birthday, not because he's a blockhead but because he's due adult wages now. Dad was disgusted by it; money-grubbers like Howard sack at twenty-one and hire a fifteen year old the next day as if it's best business practice. Colin might be a boatie, but Dad's heard he's a good mechanic; so I ask him, more for Dad: 'What job did you get?'

'Working on the trucks for the AIF,' chest puffed out even more above me. 'At the army depot in Marrickville.'

'Oh?' I blink with the shock. 'The army *army*?' That is, not marched off into this national service conscription thing?

He rolls his shoulders, awkward. 'Not really, not you know, but, um, yep.'

Oh. I can already hear the argument with his own father not going too well. Mr Quinn is of the same mind as Dad – they have a drink at the Bay on Saturday afternoons – only Mr Quinn more so; he's Irish ex-army, emigrated here to get as far away from Britain as physically possible, wouldn't be seen dead at any returned services things because there's always toasts to the King.

Colin's already bracing for it; he says, somehow defensive and aggressive at once: 'I've signed, can't take it back now. Anyway, I'm not sitting round while others get going.'

'What others and going where?'

He reels off half-a-dozen names, most that I haven't said two words to since primary, and after my 'What on earth for?' he gives me a list of reasons that sound like they might be slogans off an AIF advertisement. The Empire needs them. This time it's different. It's about the freedom of the civilised world. It's about protecting what their fathers fought and died for. 'It will be this city, this land, our country at stake this time if we don't.' He is excited and he doesn't care who on the tram hears it.

My head is saying, *You really are mental,* but my heart is with him as he speaks: he really does think he's doing the right thing. I even envy him for a moment, envy his purpose. He's set his course. His country is giving him a rifle. But millions of twenty-one-year-old Germans are getting rifles too, aren't they. I'm suddenly so lost in the hugeness of what he might be getting into, I barely hear him ask me to the pictures tomorrow night.

Still, the lie is automatic: 'I'm sorry, I'm busy.'

He says: 'Are you and that Brock bloke going to get engaged or what?' Doesn't care who on the tram hears that either. A demand, hanging there above me off the roof rail like a great ape. Arrogant boatie. As if I don't know you call us Jackaroo and Jillaroo behind my back.

'None of your business.' I shred the question with the tone of my voice and pull out my paperback. But I can't read a word. Stomach churning over with greasy pork chops, with everything, as we rattle down Anzac Parade. Colin takes a seat across the way as the tram begins to empty and I stare blankly out the window at the rain, at the road, and back down at the words in my hands, at the lines of type, making my world neat and small between them, and certain with gratitude that this war has nothing to do with me or mine. It won't touch Rock. It can't, can it. He's a long, long way away in a different direction altogether. At any rate, his father would kill him first, and my father would murder him twice. I would go in for triple if I had to. I might not be ready for marriage, but if anything happened to Rock, I –

'See you, Bernie,' Colin says, hanging off the roof rail again as we near the terminus, looking like a boy, just a boy, and I reply, 'Take care, won't you,' hoping he can hear that I mean it sincerely, before he heads west and I head north.

But every step I take up Heartbreak Hill the greasy-chops churn gets worse. As if the world is expanding beneath my feet. Like the universe expanding in that story Rock read me from one of the secret-rubbish magazines he buys – *Extravagant fiction today, cold fact tomorrow* – that we are just a hunk of rock flying round a star that's flying through space inside a balloon that's constantly being filled with more and more nothing. That he said might actually be true for once, minus the red-scaled lizard men from another galaxy that invade Earth after the balloon goes pop. Funny then, but now ... an unsafe feeling, and I don't know quite where it's coming from. I stop halfway up and look back over Coogee, at the long stretch of bay surrounded by Heartbreak Hills in every direction, lights flicking on in the banks of flats above the baths, above the cricket oval, above the little colonies of Californian bungalows, all still there ... thousands of greasy pork chops on the stove ...

It's only Coogee on a grey evening giving me a chill, and I am absolutely drowned-rat soaked. I look up at the ten or so yards of Heartbreak's steps left to go, up to my street sign. Arcadia. Nothing bad ever happens in Arcadia, does it? It's heaven on earth, on the bluff between Coogee and Gordon bays. A little Californian heaven on earth, Mrs Zoc's strawberries and cream gable next to our gumdrop green, lolly boxes with an eyesore ute out the front. It's home.

Where onions are on the stove, with garlic, coming from Mrs Zoc's. An instantly comforting smell; I wish Mum would be adventurous and use a bit of garlic, until this nose discerns that it's Monday in heaven on earth and Mum has cooked shepherd's pie: the most comforting smell in the world.

That is, until I open the door and I hear her screeching from the kitchen: 'How could you, Bill!' Pot slamming against the sink. 'What about the building society payments?'

I can't think what Dad might have done to his building society payments, his housing loan, big fat point of pride with him that he even has one, not to mention the home that goes with it, but he's done something all right. And he's angry too, fist slams the table as I walk in on them: 'I have no choice!'

Mum's cheeks are fuchsia with rage. 'We all have *choices*.'

Dad spits through his teeth: 'My conscience doesn't.'

Both of them in such a fury they either don't know or don't care I'm witnessing this … argument. They never argue. Not like this, not seriously. Unsafe feeling is now fully fledged fear.

'Mum, Dad, what? What's happened?'

Mum doesn't look at me; she's too busy goring Dad. 'You tell her, Bill. You tell her.'

But all he manages to get out is: 'Bernie love, I–' before Mum tells me anyway.

'He's enlisted. Your father has enlisted.'

'Enlisted?' I almost relax my panic: that can't possibly be true. Mum's lost her cumquats. Dad's forty-seven years old; fit for anything as he is, it can't be true. *Keep out of this war now, son.*

But it is true. I can see it in his eyes. It's not disappointment there, is it. Nothing to do with me at all. A terrible sadness, grief that was put there before I was born, grief that does break my heart as he says: 'I'm sorry, Bernie love. I–'

He walks past Mum and out the back door, closing it gently behind him.

GORDON

'Well, look who's here.' Jim Fletcher turns at the bar: 'It's Gunner Did.'

Jim is a contractor for Carlyle's, Dad's and my contractor, and I'm Gunner Did, a name Jim's called me since I can remember, for the boy who was gunner do this and gunner do that, and usually I did. A year since I've seen him and he hasn't changed; doesn't look any different from the big ringer that used come up to the verandah of wherever it was I was doing my schoolwork, wanting me to box him, *Come on, Gunner, have a go.* Only now, he's holding up a schooner to me.

I smile, 'G'day,' but shake my head at the glass; I'm looking for Dad, but he's not in this Court House line-up of townies, a dozen or so, the butcher, the baker, the blacksmith. I look at the clock above the bar: half-past six, half-past closing time, which is as relaxed here as every other rule, unless the union made it. Sergeant Brant will be in for his tea shortly, and Dad'll have gone by now, if he came in to town at all.

Jim says: 'Come on, for your twenty-first.'

I laugh: I had my first beer here at seventeen. 'Just thought I might catch Dad. I'll see him at home.'

'Home?' Jim raises his elbow off the bar and comes over to me at the door, a look on his face saying *Hang on a minute* before his mouth is telling me: 'But your dad's up at Brewarrina.'

'Oh? What's he doing there?' I'm more disappointed than surprised. Dad never stops working. I'll see him tomorrow then, because that's when he's expecting me.

But Jim is saying: 'Tank-sinking, I think he said, left more than a week ago.' He looks at me as if to say *You really don't know, do you*. I shake my head *No idea*, and he tells me: 'Said his back was a bit crook and so he was taking other work for a spell.'

That doesn't make sense, and not only because excavating earthen dams is not spell work, not work you would want to do with a crook back or otherwise, leading a team of heavy plodders back and forth across the dirt with a plough and grader, for days, or weeks on end, and with summer coming on. But still I say to Jim: 'So he's meeting up with us at Coolabah on Thursday?'

'No. He told me to scratch him till further notice.'

'Right,' I say, but there's a look between us that says there's something not quite right about this, and then a different concern from Jim, a more important one for him.

'Don't you start thinking about letting me down too, Gordie. I've got two young chaffers on this Coolabah team – where these blokes get their tickets from, I don't know.'

I do: their dads making them go shearing to get out of national service, and hopefully stay there, in a protected occupation. Jim would know that too of course, but I don't want to chat about it right now. I tell him: 'I won't let you down. But I'd better be going or I'll fall down. Probably see you tomorrow for tea, yeah?'

'All right, Gordie,' Jim tips his hat back with the rim of his glass to watch me leave. I can feel my gait is slow, creaking so as you could probably hear me coming: I didn't bank on the ride being this hard on my arse.

'You come from Sydney on that thing?' Jim laughs.

I don't turn back as I say, 'She's a beauty, isn't she,' mostly because my neck is stiff too.

'Gunner Did,' he calls above her engine, 'you might be clever, but you've got a roo loose.'

In my top paddock. I probably do: that was quite a ride, and I am dangerously sleepy now. I can only just wave hooroo. There's an inviting smell of mixed grill coming from the new Greek milk bar across Pangee Street, the California Cafe, and the light's still on there, too. But as much as I can taste their American Beauty butterscotch whirl from here, I know I'd probably only pass out in it. I keep my eyes on what I can see of the road out of town, keep awake looking for actual roos. I've got to get home. Why didn't Dad tell me what he's up to?

It's not far out to our property, if it can be called much of a one. Still Waiting, she's actually called: waiting for the flood that never comes. She sits on just enough of an elevation on this side of the Overflow, just far enough from the Bogan River to the west and Gunningbar Creek to the east to keep her perpetually in drought. As I see the first of her fence posts now I remind myself that Dad never did a walk-off from any of it. He stood his ground with the bank each time he defaulted, daring them to kick him off, and they never came either, that's how decent this land is. But he paid off the debt all the same. That's who Dad is. Tough as fencing wire. And he hasn't done a walk-off now. He'll be back from Brewarrina tomorrow and he'll tell me what's gone on then. He's sent me a note last week and it's missed me. That's probably what's occurred.

The sun is beginning to set directly behind our house when I see it, the pitched roof and verandah posts in shadow against the sky that's turned to copper plate in the dusk. Copper. That's what's in this land, and might've given Dad's life a different story if the government was interested in it. There's little diggings all over the place, made by the Chinese and which I mapped out last summer. There's also what I think might be an old ochre pit at Blackie's Camp, on the Crown land just beyond our northern boundary, but no one's interested in that either, not even Professor Richardson, and Blackie's no longer here to tell anyone about it anyway. No one's here. Moved off, or moved on, left a pile of stones for an unmarked prospector's grave. As I pull up at the gate, the wind picks up and makes a sound like a shiver, reminding me that when I was little I used to think that sound was the sound of the land, I used to think that rocks could really speak. I was probably that desperate for company at times. Now, it's just the drop in temperature and the lack of Dad's ute out the front, the lack of Tess our kelpie barking hello.

I can't get through the gate and across the verandah quick enough to get the lamp on, and when I do I push open the door and see that everything is as it should be. Always as it is with Dad: everything neat and tidy and in its place, ready to pack up when the work is on. I smile as I feel the weight of the lamp in my hand: he would have topped up the kero for me before he left. I light the big lamp on the table by the hearth, that lights the whole place, which isn't difficult: it's only one room. Dad's bed is on the far side, sheet regulation-folded over the blanket, corners as square as the joinery of the loft above it: where my bed is. Cup of tea first. I could murder a cup of tea. I get the fire on and find that the billy is full. Of course it is, just as Dad has the handles of the four cups on the dresser standing at exactly forty-five degree angles.

It's not until I'm pouring the brew into one of them that I see the note on the table, sticking out from under the base of the lamp:

Dear Gordon
I am sorry that I am not around to meet you but I had to get away to work. I wanted to congratulate you in person on finishing your university degree but I'll just have to write 'well done' here for now.
All the best,
Dad
PS here is £10 in case you need it

Ten pounds it is, folded under the base of the lamp. It's too much money: more than I could spend till my own pay starts. A warning bell is ringing quietly in my head: this is not right. Dad is a man of few words, but the ones he speaks are always clear and true. This is as clear as mud. *All the best?* Pip pip cheerio, that's not Dad. This note should state when he expects to be back from Brewarrina. It gives me the shivers enough that I check to see that my rifle is by the door. It is, where it should be. And so is Dad's, next to mine. We'll go rabbiting tomorrow at dusk and I won't remember what I was worried about.

But before I can worry some more about why Dad decided not to take his rifle up there, I have to eat something myself. I've got a headache coming on from not eating since Dubbo, and now I'm too far past it to even open a can, so I check the biscuit tin first, and find a whole fruitcake. This is good, and reassuring for two reasons: I know Dad's left it for me – a lone, unnoted fruitcake is permission for me to eat the whole thing – and it indicates that Dad continues to be looked after by the Country Women's Association, who regularly provide him with cakes and slices of all kinds when he's home. CWA special charity: he might be cranky and old before his time, but he's a good-looking bloke. They took it in turns to look after me when I was a baby. This is Mrs Wells's fruitcake, I can tell from the amount of peel. But as I tuck in, a heaviness drops over my shoulders, and it's not just tiredness. There's a good reason why the women of this district have a soft spot for Dad. I don't know much about her, my mother, other than that she was a nurse, from Bourke, her name was Caroline and they met in Bathurst when he was discharged from the army, and that's who I get my brains from. That's always seemed enough to know about the tragedy. But tonight ... the loneliness of Still Waiting is ...

What's happened to Dad?

Nothing's happened. Dad's tank-sinking in Brewarrina for a spell. And, as he would say, worrying about things you can't change is about as useful as kicking a dead dog backwards up a hill. I'm just disappointed he's not here. Crawl up into bed and go to sleep.

BERNIE

'Smile, Miss Cooper,' the photographer says and I paste one on. 'As if you've just seen a handsome surfer walking up the beach towards you. That's it. Great shot.' Flash. Smile. Flash. 'Come on, Miss Cooper.'

Sorry, not coming easily to me, not even picturing the way Rock flicks the saltwater from his hair when he emerges out the back of a wave, not even for this photographer who's quite a dish himself. It's half-past eight after a sleepless night and I don't want to be too late to my desk in at work, don't want Count Heany's disapproving grimace, that I've been up to something frivolous. Even if I'm technically at work right now, hanging about in a swimsuit getting sensationally programmed does seem at odds with … just about everything.

Dad hasn't enlisted, as it turns out, and he's not abandoning his building society payments either – he's been blooping commissioned is what's happened. Captain Cooper. I can't believe it. He's put himself on extended leave from the garage, given Mum a list of customers to write special letters to in her neat hand, and he's going to Ingleburn tomorrow, wherever that is, some paddock on the edge of the far-flung suburbs. He's going to live there. He's going to train recruits. They're building a barracks; only thirty miles away but it might as well be on the moon. He'll be home every second weekend.

How could I morally say no? he said gently into Mum's inevitable defeat on the back steps. *Can't have these lads going off without knowing what they're in for.* The inference being that he and his company had to work it out for themselves last time. *And I won't be going anywhere myself, nowhere further than Ingleburn. I'm to train them, Peg, that's all.* Mum's response was entirely lacking in hysteria: *The army will do with you what they like and you know it, Bill.* But then she kissed him on the top of his head, in the middle of his bald spot, a tenderness that surprised me, stupidly, with the idea that she was a woman before she became my mother, that she really was Peggy Doyle who went all the way to Melbourne by herself to meet Bill Cooper off the troopship, true as the six-month gap between their wedding and my birth is a secret more tightly guarded than her recipe for treacle pud. A young woman braver than me. True as Dad's conviction that he is doing the right and only thing now, again, for better or worse, for the benefit of others, for these lads, for Mum, for me, to protect everything he's worked so hard for, and so the least I can do is –

'Smile, Miss Cooper.'

And studiously apply myself to a reconsideration of my options. My choices. The foggy depths of selfishness I've sunk to lately. All my parents want is for me to be happy. For me to marry Rock. How can I morally say no?

'Come on, Miss Cooper. You still asleep?'

GORDON

'**S**heep!'

I quickly hate them. I dream of sheep, twenty-four hours a day, six days a week and all day Sunday. After one week and two days here at Yarranbulla Station, they are the enemy. I don't know how Dad has done this for twenty years and more. This is my third year, very part-time, and my last, and I am a psychopath already. The ewe I take now between my knees kicks up and gets me below the belt struggling. I take it personally. I look her in the eye and say to her: 'Do that again and I will clip it right off.' Then I nick her on the hock and have to call the broomie for tar and I'm shame-faced for hurting her. Not that I have time to go and join the RSPCA about it. I'm too busy calling: 'Sheep!'

'Only ten minutes to smoko, mate,' says this bloke called Rennicks in the stand next to mine, and he's said it as if I might need a rest.

I ignore him and pull another ewe from my pen. I don't know him. He's come up the Long Paddock from Deniliquin or somewhere, don't care – I don't know anyone in this eight Jim's put together, all of us oddly enough around about twenty-one – but this Rennicks seems to be sure that I'm some silvertail. As if someone with an education avoiding national service is somehow different from anyone else doing it. He's sure of himself: thinks he is ringer of this shed. Pig's arse he is. This is my shed. This is what shearing does to an otherwise rational man. I will kill myself before Rennicks

36

catches my tally again, and it's got nothing to do with the money, even if I am almost doubling what I banked on at this present rate. I will also continue to let Rennicks think what he likes of me; give him a look now and again, as Dad would do, and say nothing. Leave him to wonder if I might be a silvertail, or a psychopath.

He decides to have another go at provoking me, nodding out towards the homestead. 'What do you reckon of the cocky's little sheila, eh? Reckon she'd want some of this for smoko?'

He's butting his equipment into the back of his ewe's head and referring to the grazier's daughter. Her name is Jennifer Fitzgerald. I taught her her seven times tables on that big verandah over there when I was ten and she was eight, and her father is no cocky, he's one of the most respected graziers in the district, and a good bloke. So now I lose what little cool I have, and react: 'Yeah, I reckon. I reckon she would – if you bent over backwards and ate your own shit.'

As Jim yells out, 'Duckie!' from the wool room, to warn of a female approaching the shed. Too late.

Rennicks has just blown off with some language even I don't like to hear, with Jenny Fitzgerald's boots just about under his nose. But she couldn't be less interested. 'Excuse me, gentlemen,' she says. 'Gordon, I need to speak to you please – outside.'

I'd be pleased at that little run of events if it wasn't for the look on her face.

She touches my arm. Bites her lip. Before she says anything I know it's news of Dad, and it's not good.

She says: 'Someone's been found on the Darling.' She doesn't mean swimming. On the Darling River. That comes out of Brewarrina. 'There's a policeman up at the house, a constable from Bourke, wants to ask you some questions.'

I can't think anything or see anything or breathe again until I hear this constable ask: 'He's a slim man, your father? About six foot three?'

And I answer: 'No, no.' Christ no, thank Christ no. 'He's built like a bull. And he's five eleven.' A full inch shorter than me.

It's not him. I might be able to think something about relief when the adrenalin in me dissipates.

As it does, I have an uncomfortable cup of tea with Jenny and this constable on the verandah, shame-faced that I've wasted this bloke's time, embarrassed now that I put the word out with Sergeant Brant before I left Nyngan that Dad might be … I didn't know what to say and Sergeant Brant finished my question with the words *Not too good?* I said I didn't know, just that something didn't seem right, and Sergeant Brant nodded as if he might know. No one knows, though, and I'm wondering if that's the way Dad wants it. He knows exactly where I am – he made my engagements for me with Jim. Whatever is keeping him away, stopping him from giving me word, it will be a good reason. I'm just … I just want to know when he'll be back. I'm starting to get cranky with him.

'Gordon? Have you listened to a word I've said?'

Jenny is standing there with the teapot, the constable has gone on his way; I say, shame-faced again: 'No. Sorry.'

She smiles, understanding. I look at her, properly. Geez, she's got pretty, her hair seems blonder, big blonde curls, and her eyebrows look different. She arches one of them. 'I said maybe he's just gone bush.'

I have thought of that among the million possibilities, but: 'Why would he?'

'A man doesn't seem to need a reason at the moment to do anything,' she says, pouring me another cup. 'Mr Collins, from the bank, has packed it in to go trapping, and Mr Leighton, that Victor Oil man, has gone off to Dubbo to set up as a florist. Haven't seen Mr Harrington at the post office for two months now and not a word about it. You know what they all have in common?'

Not immediately, no.

'They're all ex-servicemen,' she says. 'It's a bit too much of a coincidence, don't you think?'

That makes a lot of sense. That could be a reason for Dad to have gone bush too. I am safely set up, and he doesn't want to know about this war. I have no idea if this is the truth, but I've settled on it already, even if it remains so at odds with his character it's unbelievable. There are plenty of swaggies who've been waltzing Matilda permanently since the last war. Dad's gone bush and he's not in Brewarrina, is he, not in Bourke either. Not some poor bastard fallen dead drunk in the river. I look west, across two thousand miles of nowhere that doesn't vary too much till it falls into the sea. He could be anywhere.

I hear the bell go for the end of the last run in the shed. I've just lost two whole hours without knowing where they went, and I say to Jenny: 'I think you might be right. Want to go into Nyngan this arvo? To the pictures?' It's Saturday and I want an excuse not to have to suffer Rennicks up at the pub in Coolabah as much as apologise to Jenny for not being quite all here.

She tries not to look too thrilled at the idea as she says, 'I suppose so,' and so does Mrs Fitzgerald when she hands me the key to Mr Fitzgerald's ute. He's out mustering on his cousin's property and she's got us married in his absence. Don't worry, though, Mr Fitz, that's never going to happen.

It would be logical if it did happen, Jenny and me, I think as I tidy myself up for her. Geologists don't know how to be boring next to graziers. Imagine marrying a bloke who only ever talks about the weather and sheep, now and again breaking from that to chat about dogs, or the cricket or the rugby, depending on the season. And Jenny wouldn't mind marrying a bloke who'll be away for long stretches: that's what she's expecting. When I come up to the house and see her again, waiting for me on the verandah with her cardigan over her arm, geez, I think, she really has got pretty. But it can't happen, and not only because her father would be expecting her to marry a grazier: wouldn't matter if he was illiterate so long as he had good water.

We get in the ute and Jenny makes the forty miles go by telling me all about who's doing what where, and she's happy for me when I tell I'll be going straight into work on the survey from here. She says: 'Better adventure than this army business. You know Lindsay Ferguson's gone and joined up. No other prospects, though, has he, with the farm gone to his brother.' That might be a common story too, but I don't give it any thought. Don't give anything any more thought as we pull up at the Palais in town and the first face I recognise is Merle Oberon. Staring out of the poster for *Wuthering Heights*. Of course. It's been playing at every theatre in Sydney for the last few months. I've seen it three times already myself.

Always with the same result: me spending an hour and a half telling Merle she's nothing next to Bernie Cooper. And it's no different this time.

Afterwards, we take a booth inside this new California Cafe and Jen is wanting to talk about the film. 'Wasn't that Laurence Olivier good?' she says. 'But all that deep emotion – oh the drama, oh the agony. I suppose that's art, not that I'd know. *Oh Heathcliff,*' she puts on Merle's Cathy. '*Oh don't let me go.*' She laughs: 'I was a bit glad when they killed her off. Real people just don't carry on like that, do they? Well, maybe they do in Hollywood, or Sydney,' she supposes, adding, 'or Hobart,' trying to get my attention with another shot at our Merle, but I am obviously a lot more interested in how much butterscotch sauce I got through my bowl of American Beauty. Jen gets to the point: 'Have you got a girl in Sydney, Gordon?'

'I don't know.' I'm examining a cross-section of ice cream.

However I've said that has given me away, though, because Jenny's onto it: 'Oh, I see. You're in *agony.*'

She stares at me with that arched eyebrow across the table till I admit it. 'Um, yeah.'

'What's she like?'

And that's all Jenny wants to talk about the forty miles back to Yarranbulla. 'Has Bernie always lived in Sydney?' Yes, I tell her, but her Dad, Mr Cooper, is from Gilgandra way. 'Oh good. Does she work?' Yes, she works in advertising at Chalmers. 'Oh, that's impressive, she's a *career* girl?' Not really, she hates it. 'Oh good. Does she ride?' Horses? No. I doubt that Bernie owns a pair of strides, much less boots. She wears high heels. Jen pretends to be shocked. And when I tell her Bernie can surf, that she could cartwheel across the length of the beach and then bring in a bream off the rocks for tea in those high heels, Jen decides: 'She sounds wonderful, Gordon.'

Jenny's such a good sport, a good friend, I *should* marry her. If I wasn't so in agony with Bernie Cooper.

I drop Jenny and the ute off at the homestead and walk down to the shearers' quarters just about as convinced as Jenny is that 'of course she's only playing hard to get, Gordon, unless she's blind as

well as silly'. Agony is only what you make of it. Things will work
out all right, however it happens, so let's get on with it: sleep, sheep,
cash, diamond engagement ring ...

But before I can take that good thought to my bunk, I hear
Rennicks getting stuck into one of the chaffers, a bloke called
Simon Carter. It's true he's not that good with the shears, not his
calling, but Rennicks is going on about it as if the ability to fleece a
sheep is the only true test of manhood. If you reckon wrestling and
barbering sheep all day, with fleece stuck to your sweat and shit all
over your boots is manly. 'We should get you some blades and see
how many you can butcher.' Rennicks thinks he's comedian of the
year. I'd like to see him on the blades; I'd like to shove a mechanical
handpiece down his neck and turn it on, actually. Simon is copping
it, though, he doesn't care, but Rennicks is pissed, and he's wanting
more, wanting to blue. There are four on the verandah, looking at
him laughing at his own jokes, and they're thinking as one: How
are we going to shift this idiot?

He turns and sees me coming down the track. I have every
intention of walking straight past him and through the door. But he
has to say: 'Hoi, city boy, did you get a good root in her?'

I don't say anything, and I don't think twice. I give him the
weight of all that's been on my mind and I enjoy the sound he
makes when he hits the tin wall.

But I'm ashamed of myself again by the time I hit the hay. Dad
wouldn't be happy with me. 'What was the flaming point of that,
Gordie?' I don't need Jim to yell in at me either. After this job, I'll
never see Rennicks again, probably. And I let him win. By lowering
myself to him. By letting myself be pushed that step too far. *Always
stick to your own course, son.* Yes, Dad. I fall asleep wondering if
that's obsolete advice.

*

I wake up with a sore hand, glad it's Sunday, but it's not better by
Monday, and Jim rips in at my having to pull out of Yarranbulla
with five thousand head still to go: 'Gunner Bloody Useless!'
Rennicks doesn't gloat as I knock off early: he's been docked for

bringing alcohol onto the station, lucky not to be sacked; and neither of us is particularly happy about me going back to Nyngan to see if I didn't break my knuckles on his face.

I didn't. I couldn't have. It's just sore, and Doctor McCullough is more interested in asking me: 'Heard from your father yet?'

'No.'

He gives me that same look Sergeant Brant did: sort of not knowing but knowing at the same time.

I ask him: 'Is there something you know about Dad that I don't? Is he not well?'

'Not well?' Doctor Mac looks at me over his specs, and he's overdoing the surprise. I'm sure he knows something I don't.

I say: 'I have a right to know.'

'No, Gordon, you don't, in fact.'

'Well, it's a matter of *my* health then – it's driving me mad. What's wrong with Dad? Please, tell me.'

He sighs. 'Nothing is wrong, I would hope.' But there's something weighing on his mind. I'm going to sit here until he tells me. He knows that; he sighs again, but finally he says: 'Your father'll be back. It's been a long time but he's done this before, I mean disappeared, a few times, before you were born. And that's all I will say. It's not my story to tell.'

Well, *that* I consider to be good news. Thank you. Evidence that he's gone bush. That's all I need to know. Medical opinion: he'll be back. Then Doctor Mac changes the subject, back to my knuckles, clicking his tongue.

'Not like you to be getting into fist fights, not like you at all.' Shaking his head. 'Now, unfortunately the X-ray's gone phut, again, still waiting on a part from Sydney, so I'll have send you off to Dubbo Hosp–'

'What for? I have to be at Murrawombie on Thursday.' I told Jim I'd make it there, team of six on ten, already cutting it fine, never mind the pay I've already lost over this.

Doctor Mac looks doubtful. 'I don't think continuing in the sheds would be advisable,' but he's onto my concerns as well: 'You start with the Geological Survey soon, don't you? If you need some money to tide you over, I can give you a loan.'

'No, thank you.' I almost smile, at his generosity and the fact that you can't scratch your arse in this town without everyone knowing about it. 'That's very good of you,' I tell him. 'I've got enough money, I ...' Just don't have enough for Bernie's diamond. Sixty-eight pounds, I need. I could get her a cheaper one, I could get her a decent one for a third of that price. I could get her one for a fiver. No, I couldn't.

'You what?' Doctor Mac wants to know my story.

Knowing that the answer will be back to Mrs Fitzgerald and right through the CWA in five minutes flat, I admit with no shame left: 'I'd been hoping to get enough to buy a girl a ring.'

Doctor Mac's eyebrows just about jump off his head. 'This Sydney girl we've been hearing about?' He sits back in his chair, thumbs in his waistcoat, happily married father of nine with two bob's wisdom to give me. 'But you don't need to buy her a ring, my boy. Just tell her that you love her. That's what a good woman wants. Go to Sydney and tell her that you love her!'

Of course. That makes perfect sense. And there's nothing stopping me, is there. Except ... I hear myself actually say: 'But I suppose I'd better stop in at Dubbo first.' As if I have any intention of stopping at Dubbo to have an X-ray machine tell me exactly how much of a halfwit I am. Doctor Mac's clap on the shoulder sends me back out onto the road. 'Yes, my boy, and give my regards to Doctor Wilmot while you're there, will you?'

I look at my knuckles; it's just a bruise, one that looks a lot happier than the face it clouted. I can't let Jim down, I have to get myself to work. But I can hardly close my fingers round the grip of the bike's handlebar as I head back to Still Waiting. How am I going to ride all the way back to Sydney like this? I could catch the train of course. I don't think the train comes through till tomorrow evening, though. I have to go to Sydney now, to tell Bernie that I love her, to ask her if she will marry me. Now.

No. I can't do it. I really do want to get her that ring first. Stick to my course. Keep to the plan.

Keep to the course of excuses that have stopped me from asking her before now, a month ago, a year ago. Why? Because I don't want to hear her tell me no. And that's the simple truth of the matter: I'm a coward.

I see some mail sticking out of the letterbox at the gate. Three letters. I'm hoping there'll be a good excuse not to go to Sydney in there, hoping more specifically that there'll be something from Dad. No luck here, though: they're all official-looking envelopes.

One is from the New South Wales Surveyor-General's Office and, once I manage to open it, tells me that indeed I do have another job to go to, beginning in February, so long as I pass a medical examination at such and such. Another is from the Australian Workers Union for Dad, put it under the lamp, probably rubbish. The third is for me, from the Southern Star Oil Company. Never heard of them. But they have heard of me I see when I read that they are offering me a job in New Britain, oil and other mineral exploration, in the Mandated Territory of New Guinea, a three-year contract at a salary of £595 per annum plus travel expenses, and asking would I like to come to their Sydney offices at three pm, Friday the eighth of December to discuss it?

Yeah, I think I would like to do that – £595 a year! That's almost £200 more than the Survey is offering, including a travel allowance. Oil, not exactly what I had planned fossicking, and New Guinea is not exactly on the top of my list of places to go. I hadn't planned on leaving the continent. But it wouldn't be bad to have a look at the volcanoes of Rabaul, would it, and – £595 a year! Two hundred pounds is a lot of money. Three diamonds, or a good deposit on a harbourside house at the end of the three-year contract, during which Bernie could be a company wife, in a company house full of servants, with shopping trips to Singapore, holidays in Hawaii. I am ten thousand miles ahead of myself but that sounds like a decent prospect, doesn't it? Not a very boring one. I hear the whistle of a willie wagtail and see her land on the fence post by me, not ten feet away, her white eyebrow raised on her little black face saying: *Well, go on then.*

When do I need to be there? The eighth of December. And the date today is? It's the fourth. This was meant to be. If I hadn't quilted Rennicks, I wouldn't have got this letter in time. I don't subscribe to any ideas about fate ordinarily. Life is just a series of random events and the decisions they cause. But –

The wagtail whistles again and flies off. I see there are two of them, their black feathers fanning out against the hot blue sky, and suddenly I can't get to Sydney quick enough.

BERNIE

It must be almost six now and I'm late for tea; I have to get going. What'll I tell Mum when I get there? I missed my tram. I've missed three, wandering into the park past Museum Station, to the Anzac Memorial, to sit on the steps looking over the Pool of Reflection. What for? Nothing in particular. The pool is still as glass, reflecting the evening overcast. It's Wednesday and Mum will have Dad's favourite ready, lamb 'cuddles', her little pastry rolls made from Tuesday's leftover roast and mint sauce, and she'll follow it with pineapple upside-down cake, Dad's second-favourite pud. She always knows what she's doing and she's been sticking to the routine as if it will stop time, or make Friday night come faster, when Dad will be home. Is this how she got through the last war?

I turn on the step and look up at the memorial, again. It's not a very attractive building, always looked like some sort of industrial furnace to me. Or a gigantic mausoleum. I suppose it's supposed to look like that. It's strange, though, how quickly it's become just part of the park. I pass this memorial every working day and I don't ever think about it. Lest we forget? Hmm. It's stranger that I've never been inside it. I came here on school excursion once, not long after it was opened, but we weren't allowed in because of the sculpture of the soldier, which the nuns deemed too explicit for us young ladies. I'd forgotten there was anything inside it at all.

Forgive me, Sister Columba, but I think I have to see it now. As I get to my feet I see I've been sitting right by a sign saying, *It is an offence to sit or loiter on the memorial steps.* That'd be about right. Law-breaking time-waster, that's me. I take the steps up quickly, but inside the entrance I can't see any sculpture. It's a bit gloomy in here, despite the huge windows on all four walls, or maybe because of them: the glass is amber. I peer harder but I can't see anything but an empty space above a stone balustrade, circular, like a gallery railing. I peer over that. And now I see him. The soldier.

Takes my breath away. The last of the daylight shines down over his body, the lines of his chest, his legs, the backs of his wrists. It's not his naked state that's shocking, no more shocking than Apollo on his fountain up the other end of the park. It's that he's dead. Held up on what looks like a shield, his arms lying across a long sword, like a crucifixion.

'Excuse me, miss,' a man's voice says behind me, 'the memorial is closing now.'

'What?' I turn, but I can't see anything except the outline of his sovereign hat in the dimness.

'I'll give you five minutes if you like.' The voice is kind and footsteps leave me to myself. I suppose he imagines I'm grieving.

I just need to catch my breath. I lean on the railing, and as I do I look down at the soldier again. Made of bronze, perfectly formed, and the colour of tar in this amber light, oilskin, just come in out of the rain. Below him, set into the floor, is a great golden sun. But he's still dead. He's just a boy. And I am overcome by the sadness of it.

But it's not sadness in me alone. I don't know what this feeling is. Anger? Disbelief? That we're at war again – *again*. Do people like the taste of greasy pork chops, or do they just eat what they're given? *Nothing's changed*, Dad said when he telephoned last Saturday night, spinning me a yarn about the shenanigans going on for him at Ingleburn, that he'd spent most of the week teaching a young English lieutenant some lessons in the AIF, taking this *Pommy kid* out on a march to the Blue Mountains, telling him to catch his own tea and see if the rest their company didn't know how to look after themselves and each other better than him. He had me in connipting stitches, but it's not funny here. The facts of Dad's responsibility: that he has a hundred and twenty boys in his charge, to train for war. Boy warriors. Twenty thousand our Prime Minister promises the King, Colin Quinn and half of primary school among them, and they will be going abroad to fight the Germans, or whatever the Empire requires. *Again?* Aren't we still paying off our debt to the Bank of England for our last lot of sacrifice? What would this Pig Iron Prime Minister Menzies know about war anyway? About as much as Dad's lieutenant Pommy kid. It's a place he's never been.

Neither have I. I've never even been to the Blue Mountains. I grab the cold hard sandstone of the railing. I have to do something, play my part. But what can I do? There's a lot been said in the paper these past few days about what girls might do. The Country Women's Association wants to organise a women's land army similar to what they have going in England, and others want to see women's auxiliaries in the forces this time. But there have been just as many words on why that won't or can't happen, one long column in particular arguing that Australian girls would never go for slacks and short hair like English girls. And my response to that was? Oh, but slacks aren't very flattering on me. Let that be the bottom end of my vanity. Please. But at any rate, what would I do on a farm or in the air force? There's been a registry set up for women to volunteer their services, but what services can I offer? Hughie knows, I have no practical skills.

Apart from wearing a blooping swimsuit. I have half-a-dozen copies of the Summer Sensations programme in my handbag to attest to it. Now, what might my country do with that talent? Enter me in the Miss Coogee pageant next weekend with an eye on the national title? Blawch. But then again, maybe I should, for Dad. He'd love it. He'll also love this programme photo, just as he'll love Mum being scandalised by it. *Bill, you're ruining that girl,* she'll squawk round the table come Friday night, and the comforting sounds of my parents bickering over nothing will follow, because they love the sound of each other's voices. And they love me. And they've only ever asked one thing of me. *Have you written to Gordon yet, Bernie love?* Dad asking me on the phone. Asking me, please, Bernie love.

'Can I close up now, miss?'

'What?' I almost jump over the rail. The man is back to close up the memorial. 'Oh yes, of course,' I say and dart past him, back down the stairs, back out into the park.

What's the time? It must be well past six now. Mum will be starting to worry, she'll have her rosary out. And I've been doing what, precisely? I'll tell her I went to St Mary's to light a candle for Dad and his boys, not too far from the truth, and if she says, *Get away with your blarney, Missy,* I'll tell her I've been contemplating going to mass with her this Sunday; that'll flummox her. And I might go to mass, too. That is a small and easy something I can do, at least for her.

And here is the Coogee Bay pulling up to the tram stop on Elizabeth. It must be the 6.17, and I'm going to miss it. No, I'm not. I'm changing direction sharply for Oxford Street, to catch it.

Bang on the left shoulder as something heavy slams into me, as my feet leave the ground and I'm caught around the waist with a man's voice saying: '*Oof.* I've got you!'

'I *beg* your pardon!' Automatic reflex, I push the arm away from my person. 'Get off me!'

'I'm terribly sorry,' the man says and even his smile is somehow a rounded vowel. Tall, dark and catalogue-exclusive handsome. Incredibly blue eyes. 'But I believe it was *you* who careered into *me.*'

'Do you?' I retort, straightening my jacket. 'You should look where you're going.'

He ignores that, bending down now to pick up some books he dropped. One's fallen open at the title page: *Cardiac Failure and Hypertension.* He's a doctor. The rubber tubing of a stethoscope sticking out of his suit-coat pocket is also a giveaway. And he now looks up at me with those blue eyes he seems to well know the effect of: 'Are you hurt?'

'No.'

'Good.' He stands, giving me the full blinding dazzle of his catalogue-exclusive teeth. 'Because, if you don't mind, I'd like to invite you to join me for dinner this evening. Allow me to introduce my–'

'Dinner? For Pete's sake.' I feel the cold-fish contempt fall across my face; automatic reflex. 'No. Thank you.'

I know I've missed the 6.17, but I run for it anyway. Is this all I'm good for? Attracting male attention? Arrogant young doctor sweeps girl off feet in public park. My life is a six-penny romance gone wrong. Good grief. Hughie save me.

'Oh, but miss! Please. Wait!'

Oh please. Please leave me be!

GORDON

'She is very late now.' Mrs Zoc is watching the street through the flyscreen, hand at her throat. She's more nervous than me, if that's possible. She comes back into the lounge, goes over to the side window and shrugs at Mrs Cooper, who shrugs back from her front verandah, hands in the air. Ordinarily I might laugh that they both then reach into their apron pockets for their beads.

An hour ago, I was excited, I was ready. I'd just told Mrs Cooper that I'd come back to ask Bernie something, *Oh yes, Gordon, yes!* she said without me finishing the sentence, *Go and have your bath, dear.* I did. Then I asked Mrs Zoc if I shouldn't ask Mr Cooper first, formally, when he got in from the garage, and she said, *You are stupido?* And then she told me Mr Cooper wasn't here. Told me all about it, that he's rejoined with the Second AIF. I don't know what to make of that, something to think about when normal brain function returns.

'Did you get Bernadetta a ring, Gordon?' Mrs Zoc is trying to make conversation again, none of which is helping.

'No.'

She looks nervous again. Even the cat, Piccolo, looks worried.

'No ring …' Mrs Zoc pushes the beads through her fingers a bit faster.

But then I remember, I did get Bernie a rock. 'Hang on,' I tell Mrs Zoc and go and grab it from the pocket of my swag. It's a little piece of jasper I found among the scree at the top of the Hartley

Vale stock road on my way here. I only went that route to avoid the possibility of having to walk the bike all the way up Victoria Pass, and there I was, stopped for a billy, having a bit of a fossick along the bottom of cliffs, when I found this beauty. It's speckled red and tan, with a pink mist through it, in the shape of a B, sort of.

Mrs Zoc approves of it; she cries: 'Ah Gordon, molto romantico!'

'You think she'll like it? It's jasper,' I say. That's sounds insane now. I'm going to give Bernie a piece of jasper I found on the road?

But Mrs Zoc says, confident now: 'It does not matter if she likes it or not. It is a jasper stone. It has magic powers, to bring many bambini, to bring the rain, and to send away the snakes and the spiders.' She puts it down on the telephone table and nods at it.

'I must take the fish from the heat,' she says now, apologetic at having to tend to tea, as if not watching the street will somehow delay Bernie further. Maybe it will. Where *is* Bernie? She's just tied up at work and hasn't telephoned her mum for some reason, that's probably what's occurred. That dropkick of a boss of hers keeping her back. I wish she'd give away that job at Chalmers; it's beneath her intelligence anyway. She can say goodbye to it shortly, can't she. Please.

Geez, I could do with a beer.

What am I going to do if she says no?

'Gordon.' Mrs Zoc comes back into the lounge, and the slow way she rolls the r in my name indicates she's got something important to tell me. 'I was mean to my Marco, in the beginning,' she says softly.

'Oh?' Marco is her husband – was. I look at his photograph behind her, above the mantelpiece: happy face, thick black moustache. She still misses him. She still barnies with him sometimes, slamming things around in the kitchen. I never met him. He died of nephritis a few years after they emigrated, and she blames the war for it. She's been through a lot, Mrs Zoc, ending up here with her Marco and their three sons, because America didn't want any more Sicilians, and the Fat Head, as she calls the Italian dictator, only wanted her boys dead. They're all up in North Queensland now, her sons, making a fortune in pineapples and mangoes, making their mother lonely. That's why Mr Cooper'd thought it would be good for me to board here, when Dad wrote to him asking for advice. By mutual need Mrs Zoc is the closest thing to a mum I have, but I don't know what she's telling me now about being mean to her Marco, and I don't know if she's wanting me to ask or not. Is she telling me she told him no the first time?

She goes back to her post by the flyscreen telling me nothing. Instead, she lets out cry: 'Ah!'

I'm about to find out for myself.

Bernie. I hear her heels on the footpath before I see her. The shape of her waist in her suit. The shape of those legs, up on the crest of the hill.

I grab her jasper B off the telephone table, and then I freeze, before Mrs Zoc pushes me out the door: 'Pronto!'

BERNIE

I'm so cross. Fuming cross. With myself. I've lost my bracelet. It must have flung off somehow running into Young Doctor Keen On Himself, and could just be why he chased me halfway across the park, calling, *Miss, wait!* I lost him hopping on the Bondi tram to Taylor Square. And I've lost my blooping bracelet. Something else for Mum to be overjoyed about. It's not an expensive one, only a little nine-carat chain, and the catch was always a bit loose, but Mum and Dad gave it to me for my seventeenth birthday. Why didn't I get that catch fixed? I could cry, but I'm too cross.

It's almost dark, moths around the streetlamp just come on, and it's starting to sprinkle as I pass the flats up on the corner, past the old half-dead frangipani that looks like a great big witch's hand. It used to scare me when I was little; now I'd like it to strike me, blast me off the face of the earth in a puff of smoke. *Whooomp!* Bernadette Cooper: gone.

'Bernie?'

Oh, that'd be right. Now I think I can hear Rock calling up to me from the house. Yes, of course. According to this six-penny, he's come back from Nyngan to sweep me off my feet.

'Bernie?'

Rock calling up to me again.

Oh.

But it *is* him. The set of his shoulders. His white moleskin trousers, striding, purposeful as ever, towards me.

My feet seem to go from under me. I'm still walking towards him but I have no feet.

'Where've you been?' he sounds out of breath, and worried.

'What's wrong?' I hear myself say. He hasn't come home to propose to me, has he. Something dreadful must have happened for him to come all the way back to Coogee like this.

But he says: 'Nothing's wrong. Um ...'

He reaches for my hand, and then –

Oh.

At the first touch of his lips on my cheek I fold into him, and the rest of my person takes off to wherever my feet just went.

He breathes into my neck. 'I love you, Bernie.'

Stars are exploding across the sky, through my body and into my soul. It's true, the universe is expanding. It's terrifying, and he hasn't even kissed me properly yet.

He says: 'Will you marry me?'

And I don't believe it. I don't believe it for a second, but I do. He is holding me to his chest and his heart is asking me too. *Please, Bernie.*

What should I do? Stare into the concrete footpath between our feet. 'Mmmm.'

He pulls away and holds me by my shoulders. 'What did you say?'

I look up into his eyes, lovely grey eyes promising perfect weather for anything, anything for me.

What else can I do? Everyone will be so happy if I ...

I nod.

'Are you saying yes?' His incredulity is so pure and plain.

There is nothing else can I say but: 'Mmmm, that's right.'

Before his lips touch mine for the very first time, here in the street, in the sprinkling rain, pulling me back to earth, back to him, arms firm around me, making it real, real as the shushing of the surf in the bay below us, and I knew it, didn't I. Soon as I let him kiss me, I'd be gone. This has to be as right as it feels, doesn't it? The right thing to do. For everyone. If this is all I'm good for, then make it good. I'm going to marry Gordon Brock. I'm going, going ...

He pulls away again, hand in his pocket, and says: 'Here, I got you something.'

Puts it in my palm. It's a piece of rock. And I am gone. Not a lot of maybe about it.

Still, he has to double-check. 'You did say yes, didn't you?'

'Yes, Gordon,' I tell him. 'I said yes.'

I did. Didn't I?

GORDON

She said yes. Yes, she did. Bernie Cooper said yes. And she called me Gordon when she said it so I know she meant it. I can't do anything without thinking it, three times a second. She said yes and she let me kiss her.

She lets me kiss her and then tells me to go away. Go to bed, go for a surf, go away so she and Mrs Cooper can organise a surprise party for Mr Cooper for Friday evening. I am obedient. I go away and sign my contract at the George Street offices of the Southern Star Oil Company, in town. My hand is still that sore I can hardly hold the pen, but it doesn't matter; nothing else matters because Bernie Cooper said yes.

'A young man confident of his decisions, that's what we like to see,' says my new boss as I hand him back the document. He is the chief of exploration and at this moment I can't quite recall his name. Doesn't matter, does it. Bernie Cooper said yes.

BERNIE

'I am the proudest man alive,' Dad cries, wiping his eyes. He can't stop shaking Rock's hand, which is bringing a tear to Rock's eye too: great black bruise across his knuckles, got it caught in the door of a ute, he said. Still, he doesn't let go of Dad's hand in a hurry either. My fiancé. Gordon Brock. Gordon James Brock. Mrs GJ Brock I'm going to be. A geologist's wife. A company wife, no spud-crisping for me unless I want to make a hobby of it, in New Guinea. *New Guinea?* That's going somewhere, isn't it. It blooping well is. Going somewhere married to Mr GJ Brock, who rode all the way home from Nyngan with his hand like that to propose to me. Mental.

'When? When's the big day?' Dad is asking us.

And Mum is quick and even prouder to tell him: 'Seventh of December, Bill, next December. The seventh of December 1940. That's the soonest Gordon will be able to return from New Guinea, and it's lucky number seven. Isn't that a marvellous date?'

'Marvellous, Peg,' says Dad, wiping another tear. 'Marvellous.'

Marvellous. Mum's just about got the whole thing arranged already. St Brigid's is booked and we will have lilacs and hydrangeas, and Father Gerard will let us know on Sunday what sort of offering might be sufficient to overcome the groom's state of Presbyterianism. Mrs Zoc will make the cake; Mum will make the dress. The reception will be held in the dining room at the Coogee Bay Hotel. And I don't have to worry any more about what

I'm doing. I'm fulfilling my parents' hopes and expectations for me. With a life free from worry, free from work. Rock's going to do that, taking this job in Rabaul for the money, for me, looking for oil in the jungle, to set us up with a deposit on a house, on the harbourside, my future assured with electrical appliances. I'll never light a copper on washing day. I'll have the best agitating spin wringer there is. That's what the whole parish will know by Sunday afternoon: Bernie Cooper, she'll never have to lift a finger again.

Dad raises his glass of beer over our kitchen table: 'Bernie and Gordon!' and can't wait for Saturday afternoon, to shout the bar of the Bay, all Saturday afternoon so that my father and my fiancé have to take turns pushing each other up Heartbreak on the way home, they are so thoroughly skunked.

'Oh, get inside, Bill, disgraceful man,' Mum pretends to rouse on him, and as we watch Gordon trip up the front steps next door before falling into the hibiscus, she says to me, not for the first time: 'I hope you know how lucky you are, Missy.'

I do, Mum, I do. I've got a romance full of promises that will come true. Practically guaranteed. Who wouldn't be happy with that? So, I didn't quite get to the end of maybe. So what? Small sacrifice. Maybe this is the end of maybe after all.

When in doubt, let him kiss me again. Let him kiss me too long, longer and longer, so that as soon as Dad is on his way back to Ingleburn, my Rock is through the curtains of my bedroom window, kissing me in places that make me want to scream. My Gordon. I can feel him strange and firm against my thigh and I push him away. I have to ask: 'Have you done this before?'

And he says, embarrassed: 'No. No, not with a girl.'

And I say, with the creeping terror of everything I don't know about what we're doing here: 'What do you mean, *not with a girl?*'

Mortified. 'Oh. No. I didn't mean, I–'

'Well, that's a relief,' I tease him, keeping my terror to myself. 'You know what they say about shearers.'

And we laugh ourselves silly, till I think I've spoiled it for us, till my cheeks hurt, till we're kissing again, and my terror becomes wonder against his skin, and then something else altogether as he fills me so that I am the vast warm ball of melted rock that he says is inside the earth. And afterwards, safe and sleepy in his arms, I look up at the stars through my window, wondering how it is that a man so strong and heavy in the chest could be so light upon me, and I ask him: 'What did you really mean when you said *not with a girl?*'

And he says: 'I meant only in my dreams, and I only ever dream of you, I only ever will.'

And then there is silence, except for the shushing of the sea.

*

And a Qantas Empire Airways flying boat for him to catch to New Guinea tomorrow. The eighth of January. It seems too soon, too real now. I don't want him to go. The girl who couldn't bear the thought of getting married now can't bear the thought of him leaving. Who wrote this storyline? I don't want to wait a year to see him again. Eleven months – near enough a whole year. I want to get married *now*. A lot can happen in a year. A lot can happen in a month, don't I know it. He could get eaten by head hunters, or thrown into a volcano, and I might –

Need to pull myself together. All day I've been getting caught up in this agitating spin wringer of nonsense. What's the matter with me?

'You be careful of the Japs up there, Gordon,' Mum squawks over our last Sunday roast with him, as if the Yellow Peril is poised to swoop down through the islands this second. Where do I get it from? Nonsense. Panic for nothing, for selling copies of the tabloid papers. Prime Minister Pig Iron is maintaining it's far-fetched, and he should know, big chief imitation rubbish salesman that he is, half-a-dozen plums stuffed in his mouth to prove it: *Britain has nothing to fear from Japan.* The war is in Europe, ladies and gentlemen, or will be when it actually starts; inference being: what would anyone in their right mind want with Australia anyway?

'Don't worry about any Japs, Peg.' Dad's gentle laugh is the answer, the assurance. 'They've got their hands full in China, love. Even if they weren't busy, they'd have to get through Singapore to get down this way, and the Brits'd never let that happen.'

Of course they wouldn't. Singapore: Jewel of the Empire Crown. Rock's going to take me there one day, take me shopping for sapphires and silks. And now my mind sloshes between the fantastic excitement of that idea and the idea that the Japs seem to have been at it for a long time in China. They did some terrible thing in Nanking not so long ago, didn't they?

'Bernie?' I feel Rock's hand on mine. 'You're not worried, are you?'

'No, not really, I ...' don't know what's the matter with me.

But he reassures me anyway. 'You know the Japs won't go further than China, don't you?' His eyes telling me: *Of course you do*. 'It's only logic, Bernie. You know, economic.' He explains to Mum: 'If they want to keep going with selling us all their cheap-and-nasty manufacturing, they need lots of oil for that, Mrs Cooper, and as the Yanks supply almost all of that oil, there's no chance the Japs would want to upset them in the Pacific – nor us, if we can find our own reserves and sell it to them even cheaper. The only thing that will happen then is a bidding war between us and the Yanks for the Jap contracts.'

'Well, there you have it, you can't argue with sense like that, can you,' Mum's convinced, and she looks at Dad. 'Isn't our Gordon the most intelligent boy, Bill?'

'He is, Peg, he is.'

Their Gordon. Their boy. At last they've got their boy. I paste one on. What am I? Not even a swimsuit model. I pulled out of the Summer Sensations parade last Saturday and no one died. Rock said I shouldn't stop doing all that, shouldn't stop doing anything fun that I might want to do. In fact, he demanded I give up the proper job and wear a swimsuit for the rest of my life, which Mum thought was just about the most hilarious thing she'd ever heard. If Gordon thought it was a good idea for me to parade naked down Pitt Street, Mum would agree, but still I didn't feel right about going in the show. I felt a bit off-colour anyway, stomach cartwheeling with I don't know what when I told Yoohoo she'd have to find another pair of pins for the white Jantzen. I feel a bit off now.

'Bernie, are you sure you're all right?' He squeezes my hand.

I squeeze it back and make another attempt at a smile. 'I think I'll have to go and have a bit of a lie-down. Must be the heat.'

It's not the heat, though; it's not that hot today, but I am flushed through from the inside. I have an idea, a fear, of what it might be, but I don't know enough about all that. My curse is three weeks late; you don't get your curse when you're – Hughie, I can't even think it.

I'm not in my room five minutes before Gordon's in through the window, having taken my lie-down for code, and I don't mind that idea at all. 'Where does it hurt? I'll have to kiss you better,' he says, unbuttoning my blouse, kissing my shoulder, kissing my frown and I tell him: 'Everywhere.' I can't have enough of him. I'm ferocious for him. You don't want this sort of thing if you're whatsit, do you? I remember reading something in the *Woman's Mirror*, tips on how to avoid hubby's attention when you're – You go off it apparently. But I'm not off it. What am I going to do without it for eleven months? What have I done? What am I *doing*. Not being quiet enough right at this minute. 'Oh, yes. Oh, darling.'

Mental.

*

'Are you travelling home, sir?' the reporter asks him at the flying-boat terminal, asking him if he's going all the way to Southampton, home to England, and Gordon laughs bright as the sky this morning. 'Not likely.' Kicking the swag at his feet, happy, he's so happy, and they start chatting, about where Gordon's from and where he's going. Nyngan. Rabaul. Change planes at Townsville. He's so excited to be going, to be adventuring, he can hardly stand still, and it's impossible not to be excited for him. With him. For all that it seems impossible he's going at all. World championship mental.

You are not going to cry. You will not. Not. Not. Cry.

I squint across Rose Bay, into the glare coming off the water. This is why Mum's not here: she'd rather eat glass than risk a public display. And why Mrs Zoc isn't here either: Mum's possibly still consoling her in the front yard where she started on her display as soon as the cab pulled up. It's Mr Brock and Dad who should be here, shaking Gordon's hand, wishing him bon voyage; and why are they not? I squint harder at the glare, at the not-fairs.

'Would you mind, miss?' the reporter is asking me a question now.

'Pardon, mind what?' I squint at him tucking his pencil behind his ear, grubby lead-smudged fingernails.

He says: 'It's for the *Herald*.' As if that will make a difference to my answer.

'A photo.' Gordon puts his arm around me. 'Where did you go off to then?'

'Nowhere,' I say, automatic as my hand going to his hand at my waist to press him tighter to me. 'A photo? Of course. What for?'

'A nice Aussie story, something different from the usual,' the reporter says and calls over to his photographer, who's outside taking pictures of the bay.

I pinch my nose and give Gordon a posh twangy newsreel commentary. 'It's a beautiful day out here on Sydney Harbour as Mr Gordon Brock of Nyngan is farewelled by his fiancée Miss Bernadette Cooper of Coogee, before leaving on the Qantas Flying Boat Cooee, bound for oil exploration in the deepest darkest New Guinea.'

'You are beautiful,' he whispers in my ear and I have no trouble smiling, for him, with him, wishing I could see for a second what he sees in me, which makes me feel a lot more than beautiful. What is it? This feeling. Fear. Somehow exhilarating. Some sort of possibility I'm not yet aware of. But I want to be.

'Oh Georgie, that's too outrageous!' a woman shrieks a laugh across the other side of the terminal, from the middle of a group, three chaps and three gels, near the doors to the jetty, the smart crowd, identifiable by that certain look, contrived casual; all polo shirts and twin sets, they are a pen-and-ink for a Hordern's Sporty Knitwear ad. They're gathering their coats, coats too heavy for this summer's day, must be going home, I suppose, done this flying business before, Georgie, and one of the girls turns as the flash bulb goes off again at us, peering over her shoulder: *What's so special about them?* Everything. I smile at her too. Isn't it obvious? We're a nice Aussie story. Truly. Rock bought a new pair of moleskins especially. With the blazer and tie he's an ad for Bushie's Back O' Bourke Outfitters and Saddlery, while I am –

'Passengers for the QEA Royal Mail Service, please make your way to the punt at the end of the jetty,' a uniformed man with a great booming voice calls into the room. He's carrying a megaphone, but doesn't need it. 'All aboard!'

No, not yet!

I grab Gordon's hand. Don't go. Not yet. Inside, I am all over the shop like a madwoman's lunchbox, and yet I am walking along the jetty with him, holding his hand, and then letting go of his hand as he gives me one last kiss. 'I'll telephone or cable as soon as I can. I love you, Bernie.'

'I – I'm going to miss you, Rock, my darl–' is all I can manage to tell him without throwing myself across the gangway.

One very very last kiss and he's the last onto the punt that takes him out to the plane. He disappears into its belly, the propellers start up across its great white wings and it sets out, gathering speed across the water, and then it is in the air and I'm clutching my jasper B in my pocket with my heart wanting to fly out of me after the plane as it glides up and over the Bridge.

And as it does I hear myself cry inside and out: 'Hughie save him!'

'Aye.' The man with the megaphone chuckles softly beside me. 'An aeroplane is a wondrous thing until someone you love is in it.'

I watch it grow smaller and smaller, as if this great metal pelican might somehow carry all my hopes for the future into the future. Our future. Please, Hughie. Please let these choices we've made be the right ones. The best ones. For us.

For me.

TWO

JANUARY 1940 – DECEMBER 1940

GORDON

'I suppose you don't notice the view after a while,' I say to the hostess, who's just asked me if I'd like something to drink, twice, because I can't take my eyes off the view. I'm on the edge of my seat.

She smiles, like she's used to catering to five year olds. 'Not at all, sir. It's different every journey, always changing.' She looks out the window too. 'Like an opal – I could never be bored of looking at the colours.'

An opal. That's a good description. All the blues and greens of the waterways and the dairy pastures of the Hunter we're flying over. But it'd be black underneath: there's a lot of coal down there.

'So, would you like something to drink – tea and biscuit, Scotch and crisps?'

Scotch and crisps? It can't be eleven o'clock yet. 'No thanks,' I smile at her. 'I'll wait for lunch.'

Lunch on an aeroplane. I'm on an aeroplane. Flying. Through the air. One hundred and eighty miles an hour. How good is this? When the chief of exploration, Mr Taylor, told me that my travel expenses entitled me to one return air ticket per annum, you could have scraped me off the floor. I expected to be put on a ship, third class. Air travel is that expensive – £65 to Rabaul, £220 all the way to Southampton – the directors of Southern Star are either very confident of striking oil or they have money to burn. They, and their main backers, the Service Station Association and several transport and manufacturing chiefs, are in a hurry too. Britain supplies most of our petroleum through the Anglo-Eastern Petroleum Company, who have a monopoly over the Near East trade and up until a couple of years ago had complete control over Australian exploration – there's a racket for you – and now they're charging a premium, rightly or wrongly, because war needs oil like nothing else.

The responsibility I've been charged with is like nothing else too. The job is straightforward enough: all I have to do, as the field geo, is supervise the drilling, with the aid of comprehensive Anglo-Eastern maps and data, and report back to the chief geo and Mr Taylor in Rabaul with my findings. Easy as join the dots. But the amounts of money involved, the stakes. It's a long way from university prizes for hypotheticals and orienteering. It seems like five minutes ago I was at school and now I'm here.

Looking down on where I went to school: the New England tablelands. Wheatfields stretching up along the Divide: a great wall of gum trees. Amazing from the air. I'd be down there right now, preparing to tramp out mapping bauxite, if I wasn't here, in the sky, eight thousand feet up. I suppose I'll do this a few times over the next three years. I can't wait to do it with Bernie. She will love it. I'd kiss her right now if she was here, kiss her properly, and I could, too: I'm the only one in this little cabin of six seats aft of the wings. We might explore the luggage hold next door, too. The thrills we are going to share. Can I believe my luck? No. I still can't believe Bernie lets me kiss her at all.

I look out at the Divide again now, as if I might see past it. See Dad, in want of sharing all these good things with him too. He sent word through Jim that he's got more work tank-sinking on a cattle station at Tibooburra. He shouldn't be doing that work. In Tibooburra: the end of the road before desert, all the way to Perth. In January. It'll be a hundred and fifteen degrees there today, at least. You can fry an egg on the bonnet of your ute. Dad and I have done that, too, just to do it, and it's a favourite school-holidays memory. But it's my turn to look after him now. Maybe he doesn't want to know about that most of all, doesn't want looking after. It bothers me, though. Makes me cranky, actually: I've never given him one moment of worry, and he's off – in flaming Tibooburra? Well, at least I won't have to worry about him not turning up to my graduation: I won't be in town myself. He'll find out I'm engaged and off in New Britain from the bush telegraph via a third-hand copy of the *Herald* and there's nothing I can do about it.

A golf ball comes sailing up through the cabin to take my mind from it. A golf ball? Followed by one of the gels, as Bernie calls girls like this one. Waving a putter in the air as she says: 'Ahoy there, hello! Sorry about that.' Swaying not just because of the movement of the aircraft: she looks like she's had a Scotch and a crisp, or maybe two. She throws herself down into the seat next to me. 'Oh, but hello again. I know you, don't I?'

'Um.' I'm not sure if I recognise her, maybe from uni: Bachelor of Filling in Time, or someone's girl?

She says: 'Wilma – Wilma Handley-Endicott.'

That name is sort of familiar, Handley-Endicott is a director of something – an insurance company, or is it a bank? Don't know, and care less. City money and plenty of it. But I do now think I might recall her face, from a party, back in first year, involving togas and a chemistry experiment called zombie juice made from barbital salts and Pimms. I didn't stay long at it; not my idea of a good time.

She says: 'Never mind. Want to join us? We're playing golf in the promenade saloon.' She points her putter at the passageway, towards the middle of the plane.

As much as it would be interesting to see how a game of golf might be achieved in these conditions, I say: 'Thanks, but no, I'm happy here.' Point out the window, at the view.

She shrugs, 'Well, you stay happy then,' and wanders out again, calling: 'Georgie, I can't find it. Can you get another ball, sweets?'

She didn't even look for the lost one, and that finds the Presbo in me. Playing golf, on an aeroplane, drunk in the middle of the day, probably stay that way for the next ten days to Southampton and every day. On permanent holidays, that lot. Can't stand them, people who don't work. Even the richest of the graziers' sons I know are always expected to work. But the blokes on this plane, three of them that look like their fathers own a hair oil factory, come from a different world, a different country. One called Home. I heard one say to the other on the punt up to the plane: *You can draw out the doctorate for the next ten years if you have to.* There's a way to get out of your national service. PhD in playing golf drunk in an aeroplane, for a decade.

Leaving it to Mr Cooper to put on the khaki again. No thought for whatever else he'd rather be doing, whatever else he might have had planned, not even sure he'll make it to our wedding: *Too far off to say, son – but don't tell our Bernie that, will you?* That's enough to put me off my aeroplane lunch.

No, it's not. Mr Cooper doesn't want me doing anything other than exactly what I'm doing now. Avoiding the military, and having more fun than a grown man probably should landing and taking off again at Brisbane. And then again at Gladstone. Then finally Townville, with a splash that comes right up past the window, and where I'm to leave the home service for the Oceania Mail, or will tomorrow, for a job that's just as necessary to the war effort as soldiering, maybe even more so.

'Goodbye, sir.' That nice hostess sees me out with a smile and a wave. 'Enjoy the rest of your journey.'

'Thanks, I will.' I wave back as the humidity hits me like a wet blanket lobbed from a great height. This is a hot I've not experienced before: my swag doubles in weight as I step down into the punt. I look across the water to the jetty, not sure if I should take my jacket off now or wait till I've met Mr Johnstone here, the drilling engineer, a Mr Michael Johnstone. Mr Taylor described him as a *man of the tropics*, and an old hand at exploration on New Britain; formerly of Pacifica Mining, gold prospectors. We'll be flying out together in the morning. Can't see anything much but the outlines of ketch rigging and warehouse roofs, though: looking straight into the late-afternoon sun.

'That young Brock there?' A hand reaches down for my swag at the jetty – hand belonging to a barrel chest that's got some legs to it that are as skinny as they are hairy. In shorts. I shouldn't have worried about my jacket. 'Mick Johnstone – call me Johno,' he says, and as I step up level with him I see him properly. He's got black hair like a boot brush on his head, with big wide eyes and a nose that takes up most of his face: he looks like an emu, holding out his hand to me now, and saying: 'Shit, you *are* a kid.'

He can't be more than thirty and I'm not *that* much of a kid, I'm thinking as I'm looking at the size of his hand and estimating the magnitude of the shake there. It's not too big a hand and there's nothing wrong with mine so long as you're not too enthusiastic in the grip. I should have had it looked at, I suppose, but between momentous decisions I didn't get around to it, and it's really not an issue until – Right there, that's it. About a seven out of ten and I make a corresponding sound approximating, 'Yeah, g'day.' But this Johno doesn't notice. He's already walked off with my swag.

'We've just got time to get in for a quick one,' he says, heading across the road to a pub.

I look behind me, see my trunk being pulled up onto the jetty. I suppose it'll find me in the morning with the mail. It had better: it's got my books in it, my dinner suit and, more importantly, my photo of Bernie – that one of her in the white bathers. She got a copy of it for me, and it's safely tucked in behind the cover of Professor Richardson's *Geological Formations of New South Wales*.

'Come on,' Johno says, taking off up the road and round a corner. 'Hurry up. This is North Queensland – you don't want to get caught breaking the rules up here.'

No, I see we don't. We just get into the front bar of this pub called Ramages Tatts before being locked in at six on the dot, the blinds drawn down on all the doors and windows. But *quick* and *one* are not good descriptions of what will follow. Which is rum. Bundaberg rum.

'Get it into ya, young fella,' says a bloke at the bar, a Kiwi whose name I don't catch first go with the noise in here. Works for Pacifica, I think he just said. One thing is clear: this end of the bar belongs to the miners, and mining technicians of all sorts, either coming or going from New Guinea, all about ten years older and louder than me, with handshakes that require anaesthetic. Doesn't seem like a good time to mention I'm not much of a rum drinker, not a drinker of spirits of any sort actually. Stick with beer, in moderation, except for special occasions. I still bear a scar on the back of my left hand from Mrs Zoc's hibiscus, as a reminder of my last effort with Mr Cooper.

So, when in Rome, I get it into me and discover why Ramages is better known to some as Damages. I'm halfway through my third ale chaser, necessary to putting out the fire in my throat, when I realise that any thought I had of calling in on Mrs Zoc's sons this evening will have to be forgotten, not that I made a promise to her I would. They're twenty-five miles away at a place called Two Pots via Horseshoe Lagoon, and I've just now found I seem to be missing my legs.

*

No one light a match, and someone get me a fresh bucket, please. I'm never drinking rum again, or travelling by air. This New Guinea Airways plane is smaller, older, noisier, rockier and stinks of vomit. Notably, it also doesn't have hostesses; it has a steward who looks like a shitty old salt with some experience in catering for halfwits. His eye on me. We leave the coast for the Coral Sea and I probably wouldn't mind if he chucked me out the door and into it.

'Get some more water into you, young Brockie,' the Kiwi says, holding a glass in front of me. He is a surveyor and he's called Errol, Errol Flynn, for his famous rescue of some native women and children when the volcano erupted two years ago, which he and Johno re-enacted for my edification some time last night on the staircase of the pub. Johno was one of the native girls and I was that edified I was crying with it. What Errol's real name is, I can't remember. Someone Flynn. My head is the volcano now. I can only submit to Errol's superior knowledge of alcohol poisoning and get the water in me, before passing out again. I will see the Barrier Reef another time.

'Get some fresh air at Moresby, Brockie,' Johno suggests, but I don't want fresh air when we land there to pick up fuel and drop off the mail. I will see Port Moresby another time too. I just want to sleep, and fortunately I do, like a dead man, just about the whole trip, until I hear Johno at my shoulder: 'Wake up, kiddo, we're home.'

Home? I sit up and look out the window of the plane.

He says: 'There, that's Rabaul.'

Rabaul. I can't see the town from here, only the harbour opening out as we approach from the south. A harbour that is a volcano, a flooded caldera. I can see the peaks of its vents rising up out of the water.

'That's Vulcan,' Johno points at the mountain we're banking around to the west, descending, 'and there's the new island.' He points down into the bay and I stand up to see it: a stretch of fresh pumice below us. He told me about it somewhere in the craze of last night. Vulcan is the vent that erupted, prompting Errol's heroism, creating a new island six hundred feet high, from spewing up a mass of coral reef a mile wide, raising the bottom of the bay with a tremendous undersea pyroclastic surge. I wake up fully with the realisation now: I'm seeing a live volcano for the first time. This is a place where the earth really does speak.

I go across to look out the other side of the plane. There's a streak of steam coming out of another vent ahead. 'That one's Matupi,' Johno says, and I look at him: he's *seen* a volcanic eruption. How amazing is that?

He's gone back to looking out the portside window now as the town appears, a small town, with the mountains behind it, hardly there at all. 'Beautiful, isn't she?' he says quietly, in some sort of awe.

'She is,' I can only agree.

The setting sun is lighting up the clouds above the peaks bright pink. The water of the bay is purple and the palm trees are blue. Beautiful, like nothing I've ever seen. By the time the pilot brings us down with a kiss of the hull, I might be a bit in awe of this New Britain too.

BERNIE

Yoohoo frowns at the bump below my waistband, which I'm patting by way of explaining why there's no chance I will be able to step in and do this turquoise slipper-satin gown she's just draped over my desk, for her autumn evening-wear show. It's gorgeous, but it's also an unforgiving Molyneux, moulded hip line not designed for breathing, much less this thing.

She asks it, ever the optimist: 'But it might be over by Saturday?' Shaking my head, no, it's not that sort of bloat; I make a bulging gesture over the bump to say it's only going to get worse. 'Oh.' She frowns again, slowly, peering hard at it as she takes in what I mean, and then she says: 'Yes. Well. That would explain a few things, wouldn't it. Have you been to the doctor?'

'Not yet.' Don't think I need a doctor to tell me what any dill might find out after a visit to the public library, the big one under the Queen Vic, asking the librarian with just the right amount of awkwardness for something on preparing for marriage, so that one might be directed to a well-thumbed copy of *For The Young Wife*. It's simply expressed there: yes, not getting your curse means you're either sick, defective or – I don't want to hear it out aloud. As if not hearing it might somehow make it go away. Stop the pleats of my blouse bowing out of whack with my *blossoming bustline*. Stop me returning every other day to the library during my lunch hour to see if the book might say something different, as if the dates might say I'm not about four months along, and as if I might stop wanting to buy another pound of plums from the barrow outside while I'm there. I can't stop eating those plums.

'Don't look so glum,' Yoohoo chirps. 'So, you'll have to bring the wedding forward. You won't be the first to do that.'

'I know.' My own parents managed it themselves, history repeating like – don't even mention pork chops to me. It's not the embarrassment I'm worried about, not the moral issue or what the gossips will think. It's – it's that I don't want to have a baby. Not now. And then five minutes later, when I think of how happy everyone will be, I go all fluttery inside and I *do* want a baby, our baby – I want half-a-dozen, delirious at that picture. And then I don't want one at all again. It's too soon. Too soon for what, for Pete's sake? I don't want it to interfere with my shopping in Singapore? The cut of my figure on Waikiki? I need Yoohoo to slap me.

But she says, gone all sparkly with happiness for me now: 'Have you told him yet?'

'No!' I just about yell it. I can't tell Rock. Not now. Even if I wanted to. He's incommunicado for the next several weeks as they've gone into the jungle to do whatever it is they do to look for oil. In several weeks I won't be able to hide this bump under the peplum of my jacket. We won't be able to marry in time to keep this secret. Keep it decent. I suppose I'll have to go over there, to him, arrange a very small wedding indeed, in Rabaul. Mum will be so disappointed to call off St Brigid's, and she *will* be embarrassed. Forget horrified: she'll be humiliated. It'll look like a shotgun with me waddling up to some registry, and Dad won't be able to attend to laugh us through it. And I was going to ask Yoohoo to be my bridesmaid, too; I was going to ask her to do the decorations for the reception, at the Bay, a surprise for Mum. Something to stick in the beaks. I've ruined everything, for everyone, especially myself. The one flimsy thread of purpose I had and I've ruined it. Purpose? I'm going to be a mother. That's a purpose all right. And the book says nothing about the screaming, hair-curling terror that takes me at the thought.

'Oh, but he'll be thrilled, won't he?' Yoohoo gives me a squeeze.

I nod. He will. I can see him, a picture of pure thrill. He'll throw his hat in the air, and that thought swings me screaming back the other way. Into his smile, one that tastes of caramel as I melt into him. He won't care about the circumstances. He's already got his eye on a house for us, a white weatherboard up in the hills above the town, with a cool breeze, a view of the volcanoes, and a yard where fruit just falls off the trees and into your hands. The people who are renting it are moving back to Brisbane next Christmas. Perfect for us. He told me all about it in his last call, three Saturdays ago. He's booked a telephone call every Saturday since he left, ten shillings a minute it costs, and he doesn't care. He's so thrilled doing what he's doing there, in his element, being essential and getting paid a small fortune to go hiking, and otherwise playing bad tennis at the club where he says the inmates are a bit wild, *but geez they're a grouse mob. You're going to love it, Bernie. Bathers are compulsory on the court – it's been raining that much, you just about have to swim everywhere anyway.* With our baby. In the jungles of New Guinea.

'Bernie,' Yoohoo says, because she's as sharp as she is lovely, 'if it's worth doing, it's going to be daunting, isn't it?'

I nod again. Of course it's daunting. What else would it be? And what else did I expect? It's not so very long ago that I thought kissing a boy made babies. I might not understand the science of this business much better now, but I knew what I was up for when I kissed him, didn't I. I'll get used to the idea of this consequence. I pat my bump again: we'll work things out, won't we. Baby. Good grief.

Yoohoo slaps me gently: 'And you'll never know how envious I am.' A prod to work things out promptly. Edie Peterson is sharp and lovely and twenty-seven, just hasn't found the right fish in the sea, yet. I have the right fish. The very best of them. There is no doubt about that in my mind, not one shred of doubt at all. It's time to put my skates on, catch up with my blessings, and start being blooping well grate–

'Miss Cooper.' Count Heany sneaks up behind me with a whispery creek of his door. A *wrong* fish if ever there was one. And there's only one reason I'm still here working for him: to distract me from my woes. Yoohoo scoops the gown up from my desk and disappears in a swish of slipper satin as I turn and smile at him with my secret: *I'm having a baby, yes, say the word – P.R.E.G.N.A.N.T. – and one of the great benefits of it is that soon, very soon, Master, I will never see you again.* But I remove the smile: he looks a bit grimmer than usual. Something bad has happened, the printer no doubt has made some dreadful mistake that's all my fault. He says: 'Please, come into my office.'

Please? Strange note; the Count is not one for common courtesies. But now he's ushering me in with, 'Please, Miss Cooper, sit down,' and I know something is very out of the ordinary here. Sit down? He only ever tells me to *sit*, and it's never an invitation.

I sit down and some reflex sends my hand protectively to my bump as he begins over steepled fingers: 'Some difficult decisions have had to be made in these most difficult of times, and I regret to inform you that there is no longer a need for a full-time advertising assistant at Chalmers. The directors have decided to limit stock to British-made lines for the duration of the war, concentrating more on the luxury lines, and in much reduced quantities, having now turned over so much warehousing to the Department of Army for munitions storage. As you are aware, many of the British lines, particularly in luxury apparel, come with their own exclusive advertising material and so therefore ...'

I've got the sack. He keeps droning on about it, but I'm not interested in any rationale other than my own. I can't wear a Molyneux frock and now I can't write two words about one either? I was only ever good for flogging cheap and nasty Jap underwear anyway? How dare you! Despite hating this job, despite spending the past at least six months fantasising about my departure, I now want to hit him with a brick for depriving me of the luxury of resigning.

I stand up, cut him off: 'Thank you.'

Mr Heany stands too. 'Miss Cooper, of course I shall provide you with a suitable letter of reference. You have been–'

'Please don't bother about it,' I cut him off again. 'I'm getting married.'

Gone.

I pick up my handbag, and walk out of the office, down the fire stairs. It's only four o'clock. Let this be my resignation, my one hour's worth of dignity.

No. Make that five minutes. In my present distraction of useless, if righteous, rage, I'm charging across Liverpool Street at the corner of Castlereagh, full steam with the not-fairs, when I get my left heel caught in the tram tracks, to be sure that my dignity thumps abruptly to the asphalt.

Smack on my backside.

Ow. Ow. Ow.

Right outside the steps of Foy's, audience of hundreds, attending their April Super Savings sale – pure merino dressing gowns in there down to 30/-, put one on lay-by for Dad last Friday, in taupe. It gets chilly out at Ingleburn.

Ow. Ow. Ow.

'Oh miss, my word, are you all right?' A cab driver scoops me up before I'm flattened by the oncoming Railway Square.

'I'm all right, yes,' I think. 'Thank you.'

Just a well-accomplished dill.

*

In a considerable distraction of pain by the time I get home. Must have jarred the small of my back in the fall: breathtaking.

'Those high heels – they'll finish you one day!' Mum squawks, then she clucks: 'Get into the bath and then into bed, Missy,' and I do as I'm told. 'Lie flat, close your eyes, while I get you some tea, see if it doesn't settle.'

It doesn't settle. It gets worse. Turning into what feels like curse cramps stabbing through to my spine and making me call out: 'Mum!'

'What, love?' Mum runs back in to me, turning on the overhead light as I throw back my bedclothes, trying to get up, get away from this pain, and as I do I see the blood. My bed is covered with blood. It takes a moment to understand that it's mine.

'Oh no, oh no.' Mum is bundling up my sheets, and telling me: 'Look away, love.'

Look away? I want to curl up on the floor. My legs are shaking with the pain but I look away. I look up above the bed, at the little rosewood cross there, our tiny ivory Lord suffering there forever in the middle of my forget-me-not wallpaper, and then I suddenly understand what the blood must be. The pain. The baby.

'No!' I wail it. 'No!'

'Shush, love,' Mum says gently, even though she's busy cleaning up my mess. Cleaning up me. Bundling me back into fresh sheets and holding me as I cry, as I've never cried. 'Shush, love, it's all right. It wasn't meant to be.'

'What?' What did Mum just say? Wasn't meant to be? 'You *knew*?'

'Yes, love, I had my suspicions,' she says, soft as the warm kitchen smell of her, stroking my forehead. 'I know what goes on in my laundry. You haven't had your things for a while.'

Things, what Mum calls the curse, and I see what she means: although I wash my own bits and pieces, it's her laundry and she knows what goes on it. Where I've been, or haven't. That makes me cry again: she's been waiting for me to come to her, keeping her disappointment to herself.

'It might be for the best anyway, Bernie love,' she tries to soothe me. 'You'll have another. Next year, when you're properly married. You'll see. Maybe you've been spared worse. Sometimes I do wonder if our Lord punished me for, well, you know, jumping the gun, as they say.'

Dreaming me up before Father O'Brien said Amen, as Dad always teases her, but: 'What do you mean punished?'

'Oh,' she sighs, 'I had a lot of trouble afterwards.'

'Thanks a lot,' I try to joke, not funny, the pain coming back for me again, with interest.

'Not you, silly,' Mum clucks, mystified by me as much as I am by her, and then she tells me: 'I lost four babies after you. And the last one got a bit dangerous, so I had to go into St Margaret's and have the doctor make it so I couldn't have another. Your father made me go in. I didn't want to.'

Mum. There's no euphemism for what's in her eyes now: this pain. It still hurts her after all these years.

'But it was for the best, Bernie. As this is for you. You'll see. It'll be all right.' She looks up at the cross. 'Maybe you'll be spared my troubles.'

She's asking Hughie for that to be so, praying for it. And I want to wail again: *Hughie doesn't care, Mum. He doesn't care about us.* Dad told me that himself, years ago, a Saturday afternoon, he was a bit pie-eyed and full of some worry about the garage, and I asked him why he called God 'Hughie', and he told me, *Hughie is the rain, never around when you need him, he's drought and then a flood followed by a bushfire; and calling him Hughie is better than calling him what he ought to be called.*

A baby stealer.

I've lost my baby. Our baby. I'm so sorry, Gordon. Sorry and grateful only that you'll never know about it.

I roll away and curl around my pain. Mine. And rage returns. *Sorry.* There's not going to be any wedding now, is there. I'm not going through this again. I'm going to cry for a hundred years. I have nothing now: no job, no marriage, no baby. No baby? All my horrible, sinful, selfish whingeing about not wanting my baby smashes into my spine. I don't deserve to be a mother. I don't deserve Rock. I don't deserve anything less than this punishment. I'm a disaster. The whole world is a disaster, waiting to unfold, and the unfolding begins here, right here: in me. It's all my fault.

'It was a girl,' Mum says.

A girl. Of course it was a girl. My baby girl. I'm going to wail forever.

*

I make a good attempt at disappearing into the mattress, at least until Thursday morning when I hear the front gate squeak, boots clomping up the path.

'Peggy!'

It's Dad. Come home a day early. Surprise. And you've never seen a girl pull herself together faster: he can't know about any of my nonsense. He's got more important things to worry about, such as the next one hundred and twenty recruits he's preparing for Hughie's boy-stealing machine.

'Dad!' I'm in the hall and in his arms in a heartbeat, in desperate need of his bear hug.

'Bernie? What are you doing home, and in your nightie?' he says, and as I let him make his way in, I give him a brief but embellished account of my fall on Tuesday night, about Mum being a pest making me stay in bed, lying like there's no tomorrow, apart from how sore my back still is. Not too sore compared to how tired Dad looks, though. He chuckles at my tale of calamity, 'Just as well the cabbie stopped or we'd still be picking you out of the tracks, eh?' But there's something on his mind. Distracted: he's come home to speak to Mum about something. Something serious.

'Hello, Bill,' she says with a lack of surprise: she knows what goes on in her kitchen as well as anywhere else. A look passes between them, as if Dad's done something to earn her disapproval, got some explaining to do. A long silence before Mum asks him: 'So where are they sending you?' She's holding the rolling pin as though she might hit him with it, or turn back to the shortcrust, depending on the answer.

'Peg,' he says, apologising. 'Beyond Palestine, I don't know, not really.'

No, I didn't hear that. This is not happening. Not now. I'm still asleep. I want to be still asleep, wrapped around my warm ball of pain.

'Hmm,' Mum sniffs: 'Of course you don't know where you're going – the army don't tell you anything, do they.' Turns back to the pastry.

Dad opens a bottle of beer; it's only ten o'clock. 'We flipped a coin, the other captain, Pat Sullivan, and me, to see which one of us would go. I won.'

'You won?' Mum doesn't stop rolling.

'He's got littlies, Peg. Two little girls, too small to be without a father for so long.'

My heart screams: *What about me?* I'm too small to be without my father. I want to hurl myself around his ankles to stop him from leaving me. For Palestine. I know most of Dad's division is already there, in the desert. The Sixth Div. I've heard Dad complain that it's the same story as the last war – *Hanging about getting skinny, waiting for the Somme.* Shaking his head: *Or are they busy planning Gallipoli II for us? Only Hughie would know.* No. Dad's not going there. Not going anywhere. He can't go.

It bursts out of me: 'No, Dad. You can't go.'

'Yes, Bernie, I'm afraid I have to. You don't need to worry too much on my account, though.' He starts pouring his beer, but I've caught the torture of sadness in his eyes before he looks down. He assures his perfect quarter inch of froth: 'I'll still only be minding the young fellas; you know I'm too old to do any real soldiering. I'll be stuck out in the desert helping the kids to get skinnier, marching them out to the pyramids. That's all.'

And I'm old enough now to know you're lying too, Dad.

'You'll have to make sure you get some good pictures of the wedding for me, love,' he says.

I lie in return: 'Course, Dad.'

*

The only thing that's giving Mum away is her grip on my hand as we watch the parade up Martin Place. She's so brave to come out to this, risking a display. But how could she not? This could be the last time she ever sees the love of her life. She's so stone-faced she's a statue, not seeing the way the troops pass three by three through this avenue of banks, past the cenotaph like a great snake devouring Lest We Forget, not seeing the ticker-tape snow falling all around us, only watching for the head of the next company to appear, waiting to see him.

A few feet away, a girl rushes out in front of us and flings herself at one of the boys, kissing him, and a policeman drags her off, her Breton halo tumbling off her head. There's a display for you; I'm raising an eyebrow at it as Mum's fingers dig deeper into my palm and she says: 'I did that exact thing. Twenty-five years ago, almost to the day. Your father got in such trouble for it from his captain, too.'

Ha. Well, there you go. Always more to the story, isn't there? Mum and Dad. They'd only met the fortnight before he set off for the Great War, at a tram stop, so the story I know goes, the greatest love story ever told: the boy from Gilgandra and the girl from the

Paddo slums who couldn't wait to get away, but had to wait five years, a wait that was worth it, for he was as true as his word: he came back, and he came back for her.

Come back again, Dad.

How Mum hasn't dissolved into a small ocean of display a hundred times over in the last five minutes, I don't know.

I go back to watching for Dad again, up on my toes as if that might help, and I see Colin Quinn instead. Marching with the auxiliary trades. He looks good in the uniform, making him broad and tall and, incredibly, out of what must be a thousand in this crowd, he sees me too and grins across the barrel of his rifle. Take that as a reminder that miracles do happen; will happen; must. I wave. The pipes and drums of 'Australia Will Be There' roll into 'Waltzing Matilda', and then I see him: Dad.

'Dad!' There he is at the head of his company, and all I can see is my dad. My heart would be breaking into a million pieces if it wasn't thumping so hard and fast with pride.

Mum releases my hand and waves with both of hers, shouting: 'Oh, my wonderful man!'

Her smile is the light of the world, nothing less, and with it the only choice left to me becomes clear. I can disappear into my grief, into this small warm-ball nothing of my own design, or, daunting as it is, I can be brave myself.

Life is as wonderful as it is cruel. Get used to it. Get on with it.

Be as brave as my parents are.

But can I?

GORDON

'You get paid a quid a year for it,' Johno laughs, handing me a mug of tea. 'Don't be shy.'

'I'm not being shy,' I tell him. He's trying to talk me into joining the New Guinea Volunteer Rifles, the militia up here, while we're having a billy, hanging about camp waiting for our hoisting engine to arrive for the rig. But it's a difficult issue for me. I wasn't even allowed to join cadets at school.

'There something wrong with you?' Johno's not shy about much at all. And he's not knocking me either. He's genuinely interested. He's a good bloke. I like him a lot.

So I'm straight with him. 'No, there's nothing wrong. It's that my father wouldn't be happy if I did any sort of military service.'

'Oh, righto. Fair enough,' Johno nods, pouring himself a brew, 'and that's your business, too. But you do realise you're going to have to do some kind of service, get ticked off the list, don't you? Unmarried and twenty-one, you're expected to get the national service training at least. They'll catch up with you and you'll be shanghaied back to Townsville or Darwin to do it. It's not like you're in a protected occupation here.'

'Aren't I?' I nearly drop my mug. I'd assumed this sort of exploration work would be considered essential industry – because it is. I say: 'Bull.'

'No, mate, no bull,' Johno laughs again. 'But if you join up here with us, then you can tick off your obligation – and have some fun at the same time. It's only target practice out on the rifle range and a few marches now and again. Nothing too cracked. I enjoy it.'

I know he does. When he's in town, first thing he does after drinking is get back out bush again. He goes out with his militia mates, hunting feral pigs with this bloke called Sven, a Norwegian giant who only ever wears a shirt on NGVF parade or when dancing at the club, and is otherwise a metallurgical chemist. Cracked. The Territories attract some interesting people, and I know I would have a great time with that mob doing just about anything. Except military training.

'Anyway.' Johno screws up his nose, the way he does whenever he's got bad news for you, like the native labourers aren't turning up for work because they've gone fishing, or the hoisting engine for our rig is going to remain on the docks indefinitely because the local witch doctor is blessing it. But he says now: 'I reckon it would be a good idea to make yourself handy with a rifle.'

'I am handy with a rifle,' I tell him, a bit browned at the suggestion I might not know how to look after myself. Dad gave me my own .22 when I was ten, and taught me to get a rabbit for myself, for necessity. I can hit dinner between the eyes at fifty yards. 'But why should it matter out here?' I ask Johno. You don't need to shoot anything to eat well in this country: food really does just fall off the trees.

Johno gives me that look, the emu blink that says, *Shit, you are a kid,* before he says: 'There's a war on, you dozy bastard. Don't expect the blackfellas to fight off the Krauts for us if they decide they want their colony back. They don't owe us anything, Brockie.'

'It's true.' Rico, our carpenter, joins us, rolling a smoke. Rico Micallef: he's from Melbourne, via Malta, and he's been taking contracts in New Guinea for even longer than Johno. He says: 'People here have long memories, and I don't blame them. I was down in Kokopo when the RAAF planes came and dropped the bombs on those villages – the payback for them killing those copper prospectors. Remember that, Johno?'

'Heard about it,' Johno says.

And I say: 'What bombs?' They're having me on. Not unknown for them to string me along with a tall one – man-eating pythons, giant face-sucking leeches, flying pigs, et cetera.

'Bad business.' Johno looks into his tea, not having me on. 'These two idiots, poking about where they shouldn't have been, going into a women's hut, and then everyone's shocked when they get speared. The RAAF rains jam-tin bombs down on the villages along the coast at Kokopo in response – the wrong villages too. It was pretty disgusting.'

'Oh. Right.' Christ.

'Yeah *oh right*. So you see, Brockie, it wouldn't take much for them to turn Nazi on us if the opportunity arose. You know, the Krauts treated them better than we do, the Lutherans getting their kids in school and that. We give them one school, three miles out of town at Nordup, and start interning the Lutheran missionaries. We give them bugger-all in return for all we take.'

I take a moment to consider our position a bit more carefully. My position specifically. I'm sitting on a log outside a tent, in a jungle, somewhere on the northwest tip of the Gazelle Peninsula in the middle of the Bismarck Sea, only twenty miles crow's flight from Rabaul, but twenty thousand years from civilisation. In front of me sits our derrick, the eighty-five-foot mast of our rig that will hold the drill rods, which has been constructed with the assistance of native labour, when they could be bothered, or when they've run out of tobacco. We're waiting for them now to haul two tons of hoisting engine along a track that's as muddy as it is steep, through forest that dense it could close over again come the next shower. Why? So that we can make a small consortium of professional gamblers and petrol-station owners unbelievably rich.

At a rough estimate, on this island there are maybe fifty thousand blacks. Who would really know how many there were? There are not more than two thousand of us, in the town, including Chinese shopkeepers. But here, right here, there is me, Johno and Rico, and a boilermaker who, like the engine, hasn't turned up yet.

I spill my tea as I realise: Bernie can't come and live here. I don't want her to. I can't guarantee her safety. I won't be able to look Mr Cooper in the eye and say she will be all right. Because I won't be with her to protect her should we have a situation. Once we start drilling, I'll be gone fairly solidly for six months, till we get down twenty-five hundred feet or so, into the basalt capping stone the Anglo-Eastern maps tell me we'll find or till the rainy season bogs us, and after that, if the core samples are promising, I'm to keep on down to six thousand feet, before starting on another hole, and then another, and possibly another until a decision can be made on where to spud the wells. There's my three years laid out. How am I going to tell her?

'Didn't mean to put the wind up you.' Johno gives me a nudge, spilling my tea some more. 'You can pay me back on the rifle range, ay? Since you're so handy.'

'Yeah,' I say. I look at the back of my hand, brushing the drops of tea off my knee, and I'm not sure what sort of a shot I'd be if a situation happened right now. The knuckle is still that tender in a grip. I have enough trouble with a tennis racquet. So I stare at the fire, and put in a good effort at ignoring the idea that I might have made a bit of a mistake coming to New Britain.

I'm sure I hear a twig snap behind us. But as I go to look over my shoulder all I see is a wagtail hopping about on the ground near my bedourie. She's just like the ones at home, only maybe a bit bigger.

'Don't worry, mate,' Johno says. 'Newton's second law of thermodynamics is always there for us when no one else is.'

'What?' I don't understand the joke.

'The perpetual contest between chaos and equilibrium,' he says, not joking. He tosses the dregs of his tea at the coals. 'War and peace,' he says. 'There's no escaping it. It's only natural. Everything is, isn't it, until we decide we don't like it for some reason. We like beautiful volcanic islands until they explode, we like a nice fire until it burns the house down. We like German engineering until there's a war. We like guns until we get shot. It's only perception. Everything creates as much as it destroys – humans, volcanoes, trees, ants, bacteria. Everything.'

He points up at the sky. There's a harpy eagle circling high above us. Then he thumbs over at the derrick: 'We make a clearing in the forest here for the rig, destroy a whole heap of shit for it, but that makes a place for small birds and wallabies to forage, and it makes a place for that eagle to forage too. Who's the bad guy there, mate? Everything's a shitfight, if you think about it, right down to the atomic level. Everything's good. And here's as good as anywhere for a good old shitfight, isn't it? Keep your eyes and your mind open, ay? You'll be right.'

I'll have something to wonder about for the next thousand years at least. This is why I like Johno. I think he's probably a genius. I look over my shoulder again. The wagtail's still there, hopping about, and as I look at her this time, I remember I saw one go a kookaburra over territory once, out at Blackie's Camp. Fearless. She won, too.

Johno's on his feet now. The sound of the natives' singing is coming up the track, and I'm quick on my feet, too. A train of bamboo litters is arriving: they've got all our gear. When I see they've brought up the load of our rods as well, I can't wait to get into the drilling. With any luck, we're going to get the rig going this arvo. And Johno is right: it's only perception, isn't it. Suddenly, I wouldn't be anywhere else.

'Hard work starts for you now.' Rico slaps me on the shoulder, then picks up his tool belt. He's counting the days till the end of his contract, about nine hundred to go.

I'm not. I'm thinking: yes. Work starts now. After all these weeks of planning, my job is finally about to begin.

One of the natives waves at me from under the weight of the boiler, calling out: 'Ello, boss.' But I don't know which one he is. They still all look the same to me, these ones that come up and work for us: fuzzy gold hair, white smiles, brown skin and red sarongs.

'Who's that one?' I ask Johno.

'To-An,' he says. 'And he doesn't give a shit about Newton's second law of thermodynamics. He goes to church on Sundays, like a good little black boy should.'

Johno starts jogging over to the rig, calling out something in their Kua-Nua language, and I'm stuck, as I always am, watching the way he is with them. He's been working here a long time, I know, but I've never known anyone to give the respect he does to a black, talking to them in their language, not pidgin. He laughs as easily with them as he does with me or anyone. He's laughing now, scaling up the derrick with one of them, easily as he can scale a palm trunk, racing one of them, making me wonder if he *is* one of them. He's not. He can't be. He has a degree. From Queensland Uni, too. I suppose he's just an anomaly I'm lucky enough to have coincided with.

'Brockie!' He yells down to me now. 'Stop your dozing, mate, and get up here, will you?'

*

Three weeks' drilling and my shirts have got tight from lifting and bagging rock. I don't doze. I am either at it or unconscious, triple-checking the core samples in my dreams. The blue and tan bands of the pyroclastic strata here, the ash and pumice, are consistently showing we're drilling where we should be. I'm confident, I'm sure I am, so I decide to head back to Rabaul to report our progress, to get permission to continue with this hole.

I have to go out with a native guide to get through the rainforest, and Johno arranges for To-An to take me. If he turns up. And he does, after a three-hour wait. Nine o'clock he wanders over, and I recognise him now by the chip on one of his front teeth. I've also learned that anyone would have trouble distinguishing one native from the other round here because they're all brothers and cousins from just two families, and there are three sets of twins among them. They're all mostly called To-Something, too, and all call each other *to-lai,* which apparently means mate, and does nothing to assist in their easy identification either.

'Ello, boss,' To-An waves, always with that smile suggesting he thinks the title might be a bit of a joke applied to me.

'Hello To-An.' I'm already walking, heading down the top of the pass, which has become known as the Slippery Dip after the loss of one of the rods – *It slippy-slippy, boss.* It did: all ten yards of it disappeared off the mudslide into the forest below, never to be seen again, not by human eyes anyway.

He says beside me now: 'Him rocks speak you good, ay?' Apparently I also look funny when I'm inspecting the cores, as if I am talking to them.

'Yes, the rocks speak very good, To-An,' I tell him, and he laughs – at me.

It would be good to have the language to tell him it might be funny but it's true. I'm am talking to them, in a way, at least trying to work out what they're saying to me. But the language gulf is too wide for anything much but instructions.

That doesn't stop To-An trying to chat. 'Looky him, boss,' he's saying next.

I'd rather keep my eyes on my feet in this mud, on this gradient, but I look up to where he's pointing, in case it's Ooga Booga, the vampire spider, or one of those flying pigs. But it's only a wagtail, hopping along a liana vine ahead.

'Him belong you,' To-An says, and he's not laughing. 'Him follow you. Him you clan.'

My turn to laugh at To-An: I suppose he's telling me this bird is my totem or some superstitious bull or other. Him doesn't follow us any further down the pass, and To-An stops the chat with me. His face is blank. I've probably upset him. Well done, Brockie.

After an hour or so the forest opens out a bit. The gradient declines, too, as the ground firms and the palms reach a height of a hundred feet or more. Incredible. Another world. The village we're heading to, Kabakada, is to the east, but my compass tells me we're going due west; I have no idea where I am. I might be a competitive hiker, but this is not the gum forest I know. It's so thick with vegetation. Giant lilly pillies and beech are a canopy beneath the canopy of palms, and under them is another canopy, mainly of fat tree ferns. There's no sense of the sun. The light is a green mist in every direction, all day, and I don't relax until we sight the coast, where we start following the mangroves along the North Road, the only road, travelling east at last.

It's almost three by the time we get to Kabakada, which is the village To-An and all the brothers and cousins come from. We've been walking nearly six hours. It only looks ten miles on the map, but I *know* we've walked at least twenty, and you just can't get any pace on in this humidity. I'm very glad to see the Southern Star jeep waiting for me at the back of the grass huts and frangipanis of the village. There's smoke coming up from the women's huts, but there's no one else around. Must have gone fishing, further up the beach. The keys are in the ignition of the jeep; no one to pinch it either. What would a To-Something do with a jeep anyway? He wouldn't be able to go into Rabaul, not without a pass from a boss, or the native police would wallop him, literally and conscientiously. I start the engine and tell To-An: 'See you tomorrow, at dawn, when the sun comes up, here in Kabakada.' And he laughs: 'Yeah, boss.' If and when it suits him.

I put my foot down on the accelerator. From here the drive to Rabaul is only twenty minutes, but I think I'll probably do it in ten, I am that keen to see civilisation again. As soon as I'm through Tunnel Hill and on the bitumen, catching sight of the whitewashed town and tramlines of Malaguna Road, all I want to do is have a bath. After I've called Bernie. It's the twentieth of May today. I haven't seen her face for nineteen weeks. Please don't let the wireless be out. Don't let the line be booked out either.

As I drive through town, I look out across Simpson Harbour at Blanche Bay, at the shape of the volcano. Mother Mountain and her North Daughter and South Daughter are asleep behind Mount Matupi – the one that's always steaming and groaning, always threatening to show how alive a rock can be. I want to go up there, as close as I can to the lava, when I have the time. It's only three miles away, but I can't even say when I'll be back in Rabaul again, let alone organise a hike. How am I going to tell Bernie that? That I'm not keen on her living in this town while I'm away, that we will probably only get three months together out of every year I'm here, at an optimum. I'm concerned she'll get cold feet about the whole thing. Maybe I shouldn't say anything yet, wait until after the wedding. I can't do that, though. Can I?

I turn into Casuarina Avenue, past the Pacific Hotel, the rum palace that's always full of sailors and dockers, and some very interesting people that probably had to disappear from normal society not exactly by choice. There's a brothel behind it up the top of Chinatown, where you can get heroin and Christ knows what else. But then the she oaks of this wide avenue open out into a flower garden, and I can see Bernie here, picking orchids on her way to buying some pork roasted in sweet red sauce from

Ah Ching's on Solomon Street. I can see her with a frangipani behind her ear bargaining for fish and pineapples with the marys, the native women, at their market called the Bung. I can see her picking passionfruit off the vines that grow up the stilts of the Commonwealth Bank here, an old Queensland bungalow that looks more like a holiday resort. And I want her here, I do, in this town that's not much bigger than Nyngan, but it's an amazing place. What if she just came up when I'm in town? In the rainy season. January and February it rains so hard you may as well really wear your bathers everywhere. Two or three months of amazement a year would be better than whole years of ordinariness, wouldn't it?

But first things first. I have to stop into the Southern Star office to report that I haven't buggered things up with the rig: we are drilling in the right place. The office is over the other side of the flower garden in Court Street, a smaller version of the Commonwealth resort. Mr Taylor, the chief of exploration, and the chief geo, Mr Roycox, are already having a gin sling on the verandah as I pull into the drive. It's a tough life for some. I'm sure they do more important things than changing their shirts three times a day. I just don't know what, apart from sometimes having a gin with Mr Komazaki, the Jap who owns the shipyards, ready to strike a deal as soon as we strike the black gold. In any case, town hours are unreal, especially for public servants, they work from nine till twelve, and then, after a nap, from two till four, yawning.

'Hello, young Brock.' Mr Taylor stands and waves me over as I get out of the jeep: 'I do hope you bring good news for us?'

His wireless voice is turned on full. This is not his first gin. I tell him, 'I do,' holding up my core-sample logbook. As I take the stairs and hand it over, I notice the houseboy cutting the lawn round the side, with shears: they work twenty-four hours a day. The inequity knocks me a bit sideways for a second, probably from being out of town for a while. But it's the way the world works, and not my concern today. I reel off my facts for my bosses, that the composition of the pyroclastic overlayer so far matches the Anglo-Eastern data, and the bagged-up samples are to follow for their analysis. 'Hm, hm,' they nod, as Mr Taylor hands the log to

Mr Roycox, who puts it on the card table behind him. They look a bit like Laurel and Hardy, only it's skinny Mr Taylor with the toothbrush moustache and they both wear panamas rather than bowlers. I add, for what it's worth, what I think might be one small discrepancy: 'There's some dacite apparent in the last few cores that I didn't expect at this—'

'Never mind that,' Mr Roycox says with a clap of his fat hands. 'Carry on down for the oil, lad.' There's my permission from my scientific senior. Chief geo: I don't think he even has a degree. He's certainly not interested in geology. It's Mr Taylor who got my name from Professor Richardson, not Mr Roycox, some old boys' connection from the Kings School. And the dacite doesn't really matter, I don't suppose – it's just another type of igneous rock very probably splattered over the entire island at many and various times.

Mr Taylor puts his hand on my shoulder. 'Will you join us at the club for dinner?'

No. I recognise that this offer is an acknowledgement of my efforts to make these men and their cohorts rich, but I don't want to go their club. The Rabaul Club. It's where plantation owners go to count their coconuts with the senior public nappers, in the traditional airconditioned atmosphere, so I'm told, of native boys waving palm fronds. As my father's son I couldn't accept an invitation to dine with bank managers. As plainly myself I can't either, because I'm going to the New Guinea Club, two steps round the corner from here, where my trunk is, and where I'm going to have that very long bath after I've made my call to Bernie. The service to Sydney opens at four; it's a quarter to now. I put them off with an appeal to their greed: 'Thank you but no. It will have to be an early start for me in the morning. The sooner I'm back at the rig, the sooner we recommence the drilling.'

'Good show,' says Mr Taylor. 'I knew you were our man the moment I met you.'

I'm not your man, I think, but as I say cheerio to them, I can't say to myself whose man I am. My own? Not for the next three years anyway.

The afternoon sun just about quilts me as I pull into the drive of the New Guinea. There's music already coming from the lounge, laughter coming up off the tennis courts at the rear, but I'm going straight round to the Weekender, where the accommodation is.

'A room with a bath, young Mr Brock?' the manager's wife, Mrs Chittaway, smiles from the reception desk when she sees me. I must smell bad, too. But when she says, 'A call to Sydney this afternoon?' she's frowning. 'I'm sorry, pet, the afternoon service is cancelled today, terrific storms over the mainland. But the morning service is expected to resume as normal at eleven am tomorrow. Will that suit instead?'

No. That's too late. I have to leave at dawn. You can't do this to me. But Mrs Chittaway adds: 'Ah, but I do have a letter for you, came a few weeks ago now.'

She fishes around under the desk, and I'm expecting it to be from His Majesty, catching up with me, for overdue national service. But it's not. As soon as I smell Bernie's White Lilac, my heart rate doubles. I don't know why, but I'm suddenly convinced she's calling it off, that it's a Dear Gordon letter. Halfwit. It's the first letter from Bernie. My first letter ever from my girl. I'm going to be excited, aren't I. Open it here in reception. My hands are shaking as I read:

My wonderful darling Rock
I have absolutely nothing to tell you but I had to write to let
you know that I love you, with every atom in me. I love you
come what may. I love you always.
  Bernie

She loves me. My mind goes into a spin, looping round every word, lost in the R of her *Rock*. I've never seen her name for me written out before. And she's never said she loves me before.

She loves me.

BERNIE

It looks like a budgie, not an aeroplane, spluttering out of the De Havilland hangar here at Mascot Aerodrome. It doesn't look like a plane at all, not compared to the huge thing that Rock went up in. But this – this Tiger Moth – is a training plane. For the Royal Australian Air Force.

'Ladies!' the supervisor bellows above the engine as it begins its hurtle up the runway. 'This is your machine! The pride of our war effort! The pride of the Commonwealth!'

A fleet of budgies is all I can see as another one splutters out behind it. These are the aircraft we're making, and this demonstration is to inspire our fingers to faster work. Two planes a day, seven hundred a year, is the schedule. I want to call the pilots back as they take off and up: you can't go up in the air in that thing. It's made of matchsticks and Irish linen, and I had a hand in it. You'll fall out of the sky.

I look at the faces of the girls around me: all beaming, bursting with the pride of their contribution, as the budgies whizz and swoop above us. There are eight of us wing girls, who cut and sew the linen coverings for the wings, other teams doing the fuselage, propellers and tail, and I'm the oldest of us, getting £1/5/6 per week, slave-labour wages – less than half of what I got at Chalmers. The youngest of us wing girls, Gladdy, is sixteen; she just about works for free, and is thrilled about it, jumping up and down and shouting: 'Woweeeee!' Maybe I'm too old for this. I don't want any pilots to train for war. I don't want to be a part of this aeroplane sewing machine.

We file back into the workshops at the rear of the hangar and I dread even more a return to the task itself. I got the job on the strength of my record of gainful employment and that dress-making course I didn't finish almost three years ago, but I really got it because the manager of production, Mr Dobbs, has known Dad for years from the Mechanics' Institute, and because Mrs Dobbs told Mum via the Catholic Daily natter up at the grocers that he was looking for good girls to sew the wings on budgies. I'm a fraud. I'm a good seamstress, no doubt about it, and there's no one more desiring of doing her bit, but I am –

'Oh come on, Miss Cooper, you are not a surgeon,' the supervisor, Mrs Curruthers, is already picking on me for being so slow, as she does a dozen times a day. She is the Methodist equivalent of Sister Columba: horribility incarnate. She also picks on me each morning on arrival for not wearing overalls like the other girls. Well, I'm not wearing overalls. I'm just not. There are some sacrifices my country can do without me making and one of them is overalls.

'You're the neatest,' Lena, my partner, whispers beside me when Mrs Curruthers is gone; she holds the strip of fabric taut and straight over the wooden frame as I sew. 'Not one tiniest bit of air could get through your stitching,' she says, and it's important to her at least: Lena's fiancé as well as her brother are among the trainee pilots, about to head off to Canada to learn how to be bombers. It's important to her that my stitching is more perfect than fast, so that the budgie-yellow cellulose paint will go over it smoothly, no bumps or cracks. So that the planes won't fall out of the sky.

I can't do this job. My nerves are racked rotten. But I've only been at it a fortnight, I tell myself, trying to inspire these nerves to settle down – as I shove the needle into my left thumb. *Baaa!* Ignore it. Think of Dad. And see a fleet of budgies falling out of the sky, raining down over his whole battalion.

'Miss Cooper?' Mr Dobbs is behind me now as the bell for morning tea goes. 'A word, if I may?' Lena skedaddles off outside with the others as I stand up straight, preparing to take it like a man. 'You're not quite happy at this sort of factory work, are you?'

I consider lying, but instead I say: 'Ahummm?'

He sighs, impatient but nice about it. Hard, shrewd eyes, won't suffer fools, not even Bill Cooper's daughter. 'Office work might be your sort of thing after all, no shame in that. I could make inquiries for you, if you like, with the Department of Army.'

No, please don't, is my first thought. I don't want to work for the machine at all.

'Thank you,' I tell him, 'but it's all right. I'll find something myself.'

I pick up my handbag and he says: 'You're very good, you know, just a little bit ... slow.'

Yes, I do know that, and I don't walk too slowly out the side door, into the winter sun, where one of the young airmen having a cigarette by the engine workshop whistles at me.

I glare at him. 'Shut up.'

So that the whole half-dozen of them go: 'Ooooooh. Cranky.'

Blockheads, think they're above the law in a uniform. There must be something useful I can do that's not associated with the killing of them, though. But what? I wonder as I walk up to the tram. Go to Lithgow, wherever that is, and make bullets? Girls getting paid double, shifts round the clock, hundreds more needed, to fill the arsenal of the antipodes. No chance I'd be in that, but that's about all the war work there is for a girl. With no talents. I've been scouring the papers every day since Dad left for Palestine and there's nothing – even if I did have some skill. Women's auxiliary forces are under consideration now, or might be once Big Chief Pig Face overcomes his horror of women wearing slacks – about the only point on which the Prime Minister and I agree. Other than that, there's nothing but nursing; loads of vacancies there. But that's a vocation, not a job; it's also too close to the nasty end of this business, for me.

Not something you can do for six months, either. While you're waiting to get married. Trying to convince myself that I *can* go through with it, that just because Mum had four miscarriages and a hysterectomy doesn't mean I will. History can't be that predictable.

Could be worse in store for me: I could die in childbirth. Like Gordon's poor Mum. Blooping heck. So I keep putting off making any decisions about it – can't manage to call Yoohoo to ask her about doing the reception, or being my bridesmaid, can't choose a typeface for the invitations – stalling, stalling, stalling, and disappointing Mum who wants to get on with the business of distracting herself from her worries by the only means available: my wedding. *Why don't you pop into town on your way home Friday night, love, and choose your fabric so I can make a start on the dress?* Because I can't. I am trapped, trapped the way you feel when you've got both hands full on a hot day and can't get your cardi off till after you've reached the top of the hill. What can I do? Not much, it seems, but change trams at Central.

When I finally get home, Mum's out the back in the veggie patch scraping the caterpillar eggs off her cauliflowers, again. Lost to it, unaware that I'm watching her from the kitchen window, watching her missing Dad. Mashing my heart. How can I possibly not marry Gordon? How could I do that to Mum, never mind Gordon? And yet that note I sent him, true as it is, was a warning for him too: I love you always, even if I call it off.

You can't call it off, Bernie. That is not on the menu. Just simply no, not.

Where's my bravery got to now?

I look away from Mum and down into the newspaper she's laid out by the sink ready to receive her potato peels, and see the bold type heading, *DROUGHT!* and a few columns over, *NEW AIF INFANTRY DIVISION TO BE RAISED.* I read this whole page yesterday, including the three paragraphs on the Country Women's Association continued lobbying for a women's land army, and their being told no, again: Australian properties are too vast and the work too hard for girls. Is it too hard, though? What sort of work would it be? Work that's important no doubt, in the drought, with diminishing resources of men, but not part of the machine. Maybe. I don't get as far as imagining what I might look like in an Akubra, one like Rock's with the brim turned down at the front, trusty girl rouseabout in the mythical land of Nyngan, looking for a bad storyline, when the doorbell goes.

'Bernadetta?' It's Mrs Zoc, already coming down the hall, biscuit tin in hand. She's made more of her almond shortbread for Mum, as if they can cure a sore heart. Maybe they can; they are at least criminally moreish. She presses the tin into my hands and apologises: 'I make too much biscotti again. I am old, I forget I have no one to feed but myself.'

'Oh no, not *again*,' I say. She's mad. And maybe a bit magic. The day after Dad left, she told me to sleep with my jasper B under my pillow as it would help heal my sore back, and so I did, because I am obviously mad too, and the next day, hey presto, not sore any more. I've been sleeping with it under my pillow ever since, as if it might heal everything else that's wrong with me. I tell her: 'Mum's out the back.'

'I see your mamma later,' she grins, conspiratorial. 'I bring something for you today, Bernadetta.' She reaches into her apron pocket, black linen on her black crepe frock, perennial widow all in black except for her white hair pulled into a bun, perennially elegant. But when she looks up at me again, there's a glint of fire in her dark eyes, hot-blooded as a Sicilian volcano, a glimpse of the young woman who must have made the boys of Palermo fall to their knees in the presence of Venus. 'I find this for you this morning ...'

She places a tiny clipping on top of the biscuit tin under my nose. I see what I think are the words: WORKERS WANTED. It's a job advertisement.

How could she know I lost my job this morning? The Catholic Daily couldn't have broadcast it that fast, surely. Couldn't be much more than an hour ago. Of course, it's just a coincidence. Isn't it. Read it again, properly:

WRITERS WANTED
New, innovative publishing house requires storytellers of fiction. Romance, Mystery and Adventure for serialisation and paperback publication. Send brief résumé and sample of writing no more than 20 pages in length to: Wonder Publications Pty Ltd, Level 3, 83 Goulburn Street, Sydney.

For the moment, I can't imagine how this might apply to me. I look at Mrs Zoc, who nods, smug: 'I see it in the *Woman's Mirror*.'

'*Woman's Mirror?*' As if I'm astonished Mrs Zoc can read English, never mind that it's a halfway decent magazine, but with boring serials – ones that go along the lines of Mr and Mrs Sophistication throw a cocktail party, where Mrs Sophistication meets an alluring stranger across the crowded room but ultimately decides not to jeopardise her dull but sturdy marriage and returns to reading the far more absorbing article on balancing the household budget.

Mrs Zoc points at the shelf full of six-pennies behind me through the lounge door and says: 'You are reading these all the time. Why don't you write one yourself? It will make the time go fast until Gordon comes home for you.'

I look at the rainbow spines of my romances; the current one splayed open on the table by the wireless: *The Thoroughbred*. Will Joan Markham drown in the swollen river or will Douglas McRitchie reach her in time, and kiss her with actual lip contact? I laugh: 'What on earth would I write about?' A laugh that's snipped off smartly by the fact that I can't even write a proper letter to Gordon; couldn't even find the words to tell him about Dad. About anything.

Mrs Zoc shrugs but her eyes are full of fire again: 'Write about love, bella.' As if she does the same herself every Tuesday afternoon.

'What's that?' Mum says, coming in through the kitchen.

I sing over my shoulder: 'It's Mrs Zoc – she thinks I should have a go at writing a romance.'

Mum frowns, and I'm sure the lines on her forehead have deepened over this past month. Lines that look sore. All she wants to see written is something from Dad. She says: 'What are you doing home so early, Bernie?'

I tell her: 'I got the sack. Too slow.'

And so I've got nothing better to do, have I. Might as well have a go.

*

'How quickly do you think you might be able to send us the complete manuscript, Miss, ah, Brockley?' says the gravelly voice on the end of the telephone line, a Mr Jacobs from Wonder Publications.

You are joking. I've just walked in the door from overdue penance up at the Little Sisters of the Poor, making soup, carrot under my fingernails. Brockley. That's me: Monica Brockley, concocted from my middle name and almost married one, because I didn't imagine for a second ... 'Beg pardon?'

'The opening chapters you sent us are very promising. We would like to see the complete manuscript, your novel, ah, *Paper Wings And Heart Strings*.'

'Er. Yes.' Oh my blooping stars. There is no such thing. What have I done now? It was only a bit of distracting fun. I sat down to write about love all right, with every intention of rehashing the plot of one of the simplest, *Dreams in the Dust* – wild girl sets out to snare rich grazier but falls for poor man who turns out to be rich; lots of hand-feeding of lambs and panoramic outback landscapes while she's being tamed. But then a flying boat zoomed over the top of the house from Rose Bay and I started romanticising about Rock instead, only I've called him Will Gordon, he's on the plane to New Guinea and he hasn't met me yet – because I'm the pilot, Miss Eugenia Frank, having some fun. Pretending I have nerves of steel. Gone to jelly now. 'How, um, quickly might you want it?'

Mr Jacobs grunts; clearly doesn't like questions in reply, informs me gruffly: 'As soon as possible. The company is expanding rapidly. This is an exciting time for Australian literature.'

Literature? I almost laugh. We're not discussing Penguin paperbacks here, nor Angus & Robertson's actual respectable Australian literature – this is wonky type, cheaper than nasty newsprint paper, lolly-coloured covers stamped *Complete Novel* in case it's not apparent in the reading, and I can't imagine it's very lucrative at any time. But I don't laugh: this Mr Jacobs likes my two chapters! How long did they take me – just over a week? But a whole novel? Six-pennies are usually a hundred and something pages long, twenty chapters, eighteen blank ones in mine, so I can only tell him: 'I'm sorry, I don't know.'

'Hmm,' he grunts again, irritated, and then he says: 'Well. Contact me again when your manuscript is complete.' I open my mouth to give him a bewildered thankyou but he's already said: 'Good day, Miss Brockley.' Clunk.

I stare at the telephone for quite some time. The universe is expanding again, the earth is moving beneath my feet, but for the first time in my life it's *my* universe. I'm going to do this. I'm going to write a novel. I'm going to write to Dad and tell him all about it – and he will be paralytic with laughter when he finds out I've made myself a pilot. Might be only talent for blarney, and maybe only a slim one at that, but it's mine. And somehow, suddenly, I'm ready for anything. Ready for everything. Ready to order that magnolia shantung Mum's had her eye on at Foy's, for me, for my dress, for my wedding. Because I'm going to write a novel. I'm going to be a writer. *Extravagant fiction today, cold fact tomorrow* – Rock's going to love this too, I know he will. *How good is that?* he'll say, and he'll lift me up and twirl me around in the air, for our happy beginning. This is it, this is what I've been yearning for, all this time. This is the very end of my maybe.

I run out the back. 'Mum! Mum!' She's picking broad beans round by the shed and as she looks up I yell at her: 'They like my story!'

'Oh?' Mum hasn't read a novel in her life, I don't think, but her face lights up as if I've won the Nobel Prize. 'Oh, that's marvellous, Bernie love!'

'It is!' I tear up the side path to yell it at Mrs Zoc too.

I leap the little brick wall between our front yards and scream round to her door.

Where I run smack bang into the rear end of a black suit, that turns and grabs me hard around the shoulders, growling: 'What the–'

I'm pinned with fright at his massive snarling face, bad breath steaming from a curled lip.

His fists are cutting off the circulation in my arms as he spits: 'Who are you?'

The brim of his black fedora is shadowing his eyes; I think he must be a gangster. On Mrs Zoc's doorstep? In my state of hyper-excitement, I'm sure I've crashed into the pages of a Chicago crime story. But I haven't: his grip is hurting me, and I can hear the shriek in my protest: 'Who are *you?*'

Something about the menace of him relaxes and he releases my arms. 'Detective Sergeant Price, Darlinghurst.' He pulls his wallet from his suit coat and shows me what I suppose is proof of that.

All I see is the word *police*. Something terrible has happened. 'What?' I demand of him. 'What's happened to Mrs Zoc?'

'You know the person who resides in this house?' His voice is as grim as the set of his mouth.

'Of course I do,' I answer him. 'Mrs Zoccoli, I'm her neighbour. Please, what's happened?' What *could* have happened? She looked perfectly fine this morning when I saw her bringing in her sheets.

His eyes narrow under their shadow. 'You don't follow the news?'

'What news?' I've hardly glanced at a paper or listened to the wireless for the past week; but this policeman pulls in his square chin, suspicious – of me? I try not to sound too impatient as I plead: '*What?*'

He pauses for so long, eyeing me coldly, before he finally explains, in his flat constabulary drone: 'Your neighbour has been arrested. She is an Italian citizen and, as Australia is now at war with Italy, she is an enemy alien and will be detained until such time as it may be established that she is not a danger to the Commonwealth.'

'A danger to the Commonwealth?' I look round him into her open door. This is too absurd, you couldn't make it up. I stare at Mrs Zoc's umbrella, there, hanging on the coat stand, where it always hangs. I can't quite comprehend what Italy has to do with anything here. We're at war with them now too? So what: no surprise. They're fascists just like the Nazis, aren't they? And the fascists are the reason the Zoccolis left Sicily. Shock makes me burst: 'You can't go around arresting people just because they're Italian – and anyway, she's Sicilian.' As I'm sure she's pointed out herself.

But this Policeman Detective Price or whatever his name is doesn't even blink as he enlightens me not one dot further: 'Every unnaturalised Italian is or will be subject to police scrutiny, as will any sympathisers to the fascist cause.' He gives me another long, cold stare before: 'And your name is … ?'

'Bernadette Cooper,' I tell him, not withholding the dare in my tone: *arrest me and you'll find out how much of a fascist sympathiser Captain William Cooper's daughter is.* I'm not even sure what a fascist is, apart from a bully. Bullies that need to be stood up to. I'd like to stand up to the one in front of me, but Mrs Zoc has just appeared behind his shoulder, walking towards us, another black-suited detective behind her; she's carrying a biscuit tin, the one she keeps her milk money in, and a small green suitcase.

'It is all right, Bernadetta. There is a misunderstanding.' Her voice is steady but she looks pale, frail with fear. 'If I am not back by six o'clock, please feed Piccolo for me.' Her little grey tabby.

'Of course I will,' I promise as another black suit emerges from the side path. Three of them altogether, three big, broad men arresting one little old lady? This is not right. As they head up the path towards a big black sedan on the street I burst again, with dread: 'Where are you taking her?'

I am ignored as they usher Mrs Zoc into the back seat. She disappears between their shoulders and they drive away. I stare at the empty street, as if I could conjure Dad's ute if I stare hard enough, as if I would chase gangster policemen in it, as if I could drive anyway. I try to catch and hold on to the idea that this is just a misunderstanding. Mrs Zoc is no fascist, and she'll prove it easily. Her Marco fought in the Great War on our side, and left Sicily to get away from the Fat Head's black shirts, as well as the Mafia. To be safe, you either had to join the Fascisti or go in with the Mafioso: not much of a choice. I don't remember Mr Zoccoli much except for his waxed ringmaster moustache and matching ho-ho-ho laugh; I was only eight when he died, but I know Dad liked him, a great deal, and that's proof enough for me. Mr Zoccoli was a fruit grower, who only wanted to set up his boys for the future – and finished himself off by achieving it, in Dad's opinion. Those Zoccoli boys are North Queensland fruit barons today. And they will sort this ridiculous business out.

I let myself back into the house with the key from under the rosemary pot and look for the address book in the drawer of Mrs Zoc's telephone table. But it's not there: she must've taken it with her. Not to worry, there won't be many Zoccolis out of the

Townsville exchange, will there, so I try the trunk telephonist at our exchange, who puts me through to another who tells me: 'Yes, madam, there are two numbers: one for Zoccoli Brothers Pty Ltd at Horseshoe Lagoon and another at a residence in Shirbourne.' Shirbourne – that's where Armando's new place is. He's the eldest, Manny, in the midst of protracted marriage negotiations over a good Palermo girl whose father now wants to see photographs of the house before assenting – *Stupido Siciliano* if you ask Mrs Zoc. I ask the telephonist to try the Horseshoe one first, but there's something wrong with the connection, the line must be down, she says; then she tries the Shirbourne one and comes back to me with: 'I'm sorry, madam, that line is disconnected.'

'That's not right,' I say. That can't be right: the Shirbourne house is brand new and waiting for a wife.

'I'm sorry, madam, is there another number you'd like me to try?'

'No. Thanks.' I hang up the phone and look up at the photographs above the mantelpiece, her three sons, dreamy smiling eyes beneath their father's ringmaster moustache, the gilt crucifix beneath them, a shrine to the loves of Mrs Zoc's life. Piccolo meows and nudges my ankle, and as I glance down at him I see the calendar beside the phone says *Friday June 14*, when it's really Thursday but Mrs Zoc cuts out all the thirteens, and my blood runs cold. The Zoccoli brothers: they've been arrested too, haven't they.

*

Yes, they have, I finally manage to get a straight answer more than twenty-four hours and a dozen telephone calls later from a peachy-faced constable at the police headquarters in Hunter Street, in town, with the unenviable job of fielding inquiries about disappearing Italian neighbours. Behind me is a carnival of fraying Latin tempers and threats of further arrests, and the young constable, no older than me, appears to have reached a place over the other side of exhaustion as he sighs: 'I can't say where they are being held, but the three Zoccoli men have been interned and their property confiscated due to the evidence against them.'

Don't bother asking what evidence; instead I lean on the counter, alert him to my credentials. 'What about Mrs Zoccoli, their mother – where is she?'

He tells my breasts: 'I can't say, miss. I'm sorry.'

'Give me your best guess, then,' I lower my voice: *Come on, Johnny*.

But he repeats for my face: 'I'm sorry, I can't say, miss.'

Can't sway him. Unbelievable. I'd tell him this can't be legal, treating people this way, but as I've been told in no uncertain terms and several times over the last twenty-four hours – by Darlinghurst Police, Darlinghurst Gaol, Long Bay Gaol, Liverpool internment camp, Dad's solicitor Mr McLean and the report in the *Herald* this morning – it is perfectly legal. Unnaturalised Italians have no rights – not to a lawyer, a visitor, a phone call, or even a charge. I don't know what to do now, except silently curse the Zoccoli brothers for being either too stupido Siciliano or too busy to get themselves naturalised at the twelve-year eligibility mark, and I'm about to send myself back home again to stew when the constable pushes a small piece of notepaper across the counter with another heavy sigh.

'Here – I'm not supposed to say this,' he mutters under his breath as I look down at the note, two telephone numbers, 'but try contacting the camp in Orange. It's where all the prisoners from Sydney are being sent on to. The ones in Queensland, try Stuart Prison in Townsville.'

Prisoners? Prison? This is *wrong*. I can accept the possibility that the brothers *might* have done something to warrant suspicion; they're cheeky types. Tony's got a black mark with the police – had to pay a fine once for calling out to a girl up at the Spot, but that was years ago. I can't accept their mother being treated like a criminal on any account, though, not to mention deepening the frown lines on my own mother's face. Mum is having several litters of kittens a minute. And for what? The *Biggest Round-up of Aliens in the History of Australia*, the *Herald* is calling it. And it certainly looks like it: half the coffee lounges from Foy's down to DJ's have closed until further notice, and the other half have signs in their windows like the one at our Niagara that reads in letters three inches tall: *We are not Italians. We are Greeks and we are naturalised. Long live King George!* There was no such carry-on against the Germans last September, was there. Why not? Maybe because, back then, Pig Face didn't need a public distraction from the cold fact that our government is pouring rivers of our men and money into an army that remains idling in the desert waiting for the British to tell it what to do, while the British themselves have been busy getting chased off the Continent and calling it the Miracle of Dunkirk. And there's an election due soon, isn't there? Hope it's set for after my twenty-first. I won't be voting for the United Australia Party.

'Miss?' the young policeman pushes the slip of paper across the counter at me again, a plea in his eyes, weary glance at the mayhem going on behind me: *Please, take it and go away.*

'Oh, yes, thank you,' I slip it into my handbag as I call for calm from myself: I have work to do too now, don't I. Keep my universe tight and trained around the task until further notice; before I win the Nobel Prize for Romance, I have to find Mrs Zoc.

GORDON

'She's gone where?' I ask Mrs Cooper, who doesn't much sound on top of things. Mr Cooper has been sent to Palestine, Mrs Zoc has been interned, and I think she's just said Bernie's followed her to a camp in Orange. I'm feeling the distance something terrible.

'To Orange, Gordon dear, on the train this morning.' Mrs Cooper's voice seems sad and tired. 'Bernadette thought if she goes in person she'll have a better chance of finding out if Emilia, if Mrs Zoccoli, is there.'

I can't follow what's gone on, but I can hear in the way Mrs Cooper's said *Emilia*, using her Christian name, that she's very upset. So am I. Interned? What in blazes *for*? I ask her: 'Do you want me to come home? Just say so and I will.' Somehow get leave.

'No!' Mrs Cooper gives me one of her squawks, as Bernie calls them. 'You can't interrupt your career! This internment business will all blow over. It's only a misunderstanding. It's a madhouse here at the moment.'

'Yes,' I say. 'I'm sure it is.' It is here in Rabaul too. France has signed an armistice with Germany, and since I got back into town last night I've not heard anyone talk of anything else. It means Germany and Italy control Europe north and south now, so why wouldn't Germany want their piece of the Pacific back too? The Administrator has given orders to round up every last Lutheran missionary on the island and confiscate their Bibles just in case the Nazis aren't clever enough to come up with a better disguise. I'm more worried at this moment that Bernie hasn't written to me, though, shared none of her worries with me. But why would she, I suppose, when there's nothing I can do to help from here?

'Gordon,' Mrs Cooper's voice firms up and she sounds more herself, 'you mustn't get any ideas about doing anything other than what you are doing right now. You know Bill would not approve, and neither would your father. You must promise me you won't do anything silly.'

'Don't worry about that, I promise I won't.' I have no intention of taking up arms. Last night at the bar a few of the militia blokes seemed to have turned a bit enthusiastic for it, and it wasn't just rummed-up talk. One of them, Sid Triscombe, who's Johno's CO in the Rifles, put the hard word on me about my national service. He's also a veteran, with some old score. I told him I'd do my service when I'm back in town for more than five minutes. I don't think the Department of Home Defence will disagree in the long run and I still haven't heard anything from them to the contrary. The most important war service I have to perform is to keep on doing what I'm doing right now and find oil. If Australia ever got cut off from the high-grade British supplies from Malaya ... that's never going to happen, but –

'We'll see you soon enough in December,' Mrs Cooper says, and she's bright about the thought. So am I as she adds: 'I've just picked up the fabric for Missy's special dress.'

'Good. I can't wait to see her in it.' The rain had better flaming well come on time for us so I get my leave then. Apart from the obvious, I just want us to be married; put an end to that question in my mind, sort out the details of where Bernie will live later. Make me exempt from the militia while we're at it. 'Tell Missy I miss her. Tell her I want a letter from her too. I'll phone again in about another six weeks' time.' I have to go. It's Saturday, town is packed, and there's a queue for the line.

As I sign for the call, Mrs Chittaway says: 'Rough sometimes being so far from home, isn't it, pet?'

'It is,' I agree. 'But there are worse things than a bit of homesickness.'

'Oh yes,' she sighs.

I'm not in Palestine, for one, I think as I wander back out over the lawn. I'm in a garden full of red hibiscus flowers in a tropical holiday resort. Mr Cooper is in Palestine. I wonder what for. Is Britain going to use the AIF for protecting their Near East oil reserves? Most of the older militia blokes last night were saying our troops should be brought home. I'd thought that sounded a bit of an overreaction, as if we're going to be invaded by Nazis any minute, but I don't now. Mr Cooper shouldn't be asked to serve the Empire, not again. He should be at home. And Mrs Zoc shouldn't be in a prison camp, misunderstanding or not. That is the most half-witted thing I've ever heard. But Bernie's gone off to Orange to rescue her? That makes me smile. She's never even been to the Blue Mountains and now she's charging right over them. In her high heels.

And I'd better get going myself, round to the office. There's been a continued discrepancy through these last three hundred yards' drilling in the amount of dacite I'm still finding across the overlayer. It's not matching up with the Anglo-Eastern data which says we should have hit a band of limestone by now, and I want to go over some of the broader analysis of the area to check that we're not too far off the mark of where we should be. We've just finished our palatial hut by the rig, too, and we really wouldn't want to move the whole production now if I find we are in the wrong place.

I walk round the corner into Court Street and find my chief geo, Roycox, is still in his pyjamas. It's twenty past eleven. 'Young Brock, I thought you were off back to the drilling?'

'I will be in a minute,' I tell him, and repeat that I want to go over the old Anglo-Eastern papers for comparative ore samples, because I'm sure he's forgotten our conversation yesterday: I'm sure he has gin on his Weet-Bix.

He waves me away with his fat hands. 'No need for that — you are perfectly on track. Keep on, boy. No dillydallying around the office.'

I could smack him in the mouth for that. As if he's ever done a day's work in his life. As if I am not fit enough to tear his head off from all the *dillydallying* I've been doing lately. But he's my boss, like it or not, so I say: 'I'll take off then.'

He seems to understand he's put my nose out of joint and calls behind him for one of the houseboys to drive me back out to Kabakada. I would say don't bother but I can't be bothered, and the kid looks too thrilled to be going for a drive to disappoint him. I grab a stack of old newspapers from the club before we go, and I only just remember Johno's order of tinned peaches. He loves tinned peaches, all this fruit that drops from the trees and he wants a tin of Ardmona for his birthday.

Bouncing out of town along Tunnel Hill Road, I open one of last week's papers, looking for news of the AIF, and see instead: *JAPS NEAR HONG KONG.* That grabs my attention. They've come down as far as Hong Kong now, right to the border, but the report says: *Despite the evacuation of many women and children, British officials are decrying alarmist tendencies, and say that the Japanese measures are merely precautionary against Chinese guerrilla operations.* A Jap official is quoted as backing that up: '*We wish only to continue our neighbourly relations. We are here in peace.*'

The hairs stand up on the back of my neck. No you're not here in peace: there's a trail of blood behind you all the way through China giving the lie to that remark.

The first thing I think is: shit, Malaya. They're going to go after the oil in Malaya. But that is a half-witted thought, come from someone with too much on his mind. Why would they do that? It would be a lot less expensive, and inconvenient, for them to keep on with their American contracts, put up with America's hollow complaining about their unneighbourly relations with China, than provoke a war with Britain. Or provoke a war with America itself. You'd have to be completely out of your flaming mind to do that. But another thought follows that line of logic: what if Japan took sides with the fascists? Then it wouldn't look so mad, would it? All three of them could cut off oil supplies throughout the Empire: in the Near East, across Asia. Then we would be completely stuffed.

Which is why the British Army has Singapore so well fortified, isn't it. The Japs could try it on all they like, but they'll never get through Singapore. All their oil would be cut off immediately: their air force would be grounded, all industry would stop dead. This is not the unbelievable plot of an evil alien story in *Amazing* science-fiction monthly, which I might be missing a bit after six months off it. The Japs are not going to try anything on, because above all they are not stupid. They want an economic victory over us. A more realistic line of logic says they will bide their time till the war is over, when they can flood the whole world with genuine artificial everything, probably made by Chinese slaves.

Even still, all this makes me want to step up my own game. Find this oil down here on New Britain and find it fast. Just in case.

BERNIE

'How can you not know where she is?' I groan at the dull-eyed corporal with the clipboard at the gate. Through my chattering teeth, because it is snowing. The first time I have ever seen snow, and I am not thrilled about it. I am freezing, the snowflakes are piercing my face as they fall, but at least according to the clipboard Mrs Zoc is not here: corralled by a double barbed-wire fence in the middle of a showground, showing half-a-dozen huts and sheds that look like they'd more appropriately house cattle. In the snow. Hasn't rained here for six months apparently, but now it is. In snow. There is a little girl with long chestnut plaits skipping with a rope between two of the nearer huts; poor little bare legs in the snow. I want to poke the corporal's blockheaded forehead with my indignation: 'Someone *must* know where she is.'

He looks down at his clipboard again, taps it with his pencil. 'No.'

'What?' I don't think his dull-eyed stare is a military pose; I think he is either subnormal or he is lying, or both, and now my impatience snaps: 'What do you mean, *no*? No one knows where Mrs Zoccoli is? Not a soul? She's vanished into thin air?'

'Er,' his eyes shift up to the left, and after an eternity he mumbles out of the side of his mouth: 'It's secret information, miss. We're not allowed to say.'

'For Pete's sake! Is she or isn't she here?' I am almost crying with frustration.

'Er. No, miss. She's not here, but I can't say where she is.'

I stamp my foot on the stoop of his little sentry hut and just about break off the heel. Speechless, I almost really do start to cry. I've spent almost six hours on the Western Mail from Sydney for this? I knew it would be a waste of time, and he's only giving me the same answer as the ones I received from each of my telephone calls. The prison in Townsville simply hung up on me as soon as I said the word *Italian*, while the Attorney-General's Office let me know how far a protest will get me: *We make the laws and you abide by them – THAT is national security, Miss Cooper. And no, Mr Hughes does not have time to investigate each and every trivial complaint. Unless you haven't noticed, there's a war on.* Clunk. Mr Hughes, our Attorney-General, too busy for trivial matters of justice, and why should he care anyway? Mum said he was Prime Minister in Charge of Boy Sacrifice during the previous war.

I'm about to turn around and take my infuriation with me, when I feel this Corporal Blockhead grab me by the elbow and push me into the little hut beside the gate with a grunt that sounds like: 'Here.'

'What?' Fear screeches up my spine as he slams the door shut behind us, and the first thing I see in the far corner of the back wall is a rifle. I freeze inside and out, despite the heat thumping out of the kero heater at our feet. I turn around and he is blocking the doorway, leaning across it onto a filing cabinet. I back up against the desk in the centre of the room and tell him as steadily as I can: 'If you lay another hand on me, I will scream.'

And I damned well will; I glare daggers to convince him. I don't need to be afraid of you. I've done nothing wrong, and I'm not alone: there's a Mrs Ethel Finlay of Orange CWA waiting for me to be back for tea only half a mile down the road, sister-in-law of a Mrs Meredith of Nyngan branch. I always thought Rock had to be exaggerating about the bush telegraph provided by these ladies, until Mum suggested I phone the Sydney Dee Why branch for accommodation advice. They make the Catholic Daily look positively sluggish. Mrs Finlay not only knows where I am, but *who* I am: Gordon Brock's fiancée, Bill Cooper's daughter, she even knew I worked at Chalmers. And she's not happy about this foreigners' camp business ruining her showground and putting the branch's winter cake judging out of their home. She would take this corporal out with her rolling pin as soon as look at him.

He looks at me, confused. 'What?'

I tell him: 'Don't you think you can make me disappear. I'll have you know I'm the daughter of a captain of the Sixth Div and if you harm one hair on my head the lot of them will be out for you, right?' Squint at the CMF insignia on his tunic: you're not even real army, you're just citizens' militia and don't you forget it: a koala, not for overseas export or being shot at.

'All right, I won't make you disappear,' he smirks, but not unkindly, not dull-eyed, and not that bad-looking, really, for a blockheaded marsupial. He opens the middle draw of the cabinet and flicks through the files at the back. 'I could get in big strife for this, but–' He pulls out a sheet of paper, some sort of form, a carbon copy: 'Here.'

'Oh,' I breathe out as I take it from him; it's Mrs Zoc's particulars, stamped across the top: *DEFENCE SECRET*.

He adds, a croaky whisper: 'See, she was here, but I don't know where she is now – honest. Maybe Bathurst camp, maybe back in Liverpool. See, we've run out of room here. If you go to the AMF Eastern Command in Sydney, at Victoria Barracks, you might find out something, but I didn't tell you that, yeah?'

'Yeah. Good. Thanks.' I've already tattooed the Australian Military Forces phone number at the top of the page into my memory, FO455, and I'm reading on, to the paragraph towards the bottom of the page under a title *OUTLINE OF EVIDENCE*, to exactly what I need to know if I'm going to argue that Mrs Zoc is no one's enemy. I could kiss Corporal Blockhead; until the words sink in:

Member of Fascist Party, January 1924, w. husband Marco Z. & eldest son (of 3 total) Armando Z.

Seized from Coogee property various pamphlets of anarchist literature of revolutionary nature.

All 3 sons (Armando, Antonio & Arturo aka Manny, Tony, Arthur) described as 'arrogant', 'volatile' and 'secretive in dealings' by Mr Alan Raymond, neighbour, fellow mango farmer, also of Horseshoe Lagoon, Nth Qld.

RECOMMENDATION – further interrogation as required, internment for duration.

I don't believe one dot, but nevertheless it's overwhelming. I had thought that the evidence might be something stupid, a mistaken identity, a misspelling of a foreign name, some carelessness I could step in and clear up. But this is more than a *misunderstanding* … seeing the Zoccoli names laid out in this smudgy blue official type, these accusations. No. These have to be lies. Don't they?

I hear Blockhead say: 'If you're stopping over in town, I don't spose you'd want to come to the pictures with me tonight?' Thinking he's earned one.

'No.' I throw the form back at him. 'Thank you.'

I shove past him out the door, my mind reeling with the blast of cold through my flimsy coat, the slip and slide of the snow beneath my flimsy heels as I run, fear whipping through me like nothing on earth. Who would make up such lies about the Zoccolis? They must be lies. How could they not be lies? It's just name-calling, nasty name-calling. Anyone can call names … This Queensland neighbour, Alan Raymond, mango competitor gone sour? But members of the Fascist Party, anarchist literature? I don't exactly know what anarchist means, but it sounds revolutionary. My mind is turning every which way, racing over the years I've known Mrs Zoc, how she's always kept a bit to herself, always goes to early mass, avoiding the stickybeaks. Secretive? No!

The white witches' fingers of plum trees point at me as I run past the orchard at the top of the street, towards the row of pretty pastel weatherboards beyond, white picket fences and regimental flowerbeds trailing off into church steeples and blue hills. Picture-perfect country town, but with a prison on the showground, one that swallows up little old ladies and little girls with long chestnut plaits, swallows them up with outrageous lies.

I have never been so cold, so very angry. Oh, yes, I'll be asking some questions at AMF Eastern Command and demanding to see this evidence for myself, or I'll ... I'll – I don't know. I don't know what I might do.

*

Mum has no doubt, punching her bread dough into the tin. 'If Emilia Zoccoli is a fascist, I'm the Queen of Sheba, and the only bad thing those boys have ever done is work too hard and too seldom visit their poor mother. This is the work of bigots!' And she should know. 'Ruddy Queenslanders,' she hisses to prove it.

'Fascist?' She slams the oven door. 'I'll tell them about fascist – that woman's brother was killed by those black-shirted thugs. Hanged in the street! That's how much of a fascist Emilia Zoccoli is.'

I didn't know that, about her brother. But now I do, cold runs boiling hot. 'I'll tell them, Mum. Don't worry, I'll tell them.'

Then she tells me I missed Rock yesterday and I could kick a cat. No, I couldn't: Piccolo scratches at the back door, not for his dinner, but with a heart-mashing mewl that sounds like he's crying, *Emeeelia*.

By Monday morning my steam is high as I take the Bondi tram to Victoria Barracks at Paddo, undoing my coat and the top two buttons of my blouse as I walk up to the gates to beg the stone-faced guard who blocks my way: 'Please, you must let me in to speak to someone from Eastern Command, there's been a terrible mistake.'

'Sorry, miss,' is all I get from him and the pistol in his holster, together with a 'Hey cutie' from a pack of idling soldiers beyond the wall. *Cutie?* What picture theatre have they just left their blockheads in? 'You can't just wander in,' says pistol holster. 'You have to make an appointment.'

'Well, I want to make an appointment.' At the AMF zoo.

'You'll have to telephone the inquiries office then.'

So I walk the few yards back up to the telephone booth outside the town hall to be told that I can't have an appointment because: 'There is no means at present for enemy alien appeal.'

'What?' I am stunned.

Nasal drone repeats: 'There is no means at present for enemy alien appeal.'

'You mean there is no one to tell that there has been a mistake?'

'Ah, that is correct, madam. Not at present.'

I explode: 'You can lock people up and throw away the key and no one can say boo about it? Where are we? Nazi Berlin?'

Clunk.

Don't think this will stop me, I glare at the receiver. But it has stopped me. Stopped me like a blowfly in a bottle. There's nothing I can do. I have nowhere to go. But home. I move on the few yards further to the tram stop to wait, the very same tram stop where Mum met Dad all those years ago, and as I wait that picture of the little girl with the chestnut plaits sends the chills through me again, as she does every time I think of her. You can't lock up children this way. It might not be illegal, but it should be. Is she getting enough to eat? If I knit her a pair of stockings, will they reach her? What about her school lessons? Is it her fault her parents are revolutionary fascist anarchists? Are they even fascist anarchists at all, or just plain Italians? What's a stupid fascist anarchist anyway?

'Cheer up, lassie.' I hear a rough voice beside me, growly, like a pirate. An elderly man, bent back leaning on his cane, and a crinkly smile. 'Even the darkest hour's only sixty minutes long, eh?' I give him a polite smile in return, and he says: 'Oh, that bad, is it?'

'Pretty bad.' I can't help a genuine smile.

He winks, funny old man, old suit, old hat, asking me: 'Can a silly old man help a pretty young girl?'

'I wish you could,' I tell him.

'Hoi!' he waves his cane. 'Are you calling me a silly old man?'

The face he pulls makes me near connipt, so I toss it back: 'That depends – are you silly enough to know what a fascist anarchist is?'

'Oh.' His frown is like a scrunched paper bag, regretful, and still teasing me, as if he's only going to disappoint. 'Well, I do know it would be impossible to be that.'

'What do you mean?'

He clears his throat with pretend solemnity. 'As you are speaking with an esteemed professor of the University of Woolloomooloo, faculty of Silly Old Wharfies Law, I can tell you that fascists and anarchists are the opposite of each other. The fascist is a cold-blooded animal with no heart, and the anarchist is hothead, with no brain. The one wants everything controlled by rules and laws, and the other wants bedlam. You'd have to choose which one you wanted to be, lassie.'

'Oh.' He's joking, but he's also telling me what I need to know: you can't be a fascist *and* an anarchist. The evidence against Mrs Zoc is contradictory? That's not a mistake, that's –

'Rats,' the old man says: 'That wasn't much help, was it?'

'Yes, it was,' I tell him, through bash-clanging disbelief: our government locks people up on evidence that doesn't even make sense and there's not a thing anyone can do about it.

'Hmm.' The old man taps his cane on the footpath and looks away down the line of shabby shopfronts for the tram, and as I follow his gaze, out of the confusion I see it: I see that there is in fact something I can do, right across the road in the window of O'Rourke's Office Supplies: IMPERIAL 'GOOD COMPANION' PORTABLE TYPEWRITERS SOLD HERE. BUY BRITISH. BUY THE BEST.

A typewriter. What a good and timely idea. The flight of Eugenia Frank might be suspended, but not all writing has to be. See if I don't make myself a professional pest, starting today. I have the time. I have the means. And I have the skill. I am going to write, and write: letters to the Department of Army, AMF, CMF, AIF, North, South, East and Western Command, and to our too-busy-for-trivial-justice Attorney-General.

I've already stepped off the kerb when I swear I hear the old pirate say behind me: 'Gorn, give it to 'em, lassie.'

*

When I've lugged my Good Companion up Heartbreak Hill, cursing *portable* as an outrage in false advertising with every step, Mum is waiting for me in the middle of Arcadia, waving a letter in her hand – obviously from Dad. I almost drop half a ton of British Best on my foot to grab it off her.

My dear precious Peggy and Bernie ... our faces are pressed together as I read, and Mum re-reads for no doubt the umpteenth time already, that he's in a place called Gaza on the Mediterranean Sea, at a big training camp there. And every precious word strengthens my determination to tell the truth as he serves us up the biggest load of blarney I've ever read. He tells us all about how he won first place for the *oldies* of his battalion at their swimming carnival, and how he trained for the event by chasing around the cheeky Arab boys who sell them fake beer and steal their boots, and I don't wonder where I get my one and only talent from. All fun, and full of assurance that he's safe and well, having survived the worst pork chops of his life on the voyage over. But the fact is, he's ten thousand miles away in Palestine, on the edge of a war we all know he'll soon be in one way or another, somewhere or other. The Sixth Div is not going to give Bill Cooper special dispensation just because he's ours.

Mum squeezes me round the shoulders with love for him. 'He writes a marvellous letter, your father, doesn't he?'

He certainly does. And he would also be horrified if he knew what was really going on here at home. If he knew what they've done to Mrs Zoc and her boys, he wouldn't only be angry, I know he'd be ashamed, it would bring that sadness into his eyes. He would be hurt on their behalf.

Mum folds his letter into her apron pocket with her rosary, keeping him close, and for a moment I can't move. I stare up at the gumdrop gable of our house, Dad's house, breathe in the seaweed smell of the air, our home, and my feet seem planted to this asphalt. A calm and certain force moves through me: I am ready to sit down and fight for my country too.

My campaign doesn't take long to take effect. By Friday morning, after my first volley of letters to as many departments as I could think of, the telephone rings with a Colonel Aitkins on behalf of the Minister for the Army informing me in a smooth, posh drawl: 'It will not do your father any good to criticise the endeavours of this military in this most provocative way, Miss Cooper.' A warning in his voice: *We know who you are and where you live and how to keep you quiet.*

My heart would like to leap out of my chest and bolt away, but I muster a half-strangled and shrill: 'Is that so?' Before I give him a good, petrified clunking. The last thing I want to do is get Dad into trouble; why did I make an issue of his service in my letters? *As the daughter of Captain William Cooper …* I'm a prize-winning dill.

'Who was that?' Mum says at my back, and when I tell her she flicks her dust rag at the ceiling with contempt. 'As if your father would care what the brass think! What are they going to do, court-martial him? Take his commission off him and send him home?' Then she nudges me with her hip, smiling with a warmth I've never caught from her before. 'Don't you dare stop what you're doing, my daughter. I'm very proud of you.'

Proud of me? Oh, Mum. Worth it for that alone.

And for the letter I receive the following Tuesday from a Major Fielding of the AMF, Internment Inquiries, informing me that my concerns are appreciated, that *you should be assured that adequate food and accommodation is being provided to all internees in accordance with Geneva Convention recommendations for prisoners of war*, and most importantly that *application forms for enemy aliens appeals will be available in due course*. In due course is not at all soon enough, but it means I'm being heard. Or *we're* being heard. I can't be the only one doing this. And I'll keep doing this: write straight back to this Major Fielding and ask him again: where is Mrs Emilia Zoccoli? I'm going to need to know that if I'm going to help her appeal, aren't I? And write to him quickly, before the different departments spot this common pest and squash any further correspondence.

I've just sat down to it, Good Companion now permanently planted on the kitchen table, when Mum says to me over her stock pot: 'Save me that thumping on the typewriter today, will you, love? I'd like to make a start on your bodice this afternoon, if I'm to get the beading done without a panic.'

My dress. 'Course, Mum,' I say; wedding's got a bit lost in the spin wringer lately. And Mum looks a bit flushed. Weary. I smile at her and the thought of all the beading she's planned for the bodice. Mum's means of showing what she thinks of wartime belt-tightening: clear out DJ's trims section of every last glass pearl they have in stock. I get up from the table to go to Mum's bedroom, to get my fabric from her blanket box. In five months, I'll be married.

Hurry up and find Mrs Zoc so she can make my cake. So I can turn my mind to organising everything else, make this the best wedding, for everyone. Get some good photos for Dad. Kiss Gordon. For a long time. For good.

Make a detour to my room and take my little pink jasper B out from under my pillow, press it to my cheek, cool and solid earth, and as if I might better be heard this way, I pray, *Please look after us, all of us,* before I slip it into the pocket of my skirt, to keep it close.

GORDON

'Mate, I'm not prepared to take that risk,' Johno says, standing over me as I sit on the edge of my bunk. I'm wrung out. No sweat left in me. Stifling hot and it's only just after dawn. 'Malaria or not, you look like shit.'

'Thanks.' I'm sure it's only heatstroke, though, pounding into my skull. 'It's not malaria.' I know it's not. I'm not shivering with it, I'm not that sick. I can't be. I take every precaution, smother myself in so much eucalyptus oil I am a gum tree. Besides, it's Johno's turn to go into town tomorrow for his weekend, mine's not for another fortnight, and I'm getting behind in my log.

'All the same, you have to go to the hospital and report it.' Johno taps the toe of his boot into mine. 'You're too crook to work, which makes me the boss, so you have to do as you're told.'

'But the log–'

'Can wait until you can prove that you don't have malaria.' Taps the toe of my boot again. 'In the meantime, I'm not happy to share mozzies with you. Right?'

'Too right,' says Reg, our boilermaker. 'I wouldn't die for you.'

That I don't tell him where to shove that comment proves I'm not that sick. Reg 'Smith' wouldn't do much for anyone. He's taken his New Guinea contract to make it difficult for the court to get maintenance payments from him, for his wife and four kids. Not the type of bloke I think much of.

Rico hands me an envelope. 'If you leave now, maybe you will make the mail plane. My daughter's birthday is on Wednesday. It would be good if this gets to Melbourne before then.' He has five daughters and they all mean the world to him. I take the letter.

'Good,' Johno says. 'Now, piss off.'

It's going to be a long slow walk out, with To-An and one of his cousins, Manulu, on either side ready to catch me, but the headache's already starting to ease off before we've even got to the bottom of the Slippery Dip, and I'm already embarrassed at the thought of fronting up to the hospital to get a test for something I clearly don't have. So, I'm not going to the hospital.

But To-An thinks differently. 'You sick, boss, bad sick.'

And Manulu nods in agreement, looking worried.

'What sick?' I say, wondering if I might've been bitten by something, like the six-inch millipede I've just spotted crawling across the fig root I'm stepping over.

'You sick for mary!' He slaps his knee and he and his cousin stagger about laughing. I'm sick for want of a woman, he reckons.

'Yeah. Very funny, To-An.' Though he's probably got a point: I have been missing Bernie worse than normal over the last month, not that he'd know that. But I do know he's about to get married himself, Johno told me, by way of explaining why To-An performed a series of death-defying backflips down the derrick the other day.

He hands me a banana and he and Manulu stagger about again.

I'm nearly staggering myself by the time we reach Kabakada. Not sick, only tired. That's all this malaria is: buggered. I'm confident of that. I can hardly keep my eyes open on the drive into town. But I get there, just in time to post Rico's letter, and for Mrs Chittaway to tell me: 'Oh pet, you look awful. Working like a black out there, the way you do, in this heat. You need a rest. You know, we're not made the same as them.'

'No we're not,' I yawn, and I laugh, or try to, from somewhere under this wet blanket. 'They wouldn't know the difference between dacite and limestone if ... there was a million pounds in it.'

'Is that right?' Mrs Chittaway arches her eyebrow at me as if I might be troppo.

Because, obviously, I am. In half a second my skull is pounding with the worry again. I have to be back at the rig. Johno doesn't know the difference between dacite and limestone either. Why would he? He's not a geologist. He's an engineer. I can't rest. I'm already behind. And with every rod we pull up, I get more and more worried we're drilling in the wrong place. And that if we are it will be my mistake. I can't make a mistake.

'You look like you need a drink, pet.'

I'm sure I do need one. I need to settle down or I will make myself sick. Thinking Johno wouldn't know the difference between dacite and limestone is like thinking he wouldn't know the difference between black and white. Do I? I've got permanent silver specks before my eyes from looking at too much flaming dacite. Dacite that does not mean we won't hit the basalt capping stone anyway. The limestone layer has been eaten by subterranean aliens, that's all. Troppo.

I need more than a drink. I ask Mrs Chittaway: 'Has any mail come for me?' Bernie must have sent me a letter by now. I'd prefer to call her but it's almost six; I've missed this afternoon's line.

'Sorry, pet, no mail.' Mrs Chittaway is disappointed for me.

The state I'm in, disappointment goes straight to disaster. Why hasn't Bernie written to me? A proper letter. It's been a month and I need to know what's going on at home. She doesn't really love me, does she. She doesn't care for me. And I don't blame her. I've never been good enough for her. I'm not a boring geologist these days, no – I'm a geologist with no flaming idea. What would she want with me anyway? She's always been too beautiful for me. She's met someone else. She met someone in Orange.

'Would you like me to book you a call to Sydney for tomorrow morning then?'

'Thanks, yeah, that'd be good,' I say. Troppo as.

I'll talk to Bernie tomorrow. It's just the distance playing with me. Like too much dacite in my pyroclastic overlayer. The feeling that all manner of untold shit will happen if I don't find this oil we're drilling for.

'Gordon! Where are you running off to now?' Mrs Chittaway squawks as I head out.

'To the office.' To check the Anglo-Eastern files there. The old data. I have to know we're not drilling in the wrong place.

When I get round to Court Street, though, the place is locked up. No one about at all, not even the houseboys. It's getting on for sunset; they must have left for the Rabaul dining room already. Given the boys the night off? Odd. One of the neighbours sees me from his verandah and waves; he works for one of the banks, can't remember his name. He shouts across the bougainvillea hedge between us: 'You've missed them – they went off this morning.' *Orrrf*, have another Scotch and go back to counting your coconuts.

'Where've they gone?'

'Tahiti,' he raises his glass. 'A fortnight's cruising. Said they'd be back tenth of August, I think.'

Tahiti? Roycox and Taylor, together? I manage not to ask him if they've gone *orrrf* on bloody honeymoon. Who has a holiday in Tahiti in the middle of a war? Roycox and Taylor do. These are, after all, men who said no to Rico's request last week for a pedal phone for us, after one of the cables on the hoist snapped and nearly took Johno's head off with it. A phone is apparently an unnecessary expense. But a honeymoon in Tahiti, well, that's essential. This is why the rich are rich, isn't it? Because they don't flaming well care.

I storm back round to the New Guinea, riled up. Flaming bastards. Flaming pansified bastards. *Tahiti*. While I've been working my arse off. Going mad in this humidity. Breathing soup. With the endless drilling, boring into my head. The endless grinding of the motor and the rods. Lugging and logging bag after flaming bag of rock, up to my ankles in leech-infested mud. By the time I reach the lawn of the club, I am a psychopath.

I want to murder a beer, but the first person I see in there is Sid Triscombe, Johno's militia CO. He's standing at the bar, telling a crowd of his old bastard mates: 'Couldn't believe it when I heard. Three weeks these companies are on the line at a stint. *Three weeks?* We were five weeks in the trenches in my day – if we were lucky.' All shaking their heads. Someone else says: 'Gone soft, these young blokes.' I turn around and walk out again. Don't want Sid to see me right at this moment, telling me how soft I am avoiding my national service in the middle of a war. Because I could get a bit aggressive today. I had better go straight back up to my room and lock myself in.

Back across the lawn to the Weekender, I can't credit what I am doing here at all. Why did I sign that contract? Why did Taylor accept it? I am obviously too young, too inexperienced, as well as soft – in the head. I should have gone on the Survey, stuck to my course; I should be at home worrying about what postgraduate research I'm going to do. A treatise on the wealth of New England bauxite my country doesn't presently want or need, or an exploration of how useless a whole continent of haematite could be as an iron ore resource. Instead of losing my mind waiting for untold shit to happen. Where? In flaming troppos' paradise.

'Gordon!' Mrs Chittaway flaps after me as I storm past reception. 'Here! Here, pet! There was a letter for you after all, slipped under my receipts box, silly thing.' Waving an envelope. Flaming troppo, too.

It's a white envelope. A square one. Clearly not from His Majesty. Unless he's taken to wearing White Lilac.

I grab it from Mrs Chittaway, my manners taken off with my mind, and I tear it open, taking the stairs two by two, looking for the *Dear Gordon* that's surely coming, but reading:

My wonderful darling Rock
I wouldn't be writing you a letter at all if Mum wasn't sticking pins in me – truly. We're making the bodice for my wedding dress and I've only just managed to escape her with the excuse of writing to you.

So the madness stops. Here on the stairs. It all stops still around her words.

It really wouldn't matter what she wrote. But what she says is so good, I have to read the whole thing here on the stairs. She's sorting a million glass beads at the kitchen table with her mum and telling me all about the *Department of Stonewalling*, who won't tell her what they've done with Mrs Zoc. She makes me see her with her words. Hear her voice. She says, *I'm not going to bother carrying on about how much I miss you and all that,* and then carries on for half a page about how much she does, how she can't go to our Niagara, *even though it's reopened now that the police have finally stopped harassing Mr Cominos for being a swarthy milkbar proprietor. It's just that vanilla malt doesn't taste the same these days, without you.* She misses me. The distance between us shrinks to nothing, and my bearings return, before she even tells me:

If you ever have any doubt of the worth of what you're doing, don't, my darling. The price of petrol's going astronomical here. Not joking, the traffic on the roads has halved as a result, and Prime Minister Pig Face wants to bring in petrol rationing now too. It's ironic, don't you think, that Dad is no doubt making a better living as an army captain than he would if he'd stayed in the garage with disappearing custom? But Dad couldn't do what he's doing unless you keep doing what you're doing, and I don't just mean finding petrol. I mean being safe. It's so very important to me that you are safe and well. Everything else is bedlam, I need that one certainty, because you are my love, the love of my life, Gordon – despite your having made yourself so very geographically inconvenient to me.

Gordon. She loves me and she called me Gordon. She really must mean it. That's just amazing, isn't it? That she's my girl. My spirits go astronomical.

Somehow I travel the rest of the way up the stairs and down to the end of the top verandah. Find my trunk, where my photo of Bernie is. Here she is in the cover of *Geological Formations* in her white bathers and I'm not even going to bother with a bath. I'm going to look at her until I am unconscious, and when I wake up, I'm going to go back downstairs and pick up the phone and hear her voice for real. Please.

BERNIE

All in a rush, he says: 'I've only got the three minutes, there's a queue all the way to Shanghai today, but I hope to be back in Rabaul early September, and I'll confirm it then with the powers and call you again too, but plan for me to be home by Monday the second of December at the latest – I'll just have to make that happen however I can. That date should give me enough time to get a suit, though, shouldn't it?'

'A suit?' I almost ask what for, I'm so caught up in the surprise of his call, his voice. Determined. Purposeful. Caramel.

'Yeah,' he laughs. 'A suit.'

A flood of desire in me: Rock in a dinner suit is – just about worth getting married for. I say: 'Don't worry about a new suit. The one you've got is fine.'

'No, it's not,' he laughs again. 'It's got too small in the shoulders, from all the navvying.'

'Oh.' I'm drowning in it now. 'Really?'

'Yeah really. Thanks for your letter, Bernie. Geez, it was good,' he says. 'Really good,' he adds, and I can almost feel his breath on my ear, his warmth. 'You've got a real way with a yarn. Where've you been hiding that light?'

And I haven't even told him about Eugenia yet. Slipped my mind, with all that's been happening. It'll keep. I tell him, and I've never believed in it more: 'I can't wait to be with you for good. Forever and ever.'

He groans, softly, then says: 'Um, yeah …'

'Oh yeah.' I look over at my bodice pinned to the mannequin in the lounge, Mum's first arabesques of tiny glass pearls curling down from her sweetheart neckline, passion flower tendrils, not like anything you'll find in a catalogue, one of a kind, work of art, labour of love, everything she'd have wanted for herself if she and Dad could have afforded it then. The line crackles and I remember where we are now, what we're doing, and that four days won't be nearly long enough for the tailor. 'You'd better send me your measurements, darling.'

'What for?'

'Your suit.'

'Oh yeah.'

GORDON

But that's not exactly the way things are going to work out for us. The day I book my ticket home is the day the Luftwaffe start blitz-bombing London. And the day after that, Taylor drags himself away from his Sunday morning Weet-Bix and gin to tell me in the breakfast room of the Weekender: 'All Christmas leave is suspended.'

Instead of quilting him on the spot, I say: 'I'm getting married on the seventh of December.'

'Not if you work for Southern Star, you won't be.' He taps one corner of a folded telegram on the edge of my bread plate. 'You will have to reschedule your personal affairs. The board of directors has decided that you are all to work through until you've struck the crude or gone down the full six thousand feet.'

'Through the rain?' When it comes, the drill rod is going to get bogged every six inches.

'Yes.' There's a look that comes over his eyes as he glances away. Regret or impatience, I can't tell. 'Given the changing circumstances of the war, it is now imperative to push on, and push on quickly.'

I can understand that well enough. No more cruising in the South Seas for any of the board members, either. At least one German raider is lurking around this way somewhere. We know this because it's just sunk a Kiwi freighter in the Tasman.

Shit. This time yesterday, Bernie and I were holding up the queue again planning a honeymoon in Blackheath and deciding that *she* will decide where she wants to live and what she wants to do afterwards. All I can do now is send her a telegram: *LEAVE HAS BEEN SUSPENDED UFN DUE TO WAR. DELAY WEDDING TIL WHENEVER IT CAN HAPPEN. I LOVE YOU. SO SORRY.* What else can I say? I run most of the way back to the rig, as if we might strike the crude if we get another rod in this afternoon.

There is a lot of language at the receipt of the news. Reg threatens to resign, which provokes Johno to tell him: 'Go on, then. Piss off, you fat hairy sheila.' Among other things. That shuts Reg up, for the next three weeks, until Japan signs the Axis Pact with Germany and Italy and moves down into Indo-China. 'Youse are all bleeding mad to stay here, sitting ducks,' are his parting words, and Johno brings me back a rifle from town: 'Not much choice now, Brockie.'

I shake my head: no. I don't have a choice. I'm not going to pick up a gun against another man. Not a German, not a Jap, not anyone. In the very unlikely event that they, whoever they might be, get through the British Army defence of Singapore to get down here, let them intern me. Good enough for Mrs Zoc, good enough for me. I am a civilian and they, German or Jap, are civilised people. If I don't pick up a rifle, I won't die. I will be safe. And they won't come anyway. They can't, not with any great force. America has now, very sensibly, prohibited the export of high-octane fuel to the Axis countries so none of them can fly a plane as far as Singapore. Uncle Sam will keep the Pacific blitz free and I will be getting married as soon as we pull up the first traces of petroleum on New Britain. As soon as we hit that basalt capping stone. That has to be there. Somewhere between five hundred and three thousand feet from now. It just has to be.

I tell Johno: 'Let's get another rod in this arvo, yeah?'

BERNIE

Put aside your dreams for tomorrow, Pig Face said over the wireless, *be prepared to sacrifice yourselves to the point of exhaustion.* God Save the King, full complement of plums in his mouth, and you've never seen a twenty-one year old so quick to get their name on the roll, with two days to spare, my birthday falling as it does on the nineteenth of September.

'Who would Dad vote for?' I ask Mum, though she's never been on the roll herself, and Dad's never been one much for politics other than to have cultivated a reasonably firm conviction that the King can save himself.

She says with no hesitation: 'That Curtin fellow from West Australia.'

'Right.' As I'd thought: Labor Party. I know Dad would go that way, because Mr Curtin does appear to have a dream for tomorrow, an Australian one, with a matching accent, one that doesn't involve sending every last twenty-one year old abroad. In his speech, he didn't go on about war and sacrifice. He said we need to put the brains of our nation together for self-reliance, for our own industries, our own oil and our own aeroplanes – ones with steel wings, as opposed to Irish linen – to win what he calls the Peace. Pig Face keeps having a go at him for being a pacifist socialist and not caring about the bombs in London. But who better to win a peace than a pacifist? And socialists believe women should get equal pay, don't they? Fancy that. Blooping well get on with it so that Dad and

Mrs Zoc, wherever they are, can come home and Rock and I can be married by Christmas.

'But who do I vote for here, in our seat?' I ask Mum what I actually meant to ask her. Who do I vote for in our seat of Watson? Currently held by someone from the United Australia Party, who is on the way out if I have a say in it. I need to be sure I mark the right box.

'That Jewish chap,' says Mum, again without hesitation. Religious intolerance suspended for the Catholic Daily consensus. 'Young Russian fellow, all eyebrows, married a Baptist and his mother hasn't spoken to him since.'

Right. Father Gerard confirms it on the day anyway. 'Morning, Bernadette. You'll be voting for Mr Falstein.' Mr Max Falstein. Find him on the paper and mark that box.

Most of Coogee does, and he wins. Mr Curtin doesn't, though. He loses by a whisker, and we end up with a hung parliament: we don't know what we've decided. War or Peace.

'Never mind,' says Mum, and she makes me shepherd's pie for tea, even though it's not Monday.

Never mind. It's only an election. Just like it's only a wedding. Only a formality. Truly one that doesn't matter, because I have realised over the long weeks since *I LOVE YOU. SO SORRY*, that I don't need a priest or a certificate or a million glass pearls to tell me what I've always known, through all my carry on: if I should ever lose my Rock, my heart will be rendered null and void. A dead black lump of coal, wrapped in magnolia silk, packed in naphthalene, and stamped: *YOU DON'T KNOW WHAT YOU'VE GOT TILL IT'S GONE.*

Gone. No. Not gone. It's only delayed.

Postie comes with a fat letter in October, and I run up to him like a pup, but it's not from anyone we love. It's from Colonel Aitkins of the Department of Stonewalling to inform me, at length and in reference to the enclosed copy of the Official Secrets Act, that any attempt of mine at further correspondence with any officer of Eastern Command or the Attorney-General's Department will be referred to the Commonwealth Investigations Branch. All I wanted to know is where Mrs Zoc is and when the enemy alien appeal forms will be ready. But I'm not allowed to know. It's against the law.

Knowledge, like everything, is suspended. Hung. The universe is holding its breath. Week after week, I hardly want to move from the house, in case Rock phones. In case Dad writes. In case the paper says: *THE WAR IS OVER. THE PEACE IS WON.*

Doesn't happen, of course; nothing does, except facing up to calling all of our happiness off. St Brigid's, the Bay dining room, Yoohoo, the photographer, the flowers.

Friday the sixth of December, the day before what should have been our day, I go out and sit on the step of the laundry in the sun, look up into the branches of our lemon heavy with fruit, and all I can see is the Yellow Peril step-stoning across New Guinea to take everything else from us. Despite Pig Face continuing to call that far-fetched. I don't believe him now; I doubt anyone does. If the Japs are no threat, why then is America giving money to China to fight them? Why has America put sixteen million of their own boys on notice, and why have they stopped selling the Japs aeroplane oil? The Japs say all they want to do is have a *new world order* with the fascists, as if everyone should want one of those. I shudder in the sun. What does a new world order mean? What do they really want? A new fascist order? Where there's no such thing as trade contracts, you just roll in the tanks and take what you want, like the Nazis do? Has Pig Face not considered this, or is the parliament so hung it's ignoring it? Why would they do that? Because of *our* trade contracts? But we wouldn't ever sell the Japs aeroplane oil, would we? I shiver again: I don't want one drop of Rock's sweat going to this new world of fascists, not for any money.

Piccolo settles down next to me on the step with a yawn. He looks at the paper on my knees and mewls as if to say: *Don't believe anything you read in that.*

Unless it's true. Who would know? The Department of Information is in charge of all the papers and the wireless now. Maybe they're deliberately trying to addle me. I decide to go straight to the Classifieds for some sense, see if there aren't any good sales on anything that doesn't involve armaments or serviceable twill. I've had enough of news I don't want to know about. And don't understand.

I scrunch the broadsheet awkwardly as I fold it back, and my eyes fall on a series of notices from the Department of Supply and Development, inviting tenders for work and produce at various military and internment camps, Orange, Bathurst, Tamworth … Yawn. Perhaps I could disguise myself as a purveyor of lemons and a small quantity of haricot beans, get myself inside the system, and bust Mrs Zoc out. But then, halfway down the list, I see something not so ridiculous, something that pulls me up with a start: *Purchase of Waste Food, Fat, Bone, and Dripping, ex Hay Internment Camp.* Hay Internment Camp. In all my pestering and poking about, I've never heard of that camp. I've never heard of Hay.

'Mum!' I sing out to her through the kitchen window, where she's been cumquat marmalading all morning, presents for Dad and Rock. 'Where's Hay, the town Hay?'

'Hay? Is it near Wagga Wagga, love? Don't know.'

Never mind, I'm already on my way to ask the exchange.

'Hay Internment Camp?' the telephonist repeats. 'Certainly, madam.'

She's going to put me through now?

'Hay Internment Camp,' says the man who eventually picks up, a voice that's somehow bored and busy at the same time. I imagine he's a corporal and decide to throw caution to a cyclone, going straight for a series of outrageous lies.

'My name is Monica Brockley, of Brockley and Brockley Solicitors,' I charge at him. 'I understand that you are holding a woman at your camp, my client, Mrs Emilia Zoccoli. Can you confirm this, please?'

'Yep.'

'Yep what?'

'Yep, that's right. She's here,' he grunts, as if everyone knows Mrs Zoc has been there for the last hundred years.

This can't be, can it? But I continue to charge: 'It is of the utmost importance then that I see her, as soon as possible. Can you arrange this for me now?'

'Sunday,' he grunts again. 'Visitors are permitted Sundays, from two pm until four. Just turn up.'

'Right,' I say, only just, and only just restrain myself from demanding to know how this has become suddenly all so easy. 'Sunday then.'

'Good-o. Is that all?' Apparently I'm wasting his time now.

'Yep. Thank you.'

Blow me down. Hughie, you do move in mysterious ways.

'Mum!' I sing out again, grabbing the atlas from the bookshelf in one hand and the telephone receiver again in the other, to call Central Station, to find out how to get to this Hay place, but the doorbell rings first and I open it to the postie boy, holding out a telegram.

It's for Mrs WE Cooper.

'Mum!'

She looks at it from ten paces, from the kitchen door, with a special fear reserved for unexpected telegrams, from her last war. I want to remind her: Dad's still idling in the desert, where the only war that's going on is in the form of a gang of lunatic Jews attempting to blow up a British police station in Jerusalem with a bomb that failed to go off. Isn't it? Nothing's happened to Dad. No news is good news and this news is hopefully only notification of his court martial on account of his nuisance of a daughter. But Mum's already snatched it out of my hand, ripping it open.

Ripping past me and slamming the bedroom door behind her.

And then I hear her yelp. A small, sharp gulp of pain.

'Mum?'

Silence. Nothing but silence. A silence that stops time.

THREE

DECEMBER 1940 – NOVEMBER 1941

GORDON

'There is no answer at that number, sir,' the girl says, 'I'm sorry.' Not as sorry as I am.

'Give it one last try?' Mrs Chittaway looks over at the wall clock behind her. It's two minutes to twelve. I shake my head. Not worth the trouble. The wireless would cut out as soon as I got through anyway. There won't be another line at four today, either. The afternoon service has been cancelled, as I discovered six weeks ago when I last tried to call. Mrs Chittaway gives me half a smile, with an eyebrow for the muddy puddle I've sunk into her carpet. 'Get upstairs and get out of those clothes then.'

Yes, that would be a good idea. It didn't stop raining the whole way here. I went past soaked about five hours ago. About five weeks ago, actually. There's no respite from this rain, other than when the winds pick up and drives it horizontal. I am looking forward to being dry for the next little while. Dry my feet out. They are that bad with tinea, I'm almost frightened to peel my socks off. But they're not nearly as disgusting as the leech I find sucking on the back of my left shoulder soaping up. Can't get used to them. Will never get used to them.

As soon as I'm dry, though, I go back out into the wet. I'm going to Soon's Emporium on Solomon Street to buy something for Bernie. Something cheerful, for Christmas. I see it straight-away, right at the counter: a silver hair comb with tiny flowers on it, made from chips of gemstone. Amethyst and topaz, it looks like.

Purple and gold, like my flowers from home. Nyngan. Be nice and dry there. 'Very nice, very nice,' says Mrs Soon. 'Lucky lady for this one.' Don't think too much about how very nice it will look against her wavy dark hair, or that it's made in Japan.

I choose a card, one with a white Christmas dove on it. What do I say? *Thinking of you, Bernie.* Can't get further than that. I'm not good with a letter anyway. Like Dad. Haven't heard from him all year, have I. I get him a card with some holly and shit on it, and I write: *Merry Christmas, Dad.*

'I post for you, Mr Brock,' says Mrs Soon. 'You go get out of the rain.'

'Thanks.' But I'm not out of the rain just yet. I have to go round to Court Street to report to Taylor and Roycox that, predictably, we've not drilled four hundred feet in these last six weeks, when normally we'd drill more than half that in a week.

'Why's that?' Taylor asks at the door, but he's more interested in straightening his tie. I've caught him at the shirt-change for lunch.

Instead of yelling: *ISN'T IT BLOODY OBVIOUS?* I say: 'Because the rig is swimming in mud, we've snapped two rods so far, and the natives refuse to work.' Sensibly, if you ask me. To-An and a couple of the others come up with provisions out of pity.

Taylor waves it off. 'Do your best, persevere, keep on.'

I will, and this is why I have to ask once again: 'I need to have a look at the old Anglo-Eastern files. I want to check the data for dacite in the broader area.' Solid dacite now, nothing but dacite, silver specks playing with me more than ever: *you're drilling in the wrong place, Brock.*

But Roycox appears in the hall and he's annoyed. 'Not now, no,' and Taylor adds with another wave. 'We're about to conduct a business meeting, young Brock, you can't just bowl in whenever you like, and in any event, you will be told if such geological research is needed – by Mr Roycox.'

I laugh and say: 'Yeah, and stuff you too.'

Roycox tries to pull in his fat gut. 'What did you say?'

I say: 'You heard.' And I walk off, back out into the rain. The streets are empty. The streets are rivers. I hardly notice Mr Komazaki's fake Toyota Chrysler pull up after me. I'm laughing alone, here in the street, in the rain. Past troppo. I might have gone a bit native myself now.

Back at the bar of the New Guinea, I even order a rum. In fact, I think I'll probably order three. I have every intention of getting very quickly crappered, when Sid Triscombe comes up to me, already with the stink of half a bottle in him. 'That'll put hairs on your chest, young fella,' he says, commending my glass. Then he has to add to my face: 'Might even cure that shyness of yours.'

'Shyness?' I say to him: 'I'm not shy.' I know what shyness he means, militia-shy, gun-shy, pansified, and it's only my slim hold on what's left of respect for my elders stopping me from telling him to get stuffed too.

But he has to lean into me and say: 'That so? You look pretty shy to me.'

I should back up and leave this alone. He is pissed and goading me, probably mad with the rain himself. He's also a veteran: he's spent five weeks at a time in a trench getting shot at, before I was born. I've spent five weeks in a trench getting tinea. I should go straight back up to my room and lock myself inside my trunk with Bernie's letters; the one about election day, with Father Gerard getting everyone to vote for a Baptist Jew, is so funny you'd pay to read it. Funny as her last letter was sad, about the beach feeling lonely even with the summer sun coming on, the surf club having trouble filling their patrol roster because all the blockheads have joined up. So I don't back up. I lose all hold on respect.

'What?' I say to Sid. 'You reckon I'm shy because I won't come and play soldiers with you in my five minutes off?'

Unfortunately, at this precise moment, Johno's mate Sven Jorgensen walks in for a bottle to take out with him, saying, 'Hello, Gordon.' He's got his .22 slung across his back, on his way pig-shooting. I ask him: 'Can I have a quick loan of your rifle, please? I won't be two minutes.'

'Okay, sure.' Sven looks a bit confused but he hands it over.

I don't move from where I'm standing at the bar. I aim the muzzle out the open glass doors and say to Sid beside me: 'See those coconuts up there, the nearest palm?' And I fire. Two of them fall onto the tennis lawn with a splash and a scream from the ladies lounge, as I say: 'That's how shy I am.'

'Struth.' Sid's ducked down on his haunches and Mr Chittaway is running out of his manager's office shouting: 'Good God, man!' knocking over a bucket of ping-pong balls on the way. 'You can't do that in here!'

'I'm sorry,' I tell Mr Chittaway. I mean it, too, and not only because my bad knuckle has just exploded up my arm with the shot. Sid Triscombe looks to have seen a ghost as he stands up again, staring at me, appalled. One of the native boys is hiding under a table: afraid of me. No one speaks, no one moves. Still and quiet as Mother Mountain out there, except for the chaos of ping-pong balls bouncing across polished boards in here. I hand the rifle back to Sven, and I am ashamed of myself. Afraid of myself. I tell Sid, especially: 'I'm sorry. I–'

I don't know what's got into me, except that I do. I was supposed to be getting married today.

I'm about to take off back to the Weekender to plan my disappearance via the next plane back to Sydney, before I'm chucked out, when Sid claps me on the shoulder and turns me around. The cracks in his rum-soaked face could swallow a dog, swallow me, as he says: 'It's all right, son. I understand.'

BERNIE

*P*lease *don't worry if you don't hear from me for a while.*

That's all Dad said to stop Mum's world from turning, their code for him going off to … the unimaginable. That Mum has been expecting it for all this time, through every letterless day, doesn't make it any easier for her to take. She's shrunk a couple of inches overnight with the burden. Of not knowing where he is or what he's doing, but knowing too well now that he is in danger. Shrunk another inch again since we left home for Central, for me to catch the train to Hay.

'Mum, I don't think I should go,' I tell her, again.

And again she insists: 'Of course you should go – go and put something right.'

Bring Emilia back for her. See if I don't. And Dad would agree. But Mum looks so … what?

'I'm sorry, love, I'm not myself,' she says, clicks her tongue and winces: 'Pay no attention to me.'

'Mum, you've nothing to be sorry for.' I hug her, but not for too long. She stiffens in my arms, not wanting a display.

'All aboard!' the train guard bellows up the platform, porters and passengers rushing every which way. 'Riverina Express! All aboard!'

Mum just about pushes me up into the carriage. 'Don't forget to wear your hat out there, Missy.'

'I won't,' I say, just. Mum is looking at me as if her own life depends upon my wearing a hat for the duration. I'll wear my blooping hat too, won't take it off for the whole four days I'll be gone. Give her a quick kiss and don't look at her again until I'm safely in my seat.

From where I can see she's even smaller than I thought, more stray greys through her hair than I've noticed before. Waving me away with her hankie and her pasted-on smile. Peggy Doyle, who once went all the way to Melbourne to meet her Bill off the ship, old now and she's only forty-four and not quite a half. The whistle blows as the train choofs out into the sunlight. I watch her until Sydney disappears into the mountains, into the gums. This war. Interminable, and yet it's only just begun.

*

Four hundred and fifty miles and fifteen hours away, I watch the sun coming up over a land that's all sky, and don't wonder why the Department of Army doesn't care so much about security out here. It might be difficult to escape, much less inspire a revolution, from the end of the line, after Grong Grong, Narrandera, Willbriggie and The Middle of Nowhere. Exactly the middle, too – we're halfway to Adelaide. I know Australia is wide, but I've never understood just how wide, and we're not even out of the State, nowhere near the border.

There's a tap at the compartment door. 'Would you like any last refreshments, miss? We're about fifteen minutes from Hay.'

'No thanks,' I sing out to the tea girl; I need the whole fifteen minutes to unmess myself.

Between squinting out the window, looking for the trees I'd expected there'd be in the Riverina, with its Murrumbidgee Irrigation Scheme producing millions of tons of peaches and pears for the Ardmona Fruit Company, write that in your geography book ten times, Sister Columba. But I can't see any trees at all. Only patches of scrub, over an endless plain, flat as a penny. *How far are you going today, dear?* my elderly lounge-car companion asked yesterday, and when I said all the way, she nodded approvingly. *Home, dear?* she peered at me, trying to place me in the scheme. That was a Mrs Overton, who got off at Junee last night, on her way home from visiting with her brother in Mittagong, and who, it turned out as she chatted for a State medal, is a cousin-in-law of Mrs Finlay's from Orange, who went to school with her good friend, Mrs McBride, from Gundagai, and through her husband knows Dad's Aunty Ena's second cousin Iris in Dunedoo, the CWA being as wide as the country itself.

Wide and gold, I think as the sun rises a little higher, picking out the tops of the scrubby shrubs, lighting up the fields: gold. A lumpy field of gold is what it looks like, before I see the lumps are sheep. A great big pen of them, by the side of the tracks as we slow for the station.

The engine hisses to a stop and I step down onto the platform to a chorus of *baaaaaas*. A couple of stockmen types on horseback smoke cigarettes as a dog runs across the top of the small sea of sheep behind them, and everything is golden – the spare spiky grass, the fence posts, the fleece, the edges of the men's wide-brim Akubras. I've woken up inside the pages of *Dreams in the Dust*. Fair dinkum sunburnt outback cliché. But with what appears to be another big pen strung with barbed wire a quarter of a mile up off to the left of the sheep, an arrangement of huts, a watchtower, that must be –

'Miss Cooper?' the deep voice of authority calls for me to stop wandering up the platform, but when I turn around I see it's not a guard but another stockman type striding towards me. One that stops my heart for a second with the set of his gait, the white moleskin trousers, blue Scotch twill shirt-sleeves rolled, the set of his brim, turned right down over his eyes. It's Rock, coming home to Coogee with the red dirt of Nyngan still dusting the leather of his boots. It's not, of course. The dirt here is ordinary dirt brown, and this man doesn't even take off his hat as he says: 'Mitchell Lockhart.' More instruction than introduction. I suppose he is a relation of the Mrs Lockhart that I'll be stopping with tonight and till next train Tuesday, but he doesn't provide that small courtesy of information. He points at my luggage on the platform behind me, my fawn suitcase and my Good Companion, and says: 'That all you got with you?'

'Yes.' I can't help the frown as I think what a waste of a fabulous name. Mitchell Lockhart – that's Hollywood grade. But I don't reflect on this further: every fly in town has just made a beeline for me and I'm waving at my face like a madwoman fighting her hatbox as he grabs my luggage and strides off, turning into the station building. I'd say, *Well, good day to you too,* if I dared open my mouth. He's holding the door open for me, and issuing another instruction, impatient: 'Wait here, will you.' Virtually hurls my cases across the floor with complete disregard for DJ's best cowhide and British Best typewriter, and he's about to stride back outside again as I pull him up: 'Excuse me, I am waiting for …?'

'For me to see those ewes are being got onto the trucks,' he tosses the words behind him. 'Then I'll take you round to the house.'

'House?'

'Mum's.'

'Right.' The door swings shut in my face. Mitchell Lockhart, son of Mrs, I must presume. Poor Mrs Lockhart. She sounded so pleasant on the phone, not that we spoke for more than two minutes. Mrs Carlton from the Dee Why Harbourside Branch put us in touch yesterday morning. *Aren't you our Gordon's fiancée?* said this Mrs Lockhart, chirping through my fog of worry over Dad. *Well, of course, stay as long as you like, dear.* Incredible: *our Gordon.* Nyngan is three hundred miles north of here: I know, I checked on the atlas with a ruler. But you'd think they were all down-the-road neighbours. Mrs Lockhart also sounded about as happy as Mrs Finlay at there being foreigners corralled on her showgrounds – *Hmm, nasty business.* I hope she's not nasty about Italians. There's nowhere else for me to go if she is. Mrs Overton from the train knew of her, Mrs Lockhart being the President of Hay Branch, and what did she say about her? *Redoubtable spirit, that Bess Lockhart.* What does redoubtable mean? Brave? Or terrifying.

Means I won't know till I meet her for myself. Look out at the ewes while I'm waiting, and feel no better as I watch them being herded towards the trucks, big wooden crates sitting on a siding track, being crammed into them, off to a fate I'd prefer not to contemplate. Just how many lamb dinners have I consumed in my little life? Good grief but it's heating up quickly in here. Start throwing everything out of my handbag looking for something to make a fan out of, when the door bangs open again with, 'Head off now then', and I just about hit the roof with fright.

'What?' And I startle again when I don't recognise the man in front of me now, before I realise he's taken his hat off. And then blush – deep fuchsia. Mitchell Lockhart is handsome as a lion: hay-coloured hair, hazel eyes and a tea-stain tan making him gold all over. He is a lion. He's also at least five years my senior, with a hard-set jaw that says he allocates approximately five minutes less ten each day for suffering fools.

But he smiles now, as I fluster about stuffing my embarrassment back into my handbag. A crooked smile, saying: 'I said we'll head off now then.' At least I think it's a smile. 'Long trip, eh?'

'Yes,' I reply, as he swipes up my cases, and I attempt to recover myself by nattering: 'Sheep all off to market then?'

'No.' He puts his hat back on, somehow disappearing under it, and letting the pause stretch with his stride across the room, stretching till I think *no* is all the answer I'll get to my silly question, before he says: 'Those ewes are off to relief country, near Yass.'

I don't know what that means, so I say: 'Oh?'

'The drought,' tossing the words behind him again: 'Not enough feed for them here.'

'They're *your* ewes?' I ask, like a dill. Farmers have been sending their sheep away to greener pastures as the drought drags on across the State. He's not a stockman, is he; he's a grazier. Might explain why he's a bit grim.

'That's right,' says this Mitchell Lockhart, stepping out into the sun that's now promising a hundred and ten degrees of Hades's best. We've come out of the building on what appears to be the town side of the tracks, where there's a shop, one shop, with a rusting tin awning over a faded ad for Bushells tea and dun-coloured paint peeling against a sky so blue it can only be called screaming, and as I pull my own brim firmly down on my head I'm about to say, *Goodness, it's warm,* when I see a couple of tall, graceful vanilla-trunked gums either side of the gravel drive in front of the station and remark instead: 'Oh, trees.'

'That's right,' Mitchell Lockhart repeats, giving me another long-distance pause, before nodding at a gleaming black utility parked just beyond one of these trees. 'And that's a motor vehicle.'

I would connipt at that if I knew whether he was having fun with me or not. He opens the cab door and the interior, like the exterior, is so spit-polished I decide to err on the side that says he's absolutely humourless. He's certainly absolutely uninterested in his passenger as he drives us into the town along the wide brown dirt road, but it's a town that nevertheless has plenty of both trees and motor vehicles. Small but neat and complete, even got a milk bar called the Manhattan, which does force a snort from me. American Beauty ice-cream ad in the window says they're Greeks: got to admire that Mediterranean sense of geography.

Mitchell Lockhart doesn't take his eyes off the dirt road. Ropey forearms gripping the wheel, turning left and past a cluster of rickety weatherboards, and then right down what soon becomes a grassy track, green grass, shaded by rambling old figs. A long cool bumpy drive of these lovely old figs, at the end of which he pulls up in front of *the* loveliest, most thoroughly gorgeous old stone house I've ever seen. Silver bullnosed verandah dappled by another of those vanilla gums, and willows trailing down into what I suppose is the Murrumbidgee River rolling along out the back. Gasp for want of a hundred superlatives: 'What a beautiful place.'

'Not when it floods.' Mitchell Lockhart pulls up the brake, and I'm dreading again what sort of redoubtable sourpuss Mrs is going to be, must be, when she emerges from the shadow of the bullnose, waving over a great big unmistakeable smile.

'Miss Cooper, so pleased to meet you!' Not a sourpuss but a redoubtable plum pudding barrelling towards me, string of cultured pearls and matching smudge of flour on an outstretched forearm that is possibly deadly with pin in hand. CWA poster girl. Except for the Molyneux pencil pleats she's wearing under her apron, showing that she's not regular catalogue stock. There's nothing poor about this Mrs Lockhart. Squeezing my hand, cheerful as the pansies spilling over the edges of her flowerbeds: 'My word, aren't you pretty. Of course you are. Bernadette, isn't it? How do you do?' Not giving me half a second to answer before she's pulling me across the verandah with: 'You must be faint with hunger, dear – once upon a time the Express did a decent meal, but that's all gone the way of war economy, hasn't it?' Another question I can't answer before she adds: 'And our Gordon is in New Guinea, isn't he? How terrifically exciting for him.'

Mrs Lockhart can talk for Australia. World championship chat.

Still squeezing my hand, picks it up and inspects it as she drags me down the hall. 'No ring? Oh dear, I haven't been given the wrong story, there, have I?'

She finally takes a breath, and I look down at my hand, wondering for a moment what on earth she's referring to, before I realise: 'Ah. Oh. Um. Yes, we're engaged, it's just that he didn't have the–'

'Thank heavens for that,' Mrs Lockhart pats her breast in relief as she shows me into the sitting room. 'He's a catch and a half, our Gordon, isn't he?' and I'd show her the jasper B he gave me to prove it, but she's gone, calling behind her: 'Make yourself at home, dear, won't be a moment.'

Leaving me among the chintz tea-roses and teal velveteen of this sitting room. I almost whistle as I take it all in: the Lockharts are possibly a lot less poor than first impressions. There's a servants' bell pull by the door and a gilt-framed portrait of a ram above the mantel, a ram of regal bearing that bleats imperiously at me: *Yes, we are Squattocracy with a capital S.* And look at the china laid out on the table by the bay window: yes, that'd be real Wedgwood. Possibly heirloom. Makes me wonder at the connection to our Gordon. Seems a familiar and genuinely fond one, but I don't recall him ever mentioning any Lockharts, and there's nothing squattocratic about him. I can hear him laughing with Dad at some of the landed gentry he went to school with, *funny how you can fail arithmetic but still go on to a successful career in tax evasion,* while Sister Columba defined 'squatter' for us in no uncertain terms as a euphemism for *typical thieving, pillaging Protestantism.* Oh Hughie, but there's the most divine painting on the wall opposite the hearth, of a pioneer couple holding hands by the river's edge: *yes, that'd be a real Tom Roberts.*

'About time Mitchell got himself a wife.' Mrs Lockhart barrels back in with a tray and I follow her gaze out the bay window. There's her Mitchell, carrying a saddle across the actual idyllic river view like he's going to take it round behind the back shed and kill it. How are these two mother and son? 'But it is difficult for him,' she says with an affectionate sigh. 'He so rarely comes in from Hell.'

'Pardon?' Did she just say *Hell*? 'Where does he come in–'

'Hell,' she nods. 'That's where the station is, thirty miles north of here. Hell's Flat. And it is as bad as it sounds – worse for these last few years. It's the Hell in "Hay and Hell and Booligal". You know, the poem, Banjo Paterson?'

'Umm.' I'm sure I do but I can't think of it at this speed.

'Well,' Mrs Lockhart raises an eyebrow: 'Suffice to say that the reality is not nearly so entertaining as Mr Paterson's poem.' She laughs lightly over the teapot, a chinkling sound. 'That I could wish it upon any young woman seems almost sinful. Go to Hell. Dust storms and brown snakes and accepting that you and the children will never be as important as the sheep, the horses, the dogs and the dingo trapper, in that order. Still, I do wish it. Milk, sugar? Do help yourself to a scone, dear, won't you?'

I won't need to be asked twice, I am starving and the spread looks delicious; won't need to pause for conversation either. 'Married to the flock, like his dear late father,' Mrs Lockhart manages very well on her own. 'Twenty thousand head, we have. That's a sizeable mob, if you don't know. Even in a good year he's often away, Mitch, that is, moving stock up what we call the Long Paddock, three hundred miles long all the way from Deniliquin up to Wilcannia. That's where my people are from originally, Wilcannia, on the Darling River. Have you been up that way yet, dear?'

I shake my head; no idea where Wilcannia is, and it doesn't matter anyway because: 'Oh, a wonderful part of the world, it is, on the Darling.' She looks out to the willows, and then back to me, sparkly willow-green eyes. 'When I was your age, before the war – not this one, the last one – our great fun up there was to take one of the wool boats from Wilcannia across to Bourke. It's all on the railways these days of course, but in those days, oh, the riverboats were something, and there was always a dance or a party to be had in Bourke. That was a town, before the railways – Bourke was a *marvellous* town. And we were a wild mob, don't you doubt it, dear. That's where we met Brock – the senior, that is. Oh, and could he dance? A striking figure, I'll say. If I hadn't already been promised, I–'

I stop mid-mouthful at the mention of Gordon's father, a man I know only as strikingly absent, and when Mrs Lockhart sees she's as speedy with an apology. 'Oh dear, I am sorry. That was tactless. Of course you didn't even get to meet Mr Brock, did you, and I carry on with such nonsense,' she scolds herself, before changing the subject: 'So, tell me all about this Italian lady you've come for. How awful ...'

Awful. I am caught up inside the thought of how awful, for Mr Brock. That he was happy once, dancing with all the ladies of the Darling River, before *bleeding misery*. Before Gallipoli.

'And so I don't suppose you'd be interested in doing something like that at the camp, would you? Tell me all about your accomplishments, Bernadette.' Mrs Lockhart's chatter breaks through awful.

And she's waiting for an answer this time.

'Oh? Um. Pardon me – what?'

'Mrs Werner's children, in the camp,' she tisks: *Keep up, girl*. 'They're terribly bored, and bright things, too. She'd like them taught their lessons in English. They'll be there for some time yet, as their appeal has failed. Such a nasty business. You know, she's a Jewess – that's why they had to leave Germany, why they upped sticks to Melbourne. But all the authorities appear to see is that her husband's papers say he's a member of the Nazi Party – they simply won't believe that he was forced into it, like they all were, because that's what the blasted fascists do, don't they. The man is a musician, violinist, very refined fellow, for heaven's sake. Now he's in the men's camp – over the other side of the tracks, you would have seen it coming in this morning. Thrown in with the Nazis, he is, separated from his wife and the children, and there's not a thing to be done about it. Well, that is, apart from flouting the rules to have a teacher brought in for the kiddies.' Mrs Lockhart's eyes sparkle with mischief.

The little girl with chestnut plaits skips through my mind, through a vague recollection of Nazis smashing synagogue windows in Berlin and an argument in the papers over us not wanting too many Jews coming here: don't bring your Continental window-smashing troubles here, thank you. Wasn't paying attention then; am now. But I have to say: 'I'm not a teacher, Mrs Lockhart, and I'm only going to be here for–'

'They're not all Jews, you know,' Mrs Lockhart ploughs on, 'although there's a whole shipload full of men in the same boat as Mr Werner. Plenty of Christian kiddies have been locked up as well, dear, poor little Lutheran kiddies. Hauled out of their homes in New Guinea and the Top End and thrown in prison like common criminals. They take all their lessons in their own language, of course, but their mothers would so very much appreciate a kind and pretty face such as yours to take the children for craft, dance, fun things, take their dear little minds off their predicament – the Italian kiddies too.'

'I can see you're passionately devoted to them all, but I–'

'Passionate?' Mrs Lockhart shakes her napkin at me. 'The Department of Army will know about passionate when I'm finished with them. Coming here, these city people, taking over the place, treating us as if we're simple Simons, don't know what's good for us, and questioning *my* patriotism. They'll know about patriotism, my word. My husband didn't lay down his life in some godforsaken bog in France for little children to be imprisoned behind barbed wire on his grandfather's old grazing lands!'

I might be beginning to see what Mrs Overton meant by redoubtable. Mrs Lockhart is a ferocious plum pudding right after my own heart. I think she's also just told me she's a war widow.

But still I have to say: 'I'm sorry, I'm not a teacher. I have no exp–'

'You're good with words, though, aren't you – weren't you working in advertising for Chalmers before your engagement?' Mrs Lockhart purses her lips together as if to say, *I've got your number, missy*. 'You're enormously clever, so I've heard. And once you've met the children this afternoon, you won't be able to say no. The Werner kiddies are delightful, impeccable manners, for little boys. Now, tell me, how are you in the garden, dear? I have some tomato seedlings that need to be thinned out and re-potted before we leave ...'

Good grief. What have I got into here?

*

A wide beige land. Hay is utterly beige. The sun is high now and so breathlessly hot it's leached the colour from everything, so that at first I don't recognise the camp for what it is. The huts, laid out in a circle inside a circle of wire, are painted the same beige as the dirt, as if the whole camp has been deliberately and very unnecessarily camouflaged. Hughie, but how do people live in this blinding heat at all? With no verandahs on the huts, no *eaves*. Thirty miles from Hell. Should report this to the Red Cross. I am forming a new appreciation for sheep, too, who have to spend all day in it, in wool. And starving, truly. There is not one stick of grass on Grandfather Lockhart's old grazing land today.

Mrs Lockhart hands me a box of tomato seedlings from the back of the ute. 'Take those, will you please, dear?'

I would look at her as if she's the very end of mental – these plants will surely fry out here – but Bess Lockhart is a power unto herself, a kind of sun around which everything else spins. She carries another box of seedlings herself, as well as a string bag stuffed with envelopes full of seeds for a variety of summer veg, which are destined not only for putting roses in the kiddies' cheeks but to give their mothers something to do. A food garden to supplement a healthy dose of vitamin sponge-cake, all donated by the matrons of the CWA, and an old sewing machine thrown in by a Mrs McDoughal, with half-a-dozen sugar sacks worth of remnant fabric included. These will be the best fed and clothed children in the nation if Mrs Lockhart has anything to do with sticking one in the eye of the Department of Army.

A guard appears around the corner of the nearest hut and waves to Mitchell, who is lugging the sewing machine up to the camp entrance, which is nothing more than an open break in the wire fence. How ridiculous, all this regulation army barbed wire and the guard's rifle is leaning unattended beside a garbage bin, beside an absent gate. Mitchell and the guard exchange a handshake and a word, like old friends, because they probably are, while behind them a gang of small boys are kicking a ball around, kicking up dust, joyful. They play and yell and shove each other as if they are on holiday camp, and I think, what a strange country this is: closed and callous disregard one moment, and open, boundless generosity the next. Droughts and floods.

Then I see the elegant black crepe shape step into the sun from the doorway of one of the far huts, a sharp clap of hands, calling in boys, 'Pronto, pronto!' and I almost drop my tomatoes. I run right past Mitchell and the guard, losing my hat as I go.

'Mrs Zoc!'

GORDON

'Uncanny.' Sid's still scratching his head over it. 'The way you handle a rifle. You're the image of him. Dunno how I didn't pick it before.'

That I look a lot like my Dad. I don't know, either. Probably because Sid hadn't seen me with a rifle before. I'm still holding the butt to my shoulder, out on this range that lies between the cemetery and the golf course. Sid's less impressed by the bullseye just now than the resemblance. I'm still looking through the sight, not at the target now but at the steam drifting out of Mount Matupi beyond the eighteenth hole, waiting for the urge to yell out all manner of shit to express the relation of percussive impact to pain still reverberating through my hand. Eye-watering.

'Your dad's got dark hair, though, hasn't he? You're a bit fairer than him. Maybe that's it.'

'Maybe.'

'You will give him my regards, won't you?' Sid asks me again, as he's asked me several times since yesterday afternoon. I look at him now and he's not a mean bastard at all, just an old bloke asking after an old mate. He obviously thinks a lot of Dad. He only knew him briefly. Dad's was a very brief war. They met in training, in a paddock in Campbelltown outside Sydney, a few weeks before they embarked, and didn't get a chance to say hooroo when they landed at Anzac Cove. In the scheme of things, he knew Dad for less than five minutes, but Sid's thrill at the recognition seems that much of

157

a deal, I couldn't say no to coming out here shooting with him. In this break in the rain. Miraculous what a break in the rain can do for your personal equilibrium.

I say: 'Yeah, of course I'll tell him you said hello.' If I could. I don't tell Sid that Dad's gone AWL. And I don't tell him that Dad wouldn't be pleased I'm here, on any rifle range; I don't think Sid would understand that much at all. Somehow, for Sid, his Great War seems to have been just that: the best years of his life. Beats being a shipping clerk for Burns Philp, I suppose it might seem for him. Eye-watering.

Sid finally notes the accuracy of my shot and shakes his head. 'Dunno what you were shy about. I'll have you in my company.'

'No, you won't,' I can tell him, with confidence now. 'I'm not going to be any good to you in the militia.'

'No? Why's that, son?' Sid is smiling as if I'm having him on, waiting for the next line of the joke. I don't think he's the sharpest blade in the drawer, either.

I tell him: 'I might be a good shot, but I can't fire two in a row.' Not without a rest of several years in between.

'What do you mean?'

'I put something out in my hand, in a blue. About a year ago. It's no good.' Not too good at all, I reckon as I prise it off the trigger, but I couldn't be more pleased about it. This is my exemption from national service, end of issue. I wouldn't pass the medical examination – I couldn't pass the flaming handshake. But I could send a Christmas card to the shearer that caused it.

'Oh.' Sid rolls his shoulder, awkward. 'You could have told me that in the first place, I wouldn't have given you a hard time.'

Don't point out to him that he has no business giving me a hard time about anything. He's a sad old man. Hard case. Just like my father. Same disease, different manifestation.

He pulls out his hipflask. 'Rum?'

'No thanks.' I hand him back the rifle. 'But I could murder a beer.'

I want to go back to the bar and hear him tell me a couple more times what a good bloke my dad was. Having some fun on the ship, mixing up everyone's boots in the night, putting salt in his CO's sugar bowl. A man I don't recognise. And one I do: someone who'd give you his rum ration if you needed it more than him, somehow convincing you it was yours in the first place. A man Sid last saw tearing up the steep face of a gully above that beach, firing and reloading the whole time, unstoppable. Whatever happened to him after that, I don't know, and I don't think Sid does either. I just want to hear Sid tell me how much I look like him a couple more times before I go back to the shithole of the rig tomorrow.

To help me keep sight of why I'm doing this. Oil for Empire, soldiering for Southern Star Greed Incorporated, and for national industrial security against an axis of evil that is threatening my house on the harbour for Bernie. That's why am I doing this. Isn't it, Dad?

BERNIE

'So, did you write to the wonder people?' Mrs Zoc asks me, as if we're chatting over the back fence in Coogee and not in the empty and airless hothouse of the dining room of Hay Women's Camp, six months after our last conversation. She's just told me she's already made an appeal against her internment herself, and it's failed. As if no more has happened than she's missed the tram. And now I have no idea what she's talking about.

'Wonder people?'

'The wonder book people.' She gives me an admonishing tone: 'I cut out the advertisement from the *Women's Mirror* for you.'

'Oh!' The light flickers on somewhere in the depths of broiled brain. 'Wonder Publications? Yes, I–' I would tell her all about Monica Brockley's suspended adventure with Eugenia Frank and Will Gordon, but I'm not going to be distracted from the reason I've come all this way here. 'Look, Mrs Zoc, I think I'd better be writing another appeal for you, rather than a six-penny romance. You can't stay here.'

I look around the room. We're the only people in it. I am the only visitor this Sunday, apart from Mrs and Mitchell Lockhart, who've gone to look at the bore that was drilled yesterday for the garden water, bore water that is casting a stench over this side of the camp like something's gone putrid in the belly of the earth. It has: I'm the only visitor in here today because there was a brawl yesterday in the men's camp between the Nazis and the Jews over the Sabbath and so none of them has been allowed out to see their families. I repeat: 'Mrs Zoc, you're not staying here two seconds longer than necessary.'

'Of course I can stay here, Bernadetta,' she straightens, as if I've offended her: she can write her own appeals thank you very much. 'It is not the worst place I stay in my life. It does not matter.'

'It does matter. You haven't done anything wrong. This isn't fair.' Hear the whine in my voice: don't let your pride get in the way of my need to rescue you and have us both out of here by Tuesday.

'It is fair enough,' Mrs Zoc slaps the table briskly. 'It is my own fault I keep my Marco's old anarchico magazines from years ago because I keep every little stupido thing of him he ever touch. This is fair enough wrongdoing for the police: they don't know better, they don't know that Marco was not more a revolutionary than a Shirley Temple lollipop, they don't know what it is to have to lie on your papers to be safe, either. They only want to keep this country peaceful. Peace is why we come here, Bernadetta; I will not complain again. And it does not matter anyway because Italia will not be in this war for long. The Fat Head is more stupido than anyone – as soon as the Allies get to Sicilia, it will all be finished for him. You will see. And then I can worry that my bad sons will be free to kill Mr Raymond in Horseshoe, this mango farmer who tells lies about them because their fruit is a better quality and price, and then they will be hanged, and I will throw myself off the cliffs below Arcadia. So, it is better to keep these Siciliano boys locked up for as long as they can, eh?'

She is joking of course, but I am not laughing. Her fiery dark eyes smile and she takes my hand in both of hers: 'Bernadetta, please, everything is all right for me. And for my sons, too: they are in a camp in a place called Tatura, in Victoria, they write to me that they are well, and they have a big garden there. They have other good neighbours to look after their trees in Horseshoe, too – they are picking the fruit for the Christmas markets right now. The Zoccolis are all right, much more fortunate compared to others. I am happy to stay here, Bernadetta. I am teaching the children here some Siciliano Italiano. They do nothing wrong either.'

That's very philosophical of you, Mrs Zoc, but it doesn't suit my plans, or Mum's. 'You have to come home,' I plead. 'Mum needs you to.'

'How is your mother?' Mrs Zoc asks, and that's all she will talk about now. How's Mum coping without Dad and will I tell her to go and rescue the strawberries in her yard from the birds? And then suddenly: 'Ah! Bernadetta! But you are supposed to be on your honeymoon today! Where is Gordon? Is he here too?' She just about jumps out of her seat at the idea, but then she sees my face, picks up my hand. 'Where is the ring?'

'There's been a delay,' I tell her this war's got in the way of it, and she cries: 'Bella! No!'

'Yes. Afraid so.'

'When then?'

'Don't know. Haven't heard from him in weeks.'

'Ah, well,' Mrs Zoc sighs, one hand on mine and the other under the table with her rosary going a decade a second. 'It is terrible, to be apart for so long and not knowing. But then the worse it is waiting the better it is coming together again, si?'

'I hope so.'

'I know it is so.' She nods. 'This is why I tell you to write about love, while you are waiting. Always think about love. And you didn't tell me yet, what did you write to the Wonder people? What happened?'

And that's what we're talking about, Mrs Zoc exclaiming: 'Oh but you must finish it! You must finish this while you are waiting for Gordon to come home,' when Mrs Lockhart comes back for me.

'Finish what?' she barrels in, battered straw hat over her pearls and her Molyneux.

'Her book!' Mrs Zoc announces to the stratosphere. 'Bernadetta is writing a molto romantico novel.'

'Oh!' Mrs Lockhart just about squeals. 'A romance? Oh, I *do* love a good serial. Tell me you are *not* writing a romance! Is it any good?'

'Yes, it is,' Mrs Zoc declares, hands on her hips, as pleased with herself as she is with me. 'The publisher wants her to finish it.'

'Oh? Well, dear, you *must*,' Mrs Lockhart decides, because she is as mad as Mrs Zoc: they've swapped biscuit recipes. 'You simply must. And so there, I see you *are* as clever as I've heard, aren't you. A novelist? Well, isn't that something. Now, back to business for a minute. Come and meet Anna Werner and her boys …'

*

'Mum, are you sure you'll be all right?' I ask her and I want her to say no, to tell me to come home straightaway and not help Mrs Lockhart with the Christmas party for the children next week. Not come back in January to teach the Werner boys their lessons in English, a language their mother speaks more competently than I do. Two adorable little boys who I'll bet know their tables better than I do, the littlest lisping *Mith Cooper* every day. Stay here in Hay at Mrs Lockhart's Riverbend, and finish my romance, and Hughie knows what else. Mental. Not in a good way.

But Mum says: 'Of course I'll be all right. It cheers me no end to know you're helping those poor little mites. I'm proud of you, *very* proud of you, Bernadette.' Her voice wobbles with it, so that it takes me a moment to say: 'See you Christmas Eve, then.'

'See you then, love.'

I put the phone down, a strange emptiness in my belly, gnawing, and Mrs Lockhart asks me: 'Is your mother all right with your staying?'

'Yes,' I say, and I look away, swallowing the threat of tears. Tell myself I'm just baulking at the idea of being away from home, that's all; baulking at leaving Mum, as if I wouldn't have left home this very weekend anyway. Ask Mrs Lockhart: 'Do you mind if I walk down to the river for a paddle?' I want to be alone with these thoughts for a little while, get myself straight.

'Now, that is a good idea, go and cool off,' Mrs Lockhart says. For all her steam-rolling redoubtability, she's as sharp as a tack, and I think she knows how I might feel: spun-wrung bamboozled and not used to this withering heat. She smiles, and the low sun through the bay window is making her grey hair golden as she adds: 'I'd come too, but it's cook's night off. Now, why don't you put your

163

bathers on and have a proper dip. You can swim, can't you? Of course you can, and you'll see a little beach on the bend just over the other side of the stable. That's the best spot, and don't swim past the pump. You did bring some bathers, didn't you?'

'I did.' So I do, and I've already started on the romance again before I've got past the tin shed I presume is a stable. The river is a mauvish colour against the willows, reflecting this late afternoon light. A mauve sea for Eugenia to fly across, searching for Will. It's around about chapter six and he's lost in the jungle. She's determined to find him, and she will, across this wide, mauve sea. She's interminably lonely, flying and flying across this vast sea, but she is as brave as her mum, as Mrs Zoc, as Mrs Lockhart too. Steely.

'Miss Cooper,' the gentle voice of authority interrupts my wandering. Mitchell. Leading a great big white horse out of the shed.

Nerves clang at the sight. I'm a bit frightened of horses, up close. I say: 'Oh?'

'I'll see you later, I suppose,' he says.

I say: 'Oh, hmm,' pulling my towel over my cossie. I thought he'd already left for his return to Hell – in the ute. But he's getting up on the horse. He touches the brim of his hat and I see him smirk: at my feet. I look at my feet. What's wrong with my sandals? A girl's supposed to walk barefoot through bindies out here?

He says: 'Don't know how you stay upright in those high-heeled things.'

These aren't high heels; they're wedges. But I say: 'Got to be good at something, don't you.'

'Yep,' he says, touch to the brim again. 'See you.' And he rides off.

I watch him, watch him till he jumps the far fence, on his great white horse, into the sunset. That's exactly how Rock would look on a horse. I know he can ride a horse, but I've never seen him on one. And it crashes over me like a six-foot breaker now: imagining him is all I have of him. UFN. Just as that's all Mum has of Dad. Mum looking so small on the platform, waving me away. That pained look on her face: *pay no attention to me.*

And that's it. I can't stay in Hay. I'll help Mrs Lockhart with the party for the children but I'm not going to come back after Christmas. I'm going to stay at home. Where I belong.

GORDON

'She's *where*?' I can't believe she's not there. I could kick the wall.

'Hay, Gordon; she's in Hay,' Mrs Cooper repeats. 'It's out past Wagga Wagga somewhere, love.'

I know exactly where Hay is, on the Paddock, but: 'What's she doing there?'

'You don't know?'

'No, I don't.' Geez.

'Well, that's very odd. You've not got a letter from her?'

'No.' And it is more than odd. It's March. I've had nothing at all from her for months, not since Rico brought me a letter back from town last November, the one about the beach feeling sad.

'That doesn't sound right,' Mrs Cooper says. 'I know she must have written you a dozen letters since she left – and I know for a fact she sent you a telegram about finding Mrs Zoccoli, because I was with her when she sent it, before she got on the train.'

'You've found Mrs Zoc?' Christ. I hate this distance.

'Oh yes, love – in Hay!'

'So Bernie's in Hay with Mrs Zoc?'

'Yes, but well, no, not exactly, she's teaching some of the children English at the internment camp, and–'

'What?' Static knifes through the line, just about taking my ear off as another aftershock hits, a big one. Glass smashes somewhere and Mrs Chittaway goes running. We've been having these rolling quakes all morning, since a massive one hit about seven o'clock last night. Not coming from the volcano, but from somewhere to the south. Goorias, the natives call them, a reminder of who's in charge around here. 'Mrs Cooper? Are you there? Mrs Cooper?'

I stare at the phone and tell it: 'Bullshit.'

'We'll have none of that here, thank you, Mr Brock.' Mrs Chittaway comes back with a broom in hand, and ready to use it in case I threaten to go psychotic with a gun in the front bar again.

'Sorry,' I say. 'I–'

'It's hard, pet, I know. But don't lose your head over it. The things we worry about, storms in teacups most of the time.' Her guest book falls off the counter behind her and she doesn't blink. She might be troppo herself, but her lipstick is always perfectly drawn on, not a hair out of place, even though she must be worried the next quake will bring the club down.

In the interests of not losing my head, I decide to go for a walk. I'll go and find Ernie Turner first, the new assistant vulcanologist, who I met in the bar when I got in last night. He's fun. He can't believe his luck, arriving in Rabaul two weeks before a major seismic event. As a geologist, I should be a little more than interested too. But Ernie's not about when I look in at his office on Park Street: he's already gone for a walk, up Mount Matupi, the most active vent, because he beats every bloke on this island for cracked.

And I can't get my mind off Bernie. I'm not that surprised I didn't get her telegram: there was a lot disruption to the telegram service just before Christmas, with all the wireless operators being seconded into the military and replaced by twelve year olds; the message is probably still working its way back from Timbuktu. But her letters? Why wouldn't I get her letters?

Because she hasn't written, has she. She hasn't written to me because she's met someone in Hay. She doesn't love me any more, if she ever did. It was the hair comb, wasn't it. She didn't like it. Don't be a halfwit: there is no one to meet in Hay. Graziers and shearers, and that bloke I quilted at Yarranbulla – wasn't he from Hay? Somewhere down there. Bernie's in *Hay*? That is cracked. How can I not lose my head?

The sky answers with some rain. More rain. It's March, the season should be over. But it's decided not to be. I keep walking, down to the beach, through this rain I have come to hate. I never thought I would see a day where I would actually hate the rain. I hate it now. I am shaking with hatred.

I just wanted to hear her voice, just for two flaming minutes. It's the only thing that's been holding my head on.

There's some sort of native sing-sing going on down along beside Mr Komazaki's slipways. The duk-duks are there, magic men that dress up in palm leaves so that they look like giant Christmas trees; there's about ten of them blessing canoes or some crocodile spirit bullshit, calling everyone to stop work and join in a few tunes. I hate the natives too. When's my next three-month smoko due? The earth groans again. I feel the slide beneath my feet, only a small one, and I hate it too. I look behind me at Mount Matupi. It's smoking quietly. Smoking in the rain. I tell it: go on then, blow up.

It doesn't.

The rocks have something else in mind, for me. On my way back to the rig in the morning, Johno meets me at the base of the track at Kabakada, his emu frown informing me: 'Mate, I've pulled up the drill.'

'Why?' I ask him, knowing it must be bad news. There's been an accident, the derrick's come down with a quake, or …

He takes a hunk of core from the mud-soaked sack at his feet and puts it in my hands. 'Tell me that's not granite.'

It's granite. No. It can't be. That's not possible. But it is. The earth says it is. The size and colours of the grains. Pink and black and white. Pretty bloody granite. Telling me that the whole of the past year has highly likely been a complete waste of time. There is no granite in any of the data I've been given. None. We have been drilling in the wrong place.

'Come on, mate,' Johno says. 'Come back into town with me.' We get back into the jeep. 'I'll need you to stop me from going a bit chaotic and flattening the mongrels.'

Taylor and Roycox. Yes, that's what they are, and I'm not sure I'll be capable of providing much in the way of equilibrium.

But when Taylor meets us alone on the verandah, he wrong-foots the pair of us, meeting the news with a long, slow drag on his cigar. 'What, there weren't *any* discrepancies in the data to alert you earlier than this, Brock?' He doesn't seem angry but he's irritated, as if we've interrupted him at a crucial point in a game of chess, he seems ... inconvenienced.

I'm suddenly very uncertain of myself as I say: 'I did tell you, Mr Taylor, several times, of my concerns. The dacite, I – I asked, several times, to check the previous Anglo-Eastern data for an error in our situation.'

'Well, you didn't speak up loud enough, did you, boy,' he dismisses me, and says to Johno: 'Move the rig, Johnstone. One and a half miles, west southwest.' As if this is a simple thing to do, something to be knocked off this afternoon.

Johno replies, as uncertain here as me: 'Can't be done for a few weeks yet, the wet having gone on, sir. It's–'

'Can't be done?' Taylor looks angry now. 'Can't be done? Tell that to our boys in Bardia.' The AIF, in North Africa, he's referring to, fighting the Italians in Libya. Where Mr Cooper probably is right now. I have a brief but forceful vision of the Empire's oil reserves being captured in the East, Near and Far, causing the Allies to lose the war because Brock and Johnstone didn't move the rig.

I catch Johno's eye: *All right, we'll flaming move it*. Somehow. But I have to ask Taylor, again, before he slams the door in our faces: 'Can I check the data for this new drill site then, please?' And possibly ask for more specific coordinates than a mile and a half west southwest?

'Not likely,' Taylor snorts down at me, smoke spitting out of his mouth. 'You clearly can't be trusted to interpret the data.' Then he pauses, before erupting fully: 'You are not the one who answers to the board of directors of Southern Star, to our investors, and ultimately the people of Australia who would, in the event of being cut off from British petroleum, appreciate a supply of their own oil at the very least for the manufacture of our munitions, for our troops, who are presently engaged in protecting our liberty, including your freedom to inflict us all with your incompetence. And don't think I've forgotten your impudence when last you graced us with your presence. You, Brock, will do as you are damned well told, or I will terminate your employ and personally see to it that you never work as a geologist again.'

Righto. There's the best whack of clarity I've had for a while. We'll move the rig to the moon if that's what's necessary. I look across at Johno again. But he's looking away now, that way the natives do when they get yelled at. Blank. You might think it means *Yes, boss* but it says *Stuff you.* When there's nothing else you can do. The door slams shut and Johno turns to me: 'Well, I don't know about you, Brockie, but I'm off to get slaughtered before we do anything.'

So are seven hundred soldiers of the 2/22nd Battalion. We watch them piling onto the docks from the front bar. The lower ranks head for the Pacific rum palace, and the mid-ranking officers head across the lawn up to us. They turn the dance floor into a two-up game tonight, with Sid at the centre of it, ensuring that at least one deed of our fathers will be repeated. And probably exceeded.

'Frigging hell,' Johno says to me before we're too far gone, 'this all they're giving us to fight off the Japs with?'

'It looks that way,' I say. 'But at least they brought their own band.' A Salvo band. They're striking up 'Gundagai' on the tennis lawn to distract the ladies.

'And six nurses,' says Ernie Turner, enthusiastic for them.

And proof if ever there was that the Japs aren't coming. That they'll never breach Singapore. This is just a token force, a lookout, here on the off-chance. It has to be. There's not enough of them to defend this island, never mind Australia. Never mind New Guinea.

So we can keep drinking. Tonight, there's only one thing going on around here: proving that Victorians can drink more than New South Welshmen and Queenslanders combined. Fact.

Sometime later, I wake up on the floor of our room, with no recollection of how I got here or why I have twenty-three pounds in my pocket that wasn't there before. And it's five to twelve. I've missed the phone line.

*

Six weeks of sobriety and moving an oil rig a mile and a half through thick banyan forest sorts me out. Or I've just gone past it, so that when I come into town in May and Mrs Chittaway shakes her head before I even ask about the mail, I don't lose my head at all. I accept it, sort of. The way you have to accept that your chest has been ripped open, your heart thrown on the road and run over by a lorry. Six months without a letter. There's no mistaking it now. She's called it off. We were always on shaky ground from the start, weren't we. Now it's finished. And I'm not going to book a call to have that confirmed for me by her mother. I don't need a kick to the head as well.

So I don't go to the bar at all this time. I go hiking up Matupi with Ernie instead. We spend the day talking about the doctoral thesis he's planning, on the possibility of measuring the sonic energy released by volcanoes. Listening to rocks, actually. We're scrambling up the pumice scree as we near the rim when he tells me: 'So I reckon there is a connection between the quakes and the vents. There's been a substantial increase in emissions over the past few weeks as well as these low tremors – the ones you can hardly feel. There's something going on down there – if only you could measure it. My money's on there being another significant eruption at any moment.'

I laugh: 'As in right now?'

'Oh yeah.' Ernie couldn't think of anything better. He's happy to have someone to share this with, too. The chief vulcanologist thinks he really might be insane and, not that surprisingly, so do the nurses of the 2/22nd. 'Next time, I'll bring you up at night. The lava lake really is something to see in the dark.'

I reckon I will want to do that, I think, as we find the lava lake in the light. Boiling liquid cement is what it looks like. The earth is alive and has sulphuric breath. One slip on the edge of this rim and I could fall into it, becoming the rock itself. Dacitic Brock. I say to Ernie: 'Oh yeah.'

And I reckon Ernie might be a bit of a genius, too. It's only a few weeks later that me and Johno are scrambling up to the top of the rig to watch Matupi belch up the first massive plume of ash. 'Ahhhh,' Johno is in his own awe, 'she's going to blow again, Brockie. Twice in a lifetime I'll have seen it then. I'm a lucky man.'

It doesn't take us two seconds to decide that we'll pull up the drill and go into town, and stuff whatever Taylor or Roycox have to say about it. They can sack us. It will be worth it to see the lava flow. To-An shakes his head at us when we get to Kabakada. 'You crazy fellas, crazy,' his favourite new whitefella word. And it's just as well we don't need his guidance to get in or out these days: none of the To boys will move from the village while Matupi is going off, especially not To-An: he's just become a father, grinning with that chipped tooth of his as he calls after us again: 'Crazy.'

But the lava isn't flowing when we get there, not yet. Matupi is only throwing out more and more ash as we drive in, covering everything in grey powder several inches thick. The air is yellow, stinking, and the town is deserted.

As Johno pulls the jeep up outside the club, I feel one of those low tremors and I look at the volcano. Ernie will be up there, on the rim. He's getting no danger money for it either. He's just a public servant, getting paid slightly more than nothing, while so far Johno and I have been paid a fortune, for nothing, nothing but blindly drilling through another mile of lithified ash and pumice and, lately, more flaming dacite.

I tell Johno: 'I'm going over to the office.' I'm going to demand to see the Anglo-Eastern data or I'll terminate my own contract. Taylor can't stop me from being a geologist. If I'm sacked, I'm going to go back to study. Professor Richardson will have me back, he knows I'm not incompetent. He'll be disgusted at the way this exploration has been handled.

Johno shrugs: 'All right, here we go.'

But when we get round to Court Street, there's no one there. The place is shuttered up, and the head houseboy tells us at the door: 'Bosses go to Sydney. All the bosses go now,' he says, 'back to Aussie or to Lae. Administrator boss takem Rabaul to Lae.'

'The Administration is moving to Lae?' Johno asks him, in three languages, to make sure that's correct. It is: the Administration has moved seven hundred miles away, on mainland New Guinea. The town really is empty – it's being evacuated. No one sent word to us.

The earth shakes with a more determined tremor, and Johno explodes: 'Fucking mongrels.'

Yeah, that is exactly what they are.

I tell the houseboy: 'We have to come inside.' I have to see for myself what I'm already half-expecting to see. I push past his half-hearted protest to find they've cleared out everything. All the cupboards and cabinets are empty. No note. No files. No maps. No data at all. Nothing. I could tear this place apart. Looking for – what?

'What do we bloody well do now?' Johno asks the ceiling fan.

'I don't know,' I say. 'I suppose we just keep drilling and wait for word. What else can we do?'

'Hm,' Johno agrees, as confident as I am that there is something not right here. Surely the powers of greed wouldn't shy so easily from a volcano that might or might not erupt two miles away? Not without leaving instructions for us. It doesn't add up.

I look out the window and see Mr Komazaki's fake Chrysler cruise past. On his way home, to his house overlooking the golf course. He doesn't look to be in a hurry, and I wonder what he knows.

Johno is wondering the same thing, but he's more certain. 'Japs,' he nods at the back end of the Toyota. 'That's what's coming. Not a volcano. Japs.'

'No.' I refuse to believe it. 'If they were going to do it, they'd have made a move before now – when they still had a few cans in the shed.' Cans of oil. They must hardly have enough to take a squeak from a door these days, and America is threatening to take even that amount away if they don't get out of China. Japan is as trapped as we are. I don't see how they could take on America. Mr Komazaki for one probably wouldn't be keen to go to war with anyone: he will lose his lucrative Burns Philp contract, and his golf handicap; it has to be far too much of a stretch. I say: 'They would have to be mad.'

And Johno says: 'But they *are* mad, you dozy bastard, mad and ruthless, the lot of them – shoot their own grandmothers if there was a penny in it and tell you that you forced them to do it. I wouldn't trust a Jap as far as I could boot one.' That surprises me: Johno's not one for racialist sprays. He says: 'I know where we'll find the proof, too.'

He starts running up Casuarina Avenue, up to Solomon Street, to Chinatown, and I follow. To see it's closed. Even their school is closed.

'You don't get better empirical data than this.' Johno is staring up the street, breathing hard and not just from running. 'They didn't stop trading or sending their kids to school last time the volcano blew – not even when Ah Soon's roof caved in from the ash. Because at that time, the Japs were in Nanking, weren't they.'

I clench my fists. What have Taylor and Roycox left us to? What has the Administration left us to? Nanking? Where the Jap Army showed the rest of the world how to go about mass murder. I feel that weakness in my hand. A hand that can haul a million pointless bags of earth but can't fire a rifle. I still have no intention of shooting another man, ever, but I don't want to be unable to defend myself either. I won't have to defend myself, though, will I. If it comes to it, I will put both these hands up in surrender, stick to the plan. I'm a white man, a subject of the British Empire. I am not Chinese. They won't shoot me. But it won't come to that either. I tell Johno: 'It's not going to happen. They'll be stopped in their tracks at Singapore.'

'Mate, I hope you're right,' he says, and then takes off up the road again, round to the rear of the reserve, where we find just about every other civilian left on New Britain, kitted up, preparing for the invasion. Johno sees Sven and runs over to him, but I don't follow. I watch a company of militia marching up Namanula Road, east towards the village of Nordup, through the soot, and I am stuck for a moment: these blokes are getting paid a quid a year to be prepared to fight the Japanese Imperial Army. That is crazy. And it's not going to happen. The Japs aren't coming. Not here. Not anywhere across New Guinea. There's nothing here for them. You can't fly an aeroplane on palm oil. I consider if we should halt drilling altogether: if we don't strike crude, the Japs can't have it for themselves, can they.

I don't know what I should do.

I walk back to the club, alone, and find Mrs Chittaway gone too. She's gone home to Brisbane, not prepared to risk it here evidently, and somehow that's more significant than anything. Nothing for me here other than a newspaper on the counter telling me the German Army is planning to take on Russia. Crazy. Telling me I should get on the next ship out of here, to Lae or straight home.

Home? That rips my chest open again. What is there for me at home? No one. Not in Nyngan. Not in Coogee. I go upstairs, up to the room, and open my copy of *Geological Formations*, for my photo of Bernie. What happened to you? What happened to my girl?

BERNIE

'Miss Cooper,' Alby Werner looks up at me from his reader with blue eyes that could sell snow to Santa Claus, 'is this a transitive verb?'

'A transitive verb?' I repeat, thinking: fancy anyone bothering to know. Look at the verb he's pointing at, *to give,* and I say: 'Hmm, well, why don't you hunt through my grammar book for me and work it out yourself. There's a lolly in it for you if you find out before the end of the lesson.'

He nods eagerly, grabbing the book from the end of the table and diving into it. He's eight, reading at first form level. And deceptively sweet. Leave him idle for more than ten minutes and he'll have his little brother Eric hanging by his toes off the roof edge. I'm no teacher. My work here is only to give his mother a few hours' respite from wanting to throttle him while she works on her next appeal; and to try to keep the children's English going without an accent so that they don't suffer too much when they eventually get out of here. Bit of a task as half the inmates of similar age tend only to speak German, being mostly the children of Lutheran missionaries, while the other half speaks Italian, with two Finns and one Hungarian thrown in free. Thirty-seven of them, present count, not that any of the other children stay long: most of the mothers are released as soon as they can convince the Department they're not going to bomb parliament, even if they have to leave their husbands as security. Leaving poor Anna Werner stuck here with Alby and

Eric under a ream of paper lies and stubborn bureaucracy, trapped, as Mrs Zoc remains too, and she just as stubbornly still won't let me try –

'Mith Cooper?' Eric looks up at me now with the same resolve-dissolving eyes as his brother. 'Ith thith a good picture of a doggy?'

'It is indeed, Eric,' I say. And it is a good one, too. He's only six and such a little trier he is one hundred percent adorable, which is possibly why his brother teases him so relentlessly.

'Looks like a chicken, dum-dum head.'

'Alby,' I warn, 'If you tell lies, one day, when you least expect it, your pants will catch fire. Whoomp!'

He opens his mouth to backchat me, but the voice of authority beats him to it: 'Miss Cooper?'

I think it's Ken Morely, one of the guards on duty today, come to warn me that some unexpected brass is on the warpath and I should skedaddle from this subversive childminding in the dining room, but when I turn around, I see it's Mitchell.

'Oh?' Unexpected visitation from Hell. His hat is in his hands and he looks uncomfortable, as if his mother has pushed him into church, as she did at Easter, and me too, Hughie forbid my own mother ever discover I stepped foot in that particular enemy camp – St Andrew's Presbyterian, no incense, no lightning bolt, no shame. 'What is it?'

He swallows. Clears his throat. And finally says: 'There's been a telephone call for you.'

'Right.' I'm on my feet. 'Alby, take Eric back to your mother now and no shenanigans or I'll chop off your elbows and feed them to a bunyip.' I've already grabbed my handbag and I'm out the door, asking Mitchell: 'Was it Gordon?' Has to be. Must be. Haven't heard a word from him, or of him, since he called Mum in March and they got cut off. My last letter must have worked: telling him I'm blooping well cross about it, too. Worried. I know he's no great letter-writer, an exquisite hair comb can speak well enough for itself, hardly leaves my head, but four months now with no word at all is not on.

'No,' Mitchell says, and it's a brick to the belly. I know something awful has happened, but he is now saying as we're half-running across the camp yard: 'Your neighbour, Mrs Quinn, she wants you to phone back straightaway.'

'Mrs Quinn?' My mind whirls four hundred and fifty miles an hour. Colin's mum? But the Quinns don't even have the phone on in their flat, do they? I can't think what Mrs Quinn might be calling for. She and Mum aren't that close beyond the Catholic Daily and even then only to talk about the price of fish. My heart is racing with fear as I climb into Mitchell's ute, trying to keep calm: 'What brings you to town anyway?'

'Stock agent,' he says, accelerating, racing.

'Oh,' I say. Oh no, what's happened at home? I should be at home. Why did I ever come back here to Hay? Because Mum said I must. For the poor little mites. For Alby and Eric. *No, love, you needn't come home again,* she said at Easter. *It's such a long way.* It is. Nine hundred miles return. I didn't argue. I spent Good Friday by the river with an exercise book, romancing in the dream-warm autumn air. Under a coolabah tree. I've got the story right up to chapter six now, Eugenia's mauve sea, running out of fuel, getting cross looking for Will. I've sketched the whole thing out all the way to chapter twelve, was going to start typing it all up, and now it's July, and all this while I should have been, I knew I should have been –

Mrs Lockhart already has Mrs Quinn back on the line as I run into the house.

To hear Mrs Quinn say: 'Bernadette,' her Belfast brogue harsh on my name before she says: 'My poor love.'

'Yes?' My voice is small and I don't want to hear any more. I don't want her to tell me.

'We've had some bad news. About your dad.'

No. I don't want to hear what she says next. But I do. I hear it all.

And I drop the phone.

*

'I will not hear of you travelling alone at a time like this.' Mrs Lockhart is a cyclone through the house, hasn't drawn breath.

I haven't moved from the teal velveteen settee.

Dad. Died of wounds. Mum got a telegram. Wounds received in Crete, died in Suez. In Egypt. Where? No sense, no idea. He wrote only a few months ago, at Easter, telling us he was fine, *any finer and you wouldn't see me, I'm that skinny*. Mum read the whole thing to me over the phone. He wrote about Cairo and going sailing on the Nile that's as big as a sea, and how they use their Vegemite from the soldiers' comfort parcels for boot polish. Never had so much rotten mutton in his life, and he's missing her lamb cuddles and asking her and me to write. Mum's had a turn. Mrs Cronin found her this morning; had a funny feeling, popped in and found Mum in the hall, with the telegram in her hand. She's had a heart attack. They've taken her to Sydney Hospital.

I say: 'Don't pay any attention to me.'

Me. All my life I've been so plumped up on me, on myself, overfed on my parents' attention, their gratitude for having me, just the one. Wanting to be important. To go somewhere. Do important things. But they made me important. And how have I repaid them? By not being where I should have been when they needed me. Mum needed me. And I *knew* she did. I *knew*.

'What did you say, dear?' Mrs Lockhart asks me.

'Nothing,' I say.

I have stopped. Life has stopped. Here, on the teal velveteen.

Stopped until Mum is safe.

Please, Mum.

Please don't do this to me.

*

'It's not possible to visit Mrs Cooper, no,' a nurse tells Mrs Lockhart. 'She is far too unwell at the present time.'

Not even Mrs Lockhart can do anything about it. I hear a man laugh up the end of the corridor, near the stairwell, and it rattles through my bones like a tram. It's a doctor. I see his white doctor's coat, shaking the hand of another in a suit, who is young and tall and familiar somehow. I want to say to them: how can you do that? How can you stand there chatting while Mum is …

Mum is going to be all right. Because I'm going to devote the rest of my life to looking after her. I'll keep her veggies plump and lovely while she sits in the sun, breathing in the sea air, getting better. She's lasted three days now. There's reason to be hopeful, Mrs Lockhart is reminding me, the specialist doctor said so when we got here. Please, Hughie. If I don't move on this wooden seat. If I don't breathe. Please.

We wait and wait. Forever and no time at all.

Squeak of leather on lino and yet another doctor is walking towards me. He was with the specialist earlier. I haven't caught his name. He has a sour face and thick spectacles.

He says, without preamble or a change in that expression: 'Miss Cooper. I am afraid we have lost your mother. She is dead. There was nothing that could be done for her.'

Mrs Lockhart is talking to him. I don't know what they're saying.

I stand up.

What?

A priest I don't know is walking towards me. 'Miss Cooper?'

What?

I walk in the opposite direction.

I run. Down the corridor towards the stairs. I run out onto Macquarie Street, where I rip my stupid shoes off and then I run all the way to Oxford Street, and then to Taylor Square. People swarming everywhere and I can't stop running.

What?

I run all the way home, five miles or so, and I don't stop till I get to the cliffs at the end of Arcadia, our bluff above the bays, where I stare down past the rocks below and into the sea. The winter sea, cold and angry steel sea, crashing over Wedding Cake.

I stare at the sea until I hear my mother shriek on the wind: *Come away from there, Bernadette. Come away and get inside.*

I turn around but I don't know where to go. I can't go back into my house. How can I go into my house? Ever again. Never again.

I can't bear this.

I can't bear this at all. Mum and Dad. Their story wasn't supposed to end like this. Not like this. The greatest love story ever told. Died of wounds. Dad's supposed to take Mum on a cruise when he retires, take her all the way to San Francisco. This is wrong. Wrong. Wrong. Wrong.

I kneel down on the footpath on the corner of Arcadia and Heartbreak. I press my forehead to the cold of the cement.

'Bernadette!'

Belfast 'r' in it growled. I think it's Mr Quinn, Colin's Dad. But I can't move to see.

*

'Bernadette, would you like me to open the mail?' Mrs Lockhart is asking. I don't care. She's given me another pill. 'What's this big one here? It's addressed to you.' She tears the yellow envelope open, speaking to me like I'm a child, because I am one.

She's sitting in Dad's chair, by the wireless. I don't want her to sit there. But I don't really care. She's organised everything with Father Gerard, been through Mum's address book too. I didn't like her doing that either, finding out that Mum doesn't have any family in her book. She does have family, in Paddo, but she ran away from them, from the squalor down there, and that's no one's business but Mum's. She saved her money from Cinderellering at the White Horse in Surry Hills, scrubbing the floors on her knees, till she ran away on the train to Melbourne to meet Dad off the ship.

'Oh my dear Lord, Bernadette – look.' Letters spill out of the yellow package. Opened letters. My letters, addressed to Gordon, to Dad. They are all date stamped and initialled on the front. I don't understand, and I don't care. Mrs Lockhart is horrified. Outraged. 'Your mail, dear – they took your *mail*?' Did they? Doesn't matter any more, does it. Who is they or who is me.

I've disappeared.

Gone.

Whoomp.

*

181

'There are plenty of developers always looking for land around the bays, Miss Cooper. It would be an easy matter to sell it, and for a good price,' the solicitor says.

That makes me care.

'No. You can't sell the house,' I say, a thousand years since I last said anything. Sell my parents' house? The house my dad built? His Californian Arcadia? I stare at the solicitor, stare into him, partly because of the pill, this hypnotic pill that feels like breathing underwater, and partly because I don't understand how anyone, how this solicitor, who is obviously a nice man, photograph of his family behind him on his bookshelf, could ask me if I want to turn my parents' house into a block of flats.

Mrs Lockhart squeezes my hand and tells him: 'That won't do, won't do at all, Stuart.' She scolds him, but not too redoubtably; their families are somehow connected; landed gentry, they're all connected. Even Mitchell and Rock went to the same school, they all went to the same school. I'm not connected. I'm disconnected. Wasn't even at Mum's funeral, though half of Coogee was. Was that just last week, or the week before? I've lost time too. I only remember the flowers Aunty Ena sent, Dad's aunty in Gilgandra, sending all the white carnations. And the apricot roses Mrs Lockhart bought herself. In the middle of winter. More than a hundred of them, even though she can't afford it. House full of heirlooms, Mrs Lockhart has, but no cash and it's cook's night off every night because she can't afford one of them either. And yet she's so generous. She is all that need ever be known about the verb *to give*. Looking after me, helping me with everything that needs sorting out. So many things. Mum's hankies. Dad's library card. Mrs Lockhart bought me a pretty marquetry box to put all these precious things in, things she says I'll be glad I kept one day. She is telling the solicitor now: 'It's not necessary to deal with the property matter at this juncture. It can wait.'

'But there's the outstanding loan with the building society, and the death duties owing will poss–'

'Death duties!' she just about shouts across the table at him. 'Mr Cooper's estate should be exempt from such an obscenity.'

'There will be the military rebate, of course, but the probate–'

'No buts, Stuart – find an exemption. The man died in active service. His estate should pay nothing. You're a lawyer, see to it that it does.'

'Of course,' solicitor Stuart concedes, 'I'll do my best,' and then they go over my financial crisis, again, without bothering to include me in the discussion this time. They don't need to; I understood it the first time. With everything taken into consideration, I'll have about fifty pounds to my name. Roughly nothing, not including any death duty owing. Dad had increased the loan three years ago for improvements to the garage, purchased some whizz-bang hydraulic hoist; no wonder Mum screamed at him about the payments. And the business itself isn't even profitable now, as most people round the bays either can't afford the petrol to fill their cars or are conserving it – for the stinking war. That killed my dad. That killed my mum.

Wake up, Missy. I realise I need to get a job, a paying one. If I want to keep the house, I need a job. Or I'll have to rent it out, get in borders. There are always people looking to rent around the bays. But I can't do that. How could I have strangers in our house? Strangers and their greasy pork chops.

A dull, pounding rage comes for me, through and past this underwater pill. Anger that my father fought in Turkey and in France for that house and that garage, and all of it has amounted to a big fat nothing. So that he could die defending Greece. For nothing. The Nazis have Greece, they have Europe. They have Bardia back now too, listen to the ABC wireless news. And they have my dad. And they have my mum. If I wasn't underwater, this rage would send me screaming out to the men's camp in Hay, to the huts where the Nazis have been corralled away from the others now, where I would lock the doors and set them alight, burn them alive. All my dad wanted to do was look after his boys, and now they're all gone, all dead or in prison. Colin too, and he was only driving the truck. Colin. Oh Colin. The news of him sinks into me now too. He's missing in action. The Quinns are in the worst hell of waiting of all. Waiting for this nightmare to come true.

I'm not waiting any more.

I stand up, I burst up through the surface, and then I run. I run out of the room and down the stairs and out through the foyer and onto Elizabeth Street, into the lunchtime crowds. Across the road, across to Hyde Park, I see Apollo standing above his fountain, arm outstretched like a giant traffic policeman: *Stop!*

'Miss Cooper!' It's the voice of authority, the solicitor, I think; but I don't stop.

I run along the sardine-packed footpath, along the windows of DJ's, past the dismal displays of suits and handbags all cheap and nasty these days because the best of everything – the best wool, the best leather, the best men – all gone to the army. All gone to be chewed up and spat out by the Nazis.

'Miss Cooper!'

I keep running, turning right, following the windows round into Market Street.

'Miss Cooper!'

The DJ's doorman is holding the door wide for lunch crush and I rush in with the flow. Take the escalator up to the first floor, ladies cheap and nasty hats and shoes, and I wonder if I should inquire after a job here: I used to work for Chalmers, you know, practically wrote the catalogue. Somehow I have the sense to know that I should not make this inquiry right now. No sense, however, of understanding how it is I find myself inside the DJ's auditorium next. But I'm just as suddenly glad I am: it's quiet in here. Cool and quiet, the room is completely empty, apart from an exhibition of paintings. The event poster clipped to an easel on the stage says *ABORIGINAL ART AND ITS APPLICATION*. That's nice, I think, these sort of cultural activities still carrying on at DJ's despite everything, no one turning up apart from getting their picture taken at the opening. There are small safe places in the world where nothing ever changes after all.

But then I see the paintings round the room: they are landscapes. Watercolours. There are no native dots and boomerangs that you would expect to see down at La Perouse on a Sunday afternoon. I step over to the nearest of them on my left. No, it can't be. A picture of great big vanilla-trunked gums, river gums, two of them entwined, canopies arcing over mauve hills. And red earth.

Oh Rock. I am hallucinating. I must be. My heart is thumping like a bird determined to smash a window. I peer at the card by the painting: *Albert Namatjira, Central Australian Desert.* How could this Albert know my heart, my Rock? I have never been to the Central Australian Desert, but this my heart. Oh my Rock.

I reach into my pocket for my jasper B, but it's not there. I've left it under my pillow, and I want to run home to it, I need my Rock. He's not with the army. He's in New Britain. He's safe. The Nazis can't get him. I run back to the escalators: I need to tell him about these incredible trees. I need to send him a telegram. I can't trust a letter would get through. The Department steals your mail. They stole my mail. They stole my letters to Dad and to Rock. Yes, they did: Colonel Aitkins had me under surveillance, Mrs Lockhart found out from some connection high up in the Postmaster-General's Office, but I'm not a person of interest any more. Someone must've got the guilts and anonymously sent them back. But they can't undo stealing my mail and Rock getting none of my letters. No wonder he didn't write back to me. The war has stolen my Rock from me, too. I'm not a person of interest any more.

I've lost everything.

I've lost absolutely everything.

I am weeping and weeping inside, haemorrhaging oceans of tears, but I can't seem to shed a single one.

And I know before I'm intercepted by a policeman on the ground floor: I've also lost my mind.

GORDON

'Ha!' says Johno, opening the paper Rico's just brought back from town. 'He's been rolled.'

'Who?'

'Menzies. He's been forced to resign. Good. Give someone with an interest in Australia a go.'

It would be good if the next bloke spends less time in London and more time concerned about the British Army's decision not to reinforce the garrison at Singapore. They're too stretched, told us to do it ourselves. That could be difficult as the main force of our troops are still at their disposal in the Mediterranean. Hard to be in two places at once. Alarming as the situation is becoming, though, I can't join the conversation for a minute: I'm busy thinking about the way Bernie says *pig*, the way she says her p's with a little pop of her lips: Pig Iron. Pig Face. What would she call him now? Roast Pig. I've got to stop doing this to myself. It's over. I'll get over it one day. So will Menzies.

Pointless as kicking a dead dog up a hill backwards, isn't it, Dad; thanks for sticking by me too. I could get bitter about it, if I didn't have better things to do. Like not being shitty I never bought that Ricky Triumph off Mr Cooper before I left. I loved that bike. Too bloody bad.

'Get another two rods in this arvo, Dozy?' says Johno.

'Yeah,' and consider that I only have sixteen months left of this shitty contract. Can't get that to go fast enough. I was two seconds off packing it in altogether here, just about to write to Professor Richardson, asking him if there was any chance of a position at the uni next year, or any survey work coming up, when we got a telegram from Taylor: *Keep on down. Still looking for suitable new office in lae. Contact syd office with developments if nec.* That was a month ago, and not a lot has changed, except that Rabaul is even more uninhabitable now. The Malaguna tram has stopped running. The ash from Matupi is so thick on the ground, the air almost toxic to breathe. But still he hasn't blown. He just keeps spewing up rubbish as if he's sick of everything that's going on.

We keep spewing up rubbish too, more and more dacite. I think we had a trace of basalt last week, though, black pocks in the grey. Or was that my imagination too? I have no specific data to check against for this hole at all, apart from the general indication that we should hit basalt sometime this century. And the burning knowledge that as the threat from Japan increases, so does our need for oil reserves south of Malaya. For the defence of Singapore. I still can't believe the Japs would ever be that mad. If they breach Singapore, America will smash Tokio from their bases in Hawaii and the Philippines ten minutes later. It will be a suicide move. The Japs will only have one shot, with whatever high octane they've got stockpiled. Whatever happens, it will be quick.

'Oi, Brockie, chuck us that spanner then, will you?' Johno asks me. He's fixing one of the hosepipes on the engine before we can do anything else, as we have no boilermaker now. We've gone through two of them in the last six months. No one wants that contract. Can't imagine why not. There are two wagtails chatting behind him on the bottom branches of a big balsa tree. There are wagtails all through the balsa trees here. You don't usually see them in groups like that. It's the volcano, I've worked out. The birds are waiting, like we are. Waiting for Matupi to blow. They're happy enough, though, in amongst the balsa branches. That's the thing about birds. They only have one mood. Happy. Birds are working all the time and happy about it. Otherwise, they are asleep, or dead. Sometimes I wish I was a bird.

*

If I was a bird, I wouldn't be bothered when we pull up granite again a month later. I wouldn't be bothered by the idea that to drill into granite instead of basalt like this once can be written off as an unfortunate and expensive error, but to do it twice looks deliberate. It means that the original maps and data I was supplied with were either compiled by an idiot, or by someone who did not want us to strike the oil. You just can't get that sort of geological data accidentally wrong. Twice.

'But why?' I ask Johno, not expecting an answer. Why would this consortium of old-school ties and service-station owners have us undertake this pointless drilling? Because there'll be a point to it somewhere, won't there.

'Come on,' Johno says, 'into town.'

I don't know what it is I think we're going to find when we get there, apart from alcohol, but I'm in a hurry to get going. I would like to find Taylor and Roycox and hurt them before we flatten them, actually. They are crooks of some sort; I just know it. They've set up one of those fly-by-night companies and taken off with all the investors' money. I just know it.

Johno is thinking more broadly this time. He says, taking charge, and more serious than I've ever seen him: 'Rico, you too. We stick together from now on, right?'

'Yes,' Rico says, and I can hear the *shit* in it, whatever that might be in Maltese.

We pack up the camp and carry everything we can manage down out through the jungle. We walk along the North Road towards Matupi. His plume is black and orange-bellied with fire.

If any of us have been wondering if Southern Star might not have left us out here for dead, we wonder a little bit louder when we get into town. The news at the bar is that America has put Japan under a complete oil embargo now, and Britain has finally stopped selling to them too. This means one of two things: either the Japs will accept that their entire economy will grind to a halt, or they will declare war.

'Looks like we're going to make them shoot their grandmothers,' Johno says through his teeth. Then he looks across the harbour at Komazaki's wharf. 'We should get you two onto a ship home.'

Yes, that would be a sensible idea. Except that now it's come to this, I'm not leaving Johno here. I've got nothing to go home for anyway. I realise, with some shock: Johno, and my drinking companions at the club, that's all I've got. I say: 'I'm staying.'

He says: 'I don't think that's a good idea, mate.' Looking at my hand.

I tell him: 'I'll practise left-handed. I'm staying.' And I'll aim at the sky until I put my hands up in surrender.

It's not going to come to that, I'm saying to myself even now. The AIF has reinforcements in place in Singapore. I don't think too long about the other news: questions about the capacity of the anti-aircraft guns there, the use of Tiger Moth training planes and troops with no combat experience. Singapore will not be breached. I hold this line like a rope tied to a cloud.

We put Rico on a ship, back to his wife and daughters in Melbourne. Mr Komazaki has likewise left for home, in the other direction. And now we wait. Wait for the Japs to come while we wait for Matupi to blow.

If I was a bird, I wouldn't worry. I'd sit up in the hills with the To boys chewing betel nut and taking each-way bets while we wait among the balsa trees. I wouldn't sit in the sulphur stink of Rabaul drinking rum with Johno and Sven and fourteen hundred other rifles, listening to the wireless, wondering what's going to happen next. There's been another change of prime minister at home, the hung parliament swung from Fadden, whoever he is, to Curtin, the Labor leader. Is that even constitutional, to change horses mid-parliament? I wouldn't know that either. But we all hang on his word over the wireless, listening to him deliver it straight.

Men and women of Australia, I'm not going to bullshit you. We're waiting for the Japs to come down into Singapore, so we'd better be flaming well ready for them. And in this event, should it be necessary, we will, with the assistance of our great friend and ally the United States of America, and with great regret for the violence to come, smash the bastards off the pitch.

Not exactly those words, but that's the sentiment. And he gets a cheer from this crowd, even devoted UAP supporters like Sid. I voted Labor, because you do on the Paddock seat of Darling, and it does seem a good thing to have a bushie in the top job for once, but I can't cheer for anything. I can only shake my head at Sid and those fired up by him, looking forward to the match. Christ.

Still, I go out to the range; I'm not going to bullshit myself either. I need to establish precisely how I won't be taking a wicket myself. As expected, my right hand remains a one-shot wonder, and I couldn't shoot straight with my left if you gave me a year to practise.

It's only a fairly desperate need of a distraction that makes me do what I do next. I go for a walk along the harbour foreshore, through the puddles of ash mud from the first of the rains last night, round to the Department of Lands office on Mango Avenue. To look for maps. Some decent topographical maps of the island to look at, if there are any. I just want to … I don't know, see where we are, I suppose, as if a map is going to say something different. I love a good map, don't I. It's my birthday tomorrow, too, fourth of November. Happy twenty-third birthday to me.

I just catch Ted Westby, the senior surveyor, as he's packing up his desk, off to the mainland, and I ask him if I can have a look at his map drawer for the Northwest Gazelle.

'No,' he says, veteran public servant chewing down on his pipe, annoyed at being asked for anything, even in these circumstances. 'They've all been packed up.'

I'm about to say, *Well, thanks for that,* when he points to a box in the corner behind his desk and says: 'That's a load of old Gerry paraphernalia – ancient stuff, from their admin days, a few maps in there. You can toss the lot in the incinerator when you've finished, if you wouldn't mind.'

'Yeah, all right,' I say. This'll be interesting anyway. But when I unroll the first map I know I won't be throwing any of this out. It's a map of East New Britain, including the whole of the Gazelle, with a couple of pages of notes falling out. Including a table showing drill depths and minerals found. It's all in German, but I think I know what *Geologische Daten* in the title refers to. The words *Dacite pyroklastische* feature a lot, and it's indicated across almost the entirety of the Northwest Gazelle. There is plenty of basalt too, as well as *Granit* and *Kalkstein,* which I'm fairly certain is granite and limestone. Beneath the table there's a couple of paragraphs with the title *Gelt* – gold. But I can't find any references to petroleum across any of it. Or oil. What is German for oil? Surely it's the same or close? But then I think they probably weren't looking specifically for oil at the time – this data is almost thirty years old, 1912, when aeroplanes were still a bit of an experiment. They would have been looking for gold, wouldn't they?

I turn the table over and I can't believe the answer I find.

The words, in pencil: *No evidence of oil across peninsula.*

In Roycox's handwriting.

Proof. Christ. I say it out loud: 'The thieving bastards.'

'Who's that?' Ted asks me.

And I spill my guts all over the shop, while Ted looks at me with a complete lack of interest, before saying: 'That's not proof of any value, Brock. Technically, it's not thieving if you're protecting the interests of British trade.'

'What? What do you mean?'

'Roycox, he works for Anglo-Eastern. Has done since Adam was a boy. Spent most of his career in Iran.'

This is said so offhand it takes me several moments to understand what I have been told. Anglo-Eastern Petroleum has deliberately sabotaged Australia's search for its own oil reserves, and this would probably be common knowledge to me if I drank at the Rabaul Club. I think I might be sick. Being fleeced by crooks is one thing, but being fleeced by Empire? To keep us economically dependent on them. When they won't release our troops for defence of the Pacific. When they tell us to defend Singapore – their Singapore, their Malaya, their oil – with a bunch of twenty-one year olds who are still working out how to reload efficiently.

'Mongrels. You fucking mongrels.'

We really have been left for dead, haven't we.

FOUR

DECEMBER 1941 – APRIL 1942

BERNIE

'*M*en and women of Australia,' Mr Curtin calls to me from the wireless in the kitchen, '*war demands bravery in sorrow at home as well as bravery in the face of the enemy in battle.*'

How true is that? Truer today, somehow, as I pull my dressing-gown around me. '*Ladies and gentlemen, that was a recording of our Prime Minister …*' the announcer goes on with the news, but I'm still with Mr Curtin. I like the way he addresses us: men and women. I'm a woman, and there's something in his voice that brings me something of Dad: *Come on, Bernie love, up you get.* Getting pummelled in the surf: *Don't tell your mother I nearly drowned you.*

'Good morning, Bernadette dear, how are we this morning?' Mrs Wassell asks me as I step into her sunroom for breakfast, and today I reply: 'I'm well, thank you, very well, I think.'

I look at the pill on the little dish by the glass and water jug, waiting for me, and I know I won't take it today. I don't know how brave my sorrow is, but something has changed in me. Something is different today.

'Well, isn't that wonderful to hear,' Mrs Wassell smiles, like an angel, because she is one: the CWA angel who's been minding this child for over three months now. It's time for me to leave her care. Make room for another one, like me, and like Cathy Knowles who has the other spare room here at the moment. She's twenty-four: four kiddies under six and her husband's just lost the farm to the drought. She's lost her mind, too, but only temporarily if the CWA have anything to do with it. I don't remember much about coming here, to this cool-quiet cottage in Leura, in the mountains, but I can still hear Mrs Lockhart shouting the paper off the walls at some doctor over me: *You send that child to Callan Park and I'll see to it that you are struck off.* So I didn't go to Callan Park, the asylum for really mental people, I came here; and fairly much slept solidly underwater for the first seven weeks, as Cathy is doing right now. As women in need are doing right now in the CWA rest homes all over the country, from the big seaside holiday house in Dee Why, to little open hearths like this one. Next time you buy a jar of fundraising jam, know why.

'One egg or two, dear?' Mrs Wassell asks.

I say: 'I think I might have three.'

'Good for you!' Mrs Wassell smiles brighter still: light of the world. And I'll wash up.

I'll have a look at the newspaper first, something I haven't done for a couple weeks, not quite ready then. It was full of the HMAS *Sydney* having disappeared off the wireless, all presumed lost, somewhere off the west coast, with the Japanese ambassador saying: *May I extend to you my sincere sympathy for the loss.* Giving me that feeling of wanting to run for the hills again. Till I saw the smudgy photographs of the lost sailors, too sad, and then the story of one that survived: he was put off the ship with some illness or other just before the final voyage, and he said he was going out to buy a lottery ticket at the miracle of it. I hated him when I read that then. I hated him for coming home. I had to have my lunch pill early.

But not today.

Today, I stop at the date at the top of the page: *Saturday, December 6, 1941.*

Breathtaking: one year ago tomorrow, I should have been married. We should have married on the seventh.

That pummels into my good morning with a knee-grazing thump. And with the daily dread: I have to write to Gordon. I have tell him everything that's happened. He'll understand, of course. But I can't quite imagine writing it down yet, finding all the words

I'll need. To hurt him too. He'll be so sad at the news, and angry at the cause, all the causes, of my silence. Each time Mrs Lockhart telephones, she asks me if I don't want her to write to him for me. But I say no: it's my job to tell him. Anyway, as familiar as Mrs Lockhart might be with *our* Gordon, I don't know how well she knows him. I couldn't imagine getting a letter like that from ... from anyone at all.

'Bit of bacon, dear?' Mrs Wassell calls from the kitchen.

'No thanks.'

I look up out the window, at the glorious view of the mountains from this sunroom. The reds and the mauves of the rock faces above the forest, above the valley. It's not Gordon's favourite valley, the one at Blackheath, but these are the same mountains, where we were to honeymoon, the same rocks whose reds and mauves are made of various things ending in *ite*. And they're not mountains either, are they; he told me that once, seems like a million years ago, and I can't remember what he said they are instead. I miss him terribly, terrible as everything else, shocked tearless. Wordless.

When you're back in the world, the words will come, Mrs Lockhart has said, and with them possibly the tears too. But it's time for me to test that, test myself. To move back into the world. Not home to Coogee; I'm not ready for that: I would curl up in Mum's blanket box, burrow under the magnolia folds of my wedding dress, never make my way out again. But can I return to Hay? Mrs Zoc is still there, a danger to the State, and Piccolo too, Mrs Lockhart having carted him cross country when she went home at the end of August, home to get busy for the Wagga Wagga Show, major source of jam funds for the year. Mrs Lockhart, I owe her so much: she even got a good price for Dad's hydraulic hoist to keep the wolves away from Arcadia. It's in Coonabarabran now, at a tractor workshop. But still, I feel such a weight of guilt at having been with her, in Hay when I should have been at home with Mum. What did I think I was doing? Indulging myself with this idea of being a writer, of being ... I don't know. Something what, special? Outside those who love me best, I don't exist. Do I? Would Mum be here today to tell me if I hadn't been traips–

'Here we are, three eggs on toast.' Mrs Wassell places the plate under my nose, and says: 'Oo, here, almost forgot, postie came early this morning,' handing me an envelope from her apron pocket.

A small white envelope, with a little daisy drawn on the top left corner.

Dear Miss Cooper, hear the lisp in the wobbly but determined hand. *I have been thinking of you a lot. I thought you might like this picture I drew.*

Over the page: it's a picture of a bird, a corella with its comb standing up on end, sailing above the roofs of the camp. It's very good, for a six year old. Or is he seven now?

I hope you like it. I hope I will see you again one day.
Yours faithfully
Eric Werner

I think I will see you again one day, Eric sweetheart. One day quite soon. And I see something different again. Hope: a small hand pulling me up to my feet, pulling me back to life. *I'm proud of you, very proud of you, Bernadette.* Thanks, Mum. Bravery, in battle or sorrow or otherwise: it's about being alive, isn't it. Just a fact of life. Not a choice.

GORDON

If I wasn't standing in a bar under a volcano on an island in the Bismarck Sea, an island deserted except for a tiny armed force of fourteen hundred, half of whom aren't paid-up soldiers, plus me, one cracked vulcanologist and an assortment of other unarmed public servants, including six nurses, I could almost be impressed.

The Japs. Bombing the US bases in Hawaii and the Philippines, bombing Malaya and Guam, Thailand and Shanghai. They are air-raiding the whole of the Pacific at once. On the smell of an oily rag. Literally. Ten ships, at least, and an airfield at Pearl Harbor on Sunday; two British ships off Malaya yesterday. If they succeed, this has got to go down as some kind of record of will over ability.

'Men and women of Australia, we are at war with Japan. This is the gravest hour of our history.'

'You're not joking,' says Johno.

But I still can't believe it. A shower of pumice hits the tin roof of the club and I look out across Simpson Harbour. Only a couple of fishing canoes out there under the orange sky. There's nothing for the Japs in New Britain that they can't get more easily elsewhere, and there's flaming well nothing for them here in Rabaul right now. They can't possibly succeed at their war, either. This will be all over in a week or two. They can't take the Pacific. They can't take it and hold it. This is well beyond crazy: suicidal. They will be held off at Singapore and exhausted in a week.

A plane comes in to land on the water now, sliding up to the jetty, and Johno says: 'Put your name in.'

The draw for the last seat on the last evacuation flight. The very last of the women and children of the plantation families are already waiting on the jetty with their luggage. But my attention's gone back to the Prime Minister's speech.

'We Australians have imperishable traditions. We shall maintain them. We shall vindicate them. We shall hold this country and keep it as a citadel for the British-speaking race and as a place where civilisation will persist.'

Curtin sounds so certain that Australia itself is under threat, that civilisation itself is under threat. That can't be true. The biggest threat Japan has ever posed to us is economic. They want their share of the world financial pie. You can't get more civilised than that.

'Dozy,' Johno stands in front of me, the cartridge belt across his tunic making it an order, 'you put your fucking name in.'

I say: 'No. I've made my decision.' To stay.

He says: 'Please.' His emu frown insisting: please don't make me responsible for you.

I say: 'Righto.'

I put my name in, but I don't get the seat. One of the junior clerks from the District Office does, and I'm glad: he's only nineteen.

It's only as we're watching the plane banking above the harbour an hour or so later that I see the line of logic behind why the Japs would come here. Why they will have to come here: because this war is going to be won or lost by air power. In order to get to the high octane they need for it – oil that's in Malaya, the Dutch East Indies, Burma, Borneo – they will need to hold the whole of the Western Pacific, and to achieve that they will have to take out every island, and hold each one, including this one. Including Australia.

But take a whole continent? That's impossible. And now they've brought the Americans into it. More than impossible.

As impossible things go, I duck out to the post office to see if there's anything for me in what might be the last bag of mail we'll get for a while. What do I want? Some kind of last words? There's nothing for me in the bag, though. There was never going to be. But when I'm heading back to the club, I detour across to the Weekender to check behind the counter there, just to be sure nothing's slipped down behind anything else. There's no one to object; even Mr Chittaway's gone home now, too. But there's nothing here for me anyway. Of course there's not.

So I go back to the bar, with every intention of achieving my very worst, but when I arrive, the wireless is off and one of the officers of the 2/22nd is bailing up Sid. 'What do you mean, no more beer?'

I don't know him, somebody Campbell, but he's obviously not one who's too concerned about imminent invasion: he's of the type who seem to think the government is paying him to stay up here and drink. The rest of the room is not unreasonably in sympathy with him, though.

Sid says: 'And how do you reckon that's my problem?' Not happy himself at the idea of running out of grog. Less happy that a lieutenant has just spoken to a major that way, in uniform.

'You're the BP shipping clerk, aren't you,' says this AIF idiot, pulling it over a militia man and rubbing it in.

Whoa. The bar splits in two behind this Campbell and Sid. There'd be a blue on with the next word if Sven didn't call out, waving from the door of the manager's office: 'I am on the telephone now, Sid, who do I speak to?'

Sid can't get past his riling at no one ever being able to call him Major Triscombe, before Sven adds: 'Oh shit. The telephone is dead.'

Oh shit. The blue is back on, and the band starts playing 'Gundagai' on the tennis lawn.

'Come on, Brockie, leave them to it.' Johno picks a bottle of Scotch off the top shelf and jumps back over the bar to me. 'Let's make this a good one.'

We go up to our room at the back of the Weekender, pass the bottle over the crystal set to hear: *'A Tokio news correspondent has claimed that numerous Japanese planes, laden with high explosives, dived straight at the warships in Pearl Harbor, suggesting that these airmen acted as human torpedoes. It is likely then that the same method was used in the attacks on Malaya ...'*

'That's what you'd call economical,' says Johno.

'Yeah, it is,' I agree, and I understand, with the full whack of clarity now, how they're planning to succeed.

Suicide.

We can hear a plane, a mosquito buzz high in the sky, very high. Doesn't sound like a Moth.

'That's a long-range engine,' says Johno.

So it's probably not one of ours, is it.

BERNIE

'Sorry about this, Mrs Lockhart. Miss Cooper,' Ken Morely says as he ushers us through the gates of the camp towards the admin office. Gates have been erected across the entrance in my absence, and internees are confined to quarters outside recreation hours. There's a new commandant at the camp, a Major Payne – Major Pain, Mrs Lockhart's dubbed him – not taking any chances now the Japs are in. Especially not taking any chances with Mrs Lockhart's plum puddings.

Ken takes the box from me and makes a show of poking about amongst the white cloth parcels, each tied with a festive red ribbon. My eyes are still adjusting to Hay light; I've just got off the train, having trouble with the idea of confining children to quarters, vision of Anna Werner facing the firing squad in her criminally Continental d'Orsay t-strap sandals, Alby begging: *Please, I'll never run Eric up the flagpole again.*

'What *are* you looking for, Kenny?' Mrs Lockhart rouses, ready to smack his bottom with her handbag. 'Concealed nutmegs?'

'I'm sorry, Mrs Lockhart,' he says again, and he's got worse to impart: 'You can't come further in today, either. Visiting's strictly Sundays now.'

She narrows her eyes at Ken, but decides to keep her powder dry for bigger game.

'Come on, Bernadette,' she drags me back to the ute. I watch her start the engine of this great black beast of a thing: her feet hardly reach the pedals and she has to sit on a cushion to see over the wheel. Despite the circumstances, I smile. I'm glad I'm here. I don't want to be anywhere else but in this redoubtable sun's care.

'Now, back through town, we'll stop at the outfitters – got to get you some trousers for Christmas. Can you ride, dear? I can't remember if you told me …'

'No, no.' Not a horse; not trousers, either.

She switches on the radio set before I can protest any further:

'Men and women of Australia. The call is to you, for your courage; your physical and mental ability; your inflexible determination that we, as a nation of free people, shall survive. My appeal to you is in the name of Australia, for Australia is the stake in this conflict. The thread of peace has snapped – only the valour of our fighting forces, backed by the very uttermost of which we are capable in factory and workshop, can knit that thread again into security. Let there be no idle hand. The road of service is ahead. Let us all tread it firmly, victoriously …'

'Brilliant man, John Curtin,' she talks over the Prime Minister, too. 'Alcoholic. Dreadful chain smoker. But we're in good hands now.' She speaks as if she knows him as well as she does Ken. Maybe she does.

'Our honeymoon is finished. It is now work and fight as we have never worked or fought before–'

She switches him off. Outside Drysdale's Men's Outfitters. 'Now, to business. The McDoughals need an extra pair as their Alex has been sent up north with the coast watch, clever one Alex, they've got him on code-breaking, you know, all those spy stories he read as a child. Anyway, it's left Alice short for the tomatoes.'

Crop, she means; not plucking one from the yard for a salad. 'But I can't ride a horse. I–'

'Not hard, my dear. If I could in my day, you can in yours. Only plodding on our dear little Odd Socks and there's pin money in it for you. You should learn in any case – it doesn't do not to know how to ride. How else are you going to get there? Stand on the roadside till the wind takes you? You can't have the utility unfortunately – Mitch might need it.'

Irrelevant as I can't drive a motor vehicle either. I say: 'Um. Ah.' The McDoughals' property is next door to Mrs Lockhart's, the next homestead along the river, and it's a mile away.

I can hear Dad laughing his head off. Mum's saying, *Shush, Bill.* Waiting for my answer. I would like to say I will walk; a mile is nothing. In this throat-searing heat. Don't whine: *but can't you drive me?* Back and forth with petrol the price of champagne.

Half an hour later, I've even got the boots on and Mr Drysdale is looking pleased with himself: 'We'll make a country girl out of this one yet, won't we, Bess.'

I try not to turn around to see what the back end looks like in these tan canvas slacks.

'Doesn't she look the part, doesn't she just.' Mrs Lockhart is pleased too, choosing a hat now, from the one and only brand in this establishment. *ALL AUSTRALIAN AKUBRA – THE THOROUGHLY GOOD ARTICLE.* 'She's a little Boomerang, don't you think, Bob?' Mrs Lockhart plonks a beige one on my head, chinkling with Mr Drysdale at her pun on the style of the crown. One that goes past this head: all the wide-brims look the same to me in here. They all look like my Rock.

I smile at myself in the mirror: the style does suit me, truly. Doesn't matter what I look like, though, does it. I am a changed customer, outside and in, and this ensemble is all for my service to the nation, knitting the threads of security together with tomato vines. Still, I do look behind me in the mirror. *Gaaaah.*

But at least it gives me ample to start off my letter to Gordon.

I delay my first riding lesson to go down to the riverbank, to the willows and my vanilla trunks to begin it.

My wonderful darling Rock
You won't believe what I'm about to do this afternoon …

I tell him everything, about Dad and Mum, the Department of Cruelty, and Albert Namatjira's love trees in DJ's. And I do cry. I cry and cry as a great swirling mob of corellas screech and swoop through the tops of the gums, not caring one dot about me, as the river quietly continues to creep down this bank with the drought, not caring about any of us. And then I tell him:

I could burn up in want of an apology I'll never get for all this wrecking and ruining, or I can live, in love, as Mum and Dad wished me to, and promise you, as well as myself, that I will never lose my way in grief again. Never lose my own courage again. I will certainly never leave a letter unwritten so long again. I can't imagine what this silence has seemed like to you, apart from deeply ironic that I'm now about to demand you to let me know immediately that all's well with you. I'm very worried, about the Japs and all that. Does this mean you're coming home? I hope so. To see you would – oh, enough of that for now. I've got to go and get on a horse.

I love you, my darling Gordon; I love you with every atom in me. I love you come what may. I love you always. Never, ever doubt it.

Your Bernie

I stand up. Ready for anything and everything now. Ready to reclaim my fight, in my tan slacks, however it comes.

'Bernadette!' Mrs Lockhart is leading the horse out of the tin shed towards me.

It's the little one, called Odd Socks, about half the size of Mitchell's big white one, who's called Pete, and no less terrifying for it. Odd Socks is the only horse here at the moment, though, little chestnut horse with three white socks, whose stable I was too frightened to muck out last February when Mrs Lockhart was a swaggie short of assistance, never mind the smell. You can't get a swaggie to do anything out here in the high heat, not for a three-course meal, and you're not getting me up on that horse now either.

Oh Hughie, help me. No: Hughie help us all if the nation's survival depends on the likes of me.

GORDON

I'm crossing Malaguna Road for the Bung, to get some fish for lunch. I'm in a hurry, but it's good to have something to do apart from sitting behind the sandbags at the club waiting for another raid and wondering if anyone at all is looking out for us. Or if we might have dropped off the map. Up under the figs here at their market, the marys in their white dresses are still selling their produce at their bamboo tables, but there aren't any men sitting around chewing betel and smoking today. There haven't been for the last three weeks. It's hard to credit how the marys keep their dresses so white in all the grey mud, but they do, white as their smiles: 'Good day, mister. You want fish?' Yeah, I point at a basket with what looks about twenty bass in it. Life goes on. You need to eat, and their men still want their tobacco.

I think I hear the buzz coming again, and look up behind me, towards South Daughter peak, to the airfield I can't see from here. That's where the raids have been targeted, a dozen or so planes at a time, tearing up the runway. Fifteen natives killed in one of the villages over the other side, and still no one's come for us. Natives don't count as casualties. There's been no word from Sydney. No word from any of the higher ranking officers as to a plan, though for the first fortnight they bullshitted that everything was under control. Toughen up, said Sid, only six diggers lost taking Rabaul from the Germans in his day. Be grateful the RAAF is on its way in our day to save our soft arses. It's not. They've sent ten Wirraways, which Johno reckons are good solid aircraft, but there's only *ten* of them. Or seven now, if this morning's rumour is correct: that three got shot down over New Ireland just after dawn, fifty miles to the northeast of us. The Japs have got an aircraft carrier out there somewhere, snuck down from the Carolines. We have one unarmed commercial freighter loading copra in the bay.

The mary is handing me the basket of fish when the sirens start up again now and the planes start coming over, either side of the North Daughter peak. They come over the rubber trees at the rear edge of the Bung. Right over our heads. There's more than a dozen of them this time. A lot more.

The first bomb I see hits the tram lines on Malaguna Road, about two hundred yards away. I drop the fish and start running back towards the club. Women are running too, running and screaming, babies on their backs, kids and chickens sprung out from under the bamboo tables and running everywhere too. I pick up a little bloke who's tripped over in front of me and I run with him as he screams. More bombs are screaming and falling behind us, further away behind Mother Mountain. They must be taking out the guns on the coast at Nordup, three miles east. Two small guns. Useless. There must be at least fifty planes coming over Rabaul now. They are flying boats, massive heavy engines, dropping TNT across the town. Everywhere. What are they doing? They don't need this many bombs to take Rabaul.

The roof of the post office flies up in the air. The noise is everywhere. I can't hear anything. The kid in my arms is grabbed away from me as I keep running south towards the club, to grab my swag from the Weekender. I want to grab the German maps from my trunk, too, the geological maps, the notes that will put Roycox and Taylor in prison. Odd the things you stick with in times of extreme panic, but I still reckon I'm going to accuse Roycox and Taylor of conspiring with Komazaki, and I will see them done for treason. By the time I get to the top of Central Avenue, though, the whole club is on fire.

I am stuck for a second, not knowing what to do. I look down the street, straight at Matupi. He's stopped his spewing and the sky is blue over that way. Twenty-first of January and hardly a cloud in the sky. No rain, either. Even nature has abandoned us. Something explodes out the back of the kitchens at the Weekender that brings me back to where I am. Look behind me again and there's even more planes coming over. There must be a hundred. Where the hell did they get all that fuel?

Someone is yelling above the air-raid siren: 'Fall back to Tunnel Hill. Rifles, fall back to Tunnel Hill. If you are not AIF, get out of the town. Rifles, get out to Tunnel Hill!' It's Sid. No less panicked than I am. Running, just as I am, back up through the town. Through the she-oaks, I watch two planes come in so low they look like they will collide. But they don't. They are strafing the Pacific Hotel, that is on fire too. That was the AIF garrison. That was the defence of Rabaul.

We're all going to die.

'Move your dozy arse.' Johno grabs me by the elbow, shoving my swag at me, and a rifle with it.

I'm running again, with him and the rest of his company, over back fences and yards. Sven is blacking his white hair with boot polish as we cross the western end of Malaguna Road, heading for Tunnel Hill. Christ, the whole town is on fire around us.

A way up the road, off the bitumen, I slip in the mud a few yards from the tunnel entrance, and as I get up I look back over my shoulder, at the flames. They've taken Rabaul. They've taken Bernie today too. All that I had left of her, and my *Geological Formations*. My papers. My dinner suit. My hat. It's all gone. The whole of the world, and every understanding I ever had of it. If there is such a thing as bad guys, they've won today. All of them.

Johno pulls me into the tunnel, just about taking my arm off. 'Mate, keep with me, will you.'

And now it starts raining again.

This tunnel we've retreated into isn't the best construction. It's an unlined archway of rammed black mud. I've often wondered when, not if, it will fall in, so I am not that surprised when several tons of ceiling comes away at the back entrance now. It crashes onto the road with considerably less force than the bombs we've just witnessed, but nevertheless it's blocking any further retreat for the time being. There's maybe a hundred of us in here, all looking up at the mud, not game to breathe. Except for one. The Kiwi gold surveyor Gerry Flynn, otherwise known as Errol, has joined us, from Nordup. He's doubled up laughing.

He says: 'Jesus. You wouldn't read about that, would you.'

BERNIE

I don't want to look at another tomato so long as I live. Is this fruit the right shade of red? Just on the turn from green, not too red. The Riverine Tomato Growers Association objects to my employ at this too, objects to the whole idea of a women's land army; fruit picking isn't work for girls, and I agree. My wrists are pieces of string, black as the dirt; my spine is a series of rusty hinges on the verge of disintegration, and my shoulder blades are driven through with nails every step I carry my buckets up to the crates in the shed. Fruit should be able to walk itself to market. Or let the luncheon tables of Sydney go without.

Moan, moan, whinge and moan! As my thumb drives right through the skin of the next one: too soft. Too red. More red now than green; after almost a month, this job is coming to an end. Sometime in the next hundred million years. One stingy pound a week I'm getting for it, too, and as many wrinkly too-reds as I can carry back to Riverbend for chutney. Mrs Zoc says the Italian boys at the camp should be let at it – they'll do it for tomatoes alone, for their spaghetti sauce – but of course that'd be too reasonable, wouldn't it. Reasonable as letting the Werner boys come and live at Riverbend so that they can at least go to school while their mother concocts her outrageous plots against the free world. No: everything must be done the hard way. Up and down two and a half acres of vines, two Coogee Ovals worth, or roughly half a million tomatoes, in this blithering, brain-broiling heat, from seven in the morning till hopefully Mrs McDoughal rings the bell any second now for three o'clock. With my old bush cockie bowyang straps cutting into my shins, to prevent the brown snakes slithering up my slacks and –

'All righty, Bernadette, that'll do.' Mrs McDoughal is behind me now, her voice as weary as she looks, and it's enough to make me want to say, *No, I'm right for another hour.* But she sighs, pointing down the rows towards the river: 'It's pretty much finished from here.' Disappointed at all the fruit not got to in time; it's only been the five of us to do it all – Mrs McDoughal; her sister-in-law, Mrs Denison; and her two daughters, Chrissy and Ruth, both giving up their school holidays for it, and me. But she smiles: 'You've done a good job, girl, a blessing to us.'

'Thanks,' I smile back. It's not small praise, and I know my carefulness with the colours has been appreciated. This crop and the beans they'll harvest next is all the McDoughals have got, apart from Mr McDoughal getting droving work, moving stock to pasture with actual pasture on it, which pays for the water licence and fertiliser here, and the loan on their irrigation pump. Nothing so romantic as seeing five thousand sheep being driven through the town up Lachlan Street, dust flying and whips cracking, until you see the lines on the face of the wife after the run's been sold to pay the bank back only half of what they owe, on all they have left: a patch of tomatoes and beans. *Who'd be a farmer?* Rock would say every time he came home from Nyngan, and now I understand why.

I also have to get back to Riverbend with that thought, suddenly lively. Have to get back to see if any mail has come for me, from him, and to fall on the wireless for the news, of what's going on up north. The McDoughals don't have a wireless in their house, and not because they can't afford it. They're just such strict Presbos – no dancing, no card-playing, no accidental saxophones.

'We'll start on the beans towards the end of March,' Mrs McDoughal says by way of farewell, and I've said, 'I'll be here,' without thinking, lugging my sack of too-reds for chutney over to Odd Socks. 'Take me home, girl.' I throw myself over the saddle, and the girl who was frightened of horses now curses our little chestnut mare for being such a plodder. 'Come on, Odds, you've been standing around in the shade doing nothing all day – move.'

Plod. Plod. Smack her on the rump. 'Come on.' Blooping plod.

By the time I get in, thumping across the back verandah, Mrs Lockhart has the three o'clock news on, at her station by the stove. 'Just started, dear, and no, no mail today.' I dump the sack of tomatoes on the kitchen table and don't care what's happening in North Africa or London; I've stopped still to hear:

'Australian Militia Forces and AIF are resisting the Japanese and holding positions across the western end of the Rabaul Peninsula. Although reports of fighting at Rabaul are meagre, it is known that Australian troops were putting up a magnificent fight against the invaders ...'

No news telling me what I want to hear: that Gordon Brock is not there. The first bombs fell on the fifth of January. It's now the twenty-sixth. He should have contacted me by now.

'He mustn't have got your letter, dear.' Mrs Lockhart has no trouble reading my mind through the eyes in the back of her head. 'And don't take anything from these wireless reports. If all communications with islands have been cut off, how could anyone know what's going on, magnificent or otherwise?'

That's true. He's probably been evacuated to Darwin or Cairns, as they told us all civilians were last week; could even be back in Nyngan now, or Sydney, oblivious to my need to know he's all right wherever he is. He must be, mustn't he? The company he works for wouldn't just leave him there, would they? I am whipping myself up, hopefully for no good reason. Unwind these bowyangs, breathe in the sweet garlicky aromas of Mrs Lockhart's chutney factory, as the news moves on to the United Australia Opposition getting into Mr Curtin for suggesting that Britain has been slack in its defence of the Far East. As if that isn't true, wasting our time, our resources and our lives in Greece – give me a rifle and send me to Singapore, I'll do the job, with some vengeance. Mr Curtin's such an American-loving Commie he might let me one day, too – he's got girls in the air force now. They'll be learning to fly next. Fancy that.

'Our parcel of duck cloth for the blackout curtains came this morning.' Mrs Lockhart talks over the stock report, stirring the pot while ever deciding what I will do next. 'That's good timing, isn't it? We can start running them up for the hospitals, Narrandera first, and ...' I'm not listening; I'm searching for Gordon across the mauve sea, until she prods me with the end of her wooden spoon: 'Oh dear, we've lost you to wondering, haven't we. Why don't you telephone the people he works for – they'd have a Sydney office, wouldn't they?'

'Yes, they do, but–'

'Tell them you're his fiancée and don't take no for an answer – you've every right to know.'

'Yes.' I am his fiancée. Of course I am. I tell the telephonist: 'I'm looking for the number of a company in Sydney, the Southern Star Oil Company. I'm sure the address is George Street something.'

'One moment please, madam.'

It seems to take forever, a forever over which Rock never wants to speak to me again, before another telephonist finally answers: 'I have a number for the Southern Cross Theatre Company, is that the company you're after?'

'No, Southern *Star*. Southern Star *Oil*.'

'One moment please.' Another small eternity, during which I decide he did receive my letter and he can't reply because he's married someone else, and then: 'I'm sorry, madam, we don't appear to have a number for that company.'

I nearly drop the phone. Don't have a number for that company? Where is Gordon?

'Bernadette? Bernadette! What's the matter, dear?' Mrs Lockhart is beside me, wiping her hands on her apron.

I think I might whisper: 'There is no number.'

She takes up the phone from me. 'Don't you worry, these mining companies chop and change their names and addresses willy-nilly,' and does what any woman with limitless connections would do: she asks to be put through to the Lodge, the Prime Minister's residence, in Canberra. 'This is Mrs Elizabeth Lockhart of the New South Wales Country Women's Association, calling for Mrs Curtin. It is a matter of the utmost import – no I certainly do not intend to wait.'

She waits a few moments before: 'Oh Elsie, I'm terribly sorry to interrupt ... Were you? I'd go back to Perth if I were you too, dear.

Oh, at Cottesloe? How lovely for you …' She puts her hand over the mouthpiece and mouths at me: 'Her daughter's getting married – over there.' Then back to Mrs Curtin: 'Well, I won't keep you, dear, and I'm terribly sorry to impose at all – I just want to know whom you suppose I might call about a missing person … Rabaul, unfortunately … Hmm. No, civilian … Try Commonwealth Investigations? I've burned my bridges with them, I'm afraid. What about a minister? Ah, Customs, of course … Good, dear, thank you, and I will … Oh, are you? All that to-ing and fro-ing, I don't know how you do it. Cheerio. God bless.'

Mrs Lockhart turns to me: 'Salt of the earth, that woman.' Then back to the phone, making her demands, not taking no for an answer. 'Minister Keane's office. Yes please. No, I do not intend to wait, this is of Prime Ministerial imp– Thank you.' And after a few more demands: 'Yes. Gordon James Brock is the name, have every passenger list from New Guinea scoured, please, by ship and air, from December 1940 – yes, that's right, the whole year, and then up until the present day.'

She turns back to me when she finally hangs up. 'We'll know soon enough. At least whether or not he's in the country.'

Clutch at my jasper B in my pocket. He's not still in Rabaul. He can't be. Wish I could fly, for real. Gordon James Brock. I might wonder how it is that Mrs Lockhart knows his middle name is James, along with how she knows the PM's wife, if I wasn't so at sea.

No. I refuse to believe this. I'm not going to lose Rock too. Not here on the teal velveteen, not at all. Simply not going to happen. It can't.

GORDON

'Sing your way to peace?' I say to Johno. 'Who is this designed to appeal to? The Salvo band?'

He's shaking his head, looking at the reverse of his copy of the leaflet. It's got a photograph of a naked woman on it. She's a bit blurred and soggy, but she looks a little like Jenny Fitzgerald out at Yarranbulla. Only at about the age of twelve. Not the type of girl you want to see naked.

Johno says: 'They don't know us, do they – should've put a photo of KB lager on it and we'd come out with our hands up.'

That might be funny on a different day, and if the words under the photo didn't say: *Do not run and hide! There is no escape! You*

216

will starve in the hills! There is no food or water on this island! This is an outright lie: apart from the volcano, the surface of this island is made almost entirely of food and water.

But the Japs can say whatever they like, can't they. Best estimate is they outnumber us at least five to one. Within about ten minutes of landing, they overran all AIF resistance from Nordup to Rabaul, resulting in the command: 'Every man for himself.' Those of us hiding in the tunnel never moved earth faster. And now the fastest runners among us have got here. To this swamp. Not hiding very well behind some liana hanging off a fig on the southern verge of the North Road. Thirty-three of us, mostly from Sid's company, plus a couple of bank clerks, half-a-dozen mining personnel and one vulcanologist. All equally being eaten alive by mozzies and leeches while we consider the fact that we've got no idea what to do now.

My rifle is already pointing well into the ground behind me per leaflet instruction as I say to Johno: 'Maybe we should just get it over with, go back into Rabaul and surrender.' My plan from the outset. Let's stick to it.

'No,' he says. 'Reinforcements will come. A ship will come for us.' He's desperate for that to be the case. We all are. How could it not be the case? He says: 'We should get up into the hills above Kabakada, terrain we know well, and stay there, near the village, till we're rescued. And if not ... then we'll talk about surrender.'

'Surrender?' Sid overhears that and comes over to us. He's recovered from his initial panic and some kind of delusion has set in. 'Surrender? We will die fighting or we will die cowards. We are going to head south through the Baining Ranges, down to Wide Bay, to regroup with the main AIF force there.'

I look at Johno, who's looking down at his boots. This is the last order Sid received by radio phone under Tunnel Hill; just before 'Every man for himself.' Just before the line disappeared. But Sid's sticking with it. We won't be, though. The Baining Ranges are mountains, big and steep and in parts impassable mountains cut through with equally impassable rivers, and the one place on this island where you might actually have difficulty finding food apart from crocodiles. We wouldn't be regrouping with anything other than harpy eagles waiting to pick over our bones before we got anywhere near Wide Bay, who knows how many trackless miles away, on the south-east edge of the Gazelle. Johno is having trouble with the idea of disobeying his commanding officer, though. So I do.

'We would be better off continuing west. It's country we know, there'll be plenty of food, and native assistance.'

'Native assistance?' Sid laughs at me as if that idea is madder than his. He thinks they're all dumb animals.

'Yes, native assistance,' I say. While they might not owe us anything, the To boys of the village aren't likely to turn us over either. At least they won't shoot us on sight. I tell him: 'We've got good relations there.'

Sid narrows his eyes at me as if he's going to put me in my place, say I'm a coward for not wanting to die. Shouldn't I be ashamed of myself when he last saw my dad firing his way up that gully at Anzac Cove? But something stops Sid saying anything at all. I feel it too. There's a strange sort of calm come over me. Maybe I'm deluded myself.

I say, 'Good luck, then.'

Johno and I start walking. The rain starts sheeting down, again. Errol Flynn calls out to us: 'See you in San Francisco, fellas.' He'll take the others through the ranges if anyone can. Only Sven and Ernie Turner follow us.

We keep to the trees of the verge, and after a while Ernie says: 'I hope the girls are all right.'

No one answers that. The nurses. Six of them. They'd have been caught when the Japs came over from Nordup. I know one of them, sort of. Tina, a girl from Yass. She's the sister of a bloke I once met when he was jackarooing up at Coolabah. I can't think about that.

I listen to the sound of our boots working the mud, through the rain, west through the mangroves, and I hope that we've made the right choice. I wonder what Dad would think, and I don't know. I didn't last see him firing up any gully. Fighting for his country. Whose country was that exactly? Not our country. I last saw Dad on Nymagee Street, when he dropped me off for the train to Sydney. Walking off. Back to the ute. Walking off from all this shit. I keep seeing that roof of the post office flying up in the air. Whoever was in there, they're not there now. Is Dad not there either? Maybe he died a long, long time ago. It's sad. If I die now as well, there'll be no one for the authorities to send the notice to.

BERNIE

'*O*h, for the love of MacDuff, I *am* the lad's next of kin,' Mrs Lockhart hisses at the Commonwealth Bank officer on the other end of the line, in Nyngan. Since it seems, after three days of berating the Minister for Customs, Gordon's name does not appear on any passenger lists, she's now trying to discover when he last used his savings account and where, and the bank officer is unmoved by the Lockhart name. '*Must* I speak with the manager? When you can simply verify my bona fides with Mrs Emma Wells – you *are* aware of your own customers, aren't you? Mrs Wells lives at Kyra via Mundaroo Road, this side of Armageddon, on the – Well, good, thank you.'

She looks at me, worried as I am now. 'He's going to look it up.'

I look at her, in a flummox of wonder. Mostly at *next of kin*. Is that just another fib of expedience, or ... I look at the photograph of Mitchell on the bureau; he's about sixteen or so, holding up a big fish. Is there a reason he and Gordon look quite similar in their Scotch twill, other than hailing from places called Hell and Armageddon?

'Thank you,' she says, back into the receiver, with a sigh. 'Thank you, no, that is all. Good day.'

I continue to stare at her, and she glances away, out at the willows, her cheeks are flushed.

'What?' I beg her. '*What* did he say?'

'The second of January,' her voice rasps around it, hand at her throat, and she swallows hard. 'It appears that he last made a withdrawal on the second of January. From the branch in Rabaul.'

'The second?' I hear my own voice is brittle and shrill with denial, pleading: 'But that means he still might have got out.' There was a story just yesterday in the *Grazier*, the manager of the Bank of New South Wales and his accountant, they made a daring dash for it during a rain squall as the Japs landed on the beaches, on the twenty-second, got out on the last copra boat, in the nick of time. Twenty days after Gordon went to the bank. He has to have escaped too. And somehow escaped the attention of the press as well as Customs for having done so. Or I can come around to reality: 'That's possibly as fantastic as your being his next of kin, isn't it.'

Her hand stays at her throat and she swallows again, looks away again into the willows, as if she's trying not to dissolve.

Breathtaking. 'You weren't fibbing?'

Small shake of her head. 'No, dear.'

'Oh.' Float for some time on that sound while the universe breathes out, here on the teal velveteen.

Then she says to the willows: 'I don't suppose it matters to say it now.' Then she says to me: 'Gordon is my first cousin once removed. He is my cousin's boy.'

I can only assume: 'Mr Brock is your cousin?' But I can't fathom it: why would that be something to be kept secret? I look at the ram on the mantelpiece: squattocratic snobbery against poor relations? No, not from this redoubtably generous woman.

'Oh. No, dear.' Mrs Lockhart smiles, that fondness in it she has for Mr Brock, but then her green eyes fill with some awful sadness. 'No, dear. My cousin Caroline is the cousin I'm referring to. On my mother's side, Caroline Forrest. Young Gordon's mother.'

Can't help the gasp at that: Rock doesn't know anything about his mother, except for the great slamming tragedy of her death that made it impossible for his father to talk about her, and here I am sitting with her cousin, Bess Lockhart. But dying in childbirth, that's not a terrible secret, either; it's an all-too-common tragedy, especially for rural women who can't get to a doctor. I whisper: 'What happened to her?'

'As you would know, dear, grief is a strange beast.' She warns me: 'You must never judge another for it, for what they do, in grief.'

I shake my head; I wouldn't dare judge another for that: don't have a glowing record of stoicism myself.

'After little Gordie was born, Caroline had trouble,' she speaks to the willows again. 'She was out at Still Waiting on her own with no help, and Ross – Mr Brock – he wasn't well himself at the time. Not long before the baby came, Ross went walkabout for a few months. You mustn't judge him, mind, he suffered so – his debts were mounting from that piece of old toast he was sold for land, on top of all he had endured already. But he steadied when the baby came, he was happy and full of renewed hope, that the rain would come and everything would work out. Then, when Gordon was only just a little more than a month old, the rain did come. Ross got caught fencing over the other side of the Bogan in flood, and he didn't get home that night, and when he got home the next morning, she was gone.'

Gone? Gone where? Gordon's mother is alive? No, that's not what the flood behind Mrs Lockhart's eyes is saying: there will be no happy ending to this story.

'She took the baby to a neighbour's, down to Emma Wells nearer town, said she had to go into the shops quickly for peppermint water for him as he had an upset tummy and she didn't want him jolting about on her back as she rode. But she didn't go into town; she went across to Gunningbar Creek, tethered Louie, her pony, on the bank, and that was that. They found her the next afternoon, a mile or so south of Overflow. You mustn't judge, no one can judge her.'

I shake my head again: *I never will.*

'She was a clever girl.' Mrs Lockhart smiles at that memory of her cousin. 'A qualified nurse, she was, just about to go overseas with it when she ran into Ross at Bathurst Hospital, it was just before Christmas 1916. He was being discharged from the army, sent home from the shellshock, you know. She was full of hope that love could cure anything. That's what she wrote to me. *Love can cure anything.* She'd last seen him at a dance in Bourke, and now he'd come home thin and troubled and she was going to cure him, restore him. He was a good man, Bernadette. But afterwards, well, women talk – he had a temper. It wouldn't have been easy for Caroline. Far from it. He was an angry man for a few years there. And you can't blame either of them. The war ruined them both.'

Mrs Lockhart looks up at the Tom Roberts lovers on the wall opposite, holding hands by the river, but she's looking through them, to some other place. 'I should have done more. I should have gone up to help; I should have brought little Mitch up to her, to show her the pleasure that comes of mothering, given time. But I didn't. Remember, we didn't have the rest homes for mothers back in those days – not at Dee Why, not at Leura or anywhere. And I was newly widowed myself, caught up in my own ...'

I reach for her hand in understanding, a lot now, about Mrs Lockhart's hard-wrought redoubability, and we sit for a long time, both staring out into the willows, into the Murrumbidgee glittering beyond them, until she takes her hand away, with a firm pat on mine. 'It happens most to the clever ones. The cleverer you are, the more you think, and the more you think, the more easily it can all overwhelm. Always been glad I'm not too clever myself. Now,' she stands up, smiling over and through all our worry, 'I've got some curtains to make, dear, behind in my schedule with all these interruptions. Why don't you get out from under my feet and go into town, go to the pictures, take your clever mind off things.'

I take the hint that Mrs Lockhart would like to be alone for a time, but I don't go into town. I don't want to see *Huckleberry Finn* again, or a film involving aeroplanes, which is just about all that's ever showing at the Majestic now, from romance to newsreel. Don't want a hamburger at the Manhattan, either. I want the Americans to come, for real.

So, I put my cossie on and go down to the river, slip into the cool and plunge right under, and in amongst the minnows I wonder if I'm clever enough to believe that these little fish might be able to carry my thoughts to him, through the sea: Come home to me, I'm your next of kin. Come home for me.

Hear me.

Somehow.

I straighten my body in the water, diving deeper, my arms outstretched as far as they can go. I can stretch further through this teal dream. For the love of all our parents I will stretch further and make our promises come true. I am strong. I am unbreakable. If I hold myself firmly to these convictions, to this courage; he will come home. The Americans will come and bring him home. Singapore will hold, the Americans will come, we won't be invaded by the Japs, and Rock will come home. The war will be finished and we will be married and I will be a geologist's wife and every breath I take for the rest of my life will whisper my gratitude.

GORDON

'Birua, birua,' To-An keeps telling me. Enemy, enemy, he's going off his head about it. But he's pointing at me.

'What? Where?' I don't know what he means.

He smacks his forehead with frustration, saying something in Kua-Nua next, which I can't understand at all. I've gone for a short walk with a shovel, and Johno is not fifty yards away, at our camp above Kabakada, but To-An needs to get the message across right now.

He slows it down for me, in pidgin: 'Him get kakaruk, him get pigs, takem all, takem marys, four marys, crazy fellas. Birua, birua, you fella takem, white man takem–'

White man. Now I understand him, and share his alarm. We, crazy white men, have gone into the village, taken the chocks and pigs and four women. But we, white men, can't be that stupid, can we? To make sure, I say: 'No, this isn't right. They must be Jap fellas, him birua, him enemy. Him takem.'

'No, no, no.' To-An smacks his forehead again: *You idiot, boss.* 'You takem. *You* fella.' If that wasn't clear enough, he looks away as he adds: 'Jap fella good fella, givem tabak. He pay more better for work.' The Japs give them more tobacco and better pay. Of course they do. 'You fella go. Go! Now! Duk-duk makem poison long, you fella.'

We've got to go, the duk-duks have put a curse on us. And To-An doesn't want to catch it. He's probably come here against the wishes of his elders too.

I nod, while the rest of me gets on with screaming: *WHAT? NO! GO WHERE?*

He says something in Kua-Nua again, but doesn't have time to explain it. He grabs my arm. *Go now,* his black eyes are drilling into me. Shaking me. 'Bird. Look bird. You follow him – him belong you.' Then he lets go of my arm and disappears back into the trees.

I don't look for any bird. I've never moved so quickly across fifty yards, and when I get back to our camp, to Johno and Ernie and Sven, I've never talked quicker. We've packed up in about two seconds and we're off: south. The only place we can go now where we will be able to keep hidden: the Baining Ranges.

Johno is upset. 'Fucking AIF fucking bastards. No fucking discipline. Not a fucking brain between them. Fuck. Fuck them.'

Sven tries to quieten him down. 'It's okay, Johno.'

'Fuck off. It's not okay.'

No, obviously, it's not. We walk on in silence, at a fairly quick pace.

After a while, Ernie says: 'Well, there are some interesting quartz formations in the Moai-agi Gorge that will be good to see.'

That makes me laugh. Like a crazy white man.

'Not flaming funny, Brock,' Johno chucks it back at me. I've never seen him angry like this before. Like he might actually flatten someone. 'You think that the Japs will continue to be nice to Little Black Sambo after we've all gone? And before we die, I'd like to remind you that they have a name. The To-Lai. They're called the To-Lai. Right?'

'Right.' I'm not entirely sure what he's on about, and I'm not going to argue. It's been a difficult a few weeks. Waiting for nothing. No one's coming for us. Just the Japs. From Johno's previous gathering of intelligence, from Kabakada, there is a small mountain of forty-four gallon drums at Rabaul now. The place is one big airfield. Whatever's happened out there beyond this island, they've got their high octane, and New Britain is some kind of base for them. I understand the attraction now. It's the geographic centre of the Southwest Pacific – if you include Sydney.

We keep up the pace. And the silence. The jungle isn't too thick here, but it won't stay that way for long. Johno keeps looking up at the sky. The day before yesterday he saw what he thought might have been a couple of Wirraways come over, but they were too far away to be sure. There was some anti-aircraft fire and a couple of explosions that could have been bombs dropped or planes shot down. He scrambled up one the tallest of the palms with the binoculars, but couldn't see. It's hard to credit what's gone on, or what hasn't. Have we been cut adrift? Not just us on New Britain, but Australia itself? Is my country being invaded by the Japanese right now? My actual country. How can I put my hands up to that? But what can we do to fight them here? We have three rifles, two cartridge belts and one spare box of bullets, between four of us. One of us can't fire two in a row, and another, Ernie, really is gun-shy; one of his schoolmates was killed in a shooting accident, hunting deer in the Snowies. And for Johno I know it's worse: for him, New Britain is his country. Or has become his country. I don't know why. I'd better ask him about it sooner rather than later, hadn't I.

We keep on southwards about two miles, crossing the old track that goes up to the first of our rig sites, up to the old Slippery Dip. It's already almost completely grown over. There's no sky here to look up at. I think I understand Johno's shitfight philosophy of chaos and equilibrium now, though. Whatever happens, this is Nature's game. We're all dumb animals, aren't we. Everything creates as much as it destroys. No bad guys. What's the difference between our blokes stealing four black marys and the Japs stealing our six white nurses? Two women. And a volcano that won't erupt when you want it to. Rain that stops to make life easy for your enemy. How can you fight that? You can't. Don't need science to tell you. Johno's wrong about Newton's Second Law being there for us when no one else is. Science is irrelevant out here. But I don't challenge him on it. I could turn to prayer any minute. I don't want to die. I think about that little wagtail I saw at Blackie's Camp challenging the kookaburra. Winning. Fearless. But we're not birds, are we. We're a bit dumber than them.

We make our camp, just before dusk, in one of the hundreds of caves at the base of the ranges, and as the others start hunting around for kindling I start cutting up my spare singlet. I wrap this strip of blue singlet around the top of my hand. I don't know if it will do anything to help absorb the impact of discharge. I don't want to kill anyone. But I will if I have to. I just don't want to die.

Sven gets the fire going, and then we all stand there looking at it. No one's keen to chat. No one game. Johno is still steaming. I look at Sven: shirtless giant, his natural state, and his face and beard are grey with boot polish. At least we look frightening. Not one of us managed to pack a razor.

A scream tears up through the back of the cave and something darts out through the smoke. It's only a cuscus possum running for its life, but I'm already tripping backwards, over a log. I land on my arse. Sven and Ernie could die laughing.

But Johno doesn't think it's funny. 'Fuck this,' he says. And walks off.

I follow him, down to the rocky bank of a creek. He stands there with his hands on his head, telling the water: 'Fuck.'

I say: 'Stop saying fuck – you're upsetting me.'

Not even that makes him look at me. So I stand right beside him. 'What?'

'Nothing worth discussing now.' His arms come down by his sides and he pushes out a breath, like he's run out of steam.

'Why not?' I ask him. 'What's changed from yesterday, this morning or tomorrow? Really – we're still stuffed.'

'This morning, I still had a life, something of it.' He closes his eyes.

'What do you mean?'

'Back at Kabakada,' he says, and it's a while before he lets this go. 'Lil, her name is. Was. Lilla.'

A girl. Whoa. That'll do it to you. I've never thought of Johno with a girl. A native girl. To-Lai girl. Somehow, that's not surprising. It explains why he never liked to stop in town for too long, always wanting to go bush. But it is … not good for him, today. Not good not knowing if she might be one of the girls taken from the village. Not good at all. I say: 'Things could still turn around and …'

That makes him look at me. 'Bullfuckingshit. Whatever happens, it's finished with her now.'

It probably is and he's flattened over it. I look at his emu face. No time like the present to ask him what I'm wondering: 'Are you To-Lai too?'

'No.' He looks down at the rocks. 'Not To-Lai.' It's a while before he lets this go too. 'My grandmother was a Thursday Islander. Her father was a Dutch pearler, and she looked white, more or less. We were brought up to say she was a Portuguese from Timor. Anything but a black. Melanesian is too close to Abo in Queensland. She taught me to sail, my gran, she taught me to read too, and I could never tell anyone, *Guess where we went for the summer holidays – spearfishing in the Torres Strait.* It's all bullshit.'

'Yeah.' And not just in Queensland: you don't want to be black anything in my country either, roped off on the missions. I look down at the ground too, remembering one particular moment of bullshit up at Brewarrina with Dad. We saw a fight outside the Royal, a black stockman being quilted into the dust. Dad was shaking his head, *You can't refuse a hardworking man a beer*, but we kept walking, looking away. I tell Johno, as if it could make a difference: 'I'm sorry.'

'So am I,' he says, angry again. 'Sorry for myself. Even here, on New Britain, where a black man's got a bit of pride, I still would never tell anyone, not until I met Lilla. Ashamed of my own grandmother, scared I'd have my qualifications taken off me if anyone ever found out. That's how I was raised: don't tell or Dad will lose his job.' His dad is a steamer captain, on the Townsville to Brisbane run. I've never seen a black man on a steamer. I've never seen a black man on a tram. Johno looks at me again now, but with some agony I do recognise: 'Then here, I'm too scared to ask Lilla's father for her because I'm not black enough. I'd have been married by now if I wasn't so gutless. I could have–'

'You're not gutless,' I say, and stop short of telling him he can't compete with me there. I didn't put up a fight for Bernie, did I. Didn't get on a plane and go home for her when I could have. Too scared to. I tell him: 'We're all idiots.'

'Yeah, yeah,' he says. 'I love you too.' And he's finished this spit. He lets his shoulder hit mine as he turns and we start walking back. 'Doesn't make it any easier to take, though, does it.'

'No.'

And we're still stuffed.

BERNIE

February. This month is the cruellest, in temperature and circumstance. The air is crispy with heat and it's only just after dawn. Sunday morning and I haven't slept except for a horrible dream, running through some maze of foreign streets with a bolt of sapphire shantung unravelling behind me, in flames. Because Singapore has fallen. The jewel in the crown of the Empire is gone. Truly. Darwin has been bombed too, and with it Sydney seaside property values: you couldn't sell Arcadia now for five bob with the wireless thrown in. And still the Americans haven't come. Because their hands are full in the Philippines, and of course there was that business of them losing half their ships and planes in Hawaii while I was underwater, wasn't there.

I don't want to get up. But I have to. These Japs won't get to me. Can't. I will stretch my hope three times from here to Jupiter and it won't break no matter what they do. At least it is Sunday and Mrs Lockhart is religious enough that the wireless is not switched on, so I can't hear that anything worse has happened. But still, Sundays I can hear the silence stretching, from all the personal ads I've put in the papers, from the Sydney *Herald*, to the *Northern Standard* in Darwin, the *Courier Mail* in Brisbane, *Townsville Daily*, *Cairns Post*, and the Rural Press across the northwest from Armidale to Broken Hill: *Bernadette Cooper searching for Gordon Brock call urgently Hay X 43.* A continent of silence.

Apart from the bombs dropping on Darwin, about which the Department of Information is saying: *What's a few bombs to us? No one died.* Just as no one's died in New Britain either. Department of Lies.

Get up: I'm not giving in to this.

Neither is Mr Curtin. He's made the US Army an offer of heavily discounted pork if they help us. How could they refuse?

Stop it, Missy.

Losing hope is an indulgence I've got no time for. Or at least I've got better things to do. There is always plenty to do, even on a Sunday in a little country town. Go to church with Mrs Lockhart and be reminded by the calm and gentle certainty of the Reverend Shepherd – truly – that I have two hands and a heart to help, and no giving is too small a gift. That way salvation lies, and the other way of eternal pain is reserved for the manufacturers of munitions, and the bank managers and pressmen who facilitate their devilry. Yea verily, those suffering with this drought suffer just the same as those who suffer bombs, only a lot more quietly and never in the news at all. Rejoice that you are not a sheep. Or a bean. Be happy for an hour or so listening to Mum and Dad bickering over my state of Presbyterianism.

Then, after lunch, while Mrs Lockhart dutifully breaks the Sabbath running up ever more blackout curtains ahead of the Jap invasion of these pitiless burnt-toast plains, I'll plod over to the camp on Odds, and I'll spend the afternoon with the Werner boys, doing something listless. Even Alby is spent in this heat, can't be bothered looking at his little brother – does one need more evidence that Hughie can be merciful? I'll read them a story, Paterson poems in an accent so broad my jaw won't move at all, or I might just lie on the floor of the dining room breathing in the charcoal air and listening to Mrs Zoc tell me that she is one hundred and fifteen percent certain, bella, that Gordon is all right. He has to be. She says: *I would know, Bernadetta, believe me, he is like a son to me, he is my good boy, I would know.*

Know that she is a madwoman and that I am too, as I go to the dressing table now, automatic reflex picking up my hair comb, the one he gave me, pressing the little spray of amethyst daisies to my lips, *Thinking of you* ... And no one in this town will say it's too sparkly a thing to wear to church, because everyone the length of the Paddock from Deniliquin to Wilcannia knows why I wear it: because they're all mad enough themselves to know that if I wear it religiously I can make him safe. I fix it into my hair now before I've even got dressed, a little spray of mauve sea, and my Good Companion looks at me, from where it sits on the floor beside the wardrobe, in its case, untouched since ...

Something nags at me, that I should write against this. But I don't know what I mean by that. I don't know what I might write. Not Eugenia's flight of fancy. That's gone too. Something else. Maybe something true.

Open up my marquetry box of precious things, my portable Arcadia, and I take out the newspaper photograph of us that sits on top of Mum and Dad's bits and pieces, and I look into his lovely face, his lovely eyes, full of promise, ready for anything, and I'm sure he must be all right, too. Out there ... somewhere ... I lift the clipping out of the box, to read our nice Aussie story that I know off by heart – *Gordon Brock of Nyngan with his fiancée Bernadette Cooper at Sydney Flying Boat Terminal, Rose Bay. Mr Brock is on his way to New Guinea* – and Mum's wedding band falls out from one of the folds behind it. Plain, gold. Rose gold so coppery it became the shape of her finger over time; they couldn't afford better, couldn't afford an engagement ring either, but this one alone is perfect, a perfect wobbly circle, perfect because Dad bought it with every hope and promise in him.

Courage. Put it in my pocket with my jasper B, and for another day it's mine.

GORDON

'**O**h yeah!' Johno shouts from the top of the palm. 'It's them!' Scrambling down again so fast he's already packed up and taken off after them. 'White stars at the tails – it's them all right.'

Americans.

Sven is ready to take off too. 'How many?'

'Three of them, come up from the south. They're here for us.'

Three American planes. By the look of Johno and Sven, it might well be three hundred. I suppose that's what a month of nothing much but desperation will do to you. I wouldn't know. I can't share their enthusiasm at the moment. I have the flu. Two years living in the tropics and now I get crook. Probably from a month of living on feral pigs and bitter limes, inside a cloud, on the spine of the Baining Ranges.

I have to say: 'Hang on a second. What exactly is our plan?'

'To get going,' Johno says, with the look on his face saying, *And don't you bloody well hold us up*. 'We have to get down to Wide Bay. Be ready for them – that's where the force'll make land. And that's where our mob will be.'

I don't know if it's just being crook that's making me concerned for the soundness of this idea. It's been a long time since we last saw Sid and we've been through this excitement now three times, sighting more RAAF Wirraways, five planes in total, one meeting a fiery end in the side of a mountain, never to be seen again. I don't trust that anyone's coming, or what we might find at Wide Bay if or when we get there. But I don't know who's more cracked: him or me.

'Why don't we wait till some more come over?' Ernie says, somehow having become the least cracked among us.

'No, not this time.' Johno's that sure. Or is he just wanting to be? 'This time they're coming.'

I'm just as unsure. 'But what if–' I can't finish the thought because I'm coughing my guts up.

'What if *what*, Doze? What if we get to Wide Bay and there's Japs there, or no one there at all? I'm pinching a fucking canoe and getting out of here, that's what's going to happen. I will get us to the mainland. You can stay here with your flu and die that way if you want, but I'd rather you stuck with me.'

'Righto. You don't have to yell.' There's a six-inch drill grinding through my skull as it is.

I start rolling up my swag around my bedourie, trying to recreate a map of the Gazelle in my mind. If we keep due south from here, what would it be, fifteen, maybe twenty miles down to the coastal flats? But if we can't keep to that course, then we should probably stay west. Southwest. Then the worst that can happen is that we'll come out of the ranges into central New Britain and have to head east, to avoid the very proud tribesmen that live there. They don't speak Kua-Nua and they eat people they don't like. And that is another good reason to try to get out of the ranges generally, as well as the reason we've had to keep moving through the mountains all this time anyway. The Baining tribesmen up here don't speak Kua-Nua either and only just enough pidgin to tell Johno to keep away from their villages. I've got the shivers. My hands are shaking as I fix the buckles of the swag over my hand shovel, and not just from fear. I'm so flaming cold. I don't want to walk anywhere. We haven't dried out at all since we crossed a creek almost a week ago, and my feet are now made of an alien pulp that should be sent off for biological analysis.

Ernie picks up my swag with his, and Sven says: 'I'll help you if you get tired.' Carry me? He could too, but the idea makes me cranky. I take my swag off Ernie: 'I'm not that crook.'

Yet.

By the next morning I'm tempted to let the jungle harpies have me. I'm too crook. We must be nearly there. The walking has been relatively easy. We're down to about two thousand feet elevation, I reckon, and there'll be bananas somewhere for me today, if I could raise my head off the ground. Beyond the next ridge I'm sure we'll see the coast, but I'm not going to make it. I don't want Sven to carry me. It's not reasonable. I've lost some weight, but I'd still be near twelve stone. I'm a liability.

'Get some more hot water into you.' Johno's making a billy when he says: 'What's that sound?'

Even I listen. Sounds like heavy fire, at a distance. Machine-guns. Maybe anti-aircraft fire. Coming from over the other side of the ridge. But we can't hear any planes. Can't see from here either.

'Shit, that must be them,' Johno says.

Forget the billy, I have no trouble getting to my feet now. It has to be them. Or someone. Come for us. What else could it be?

We get going, quickly, to get round the ridge, and the firing continues through the morning as we do. Intermittent. Not like a drill. It's random. It must be a battle.

But still, we can't see anything when we come out onto the lowland, at the back of a copra plantation. The guns seem to have stopped now too.

Sven points through the rows of palms, down a drive, at what looks like the roof of a big bungalow. 'I think I know where this is – on the north side of the bay. There is a beach on the other side of the plantation.'

Johno looks down along the bougainvillea hedge that runs behind it like a loose border. 'We'll keep to the cover here, though. Follow it round.'

We follow it round for about half a mile.

Till Sven puts out his hand and stops.

The four of us stop dead as one animal.

They can't see us, but we can see them. Through the pink flowers of the bougainvillea canes.

Japs. This is the first of them I've seen. They are small. I'm shocked at the size of them. Little men in yellow-brown uniforms. About twenty of them.

They look to have caught and bailed up a party of half-a-dozen AIF, taken their guns. One of them is that Lieutenant Campbell, with his hands up, but I can't see the faces of the others. One of them is kneeling. A rifle is being shoved into the middle of his back, and he's getting screamed at in I don't know what language. His hands are tied behind him. He's still holding a piece of white material in his left hand.

He is shot in the back of the head. His blood shoots out across a stack of cut palm stems near him. Red blood on the gold stems.

Another of the Japs steps over him, straddling him, and drives a bayonet through his back.

I don't understand what's happening. Why would you do that? He had surrendered. Why did you kill him? There are more of you than us. I don't understand. I can't move.

Until Johno grabs me. Dragging me. Down along behind this bougainvillea maze. The thorns are ripping up our legs. Thorns that I can't feel. We keep running until another half a mile or so on when we see a pile of militia uniforms, stacked liked dead sheep in the middle of a clearing. There's maybe a few dozen of them, chucked around the base of a pole, with another man nailed to it above them, half eaten already by the harpies. Ernie has to stop to throw up.

I would too, if it wasn't for the sound of rifles being cocked above us. And someone shouting. Could be a dog barking for all we understand.

Little yellow dogs. Two of them.

Only two of them, coming down at us from an outcrop of granite boulders. I can take the one on the left from here, I know I can. I have my finger on the trigger: I will kill him. I am going to. If it's the last thing I do I will kill this little mongrel.

I fire and I don't feel a thing. But all three of us have missed him. How could I have missed? Missed both of them, while the other one has got a shot in.

He has shot Ernie through the chest. Ernie has fallen to his knees beside me, holding his chest; his eyes are screaming: *Why?* So am I. He's an unarmed vulcanologist. He talks to rocks. Why did you kill him?

Before I know what I've done, I've reloaded, and Sven has got a bullet into the one on the right, hit him in the shoulder. Not good enough, but before me or Johno have another go, there is a collective discharge of fire, from eight of them now that I can count. They keep firing at Sven. Into him. He is a very big man, but they keep firing into him. Don't they know he's probably already dead? Am I dead too? Have they shot me too? I wouldn't know. I drop the rifle. Put my hands in the air.

I must still be alive because I feel a shove behind me, something ripped from my swag. Barking at me, into me, and my shovel is thrown into my hands.

'Digga! Digga!' The little man is screaming up at me. His spit hitting my face. Black slit eyes. Teeth bared. Is this a man? He is so clean, neat and tidy. I stare at the little yellow star on his yellow cap.

'Dig,' I hear Johno say. 'Dig, Brockie.'

What? I look at Johno, begging me: *Please.*

I don't understand what's going on. Dig what?

I don't get to find out.

There is another discharge of fire.

And that's the end of us.

BERNIE

Up and down the rows of beans, Rock's not coming home. Mrs Lockhart is sewing rabbit skins into her quota of a hundred vests for airmen, but Rock's not coming home. The United States Supreme Commander of the Pacific, General Douglas MacArthur, has finally arrived to have his photograph taken with Mr Curtin, for a hundred million tins of pork and beans, but Rock's not coming home. It's too late. Two months too late.

The Japanese lined them up and tied their hands behind their backs with fishing cord and ordered them to march into the bush; some were shot, some were bayoneted.

Only three have survived the New Britain massacres to tell the tale to the *Canberra Times*, and none of them is called Gordon Brock. One of them, who escaped from a place called Tol Plantation, said that all their identification papers and tags were taken and burned. That's it, six-pennies' worth of hope tells me, that's what's happened: he's wandering around out there unidentified and unidentifiable. He has amnesia. He's drifting out across the Coral Sea on a bamboo raft, notify the Coast Watch.

But reality tells me it's time to face facts. It doesn't matter how wonderful and capable I think Gordon is; what chance would he have had? The Japs don't trade in punches. They tie your hands behind your back and bayonet you. Just as the Americans aren't here to rescue anyone but themselves – they've only come because they've lost the Philippines and need a place from which to try to win it back. If it wasn't for that, Australia would be sacrificed, full stop, and Britain would be forced to pay a little more for inferior American beef and wool. Who would care? Only a handful of people who don't matter, down round the forgettable side of the earth.

It's just as well I'm picking beans ten hours a day for the McDoughals. I'm too tired to be overcome by anything much but sleep at the end of every day. Be thankful for small mercies. Yes, yes, yes. At least it's not a hundred degrees today; the breath of Satan is cooling with autumn. And I'm alone with my despair; the others, Mrs Denison and her Chrissie and Ruth, won't get here until next week. Meanwhile, I'm the fastest bean-picker Mrs McDoughal's ever seen. Searching for my courage in the leaves. If I can pick them fast enough, Hughie, will you reconsid–

The horn of the ute toots over the other side of the field, near the homestead. Mrs Lockhart. And someone else, another lady. Oh? And two little boys, one of them jumping headlong off the back: Alby. It's the Werners. Anna Werner running towards me, in her crimson D'Orsay t-straps, pretty fern print sundress, waving a letter, as if she's won a trifecta at the races.

'Bernadette!' she's breathless with it. 'My brother – my brother, he is found!'

That doesn't immediately make sense to me, not until I remember that one of the reasons she's remained in internment for so long has been her inability to prove who she is outside her husband's false membership of the Nazi Party.

'Oh,' I say. 'Isn't that good.'

Mrs Lockhart gives me a sharp frown: *You could be a bit more pleased for her, couldn't you?*

'Yes.' Anna is thrilled to pieces, hardly able to keep it in. 'He escaped – he came through Denmark in a truck with furniture and then on a trawling boat across the North Sea. He is in London. He's been there for months – but we only found out this morning. They gave me some letters from him and said now we can go!'

Well good for you; my soul shrivels very quickly with the most hideous envy.

Eric throws his arms around my waist, looking up at me with those irresistible blue eyes. 'Will you visit us in Melbourne, Miss Cooper?'

And not even that gets through. I say: 'Course I will, sweetie.' But I don't mean it.

Mrs McDoughal is magicking up a spread of scones and cordial on the verandah to celebrate, and Mrs Lockhart marches me inside for a word. 'I know that you are upset, as I am too, but don't you forget that woman has fourteen other relatives who haven't escaped from Germany – including her eighty-seven-year-old grandmother. Straighten that back, girl – Anna thought you might take heart from her good news. So take heart.'

So I do. Try to. Mrs McDoughal's scones are almost as good as Mrs Lockhart's, but they taste like sand today. Stuff one down and wave the Werners away. They'll be staying at Riverbend tonight, before they get on the train tomorrow, back to their lives. Minus her husband Franz, of course, who's still a fake Nazi, just as Mrs Zoc remains a dangerous fascist-anarchist, but at least Anna's husband is safe in prison – he's got a little orchestra going in there, one that's dwindling daily as the Jewish boys keep getting released so they can go off and join the AIF.

'Well, I'd better get back to it,' I tell Mrs McDoughal. I'll pick beans till sunset and then sleep out with the brown snakes.

'Oh no you won't, Bernadette,' Mrs McDoughal shoos me off, expertly putting aside her worries, for her farm, her droving husband, and her son, youngest and only, somewhere in the Top End on Jap watch, to share another's good news. 'Have an early mark today. Go on. Go home and enjoy the rest of the day with the Werners.'

Throw myself over Odd Socks thinking this'll give me half an hour's avoidance, but she decides today is the day she'll go for a little trot. She can't wait to get home. When we do I decide she'll be needing a long brush out in the stable this afternoon; as if I am anywhere near competent at grooming her. Doesn't matter, does it, Odds, thought that counts; main one: please don't let Mrs Lockhart send the boys out into the yard. I want to be alone, with my miserable trifecta of loss. At least until tea.

But I can't even manage that. Halfway across the yard I see that Pete's in the stable shed. I'm not going in there now for anything. Big white stallion still frightens me silly. And this is why Odds was in such a hurry to get home, I see. She snorts excitedly: she's got her boyfriend back for a visit. Can't wait to say hello to him. Good grief. She practically pulls me into the shed.

'G'day, um, Miss Coop–' blue Scotch twill reaching out of the shadow of the overhanging roof, taking Odds's reins from me.

'Mitchell.' I'm rude to him: 'You can call me Bernadette – it's easier.'

'Right. Good.' He manages to say half of it audibly: 'Dette.'

I say: 'What are you doing home?' Though I don't care.

'Easter. Come home early. See the stock agent tomorrow.'

Tomorra. 'Right.' And then I remember I did know that: he's got to sell off more of the flock; something about getting rid of the wethers, useless boy sheep, not worth their feed. That suddenly makes me so sad, and tired of being sad, I –

'You want to go fishing or something this arvo?'

'What?' In the dimness of the shed, in my wanting, he even sounds like my Rock. I could say: *You want to really upset me, then yes, let's.* But I've no doubt his mother's put him up to this, so I say: 'Don't worry, Mitchell, I'm sure you've got better things to do.'

He's already got Odds's saddle off for me and he says, tossing it over his shoulder: 'I was going fishing anyway. Don't come if you don't want to.'

'I won't.'

He turns around from hanging the bridle. 'You all right?'

'Yes.' I'm sure that was convincing. My fingernails are shockingly filthy, aren't they. If I stare at them for long enough, this wave of grief will pass. Or Mitchell will go away. He doesn't.

I can feel him walking towards me; his voice is a warm rasp of concern: 'He'll be right, I reckon, Gordon. You know, at school, with the five years between us, I was supposed to look out for him, Mum being an old friend of his dad, and both of us without brothers, but he didn't need me. He's pretty good at looking after himself. He's got good bush sense, too.'

Mitchell would know that's a pretty useless offering, but he wants Gordon to be all right, and I do appreciate it, coming from one who'd no more waste a word than a drop of water. I look up at him, his lion jaw and sharp hazel eyes, not like my Rock much at all, not up close. They don't even know they're ccusins. Second cousins. Doesn't matter, does it. It's care that counts. We're all family, somehow.

'So you want to come fishing, or not?' He gives me his crooked smile. 'Get away from Mum's yacking and carry on for a spell.'

'All right.'

We walk up along the river's edge, under the coolabahs and almost back to the McDoughals, to the old tumbledown wharf where, once upon a time before the railways, the wool steamers would pick up the Lockhart clip. We don't talk; we throw the lines in and wait, disappear under our wide brims, ignoring the water creeping ever lower down the banks, exposing the roots of the big vanilla gums. I meditate instead upon the great mystery that is country boys' preference for white moleskin trousers; ride a horse thirty miles in from Hell and not a speck of dust on them. I lose time altogether until, just as the sun starts setting, I get a tug on my line and I pull up a big silver perch.

GORDON

'What is your name?'

I know my name. *Brockie, it's me – it's Gerry.* Errol Flynn, shaking me awake: *You've got to get up, mate. I've got us a dinghy, down on the beach. It's only two hundred yards.* There was just enough daylight left for me to see that we would not include Johno. He wasn't carrying a spun steel shearer's bedourie oven in his swag, like me. His face. He was wide awake and dead cold. I'd landed on his arm. I didn't want to leave him there. He still felt warm on that bit of his arm. But I got up and ran with Errol. I could hardly breathe, kneeling in the sand. Errol pulled me into the dinghy. Because I've got pneumonia. I know that as well. I was winded, too, from the bullets hitting the bedourie. Errol unrolled my swag on the dinghy and found two of them inside, gone right through the lid. *Strike me blind, someone's looking after you, aren't they.* They are. Not a scratch on me. Now. They healed.

'Are you AIF or New Guinea Rifles?'

Neither. I'm a geologist. With pneumonia. In Townsville, in the hospital, and I'd be dead if it wasn't for my bedourie and Errol Flynn and sulfapryridine. I'm getting very well looked after here. I'm on the mend. The curtains are black but they're open and the breeze is nice. I don't want to talk, though. Didn't Errol give them my name? He left me at Cairns. There was an air-raid siren going and he said: *See you in San Francisco, Dozy. You'll be right.* I don't know how I got to Townsville. I remember the smell of the sea in the bottom of that dinghy, though. Crook. A lot of sea and coconut milk and then I nearly slipped on the rope ladder boarding the ketch that picked us up. Some old salt with tattoos up his arms was shaking his head: *You rowed from Wide Bay?* Errol did. He rowed so far he missed the mainland of New Guinea and might have got us to Townsville himself, if the ketch hadn't nearly run over us in full sail. It was getting away from the Solomons. I couldn't row; couldn't scratch myself. I've been crook for a long time. I don't know how long. I don't know what day it is. But I know who I am. I'd hand over my wallet and show you, if I knew where my wallet was.

'You are quite safe. My name is Ackerman. David Ackerman, and I'm a doctor. You're in the hospital, in Townsville, and you're quite safe.'

I look at the doctor now. It's a different one today. He's young, about my age, and his teeth are so straight and white he should be in the pictures. They're amazing teeth.

He says: 'I'm an army doctor, a lieutenant, you can tell me. What's your unit?'

I shake my head, close my eyes.

I'm not military, and I'm not safe. I'm running through the bougainvillea thorns again. The pink flowers and the gold palms on the blue sky. Red palms, yellow stars. When I can speak, when I can hold a line of consciousness, I know what I am going to do.

'It's not uncommon to lose speech from the shock of a difficult experience. It's called nervous–'

'No.' That gets me talking. I know what he's getting at. There's nothing nervous about me. I missed that shot. I missed hitting that little mongrel. We were surprised and I was crook. I won't miss again.

'Ah, good. That's the way. What's your name then?'

'Brock,' I tell him: 'Gordon Brock.'

*

'Notwithstanding your general ill health, Mr – ah – Brock, you have a significant impairment in your right hand.' This military doctor is middle-aged, short-sighted and overweight and he's calling me unfit for service. It might be true that I'm not up to my normal state of health yet, but I'm not too far off. My lungs are clear and I have no impairment.

I argue: 'It's not significant at all. You haven't seen me shoot – there's nothing impaired about my abilities there.' I just wasn't quick enough, practised enough. I will practise and I will get fit. I have every motivation for it. They killed Johno and Sven. They murdered Ernie. They killed all of Sid's party, except for Errol, who only survived because, as he started to run, he stumbled off the top of that ridge and fell into the middle of some banana trees. I think about what they might have done to those nurses at Rabaul, in light of what they did to us. There's dumb animal. And then there's wilfully depraved. I think about what they've done to Darwin. That Lieutenant Ackerman told me he's been learning a lot about burns lately, reckons at least a hundred were killed, some come from Broome too, and it's all been kept out of the papers. He could understand my need to get into it. The mongrels are going to invade us, sometime probably quite soon. I tell this doctor: 'My hand doesn't give me any trouble.'

So he puts down his clipboard and squeezes right behind the knuckle again to demonstrate otherwise: an electric shock up my forearm.

I say: 'It doesn't give me any trouble in the heat of firing.' I didn't feel a thing when I fired. I know I didn't. It might have been the effect of adrenalin but it worked.

He says, to my hand: 'It is my responsibility to ensure that the Commonwealth of Australia does not spend a penny on time-wasters.'

End of argument. I can't believe I'm being rejected. I've never been rejected on my abilities at anything. You can't reject me. With an audience of a dozen eighteen-year-old farmhands lined up behind me in this office at the town hall all thinking: Geez, I'm glad that's not me. Bullshit.

'It might be reparable, supposing it is what it feels to be, an old injury, poorly healed; I can refer you to a surgeon in Brisbane,' this doctor says, still not bothering to look at me directly, 'but it would be at your own expense and in your own time.'

No. I don't have time to waste – yours, the Commonwealth's or mine. I'm not going to another hospital. I put my shirt back on and I could quilt myself for not having had this seen to when it happened. Why didn't I stop at Dubbo for that X-ray? One, because I was embarrassed about fighting. And two, because I was in a hurry to get back to Coogee, to Bernie. How relevant are either of those things in my life today?

The doctor is looking down at my form now, on the clipboard on the desk behind him. Beside it is a stamp pad and three stamps. You are not going to reject me. You are not going to bloody well reject me. I'm right on the verge of asking him for the referral to Brisbane when he looks up from the form.

'Geologist, eh?'

'Yes,' I say: 'Why? Is that important?'

'Important to the CSIR at the moment.' He takes off his specs to look at me now as if he's just recognised a fellow human. 'They're recruiting all manner of scientists – geologists, chemists, physicists and engineers, all the technicians they can find. Get yourself down to Canberra and you'll have a job before you walk in the door.'

The Council for Scientific and Industrial Research. Go and join the public service. In Canberra. Go and sleep in a lab. Not likely. Let's not put too fine a point on it: I've got a score to settle.

I ask him: 'Do you know what sort of projects they want people for at the moment?' Apart from their usual of how to make sheep breed in triplicate without entirely eradicating the topsoil.

But he says, raising an eyebrow at the halfwit: 'Defence projects, I would imagine.' He hands me back my form to dispose of. Thanks for that. 'If you want to serve your country as a scientist, I'd hop to it if I were you.'

All right then, the CSIR I suppose it is. Can't think what they'd want geologists for in defence, but I may as well find out.

I go back out into the street, back up Flinders Street, towards the foreshore where the Qantas terminal is. I've got eight hundred and seventy-four pounds in my account, established with my identity yesterday. I'm a wealthy man. Southern Star did pay this idiot well. Why not go by plane? There's plenty here. The whole of Townsville is an air base now. You can't get into a pub, which is good. I don't want a drink. I do want a drink, actually, a lot of drink, but I'm not going to have one. I don't know what I might do if I had a drink in me. All the same, I have to pass Ramages on the way to the wharves, and the anger that overtakes me as I do has no name. This is where I met Johno. What do I do with this anger? Write to Johno's father is what I should do. I know he works for Union Steamships, and there'd be an office here I could drop a letter into. But I can't do that. Not yet. A fight spills out of the front bar into the street, between the RAAF and the Yanks, and I could join them, on either side. I can't believe Johno's gone. I don't know what to do with this – chaos. The violence wanting to rip out of me.

Keep walking, to the terminal, to the booking agent. Get a ticket. Townsville to Sydney on the seaplane this arvo at three, then change at Mascot 7.15 tomorrow morning, for Canberra. Too easy.

I walk back round the corner towards the hospital, back to the outfitters across the road from it and kit myself up with a new swag. I need new everything. Jacket, tie, look like I'm applying for a job. I'm unemployed. Flaming hell. Probably not for long, but five minutes is embarrassing enough. This borrowed shirt I've walked in with is embarrassing enough. I think I should go and thank that Lieutenant Ackerman, for looking after me. Nice bloke; from Lithgow originally. But I don't go and find him. He's that good-looking and sure of himself I can't look at him directly without thinking Bernie married him. Someone like him. I walk back to the foreshore, go and sit on the wharf, and wait for the plane.

On board, I spend the afternoon watching the cloudless sky for Jap Zeroes. Then, after Brisbane, as Queensland becomes New South Wales, I watch the sunset over the Divide, over the drought of the northwest. That's not my concern. Not my country any more. Not a lot of colours going on out the window. Nothing for me down there any more. Just as there's nothing for me in Sydney either. When we hit the water at Rose Bay, I consider going to Coogee. It's only three miles from here, and I stand on the jetty for a minute, in two minds about it.

Mrs Cooper would be thrilled to see me. Maybe Mrs Zoc, too, if she's home, from that internment bullshit in Hay. Surely she would be by now. It's almost seven. They'd be finishing their tea.

But I can't imagine knocking on the door. I can't imagine having a conversation with them. I can't imagine saying hello. What I might do when I find out who Bernie's with. Seeing her.

That makes me break out in a sweat. Not in any good way. A cold sweat, here where I last saw her. Saying goodbye, here. We were so happy then. But that was then. She doesn't want to see me now. I'm long forgotten. And to see that written on her face, in her eyes, that's a rejection I couldn't take. It would finish me. It's hard enough getting my breath back over it, right now. This pain in my lungs that's not pneumonia any more.

But somehow I do breathe. Somehow I'm in the cab, going out to Mascot, and then I'm in the hotel, the Lakes by the aerodrome. Where I can't get to sleep. I'm not thinking about Bernie. I'm listening to the planes going all night long, waiting for the sirens to start up. Somewhere, inside the long dark tunnel of this anger, I pass out. I don't wake up properly until we're nearly landing again, flying over the Goulburn district. It looks like it's had its grass removed. This is prime grazing country; the drought is bad. I look out the window for Lake George, but it's disappeared too. There is some suffering going on down there. That's not my concern. Not now.

'Where to?' says the cabbie on the lonely paddock that's Canberra Airport.

'The CSIR.'

'Black Mountain?'

'I suppose so.' I don't know Canberra well. Only been here twice, to play tennis against Grammar at school. No other reason why you'd come.

'Busy out there lately – you working there too?' the cabbie asks, wanting to chat.

'Maybe.' I don't want to chat. I look out the window, at the bush. At Canberra. It's not called Bush City for nothing. The centre of town, where the shops are, is not more than two miles wide. Who else has a national capital like this one? What am I doing here? No one in the streets, all shut up in their offices napping for their country, round an artificial lake that famously hasn't been built yet because of this flaming war. Out the other side, we're into the bush again. Then out of the bush, this big concrete bunker appears. Two of them. Like an extra-galactic alien laboratory for the study of life on Earth. One that landed shy of its target.

'Here y'are,' says the cabbie.

'Thanks.'

Pick up my swag and find a signpost. I find two: *Insectarium* or *Administration & Soils Department*. This was a pointless exercise. I am cracked. But I head in through the Admin revolving door anyway. May as well find out how pointless and cracked, since I'm here.

The foyer's surprisingly busy. The sound of footsteps and conversation reminds me of rushing between lectures at uni. It's almost comforting, to be somewhere, for the first time in so long, that seems familiar. In a good way.

I go up to the counter and wait at the inquiries sign till one of the ladies behind it comes over and says: 'Can I help you?'

'Am I in the right place to inquire after war effort work? I'm a geologist,' I say.

She smiles: 'You are indeed. All the positions currently open are pinned to the noticeboard on the left, over there. The priority positions are marked with a red dot. If you see anything you're interested in, come back with the position number and we'll make you an appointment.'

All right. I go over to the noticeboard, where there's dozens of jobs, lots with red dots. Metallurgists wanted for aeronautics in Melbourne. Chemists for experiments with rubber plants at Queensland Uni. A junior biology technician wanted for dehydrating vegetables in Sydney. Not many jobs in Canberra itself, unless you want to study moths for the Wool Board. And nothing for me, that I can see. Except for one small notice for a surveyor to go out to Port Hedland for haematite exploration in the Pilbara, in Western Australia. I nearly laugh. Someone doesn't think the idea is too wild of accepted wisdom any more. But then I suppose now would be the time to get someone to go and have a proper look, wouldn't it. Not me, though. I'm not doing survey work. Not now.

Still, I look at the notice again. Haematite. My honours paper. That seems like a long time ago. But it's not five years since I was looking at this sample of high grade ore that had just come to

Professor Richardson from a gold exploration site north of Alice Springs, from the Centre. The red bands of iron oxide through the black looked like arteries. Maybe I should –

'Brock? Is that Gordon Brock?'

I turn to see a familiar face. It's one of the physics lecturers from Sydney. What's his name? Sherbel, but Professor or Doctor, I can't remember which. I didn't have him as a teacher and I don't really know him for anything other than that he is a small, tight-sprung bloke, fit from riding a bicycle everywhere. He's got one of those faces that always looks surprised and a bit excited – cracked in that way most physicists are.

He's holding out his hand to me now. 'Brock, good to see you again.'

Again? I've said two words to this bloke my whole life, but he knows who I am. I extend my hand: 'Prof, um, Doctor Sherbel, isn't it?'

'One and the same. Call me Charlie. Ha.' He's excited all right. 'Heard you were in New Guinea. Richardson will be glad to know you've got back to us in good shape. Looking for a job, eh?' No chance to answer that before he's giving me the worst handshake. If he is not a world champion arm-wrestler, he should be. I'm seeing stars as he says: 'U-235.'

'U-235?' Please let go of my hand now.

'That's the one,' he says, finally releasing it but no less excited. 'U-235.'

'Um ...' I'm not following him. He has a doctorate in cracked. I know what U-235 is of course, the isotope of uranium which might be able to sustain a chain reaction of fission, the release of molecular energy on splitting an atom. It's all anyone talked about at the beginning of '39, the discovery of U-235's instability and how its intense radioactivity will be used to make death-ray guns to fight off the red Lizard Men of Ergamon when someone works out how to extract enough of it to test the theory. But all I manage for Doctor Sherbel is: 'Ah, yeah, 235, as in uranium?'

'One and the same, Brock, one and the same.' Doctor Sherbel nods, his vice-hand taking me by the elbow now. 'Uranium. The destructive potentialities of uranium.'

I can't imagine them. But Doctor Sherbel is imagining them, and probably not as science fiction.

He says, already pulling me down a long corridor: 'Interested?'

Uranium. It's a miracle mineral. It can cure cancer, at least radium bromide can. The radioactivity somehow shrinks the bad cells and makes them disappear. Mix it with a fluorescing agent and it makes clock faces and expensive champagne glasses glow in the dark. But don't lick the paintbrush or it might give you cancer. Uranium. It's a very heavy metal. What would those U-235 atoms really do, splitting, ping-ponging against each other with a force … I can't imagine it, that chaos, but I want to. An energy, a destructive potential, more powerful than anything I can put sense to. I'm interested.

'Yes,' I tell Doctor Sherbel, 'I'm very interested.'

FIVE

MAY 1942 – FEBRUARY 1944

BERNIE

'He's home – Bernadette love. He's home!'

I could drop the telephone. Mrs Quinn is so overjoyed she's let herself in to Arcadia to phone me. Can't blame her: Colin's been missing in action for almost a year. I haven't given him a thought for ages; I'd given him up for dead. And now he's home?

'He turned up on the doorstep, crack of dawn this morning, nearly killed us with the fright of it. Telegram didn't get through, all them Americans clogging up the lines at Easter. He got himself to Egypt, our Col did – hiding in Greece all that time, he was, having a holiday. There's an Irishman for you. They're going to give him a medal. Can you believe it?'

Yes. I believe everyone's going to come home but Gordon. And my mum and dad. Come back from the dead, evade capture. Come on, Missy, nerves of steel, tell Mrs Quinn: 'That is the most marvellous thing I've heard in so long, I could cry.' And I could: this hurt is excruciating.

'They've given him two weeks with us. I thought I'd see if you might like to come home and celebrate, at our place, this Saturday – only a small party, but it will be a happy occasion, I can promise you that. We need a happy occasion, don't we, love?'

We do. But I don't want to celebrate with you. I have to, though. I have to start accepting; facing Arcadia might well be the place to do it. Tell Mrs Quinn and quickly: 'Of course I'll come, thank you so much for thinking of me.' Giving me a telephone account I can ill afford, too; I should have cancelled the subscription. 'I'd better go now, though. See you Saturday.'

'See you, love, I'll be so looking forward to–'

Press my finger down on the cradle so it doesn't clunk on her.

'What was that about, dear?' Mrs Lockhart puts her head around the sitting-room door.

I say: 'Mrs Quinn, their Colin, he's turned up, in Coogee.'

Mrs Lockhart's smile is full of sympathy as I wipe away the evidence with my cardi cuff. There's nothing to say about it, apart from: 'So you'll be going off to Sydney to welcome him home?' Because she has telescopic ears to go with the eyes in the back of her head.

I say: 'Yes, I suppose I will.' Unless you can find a compelling reason for me not to make the nine-hundred mile round trip into the heart of my sorrow and back.

'Oh, it'll do you good, dear,' she says. 'I am glad, I must say, and I have an ulterior reason to go with it. Now, we need a dele-gate from Hay branch to attend the national conference on the fifteenth. They're holding it in the Grace's Ballroom – you'll have a great time with the girls, I know you will. Mina Carlton'll look after you down there, you know, from Dee Why? Of course you do. Someone's got to go for us, don't they – you know how important it is that we have as many from the far west as we can get, so our needs are heard out here. And as well, I've put you in to model the proposed uniform – you've done that sort of thing before, haven't you, dear?'

Would it matter if I hadn't? I laugh, with that sort of sweet hysteria that rolls over tears. 'Of course,' I snortle, and I do know how important it is. The Women's Land Army is at last about to become a reality, a national organisation, with a proper wage, ranks and an official pin, as well as a uniform, instead of the ad hoc way things've been done to date, and always short of hands out here. City girls want to go and pick pears in Leeton for a trip away with friends, just like on the peachy posters, or work in the cannery and go to dances with the boys from Narrandera aerodrome. They don't want to pick boring beans at the end of the line or muck out stinky stables and spend Sundays being grateful for it. As I have, and I'm a bit chuffed now to be asked to go to the conference. I've never done anything like that before, represented anything or anyone.

'Oh, I knew you would.' Mrs Lockhart squeezes me round the shoulders. 'Have I ever told you how indispensable you are, Bernadette darling? You're like a daughter to me, and I'd so very much like to come along to Sydney with you – I need a trip, I do, my word are we going shopping one day – but with things the way they are with Mitch, I can't get away. You know how it is, don't you, dear.'

I do; things are grim with Mitch. But she's never called me indispensable before, or darling. Like a daughter to her. That is a blast of sunshine into the dark depths of me. While Mitch would like a little less sunshine. He's in Canberra, probably on his way back now, from a meeting at the Agricultural Council yesterday, making his own submissions of need, and extending his overdraft while he's there. What's left of his mob out on the Paddock is going to have to be handfed now, and if he can't extend the overdraft, he won't be able to pay for the shearing of them either, not to mention how much it's costing him to keep his best breeding stock in Yass. It's a dreadful business for him, for all the graziers, and since what they lack in pasture they make up for in pride, there'll be no women's land anything allowed near a sheep station round here. Not even me: before he left I asked him if I could help with the fences that needed mending up at Hell and in the silence that followed we all decided to ignore that I'd opened my mouth at all.

Mrs Lockhart's hands are still on my shoulders, here on the velveteen teal, as I notice a great big cloud forming over the tops of the river gums. A blustery wind through the leaves and a hulking, brownish thundery-looking cloud that has me grasping her hands with the thrill of a prayer about to be answered in bucket loads. 'Oh look! Look, that's rain! An almighty lot of rain!'

'Oh no, dear.' Mrs Lockhart has ungrasped me and is already running down the hall and out the back. 'The washing, Bernadette. Bring in the washing!'

I follow but I don't see the need to panic; we've only got spare sheets on the line, a tablecloth and a few napkins. 'A bit of rain won't matter, will it?'

'That's not rain, Bernadette – that's dust, coming in from the Centre. We've got five minutes,' she warns, and a plum pudding cyclone has never moved at greater speed, getting me to unpeg and throw the linen at her before she says: 'I'll go in with these and shut the windows. Start bringing everything not nailed down into the house, dear, the cane chairs, the planters, everything. Hurry! Hurry!'

I have no trouble hurrying as the cloud quickly changes from brown to red, rolling towards the house with terrifying speed. A great, howling, angry red cloud is billowing out of the belly of the devil, and it's going to crash right over us. It will surely kill us. I scream: 'Oh Hughie help me!'

Hurling the cane chairs and cushions off the back verandah and in through the kitchen door, I remember Odd Socks: oh no, she's not nailed down. 'Oh my God!'

Forget lugging in the planters, I run across the yard for her; she'll be under the willows at the bend, where she usually spends the afternoon, just up from the pump. I've got to get her in the shed. She can't stay out in this, surely. We'll shelter in the shed. Oh, but as I'm running past it I see the tin panels lifting at the side with the force of the gathering gale.

And now can't see anything at all. The whole world has gone a deep shade of apricot. Screaming apricot air that is stinging my skin. Everywhere. It's going to tear my cardigan off. It's going to tear my skin off.

I crouch down on the ground, cover my head with my arms, make myself as small as I can. I am so frightened I can't even blaspheme. I cower there for what seems forever until I realise the wind has stopped screaming. Slowly, I dare to look up.

And through the apricot haze I see the shape of Odd Socks, over by the willows, she's all apricot but otherwise apparently unscathed, and then I see the ute, Mitchell's ute, apricot too, rolling down the drive, home from Canberra, rolling off the drive and across the yard towards me, pulling up a few feet away.

The door of the ute opens and he staggers out holding his side. I jump up: oh no all over again, something has happened to him, something really dreadful, before I see he's laughing: laughing so hard no sound is coming out.

'I fail to see what's amusing here, Mitchell.'

When he can manage it, he smacks his pristine moleskin knee. 'You've got no idea what you look like.'

'What do I look like?' A smirk betrays my indignation, as another gust wants to knock me sideways.

He says: 'You – you looked like a little red rock. I come in and I'm thinking what's that on the ground by the shed? Then it moves. It's Dette!' He starts connipting again; a proper laugh. I've never heard him really laugh before. It's a wonderful sound.

Until he says, over the wind: 'You're beautiful, Dette. Just beautiful.'

Heat rises up from my toes, scoops through my belly to land in my cheeks, unwanted. Don't look at me like that, Mitchell Lockhart. I'm not ready yet. Not ready for that sort of thing, not at all.

*

I use the excuse of the dust storm to avoid him by going off to the camp to check on Mrs Zoc, though it's only Tuesday, and Ken, on the gate, is saying: 'Miss Cooper, you know that's not possible. I'll get into trouble.'

I call on my own bit of redoubtability: 'Don't be boring, Ken, I have to speak with Mrs Zoc now – I won't be here on Sunday. It's urgent. I'll tell the Red Cross you wouldn't let her speak with her advocate, that's against the Geneva Convention recommendations, and then you'll be in trouble with more than just Major Payne.'

No idea what I'm talking about, but it works. 'All right, just for ten minutes.' He lets me through and it's not long before I hear: 'Bella! What a storm was that, ah?'

'Mm, it was.'

'What has happened?' She's spotted my long face before I've even let it fall.

'I'm not sure,' I tell her. 'Mitchell. Funny feeling for him, baaaa, don't know. Strange.'

'Ah! No, Bernadetta. No!' Mrs Zoc is as horrified as I am. Good, that's what I came for: to be put right off. She says, two hundred and fifteen percent certain: 'You must not lose hope for the one you love. God would not take your mama and your papa and Gordon too. It is not possible.'

That's just what I don't need. I say: 'I have to let him go, in my mind. The suspended grief is making me a madwoman.'

'Si, it does do that,' she nods; she's worn these shoes herself. 'But don't you let him go. Think about him. Dream about him. Write about him, bella. That is what you must do. Tell him all of the things you would tell him if he could hear you. Talk to him. He will hear you and he will come home.'

And then I will be as whacky-doodle-do as you. I tell her: 'I'm going home myself, on Friday. Colin's back – Colin Quinn. He–'

'Si!' she claps her hands for joy. 'If that stupido boy can come back, Gordon can come back too. But can you do me a favour, please, at home? Put some poopy through my garden and turn it through the soil. I think I will be home in one year myself. Maybe not this spring, but the next one.'

Of course you will.

*

But still, something makes me lug my Good Companion onto the train with me on Friday. Write to him. Yes, not a bad idea. I should write to him. Write him a long goodbye.

After I spend the trip thinking about Mitchell, about how like Rock he is if I'm not looking at him properly, the width of his shoulder, his stride, the tea-stain tan of him, and the sense it would make if we – what? I would be Mrs Lockhart's daughter for real then, and I could help him out at Hell. He needs a wife, to look after him, if not mend his fences. Could I love him in that way, though? No. It is a thoroughly horrifying idea. He's like a big brother to me; and he'd always be second best, wouldn't he. I would be the worst wife in the world for him. But his crooked lion smile, calling me beautiful, calling me Dette, the way he does, makes my belly flip. Because I *want* to be loved, I suppose. Because I miss Gordon, and I'm becoming desperate to relieve the ache of it, even as I can't let go of my charms that bind me to him: my jasper

B, my hair comb, Mum's wedding band. Round and round it goes. Fifteen hours, all the way to Central and onto the tram. Whatever happened to that girl who didn't want to marry anyone at all?

Arrival in Coogee gives me something else to think about. The beach is empty and not for winter coming. It's three o'clock on a Saturday, a perfect sunny autumn afternoon, and barbed wire's been strung along the sand, all the shop windows newspapered and duck-clothed, the Niagara shut up with a sign in theirs: *CLOSED UNTIL FURTHER NOTICE. THANK YOU.* The balcony of the Aquarium hall is blacked out, as is the ballroom of the Bay. Because the Japanese are coming.

Hatred like nothing I've ever known fills my chest. I hate them so much I could shake apart with it. You're not going to take my home, Japs, I promise the surf off Wedding Cake. I wish I could fight them, show them just what I think of them. Of their new world order, destroying all of mine. *They tied their hands behind their backs and ordered them to march.* I hate you. I yell it into my centre as I take the steps up Heartbreak Hill. I hate you.

'Bernie! Hey, Bernie!' I hear behind me. My heart lurches as I turn on the steps: how long has it been since anyone's called me Bernie? 'Slow down, will you!' It's Colin, jogging up to me, grabbing my Good Companion and my suitcase with manners he has somehow acquired over the past three years. 'You walked straight through me outside the Bay,' he says, giving me an awkward kiss on the cheek, all beer fumes and cigarette smoke ingrained in the wool of his tunic.

'Did I? Sorry, Col.' I take in the sight of him, the look in his eyes, a tiredness, not quite my old blockhead boatie boy. But he is here: I suddenly realise how marvellous that is. 'You're home, you are. Well done.' I drop my hat box on the steps and hug him, because he's here. 'It's wonderful to see you – welcome home.'

'Thanks.' He hugs me back, a bit too long.

I pull away. 'Your mum says you got a medal – what was that for, drinking?'

'Nah.' He looks away, up the hill and starts walking; doesn't want to talk about it, but it's not like him to avoid a brag. Probably got it for something awful. I feel awful for mentioning it; only got a handful of days before he's going to be sent back to it, likely New Guinea, to fight the blooping Japs for real. Everything unspoken slips between us like a third party; he doesn't mention Dad, or Mum, and I'm grateful. More so that I think he was looking out for me down at the Bay, waiting to walk me up so that I wouldn't be alone.

Here, at the doorstep of our gumdrop green Arcadia, where I see the garden has been well cared for, banksia rose clipped back; Mrs Zoc's yard too, hibiscus nicely pruned. The work of Mrs Quinn and Mrs Cronin, I'll bet. That's so good of them. It gets me in the door, and I know there've been Catholic Daily angels busy in here too – everything smells fresh and clean. I put Good Companion down on the kitchen table and see the hamper that's been left for me: steak and kidney pud, baked beans, orange cup cordial, a precious block of Cadbury's …

My eyes well up with all my good fortune at having so many good people in my world.

Colin leans on the ice chest. 'So, you and that Brock fella didn't get married?'

I stare at him: blockhead. Doesn't he know Gordon hasn't come back from Rabaul? Probably not.

I say: 'No, we didn't.' Then something makes me say: 'Not yet.' Something else again makes me add: 'Come on, let's get to your place. I want to thank your mum and then get skunked.'

'Fair dinkum?' Col likes that idea; still thinks he's in with a chance with me. Incurable blockhead, and I've never been skunked in my life. I think I just need something, out of all my wanting, to give way.

By the time we walk down to the Quinns' flat on Dolphin Street, the party is in full roar, or at least Mr Quinn is, Belfast brogue unintelligible. 'Barrrdat, Barrrdat, love.' He envelopes me with his whiskey embrace, pushing me down the hall into the tiny lounge room, tinier for its black-papered window and crammed with Colin's three older sisters and their families, his little sister Maureen and her gaggle of friends. Mrs Quinn's brother, Slick Mick Heggarty, is here too: he deals in sly petrol coupons, and possibly sly chocolate, under the counter of the Oceanic, and tonight he's managed to squeeze in a three-piece ensemble here – banjo, fiddle and accordion reeling madly.

'Just a small party, Mrs Quinn?'

She laughs, revelling in the very centre of it, all her chicks in the roost. 'Oh love, it's so good you could come. Don't you look a treat.' Thrusts a lemonade shandy in my hand.

Then another. I think she'd like her Col to be in with a chance too.

Halfway through the third, I raise my glass to him across the room: *Yep, I reckon I'm skunked.* Enough to have a dance with you.

*

Some time, I don't know what time the next morning, it happens. Something breaks open inside me, in the kitchen as I'm bolting the chocolate for breakfast, and I sit at the table, with my headache and sore throat from yacking above the music, and I raise the case off my Good Companion.

I'm still wiping tears from my eyes, laughing blarney tears, from last night, Slick Mick recounting the time my mother hit him across the head with a bag of onions in the street for selling her fake Solvol soap during the Depression that took the enamel off the sink never mind the skin of her hands, when the words come, just pop into my head.

I roll a sheet of paper in round the barrel and I type: *She looked out from the cliff top at the end of Arcadia and wished she could fly.*

It's so quiet after the full stop I can hear the sea crashing into Gordon Bay.

And then it begins to pour out of me, out through the wound in me. I punch and punch the words down, letting them tear out of my grief, my anger, my powerlessness. I don't know what it is I am doing, apart from … telling my truth. Because I must. Through these bursts of words. My words. And it feels like I'm flying.

Because I am.

I am the sun, she told the sea, flying far, far across you to kiss his shoulder and turn his skin the colour of the land. My country.

Our country. In this house, love trees growing together, in the desert by the sea, fishing on the rocks under the island, his hand moving over the golden honeycomb sandstone, moving over me.

I am the earth, she told the sea. We are the earth, the sun, the moon and the stars, exploding across the sky, across the universe, to be beaten into these pages as words shouting out of my core, pages that will be swept up in the wind and spun into dreams by a thousand steely winged gulls who will take them to him, protect him, wherever he is, and bring him back to me.

In ten million tiny glass pearls of truth, fragile and indestructible, bring him back to me. I will write and write and write for him, for our lives. I will write and shout for him across all land and sea and I will not sleep. I will write and call and call and call until I am awake inside this dream. Until he is here with me.

And I do. Turn the paper over. I stay inside this dream all day and into the night, and just when I think I might put some baked beans on the stove, I hear a long, lonely *boom* noise followed by a *pop pop popping* that makes me get up and look out the back door. A searchlight beam sweeps across the sky a few times, from the direction of town, and although it's probably just some sort of military exercise, setting the dogs off, a thousand woofs and yaps, I let myself imagine it's the Japanese tonight. They've come – they're bombing the Sydney Harbour Bridge and picking their way across the Eastern Suburbs to Coogee, and I'll be here to meet them.

I let the anger roar through me and out of me, roar onto page after page, all the way into the morning, when I run out of paper and have to go all the way up to the stationers at the Spot and empty my purse of coupons to get some more. Cheap and nasty typewriting paper, too. Rationing, for everything: hate the Japs some more.

When I get back, the telephone is ringing, ringing, ringing. I look at it: how many times did I stand here talking to Gordon, twirling a lock of my hair, or watching this phone in its little recess in the hall, waiting for it to ring? I don't want to pick it up now; I don't want to hear it's not him. But whoever it is, they're persistent. Pick it up.

'Oh Bernadette, I thought you'd never answer!'

It's Mrs Lockhart. 'What's wrong?' I ask her; she sounds a bit frantic.

'Are you all right there, dear?'

'Yes,' apart from being a madwoman, caught up inside this strange dream. 'Why?'

She says: 'The Japanese submarines, in the harbour–'

'What?' The chill roars straight into my bones. 'That *was* them?'

'Is everything all right, dear?'

No. 'Yes, I've just been up to the Spot.' Just another day out there, it seemed. 'What's happened?'

'Mina Carlton's just telephoned me, she didn't have your number there–'

'What? What's happened?'

'Her sister-in-law, Gilly Cruickshanks, she's over at Point Piper, and she's said they came right in and blew up a ferry, little submarines. They fired some shells over and one hit a corner shop at Rose Bay, but none of them exploded, although some poor fellow broke his ankle falling down the stairs with the fright of it. But you're all right, that's the main thing. You are all right, aren't you, dear?'

No. My fist balls: come here and fight me, you creeps. But I say to Mrs Lockhart: 'Yes, I'm all right. Is the CWA meeting cancelled, though?'

'Oh no, dear,' Mrs Lockhart says emphatically. 'Take more than a couple of submarines to put the girls off. Anyway, Mina said they couldn't hit a warship at Woolloomooloo, and that's a fact. Now, you telephone if you need to, and keep those curtains drawn in case they get their eye in. Please.'

'I will.'

'Bye bye now, darling.'

'Bye bye.'

I go back to the kitchen, but I don't sit down right away. Submarines, sneaky little submarines, creeping like slimy eels through the depths of the harbour in the night. I want to blow them up, but instead I take Mum's good Noritake tea service out of the dresser and take it out the back and smash it to pieces. And then I write about that.

I smash it into the keys until Colin knocks on the door in the evening to tell me his leave has been cut short. I let him hold me too long on the doorstep of Arcadia; I let him kiss me, and I kiss him back, kissing Gordon. That's awful, but that's what I do. I pretend he's my Rock, though he smells of Turf cigarettes. I tell him: 'Come back in one piece and I might give you another one.'

'See you, Bernie.' The look in his eyes calls me cruel. I am.

'Bye bye.'

Then I sit back down and write about that. I write about kissing Gordon. For days. The Japs don't return for another go and I keep writing about kissing as if that is going to keep them away. There were twenty-one Navy boys on that ferry they blew up. All gone. I write until I find I've written fifty-three pages. That's almost half a six-penny. But this isn't any six-penny. I've got no idea what this is.

I'm not altogether certain of the date, either. So I turn on the wireless, for the first time since I left Hay, just as the beeps go for three o'clock. '*Good afternoon, boys and girls. Today is the fourteenth of June, 1942, and welcome to the Children's Hour.*' I've written fifteen days away. And I'm suddenly very tired; it's the CWA meeting tomorrow and I'd better get some sleep. I've slept of course, but only inside the dream, a restless, feathery sleep. Now I curl up on the sofa, let the soothing wireless man tell me a story. It's the adventures of Snugglepot and Cuddlepie today, the little gumnut babies setting out in search of humans ... cicadas singing through the hot, hot night, drifting out through the bush ... Where are those terrible humans?

*

I'm running late, already nine o'clock, running up George Street, missed a tram, coming up to the corner of Goulburn Street, when I wonder if I should send my pages of madwoman dreaming to Wonder Publications, ten doors up that way. Don't be a dill: the only person who might be interested in what you've done is the censor. Get on the next tram and jump off at Broadway, hurtle into the conference as the great flock of matching hats and gloves is about to sit down to business.

Mrs Carlton catches me from behind as Mrs Wassell waves to me from a table at the rear. 'I thought you'd never show up, Bernadette – here, quickly.' A uniform is thrust into my hands, olive drab, just my colour, *blawch*, and five minutes later I'm on the stage, the flash bulb is going off in my face and I'm smiling for Australia. For the Australian Women's Land Army, and very pleased about it too.

My mind, though – it's back at the kitchen table, with my heart. My dream: corellas swirling through the leaves of my vanilla love trees, bursting out of my soul. It's all I want to do. The only place I want to be.

GORDON

'So, you'll be applying to come to California with us, won't you, Brock?' Charlie Sherbel comes up behind me in the canteen queue. He's more excited than usual, because in his mind he left sometime yesterday. Who wouldn't want to go to Berkeley University to study atomic energy with the United States government paying your way? Me, probably.

I say: 'I don't know, Charlie.' I want a practical application for revenge, but I don't think I'll find it in a laboratory. I'd go over there and look at the cyclotron particle accelerator and go, geez isn't that amazing. Smashing an atom. How about that. And then I'd want to get outside and use it. But how are they going to use this energy? This destructive potentiality? A couple of the chemists here are convinced that the radioactivity will be dispersed over land to make the soil infertile. Charlie is just as convinced it's going to be made into a super-incendiary bomb. But it could really be a death-ray gun for all anyone knows. I don't think I can sit and do lab work, probably recording endless data on U-235 extraction, without knowing what it's for. This is why I'm a geologist and not a physicist. I am also a bit ragged. I still can't sleep properly. I wake up in the night running along the back of the plantation and I can't get back to sleep. Caught up in the canes. I need to get going with something. But I don't know what. Go and get rejected by the army again.

'What can I get you, then?' the lady behind the counter says, and I'm thinking I want one of those death-ray guns, while Charlie answers for me: 'Egg and lettuce, thanks.' He looks at me: 'Two?' That'll do. He takes the tray. 'Professor Oliphant was obviously impressed by your question on uranium at the lecture yesterday – I think your application would be successful.'

That's flattering of Charlie to think so. Professor Marcus Oliphant is physics royalty, lately famous for giving the Luftwaffe a quilting at the Battle of Britain with short-wave radiolocation. He's from Adelaide originally and he's home for the next few months to advise the CSIR and to poach scientists for the atomic project. We had to sign a secrecy document just to attend the lecture, during which I'd asked if the energy given off as uranium breaks down is in direct relation to the heaviness of its nine-two proton-packed nucleus, as in $E=mc^2$, which is pretty obvious really, at least to anyone under the age of fifty. After that, the professor talked a bit about a new synthetic element called plutonium, that's even more unstable than U-235, went on and on about the possible peace-time applications of the energy, while I stared out the window, wondering if I should take up another position that has actually been offered to me: field geo for a national bauxite survey. It'd be just as relevant to the war effort, and probably of greater national interest, the idea being for Australia to develop its own aluminium industry, instead of importing from the US. It'd be good to make our own aeroplanes out of our own metals, among many other things, but the American Aluminium Company, which has a monopoly on our imports, is stalling that project by not sharing their plant technology with us. A racket that sounds familiar.

I say to Charlie: 'I'll think about it.' A lot to think about, when you're having trouble concentrating on anything at all. I look at the egg and lettuce as we sit down. I don't want an egg and lettuce sandwich.

Charlie bites into his and says around a mouthful: 'I've heard a rumour, won't say where from, that Oliphant's been in the ear of the PM about uranium exploration here – Flinders Ranges. That'd be more up your street, wouldn't it?'

It would. Although I haven't been there myself, I know there's plenty of uranium in those ranges, in South Australia, old workings mined for medicinal radium, till the company went bust. I could pick uranium up off the ground there and personally deliver it to California to make death-ray guns. I'm not interested in rumours, though. A strange sensation shoots through me, some weird electric pulse. I've got to get up and get moving – right now.

'You want a hit of tennis this afternoon?' Charlie asks me.

'Not this arvo, no. No thanks, mate.' I get up. I don't need Charlie to thrash me at tennis today; don't need to be reminded of what a piece of bullshit my hand is.

'You all right?'

'Yeah.' No. No, I don't think I am. My mouth has gone dry, like I have been running, running for my life. Don't know what's going on here. I say: 'See you later.'

I walk out of the building and see Charlie's bicycle, standing against a tree. I could knock it off it and just ride. Ride into the gum forest of Black Mountain. Don't. Walk towards the town instead, try to clear my head. Calm down. Find my equilibrium. Johno laughs. I should see about getting my hand fixed, shouldn't I. To do what, Brockie? So that I can go back to that spot, that exact spot behind the plantation, and have a proper go. I want to kill the mongrel. I'm not going to find him in Canberra, though, am I. There's nothing at all going on in Canberra. It's lunchtime, on a Wednesday, in the springtime. Not a soul to see. I could walk across the invisible, artificial water of the non-existent lake to Parliament House unobserved, to ask the Prime Minister myself: send me to the Flinders Ranges. And leave me there, please. My mind is demonstrating some kind of fission. Splitting apart.

I'm tired; keep walking. I've been tired for three years. I've had it. I need a good sleep. A solid sleep. Leave the Japs to our eighteen-year-old farmhands at Kokoda. They don't have a choice – they've been conscripted. I'm choosing to go to Ainslie. To my house. I'm going to walk the five miles to sleep. How could anyone not sleep in Ainslie? Empty streets. Two lines of brick boxes and mowed lawns and polished sedans, each one with an identical carport. If you ever do see another person, they don't say hello. They don't look at you. This isn't a town. I don't know what this alien place is. Even the birds here, little blue swallows that fly around the bottlebrushes, don't talk to you. How can anyone live here? I've lived here for almost six months, going into the CSIR every day, a spare wheel analysing the mineral composition of dirt samples for the Soils Department to see that, yes, unsurprisingly we've got a lot salt going on there. And when I'm not doing that, I'm remembering I've never been that interested in physics. That's cracked.

I've got to get out of Canberra.

I go into the house and switch on the wireless, out of habit, just for a voice.

'The labour crisis is continuing throughout rural industry. In particular, shearers are in low supply in the North and Central Western districts, as well as the Riverina. Despite the severe drought conditions ...'

Shearing.

That's it. Why hasn't this occurred to me before? That's what I have to do. There is no other sleep like the one you get shearing. Sort myself out in the sheds. Man against sheep. At home. I want to go home. I have to get home. Because that's where I am. Back before I ever thought to kill anyone.

I have to go home to find Dad. I have to know what happened to him. That will sort me out, more than anything.

Five minutes, I've packed up my swag and I'm walking up Northbourne Avenue, the road out, waiting for a ride up the Paddock.

*

The death rays might have got here before me, the country is that dry. I've just got off the back of a ute on Nymagee Street, and I'm crossing to the Court House to find Jim, when I hear: 'Gordon! Gordon! Is that you?'

It's Mrs Wells, waving and running out of the greengrocers behind me. She stands in front of me, looking me over. Looking all over my face. She doesn't know what to say next. There's something sad in her eyes, and I'm sure by it already that Dad's not here. I know he's gone. I need to know where.

'Oh Gordie, darling heart, look at you. Is it really you?' she says, as if I'm five years old. She's puts her shopping on the ground, then has to stop herself from getting her hankie out to clean my face. She is such a good woman. Looking after me when I was little. Looking after Dad.

I tell her: 'Yeah, it's me.'

She's nearly crying in the street. 'We've all been so worried about you. But look at you.' She touches my arm to see that I'm real and decides: 'You look all right. Are you?'

No. If I was five, I'd run up to you crying. I'd go and hide round the back of your skirt.

'I'm all right,' I tell her. 'I've come home looking for work.'

'Oh? What, shearing?'

'Yeah.'

She gives me a frown: *rubbish*.

So I say: 'I'm in between other work.'

'Oh, is that right.'

'Gunner!' That's Jim, head out the door of the pub, shouting over the road. 'What are you doing here?'

'Looking for work.'

'Well, aren't you a sight,' he says. 'You don't want to get yourself up to Yarranbulla this arvo, do you?'

'Not this arvo. I want to get home for a spell first.' I'm that tired now, I don't know how it is I'm even standing. I have to get home. I have to know what's happened to Dad.

'Right,' Jim says, scratching his head under his hat.

'Anyone going up that way?' I ask him.

'Ah Gordie,' he says. He looks like he's going to come over for a word, but he changes his mind. 'Hang on.' Goes back into the pub for a word in there, and in a second his head is out the door again. 'You can take Billy,' he says. 'The black mare round the stable. Bring her back for tea, yeah?'

'Yeah.'

Billy is up for it and she picks my purpose straight off. My heart goes nineteen to the dozen with hers the whole way, and then, passing the first of the fence posts, I see what I think looks like Dad's ute out the front of the house. Am I imagining that?

No, I'm not.

It is Dad's ute.

I have never been more happy to be wrong. This was a good decision, not so cracked after all. Dad's home. Billy's over the fence and I'm across the verandah yelling out: 'Dad!'

But there's no reply. No Tess barking, either. I push the door open and there's no sign he's been here at all. Only a shingleback lizard under the tank. I go round to the ute and look at it. I think I see what's happened. Someone's found the ute and brought it home, probably by Jim. Not for Dad, but for me. Where did they find it? Where did they find him? Brewarrina, Tibooburra? How long ago? The cans of petrol on the back are still full, as if he didn't get further than the back fence. Maybe he didn't.

I go back inside. The mail I left there three years ago is still on the table under the lamp, with a couple of extras brought in, probably by Mrs Wells. There's my Christmas card to him from Rabaul, and two more newsletters from the AWU before someone's told them Dad's not union any more. And there's a small package for me. I open it. It's my university medal, with a letter I don't read. I close the lid and put it in the dresser drawer, where I pocket the keys to the ute and grab my rifle.

I look at Dad's, alone by the door now. How could no one tell me this? Dad's dead and no one can mention it. I know why that might be, because it was his decision to walk off for good, and it's not as though that possibility hasn't crossed my mind a thousand times – this morning. But no one telling me? Bullshitting that he'd gone off for work. What, hoping I wouldn't notice given enough time passing? If I was angry before, I don't know what the state of me is now.

I grab my swag off Billy's back and chuck it in the ute. For a second I think it's wrong to leave her here, one of Jim's good horses, before I think: stuff that, stuff Jim. I unbridle her and hope she finds a break in the fencing before he comes looking for her.

I start up the engine and put my foot down. What I wouldn't give to hear Dad getting into me for it now: *You'll break a flaming axle one day, kid.* I put my foot down further even though this road is cracked up to shit. I don't want to hear myself think above the engine. I don't want to think any more. Think anything.

I drive straight through town. I can't stop here any more. But where can I go? West, I decide without thinking. Turn right onto the Barrier, the stock road heading out to the top of the Paddock, out to Wilcannia. I don't know anyone up there, but I know there will be work: shooting sheep if not shearing them. As I drive, there's only dust, behind me and ahead. No little purple flowers by the road today. Not even an emu to watch me leave.

Sixty miles on, coming up to Cobar, I hear myself laughing: Wilcannia? Shearing? I couldn't handle the shears over a two-hour run, let alone a whole day. My hand won't do it. I could shoot one sheep every two hours. I could shoot myself. Or I could just keep on driving. Keep driving till I stop. Drive to Ayres Rock. Drive to Perth and then drive into the sea.

BERNIE

I look across the river, mystified and frustrated that Dad never thought to teach me a thing about mechanics. The McDoughals' irrigation pump has gone on strike. There's no blockage that we could hear in tapping the pipe up from the river, so it must be in the mechanism – centrifugal, apparently. Fancy that.

'Damn and blast you!' Mrs McDoughal kicks the motor, and my hand flies to my mouth. Mrs McDoughal just swore.

'Bernadette!' Now here's Mrs Lockhart charging down the row as if I might be responsible. 'Bernadette Cooper!' Oh dear. That tone implies: *Stop what you're doing right now and look at me, young lady.* One to make you stand up and open your mouth to say it wasn't me who did it.

'What?' I squint into the sun.

'What?' she repeats, opening and then closing her mouth, words momentarily suspended.

'Yes, what. Is it?' Oh no, what could I have possibly done?

'That thing,' she points behind her. 'That thing you've been typing at since you got home from Sydney. I read it.'

'You what!' I shout. 'You did not read it. That's private!' Oh Hughie, my hand flies to my mouth again, for what's in that *thing*, that pile of dreams. Me. Gordon. Kissing. All manner of other things that are very, very *private*. 'No, you did *not*.'

'I did,' she says, thoroughly unapologetic. 'And it's quite the most astonishing thing I've ever read. Oh darling, I've spent the day in floods with it. Floods and floods. Couldn't put it down. I've never read anything like it. I thought you were writing a romance, that adventure about the girl pilot, but it's …'

'What is it?' says Mrs McDoughal, looking from me and back to Mrs Lockhart.

'Well, Alice, it's a … well, I don't quite know what you'd call it,' she says, and she searches the coolabah above us for the words. 'A love story, I suppose you might say – a *true* love story. Quite the loveliest ever written. It's swept me right up and away.'

'You've written a love story? Oh, aren't you clever.' Mrs McDoughal leaves off her despair at not getting the water up to the tomatoes and claps her hands together. 'You kept that light under a bushel, didn't you?'

Doesn't Hughie know it. I'm lit up fuchsia with all bells ringing at the thought of Mrs McDoughal reading a word. I stand there gawking, and as I do the pump splutters back to life, giving me a face full of diesel smoke.

I shout above it, at Mrs Lockhart: 'It's not even finished. It doesn't have an ending.' In fact, I don't think it even has something that might be considered a story.

'Doesn't want one, my dear,' she shouts back. 'It's brilliant. Perfectly brilliant. Just as it is.'

GORDON

I start to run out of petrol in the desert sometime late on Saturday afternoon. It's only a few miles outside Broken Hill, and that's about right, I reckon. I've calmed down a fair bit. Probably because I slept last night. Just me and the stars. Properly alone. I slept like a dead man. I'm going to find a phone in town, call the CSIR, tell them I'm going to take that bauxite survey job, with the Geo's Office. I'm just not made for working indoors, am I. I'll phone Charlie, too, and explain. Apologise. After I've found a pub, though. First, I'm going to get more crappered than is good for me.

The first pub I find is a place called the Pig & Whistle, and inside there's about a hundred miners just come in off shift and going hard. It's a tight squeeze. Suits me. They can hold me up in a minute. I haven't had a beer in … since we ran out in Rabaul.

I'm just about to catch the barman when I hear behind me: 'Oi! Oi! Dozy! Dozy Brock.' I think it's a trick of perception again, from thinking about Rabaul just now. But I see a hand in the air in the middle of the mob.

It's Errol. Errol Flynn. Kiwi surveyor and part-time professional rescuer of women and idiots.

'Jesus. Mate.' He smacks me across the shoulder. 'I've been looking for you. Bloody hard to find and then you turn up out here? You wouldn't read about that. Jesus. Look at you. Looking a bit less shit than the last time I saw you.'

'Thanks,' I say, and that wound-up feeling I've been carrying around all this time just goes. The relief at seeing him, it's like a keg's worth. My face has got shocked into smiling. I ask him: 'Why were you looking for me?'

He says: 'I've still got your swag, haven't I, and that bloody camp oven with the air vents. I want to get rid of it, ay.' He's joking, and not joking, and I might need holding up from that. He changes the subject: 'What are you doing here anyway?'

'Nothing. About to take a bauxite job.' I suppose. Maybe. Am I? Change the subject: 'What are you doing?'

'Underground surveys, silver and zinc, boring as a box of nails. About to take a uranium job, though. Should be some fun. State secret.' He taps his nose and winks like a clown. 'Dunno why but – it's only uranium.'

'Bullshit.'

'No. But hey, they're having difficulty finding a field geo out of Adelaide for it – the location is a bit remote. You wouldn't want to come out with me, would you?'

I laugh: fully, in a good way. Back in myself. At last. 'Would I? Course I flaming would.'

There might be no such thing as fate. Life is just a series of random events and the degrees of insanity caused by them. But this is exactly where I'm meant to be. Isn't it.

BERNIE

'Emma, oh Emma, that's such good, good news,' I hear Mrs Lockhart shriek into the phone. 'Thank you so much for thinking to telephone me with it. How *is* he?'

I stop what I'm doing to eavesdrop harder. I'm tying the string bow on my pages of dreams, going to give it to Mrs Zoc to read before I give in to Mrs Lockhart's insistence that I send it off for some stranger to appraise the most intimate details of my longing. I think she's speaking to Emma Wells, of Nyngan. Do I dare to hope he heard me calling him and has responded accordingly? Course I do. I am flung somewhere between a great vault of joy and a collapse into kneeless relief.

But Mrs Lockhart's happy squawking has dropped away. 'Hm … Mm … Oh … No. Not at all … Oh dear … Oh no … Oh our poor darling boy.'

What's wrong with him? Something awful. I find my knees under the dressing table and race across the hall into the sitting room. Mrs Lockhart's eyes are filled with concern as she looks at me, waves for me to sit by her. I know they're talking about Gordon. She says into the phone: 'Yes dear, of course – no, none of us can afford it these days, believe me, but you call again and have the charge reversed if any other news come to light, don't hesitate. Please … Yes, dear. Bye bye now. Oh yes, there was a reasonable turnout at Wagga … Ha! … Love to Kathy and hers … You too, dear. Bye bye.'

My heart won't take another beat till she tells me: 'Yes, that was the news we've been waiting for. Our Gordon is home, and very much alive. But he's not well, not in a good way at all. Taken his father's old utility and gone off, sped off through town like a maniac. Emma doesn't know where. Last word, he was looking for work shearing, so she's tried everyone she can think of, put the word out to all the stations, the length and breadth, but no one's seen him since.'

The first breath I take is a sharp one: you've come home and you haven't let us know. How damn blooping dare you, Gordon. Even if he was cross at not getting a letter from me, thinking I'd called it off; even if he went round to Arcadia and found no one there and thought we'd all abandoned him – oh! Not letting anyone know – for *all* this time. That's not sulking for Australia. That's cruel and terrible. The second breath I take is a painful, angry one: something cruel and terrible has happened to him. I know it has.

I go back to my pile of dreams on the dressing table and finish tying the bow. Don't think I need a second opinion from Mrs Zoc any longer. I'll match my Rock for maniac: I sit down and type a letter to Wonder Publications.

*

Don't hear anything from either of them. Through summer's tomatoes and the autumn's beans, there's a rasp in the rhythm of the irrigation pump as she takes in more and more Murrumbidgee mud: *Let him go.*

Mitch comes home for Easter on the Good Friday and finds me in the water, checking to see when we'll run out of the stuff here at Riverbend.

'Hey,' he waves his hat at me, 'don't you go out beyond the pump line there.' Making fun of his mum's perennial warning.

I smile back, sort of, and look out at the danger: the snags. They're so exposed now you could almost walk across from bank to bank on them.

When I turn back to Mitchell, he's taken his shirt off, so that I have to look away again.

He says: 'Mind if I join you.' Not asking.

'Just getting out,' I say, and lie: 'Getting a bit cool.'

Don't look at him as I go to pick up my towel. Then do: he is tea-stain gold all over his chest too. He says as I pass him: 'You can't keep up this worry forever. Maybe he doesn't want to be found.'

That makes me prickle all over with some kind of chill. Doesn't want to be found? Just like his poor father, perhaps? Who knows what happened to him? History repeating bleeding misery. I don't say that, though. I snap: 'You don't know anything about it. Do you.' Neither of us do.

'No,' he says, embarrassed and I don't care. 'I just mean–'

'Bernadette!' Mrs Lockhart calls across the yard. 'Telephone!'

And I run back to the house, barefoot over the bindies, telling Mitch, telling Hughie: *See, it's him now.* Who else would telephone on a Good Friday? It must be Gordon.

'It's the publisher fellow – Mr Jacobs.' Mrs Lockhart is sparkling with anticipation, pushing me down the hall.

'Oh.' I don't want to speak to any publisher fellow now; not until I've recovered my enthusiasm from somewhere in this Murrumbidgee murk. But I pick up the phone. 'Hello, Bernadette Cooper speaking.'

'Ah, yes, good afternoon, Miss Cooper. It's Abe Jacobs from Wonder Publications here. Now, yes, your novel. My apologies that it's taken so long to get back to you, but ah, now that I have you on the line …' His voice sounds different from the man I spoke to all that time ago, not so gruff. But he is just as impatient: 'I'd like to make you an offer.'

'What?' Somewhere I am happy at this news, stunned and hurling myself round the sitting room with excitement, but for the most part my heart is squeezing around it as a failure.

'I said I'd like to make you an offer. An advance of fifty pounds – we can go through the details later. Is that attractive to you?'

Fifty pounds; I don't know what that means at the moment. But I say: 'I suppose so.'

'Good, good. I'll have the contract drawn up and mailed to you for your consideration. You'll see on it that the publisher will appear as Myrtle Books Pty Ltd – that's our literary imprint.

Our company has expanded a good deal since we last spoke.' He's pleased with himself, and then kind and warm. 'One of the only advantages of this terrible war, I'm afraid, all the tariffs and embargoes on American books, the British paper shortages … It's a good time for Australian literature. But tell me, it wasn't clear from your letter, will you be writing under the name of Monica Brockley or Bernadette Cooper, or … ?'

'Um …' The mud drags at my soul. How thrilled would Mum and Dad be if they were here? *Literature* … Mum wouldn't know what that meant, and Dad and I would have fun with her, not knowing what it meant either. I wouldn't know literature if it bit me on the nose in good light. I tell this Mr Jacobs: 'Bernie. My name is Bernie Cooper.'

'Ah! Very good – nicely ambiguous. Bernie Cooper it is. And have you thought of a title for the novel?'

'No. I …' can't speak.

'Never mind, Miss Cooper. That can be discussed later. It's a little overwhelming, mm?'

'Mm.'

*

It almost rains in the first week of September, two fat drops, and my page proofs come in the mail. Page proofs for a novel called *Too Much To Lose*, a title Mr Jacobs has chosen to reflect our collective yearning for victory, particularly amongst the women he's gambled on buying it. Mr Jacobs has also taken a sharp red pencil to the wilder flights of my imagination and my language, and now all that's left to do is decide on whether to give the elusive hero a name other than Gordon or change it to the more enigmatic G, before I send these dreams back to Sydney to be printed. In January.

January 1944. I can't believe it's going to be 1944 in January. How did that happen? It's all unreal.

But I can decide upon G. Enigmatic and impossibly distant, he possibly long ago ended our love story going off into the sunset with someone else. Most recent last news: someone who knows someone who knows Mitchell ran into Gordon in Broken Hill, said they'd heard he might have gone off to New Zealand with some government posting. He seemed well and happy enough, they said. How can he possibly be happy without me? Because he's moved along with his life, hasn't he.

Time for me to do the same. I run my finger over the title again: *Too Much To Lose*. At least I have this, don't I? I'm about to become a published author. I will be excited about it. Eventually. One thousand copies with my name on the cover. In January. Only four months off, printing manpower willing. And it's going to be a little six-penny after all. But a posh one, just like a Penguin, only Australian. Antipodean as all genuine penguins are, said Mr Jacobs, and printed on the nastiest sheet newsprint available. Mr Jacobs said he needs to make a penny off me while he can – before Angus & Robertson pinch me off him. Wowee. But all I can seem to see is one thousand pairs of little newsprint wings beating out across the country: *Rock, please. You can't end it here.*

What am I going to do between here and January to distract myself from the limitless impossibilities? There's no farm work at the moment to lose myself in, not now that the authorities have finally seen the sense in releasing the Italian boys to do it: Mitch has had a couple fencing for him recently, and Mrs McDoughal's got three of them planting out the toms now, three dreamy-eyed slaves, one of whom is doing his Valentino best to woo her niece Chrissy and give the bush telegraph a scandal to send flying up and down the Paddock. Tongues long enough to lick their own toes out here – for a handsome foreigner. Could well be what Mrs Lockhart is nattering about right this moment: she's up with her sister Ivy in Wilcannia, for a few weeks, or so. With the emphasis on *so*. Ivy's not been well, with headaches and dizzy spells. Leaving me on my own at Riverbend, lonely with the plain old blues.

I should lose myself to wondering what sort of a story I might write next. Mr Jacobs has asked, twice, and I don't have a clue. Because I'm not really a writer, am I. Fluked this one. Fooled you all. I wander into the little sunroom between the back verandah and Mrs Lockhart's bedroom, to pinch one of her magazines there; could I write for one of them? Write a silly serial? A proper romance. Flick open the one on top of the pile that tells me: *Less*

Butter and Sugar – it's doing your family the world of good. The blessings of rationing. Let's count them: be grateful I have no children moaning that they want butter on their sandwiches and sugar on their porridge. Our baby, if it had lived to become one, would be around about turning three now. That hurt spears into me, has me reaching for my jasper B and Mum's ring, and then just as quickly tells me it's time I took them out of my pocket, took the comb from my hair too. Put all charms away, in my box of precious things. Past things. Get on with the future. Whatever it brings.

*

'Bernadetta!' Mrs Zoc is running across the yard and up to gate to meet me. 'What did I say, bella! What did I say!'

Her smile just about knocks me over, before she does. Italy has capitulated and the camp is in such a riot that Ken has a paper party hat on, a stripy one, all the guards do, and not just because Major Payne is not around to put the kybosh on a celebration. Fifty Italian women and attendant children intent on kicking up their heels: I'd like to see any man have a go at stopping them from doing so. They're just about the only families here at the moment, too, apart from a handful of genuine bona fide Nazi mothers who don't join in anything, so the guards are kicking up their heels a bit too.

I hug Mrs Zoc back. 'Tell me, what did you say?' Although I remember her prophecy exactly.

She says: 'Aha! I said to you we would be free the next spring, and it is the next spring! I know these things, bella, I know.'

'Aha.' I laugh. Yes, Mrs Zoc, you really are a fortune teller.

'Aha,' she shakes her finger at my doubt. 'I tell you we will be free. I tell you that Italia surrenders when the Allies free Sicilia. I tell you that you will write the book about love for the Wonder people. This all has happened. Now Gordon will come home too.'

'Gordon is home,' I remind her. Wacky-doodle-do.

'Home to *you*,' she throws her hands in the air. 'It is over! The war is over!' She stamps her feet in the dust and dances a circle around one foot, like a compass. She's no elderly woman of sixty in widow's black crepe, she's the girl who made the boys of Palermo faint. I watch her, somehow liberated too. Three years she got for not throwing out her husband's old anarchist literature, and for them signing up as members of the Fascist party to avoid being shot on the way out of Italy. And today, as she completes her compass circle, she shouts: 'I love Australia! I love this country!'

She holds no regret, no bad feeling. She's just so happy it's over. Let it go.

The war is over here in this little quarter of this little town of Hay. Ken is dancing around inside a circle of ladies. Their men are working in our fields; some of them out in citrus orchards owned by Italians who came out after the last war to dig the irrigation channels here. One of the children runs up to me with a bowl full of almond shortbread – where did they get the butter rations for them? Some kindness from someone, somewhere here. For a moment my whole world is filled with good people. Our only enemies, the Nazi men and the Japs, are separated from the rest these days, behind bars in the old gaol on Church Street, and I hope their new world order is causing them to tear each other apart in there. But here, there is peace. Mr Curtin's war for peace is won. He won his election last month in a landslide, because he calls ladies women and reckons that their eighteen-year-old sons are old enough to vote if they're old enough to kill. To win this peace. It's what everyone wants: the happy ending.

Piccolo rubs my ankle and meows as Mrs Zoc grabs my arm. 'Ahhhhh, but bella, I hope my bad boys are not allowed to go back to Queensland too soon, ha?'

Manny, Tony and Arthur, her mango gangsters. 'Do you think they will murder that neighbour?' Whatever his name was, the rival farmer who slandered them.

'Noooo. I don't really think so. Antonio has promised me again in his last letter that they will only poison the trees.' I'm not sure if she's joking or not. She's not; she adds: 'They have a friend now from Tatura camp, who will buy that land when the sale is forced. This friend, he wants to grow the peppers there anyway.'

There's a tidy revenge.

'Besides this,' Mrs Zoc throws her hands in the air again, 'they promise me that they will do nothing to make me fail to become Australian. I made a promise between me and God that I would become Australian when the war is over. So, now it is over!' She stamps her foot. 'I will be Australiana!'

She's delirious. Contagiously. Australiana. I could take flight again any second.

But we are still at war, I remind myself. Keep both feet on the ground. Colin is still in New Guinea somewhere, as hundreds of thousands of our boys are. There is wire still strung along our beaches, guns on our jetties, arsenals hidden all through our hills, and you can't even have a cup of tea without considering its weight in coupons. But for the first time, I will dare a prophecy of my own. For the first time, I believe we will win this peace. We might not be many, but we are too vast to take. Too vast in spirit.

*

Ken has never moved paper along the line faster, to get the Italian families out of here. Not two days later I'm on the platform seeing off Mrs Zoc, and Piccolo in his cage, and I'm promising: 'I'll come home for Christmas, to Arcadia, to spend it with you.'

She holds my face in her hands. 'You can come home, or not come home for Christmas, bella. It does not matter. Don't you worry about me. Everything is good now. You will see. You will see.' The fires of Sicilia bright in her dark eyes assure me. 'He will come for you now. Soon.'

No, he won't.

But it's all right, isn't it, Odds, I ask her where she's waiting under the vanilla gums by the station. She snorts and stamps her foot, but not because she cares. She's keen to get home. I wonder if Pete might be there, but I don't wonder too much. I've just caught a glimpse of what I will write about next, a new story, something about things ending … Finding yourself at the end of the line after Grong Grong, Narrandera, Willbriggie and The Middle of Nowhere. Maybe. Lines popping into my head all over the place, not easy to grasp and keep, apart from one going round and round all the way home to beat of Odds's trot: *The river laughed and I turned around to see it was laughing at me.*

Till I see Mitch waiting on the front verandah for me.

He's looking grim, hard-faced; demanding: 'Where've you been, Dette?'

'Seeing Mrs Zoc off.' And don't you address me like that.

But he's not interested in the answer anyway. He takes off his hat and rubs his forehead, ashen with worry. 'I need you to come up to Hell with me, I need your help.'

'Why? What's happened?' It must be terrible if you're asking me, asking a girl.

He says: 'Snowy come off his horse yesterday – it's a mess.'

'Oh?' Snowy is one of Mitch's most reliable blow-in rouse-abouts. I'm sure he's a fine man, but don't ask me to look after him, or any mess of that sort; I'm not a nurse, I wouldn't know the first thing, and I am certain that 'mess' means complete and utter gut-wrenching catastrophe.

But before I can suggest I telephone the hospital, Mitch manages to get the rest of his sentences out: 'Yeah. He'll be laid up 'til Christ– Sorry. I've got no one to help me with the lambs coming now. I can't get any other labour, not from anywhere. You'll have to come up with me,' he says through clenched lion jaw, the inference being: *Please, don't make me ask.*

'Of course I'll come,' I tell him. 'Let me pack a bag. Of course I'll help you.'

He says: 'I'll go round next door and let Mrs McDoughal know what's going on.'

He speeds off in the ute as I run into the house, and I'm frantic with concern as I throw things into my suitcase: you poor man. The worry on his face, in the deep lines on his forehead. He's too young for such lines. He's only just turned thirty. Those lambs, you'd think they were his children, and they're not even his best ones.

I have a selfish thought as I clip the case on Good Companion, hoping Mitch won't mind me thumping it: I wonder if I'll be there with him over the summer and I'll have to miss going to Sydney for the party Mr Jacobs is throwing for me at his wife's cafe, the Ginger Jar, for my non-existent love story. I'm so nervous about that party; it's in Kings Cross. Oh so Bohemian. What will people think of me, and my book? I don't want to know.

I'm nervous about being alone with Mitch, too, out there, miles from anywhere. Apart from a pub. That's only ten miles from the homestead, apparently. No phone. No electricity. Where the country is so wild half the stockmen are Aborigines and the brown snakes are plentiful. Where I'll be doing what to help Mitch? Feeding the lambs, I suppose. I don't know.

But my nerves twist and shoot into some kind of thrill in tea-stained glimpses. Alone with Mitch. A new adventure. Can I dare to imagine that? Maybe I'm ready now. Ready to move along.

I take my jasper B out of the pocket of my strides. I look into its pink and caramel stripes and splotches, and I kiss it, for the last time. I place it into my box of precious past things, with Mum's ring, and my hair comb.

Goodbye, Rock.

I love you. Always.

But it's time. It's time to say goodbye.

My lovely one that got away.

GORDON

'Will you have a good look at *that*.' Errol takes the lid off the bedourie and shows me the damper he's invented especially for the day. It's a giant currant bun, but made with quandongs. That looks as good as it smells. 'That *is* Christmas,' he says.

'That is Christmas,' I agree, and I look at the lid by the toe of his boot, in some kind of thanksgiving. Those two bullet holes in it. Somehow Errol has made it seem like all bedouries are made that way. Or should be. It's taken a year, just over, to be able to look at it without wanting to bolt. Errol's not one for a backwards glance, though, or wasting a decent bedourie with air vents. I raise my mug of tea to him: 'Here's to the good life.'

To being alive. Because you're a long time dead.

One of the camels grunts in agreement, and I look behind me, to the sunset on the Flinders Ranges. How lucky am I? Sitting here, under a quandong tree, on Christmas Day, watching this sunset, with a view out to Mount Painter. The summit is glowing like a molten arrowhead. It's taken almost a year to get here too, the wheels of bureaucracy have moved that slow. You wouldn't know there was a war on, except for the amount of time politicians waste on getting universities to make pointless investigations into ridiculous ideas. How many bombs dropped into the vent of Matupi will it take to blow up the Japs at Rabaul? None, you idiots. That'd be about as useful as dropping a lit match into an already raging bushfire. But I still had to spend three months putting it in a report, in want of an actual vulcanologist to do it, while we were waiting for approval for this expedition from the various departments involved – that took eight months, with two forgettable tungsten surveys in between.

Teaching me something about patience. We're here now, and the combined air forces of Australia, New Zealand and the US are getting on with bombing the islands by the usual means, while me, Errol and our guide, Tim Gottlieb, go out and get some uranium, for death rays. Instead of hunting little yellow mongrels in the jungle, I've spent a decent part of this past year studying the little yellow streaks and clouds of old pitchblende samples: I know what I'm looking for. Officially, though, we're diamond prospecting for a company called Pontoon Minerals, a joint venture with the South Australian Government who would like a tourist trail put through up here. Easily believable. Great hiking country. These views ... the colours ...

Tim walks across the postcard of Mount Painter, and I say to him: 'It's no wonder you think the world was created by a giant rainbow snake – look at that.'

'Yeah,' he says, without looking, squatting near me. 'He likes red around here, too. The red of the rocks. You know, my people, the Anyamatana people – that name means the rock people. These ranges are the rock paradise.'

'You're not wrong.' These ranges are a geologist's paradise. A favourite rambling ground of Mawson, as in Mawson of the Antarctic – he'd rather be here than anywhere else on earth. A pilgrimage you have to make at least once in your geological life.

Tim waves a hand at the fire. 'You find the paradise you're after and you gelignite him, ay?'

He laughs, taking a hunk of quandong bun from Errol. I've never met a man like Tim Gottlieb. We met three weeks ago now, just beyond Hawker, a one-pub no-Abos town on the Ghan train line at the foot of the ranges. He said then: *Welcome to my country. My name is Tim Gottlieb. I am an Anyamatana man and I have learned my Bible lessons. The Lord said: Blessed be the meek for they shall inherit the earth, except for what gets leased from the*

Department of Mines. Errol hurt himself laughing – mostly at the look on my face. At a black man, having a go like that. And it's true. He's thirty-six and he'd have seen it a hundred times. We find what we want, mostly copper, and his people get moved off the land so we can blow it up and cart it away. The same will happen if we find the high-grade pitchblende we're after, and mining is viable. Merry Christmas. Not a fair exchange, and there's something about Tim that's got hold of my wanting to do something for Johno. Don't know what, though.

'That why they call him Dozy, Errol?'

'What?'

'Where do you go, when you go quiet like that, ay?' Tim's not having a go at me with the question, I don't think, handing me a brew. 'What are you looking at?'

'I don't know. Nothing.' A bit embarrassed. And not; I tell him: 'I was thinking of a mate I had once. You remind me of him.'

'Good bloke?'

'Yeah.'

'Well, that's all right then.'

I take a mouthful of quandong bun; it's all right too. Tim's kelpie, Fritz, is trying to convince Errol to give him some, wagging his tail, begging. Succeeding. I'm thinking about Johno's Second Law. Chaos and equilibrium. I want to give away the chaos part of this system altogether one day. After this survey, maybe I will. Do something different anyway. What would I do? I don't know. Go and plant saltbush up the Paddock? Someone probably should. It might be natural, but we take more than we give from this land. I want to create more than I destroy ... I should write to Johno's father is what I should do. But I can't, not yet. Just can't.

I look the other away, out to the hills, due west. They're not marked on my map, and we seem to have skirted round them to get here from Leigh Creek colliery, about sixty miles back, where we left Dad's ute in favour of the camels. It's a nice trick of the dusk that these hills are about the same colour as a quandong right now, and I ask Tim: 'The rainbow snake likes blue out that way?'

'I wouldn't know what he likes that way – you don't want to go there.' Tim tosses his dregs at the fire.

I ask him: 'Why?'

He says: 'Bad spirits in that country.' And he's not having us on at all.

'What bad spirits?' Errol asks.

'Can't say,' Tim tells the ground at his feet. 'It's just the law. Go to that country, Akurra will get you, the rainbow snake, he'll catch you, suck out your spirit and leave you there. The whitefella call them Gammon Hills, but no whitefella will go there. I'm not allowed to go there either.' He looks at me: 'You reckon this is blackfella bullshit, don't you?'

'No,' I tell him, and I'm not having him on, either. What you reckon and what you actually know are usually two different things, and I don't question blackfella bullshit as I once might have. I've come to understand that there's usually a logical if not immediately obvious reason behind just about all bullshit and I'm prepared to accept Tim's as gospel. We won't be going out to those hills. At least not with a guide, not unless we'd like to take our chances finding water on our own.

*

We reach the end of our tourist trail just before midday the next day and Tim says, 'See ya's later,' going off with Fritz for water, leaving us to it.

I toss Errol a pick, and he says: 'You're a hard man, Doze – it's a public holiday, and it's lunchtime.' As keen as I am to get into it.

Most of his preliminary work is done now, for the road, and my own is just beginning, on the pitchblende deposits. They're all already mapped out for us, in old diggings that run across an arc of ridges less than three miles long. It's hardly a speck on the surface of the earth but this place used to turn out £12,000 worth of medical radium a month. Before the Belgian Congo monopoly decided no one else could play. Now, every old hole across the free world has been reopened for business, all looking for high-grade, for California. We know there's another party looking at a site somewhere over the border, back near Broken Hill, but we don't know who they are, or exactly where. Nevertheless, the competitor in me takes over: I want to finish first.

We start in the pit nearest our camp, which happens to have the shortest adit of about a hundred and fifty feet, and we're not expecting to find anything today. This hole, called Little Gem on my map, hasn't turned out anything since 1924. But we have to go in them all, thirteen of them; might as well get this Little Gem out of the way. The adit is steep going in, though, a decline inconveniently not indicated in the data. It's quickly pitch-black too, and I think we're going to need more than our two-cell torches to see anything in here. I'm just about to turn back for the carbide lamp when Errol shouts: 'Jesus!'

I watch his light tumble away ahead of me. He's slipped on something, and taken a significant amount of rubble with him by the sound of it.

'Are you right?' Shit. This is not good.

But his light jumps up again. Then bounces around the walls of the adit as it tails down near perpendicular, and he yells up at me: 'Holy bleeding eureka! Brockie, come and look at this.'

I slide down on my arse to see that in his hand he's holding a piece of rock that, even under the two-cell, appears to have not so much a yellow mist as a fat vein in it. A yellow crack of lightning.

'Whoa.'

I scramble back up into the light to check: yes, this is the business. And it was just lying on the floor of this adit, in a mine of historically little output. So said the data. But this is the highest grade uranium I've ever seen. When I go back down I see there's a lot more: looking at us from the granite walls.

After we get five, then six, samples of the same, I say: 'I think we should just get the miners straight in here. Get this to Adelaide now and get it going. Don't you reckon?' There doesn't seem to be a reason to wait.

Errol says: 'Suits me.'

We climb up and out again and Tim's back, already got the billy on, and he says to me: 'You look like you been chased by Akurra. You find what you're looking for in there?'

Errol shows Tim a piece. 'This – see the yellow? That's what we're looking for.'

I look at Errol: *Shut up about it, will you.*

Tim doesn't notice; he's nodding eastwards. 'This colour rock?' Pointing over at an outcrop about a couple of hundred yards away. 'Plenty of this one over there. What you want it for?'

'Medicine,' I tell him.

'Must be powerful medicine,' Tim laughs to himself in a way that says he's accustomed to being lied to.

Guilty I might be, but that's not my concern at the minute. I tell him: 'It is powerful. We need it. And we need to get back to Adelaide now.'

He shrugs and starts packing up the camp he's just laid out, all our bullshit. He picks up Errol's theodolite and dances it up to the camels. 'Come on, we're in a hurry, Betty.' Having a go at me. He probably hates me. I'm tearing over to that outcrop for a quick look, aren't I. It's a flaming open pit of uranium. You can, virtually, pick it straight up off the ground. I take a few more samples and run back to the camels.

'You planning to run to Adelaide, Dozy?' Tim says, laughing again, straight at me.

It's four hundred and twenty miles to Adelaide from here.

*

It's three days on foot to get back to Leigh Creek, back to the ute, and then another couple of hours' rough driving to drop Tim back where we found him, on the Barndioota Road north of Hawker. 'Here'll do, fellas, thank you.'

He gets out. In the middle of this strip of gum forest that sits between the Lake Eyre salt pan and the Strzelecki Desert, the size of Scotland. He says: 'Ask for us at the hotel if youse want me again, ay. I'll come for you.'

He starts walking away, Fritz close at his heel, back up the road we've just come down. Suddenly this doesn't seem right. Dropping him nowhere, asking for him via a pub he can't enter. I lean out the window: 'You don't want a lift home?' Wanting to tell him I'm not like the rest. I'm not just another thief. It's not that simple.

He just waves his hat and keeps walking, doesn't turn around. 'No thanks, Dozy.'

'Don't take it to heart,' Errol says. 'He's probably just protecting his family, from any government man – you know, worried they'll steal the kids.'

'Steal what? Bullshit. Who steals whose kids?'

'The Protection Board, or whatever it is.' Errol looks at me like I've been living in a cave. 'They take the kids, the half-castes, and put them in convent schools and that, civilise them. 'Spose the children would be given an education, but I wouldn't be happy if it was me or mine.'

'No.' I put my foot down. Education, pig's arse. It sounds like just another way of clearing them off to me. The uranium ore in the back of this ute will do the job just as well, and I don't like that. It's not right. Not my concern; but it is. What can I do about it? Don't know. Ignore it for the next five hours' driving.

We get into Adelaide at about half-past three and all I'm set on by then is dumping this bag of ore with the Department of Army. Here that's in an office of the Chemistry Department, with *Doctor WW Rochester* in gold lettering on the door, and a Major Clive Gibbons on the other side of it. I'm pretty sure this bloke doesn't have any scientific qualifications, but whoever he is, he's the one to tell us what we're to do next.

I tell him: 'This is what you're after. It's all over the Mount Painter site. We could get going with the mining of it right away. There's already an existing crushing facility out there and the ore could be brought up by camel train, as it used to be, until the road's graded. There seems no good reason to delay.'

Major Gibbons holds up a hunk of the pitchblende and says to it: 'Yes, well, let's see.'

Let's see if it doesn't make the Geiger-Müller particle detector go mad. Go on, send it round to the Physics Department.

Errol and I stand there, waiting.

But Gibbons just shoos us out the door. 'Yes, well, you can go now. Don't wander too far. I'll be in touch with your further instructions.'

Right. I get a rush of blood at that as we leave the room. There's thousands of kids taking bullets in mud up to their knees for you at this present moment and you say: *I'll be in touch.*

Errol claps his hand down on my shoulder as we head back out into Adelaide's blast-furnace heat. 'Don't know about you, Dozy, but I need a root. Want to come?'

I have to laugh. Errol's got more equilibrium than is natural. But I have to say: 'No thanks, mate, you can have that pleasure to yourself.'

He gives me a worried look, as he always does at my reluctance with this, as if not wanting to visit one of Adelaide's brothels of good repute is beyond his understanding. 'I don't know how you do it,' he shakes his head. 'See you around seven for tea?' And he's off.

Leaving me to not know how I do it either. It's as if that one part of me hasn't woken up, as if the Japs took Bernie's photograph and all my interest with it. Or probably more accurately, Bernie took it herself and chucked it. I'll get over it, eventually, when I meet someone else. Probably not in a brothel.

*

Adelaide in the middle of summer is like Canberra at a hundred and ten degrees. It will strip the will from any man. We've had four unrelenting weeks of it. We've got the miners teed up, as well as an engineer from Roads and a quantity surveyor, and I personally would like to leave for the kinder climate of the ranges, but, at the last minute, we've been told to wait. Not a military holdup, but the South Australian Department of the Interior. We've been waiting these past three days for a journalist and photographer to come from Sydney, to join us for the purposes of publicity for the tourist trail. Good on the Premier for wanting to encourage the nation to spend their holidays and any money they have in his State. You'll find me playing with the particle detector to check if I'm emitting any sign of energy at all.

All the things we could be doing instead, up in the ranges today. Even without the mining. We could be fitting a new belt on the crushers. We could be going on a fossil hunt. We could be *not* in Adelaide. Waiting for a couple of jokers to come down from Sydney.

So, I'm not too happy to start off with when I decide to waste some time going round to the law school to ask a couple of questions about leasing rights and compensation. If we're going to continue to move Aborigines off their land, surely they're entitled to something more in return than sugar and flour and tea on the missions. A farmer wouldn't cop it. This is the modern world. We're not a colonial outpost any more, despite all Adelaide's appearances.

The lady at reception directs me with her best wireless voice to a Professor Todd, and when I find him, he smells like a swaggie after payday. Asking me across his desk: 'Compensation for whom?'

'Um, anyone. But natives in particular.'

'Natives?' He blinks at me as if I just asked after the red Lizard Men of Ergamon. 'There's no right of compensation for natives – they don't own any land.'

'But they live on it,' I say. 'What's the diff–'

'The difference is, natives don't *do* anything with the land.' He sways in his seat, slurring his words over centuries of judicial drunkenness. 'Never have. Never will, my boy. Our British forebears found this continent in the state of terra nullius – that is, the empty land. A land empty of people. Natives might be human, but they are not people in the sense that you and I understand what it means to be a person, a Briton as you or I, part of a greater society or polity. They are not citizens. They don't vote, they don't make or do anything at all that contributes in any meaningful way to the civilised world. You tell me, boy, what's the difference between an Aborigine and a kangaroo?'

A fair bit, I'd say. But I can't say anything. I've just understood how a consortium is stealing an entire continent. It's probably a good thing my will is a bit spare today. Not a person? Johno's not a person. Neither's Tim Gottlieb. This is wrong. But it's the law. I shouldn't have asked.

I say: 'Yeah, thanks.' And walk away, telling the flagstones I'm no flaming Briton. I'm a Scot, with Dad's grandfather come out here via New Zealand, and there is nothing I can do about this terra nullius bullshit, except put a pebble in my shoe for it. Remember it, for another day.

And go to the pub. I haven't had a drink in the daytime since I met up with Errol at that Pig & Whistle in Broken Hill. But I'm going to have a least two this day, and then I'm going to go and sit in a cold bath and stay there until that photographer and journalist turn up. I'm used to the desert heat, I grew up with it, but there's something about the way it bears down on you in Adelaide. It's wrong too.

I walk across the university lawn with extra gravity in both shoes, heading for the Stag Hotel. You wouldn't know there was a war on here either: I'll probably have the veal schnitzel for my lunch. It's just after one, so I'm expecting I'll run into Errol, but he's not in the front bar when I walk in. The barman sees me and nods in the direction of the lounge, indicating he's out there. Probably with a girl. I don't want to meet his latest conquest, not on an empty stomach: they all fall for him, nice girls and prostitutes alike. I don't know where he finds the energy for it at all.

I'm just about to order my first beer, when Errol's head appears at the door of the lounge, looking about – for me. 'Doze!' Waving for me to get over there. He looks a bit excited.

'What?' I go over to him.

'They're here, the people from the *Herald* – just picked them up from the airport. Come on.'

'Oh. Good.' Tell me when I should care.

'Find your happy face, will you?'

I find more than that.

Two seconds later I'm being introduced to the journalist and the photographer from Sydney and being whacked for six.

'Hello. Gordon, isn't it? I'm Glynis Kay, I'll be taking some pictures on the trail. Call me Glyn.'

Glyn. And you're a girl.

For all that I am unimpressed by men who have difficulty shaking the hand of a woman, I'm having difficulty now. I'm thinking: no chance. You are not coming up on that trail with us. Somehow I maintain the wherewithal to recognise that this reaction has been provoked in me because she is extremely pretty.

Long blonde hair that curves around her face. No, she's not pretty. She's … oh shit. This reaction is nuclear. Don't look at her breasts. I keep my eyes fixed on hers. What colour are they? No idea. They're not looking away from mine. Don't look at her breasts. Shaking my hand.

I somehow manage to say: 'Yes. Pleased to meet you.'

I think I might've just woken up.

'Glyn.'

*

She's twenty-eight. Three years older than me. Feels like thirty. She's rolling a cigarette. What girl rolls her own cigarettes? A girl who rolls her own cigarettes, Brock. Get past it. She's a professional woman, respected in her field, and not the first one I've ever met. My paleontology lecturer was a woman, Doctor Ida Brown, and she was frightening too. But for different reasons. This Glyn Kay, she's got ten men and one kelpie paralysed from the jaw down, this first night out from Leigh Creek. The firelight is making shadows over the buttons of her blouse. I've got no idea what she's talking about, but she's just said something to me.

I say: 'Pardon?'

And she says: 'So why do they call you Dozy then, Gordon?'

'Um …' This probably tops my list of uncomfortable silences.

'Ah, that'd be obvious, wouldn't it?' Errol jokes over it, but she doesn't laugh. She doesn't look at him.

'Story for another time,' she smiles. At me. She says the word like it might have a different meaning in her language: *tiiiiime*. She's English, upper crust, but she's not a gel. She's something else. She grew up in Africa, taking pictures of giraffes. Stop looking at her breasts. Keep looking at her eyes. They're blue.

I say: 'Yeah.' Forgetting whatever it was she just said.

Tim leans across me to turn a log. 'Getting hard to watch you two, Dozy.'

He and Errol think I'm in with a chance. Where this thought lies on the scale of frightening, I don't know. Nothing's going to happen anyway. I have the close company of four miners, an engineer, a quantity surveyor and a journalist to prevent it. Fritz leans in close to me too. Nothing's going to happen here, except my understanding of why it's not right for certain women to work in certain fields.

I've lost the thread of conversation altogether when I hear Les, the journo and her boss, say: 'It would be good for Glyn to get some shots out at the hot springs – they are going to be a great attraction for the trail. Could that be arranged when we get to Mount Painter? I'd like to spend some time having a look at the mine workings, for my personal interest.' For the Departments of Army and Information: he's in on the secret; she's not. 'And we're on such a tight schedule. You're not interested in the mines are you, Glyn?'

'No,' she laughs. The miners are crushed. She has a smoky laugh. I could listen to it all night. She says: 'Are there more paintings out at the springs, Tim?' Cave paintings, she's asking. She held us up today for a bit, taking pictures of an ochre wallaby and calcite tracks under a sandstone overhang. She's keen that Les include something on the Aboriginal art for the paper and Tim couldn't be happier at her interest.

He says: 'Yeah, lots of paintings, Miss Kay. I'll show you all around up there, the spring at Paralana. Only about six mile, easy walking. But we would have to camp out, maybe two days, if the weather's not good.' There is no such thing as not good weather up here, Tim. 'We would need company, ay,' he says, meaning you can't have a white woman going out on her own with a black man. He looks at me: 'Dozy, you want to see them rocks up there, too, don't you?'

Bastard. 'I – but. No. I can't go off on some excursion, I'm the geo–'

Errol says: 'We'll be blasting, Doze, don't need you getting in the way for the first couple of days.'

Nine men and a dog looking at me – *go on* – as if I've got to do it for the team.

I know what's going on. A conspiracy. I say, 'Yeah, all right.'

I suppose it's a bridge I've got to cross. Nothing's going to happen, except for spending a couple of days with a girl. A smart and pretty girl who's saying, to me: 'Oh, well, it's decided then.' Looking under that curve of blonde hair that falls across her face, a little bit shy herself. Yeah. This'll do me good.

*

'Just keep following the track up, will youse, I've got things to do for a minute. I'll catch up,' says Tim ten minutes after we set out from the pits. The first of the charges is let off in Little Gem and Glyn says: 'So you didn't tell me, where's the nickname come from?'

'Ah, just, um.' I can't answer that. Yes, I can. I force myself to. 'It's a name a mate gave me in, um, Rabaul. A few years ago, in New Guinea. He's not around any more.'

'Oh, I see.' It takes her half a second to put it together. 'I mean, I don't see but, you know. Please, don't say any more. I'm sorry I brought it up again. I'm too curious sometimes. Mind if I call you Gordon then?'

'No. I prefer it, actually.' Her hand brushes against the back of mine and it's all right. It is good. I'm glad she's curious, and that she could keep a conversation with a fence post going if she had to.

She says: 'So tell me, you said you're from Nyngan – where exactly is that?'

I tell her: 'Between Dubbo and Bourke, over the border in New South Wales.'

'Bourke? I've heard of Bourke – that's a wool town, isn't it? You're a country boy; I knew it.'

'You did? What gives me away?' I laugh, for the first time in her company. I like the sound of our laughing together. I'm falling for her. Her hair is tied back from her face with a scarf and she is even more pretty. Glynis Kay. It's very good to be here with you. She has little feet, and a big swag on her back, but she keeps step with me.

We don't stop for cave paintings, or even photographs of the view. You wouldn't want the weather to change, would you. Somehow her hand ends up in mine and we've chatted away six miles, following Fritz, and then Tim's saying behind us: 'It's only a few yards over there, you see them rocks sticking up – that's the pool. You go a have a look. But don't drink that water – it's

Akurra's, no good for you. I'll get us some fresh water – I'll be a while. An hour or two.'

'All right,' I say.

Glyn says to the rocks: 'How lovely.'

We can see the spring steaming up from the granite boulders ahead. You could power the Transcontinental Express off the steam between us. I could love her now. I have to love her. I will.

But I'm not going to rush it.

I ask her, rushing it: 'You want to go in the spring?'

'Oh, I don't know,' she says, and her voice is as shaky as I am as we walk round the rocks. The granite here is pink and there are red dragonflies in the grasses at the edge. 'It looks very hot,' she says: 'Would it be safe to go in?'

'Um, I don't see why not.' I've started unbuttoning my shirt. 'I'll test it out first, if you want.'

'Mm,' she smiles but then she looks away from me, saying: 'Why is the spring so hot anyway?' Unrolling her swag onto the rocks and setting herself down on it. She doesn't want to go in the spring. Fair enough. I stop undressing myself.

'Um,' I say, trying to remember what she just asked as I sit by her. The spring. Hot. Why. Conversation. I say: 'It's probably the radioactive decay. I mean, the energy coming off all the pitchblende round here, as it breaks down. I mean, the uranium oxide … in it.' Sound a bit more thrilling, go on. 'Um. It makes the rocks get hot.'

'Mm.' She leans away from me. She's looking in the pocket of her swag and takes out a book. 'It's such a beautiful spot. Here. Isn't it.'

'Mm.' Geez. What do I do now? I want to kiss her. I want to love her. How?

She looks up from her book and smiles at me again. I will never understand what women mean with anything they do or say. I'm sure she wouldn't mind if I kissed her. I think she wants me to. But how? She's probably as nervous as I am. Take it easy. Whoa. Stop this line altogether. I could have got this completely wrong, couldn't I.

Ask her: 'What are you reading there?'

She says: 'Oh this?' Turning the cover towards me with one hand and reaching up to touch my face with the other. The touch of her fingers sends a radioactive wave through me, taking me out past Alpha Centauri. I am going to love Glynis Kay, right here, right now.

I look down, to steady my breath before I kiss her.

I look down at the book she's holding in her hand.

The title: *Too Much To Lose.*

By Bernie Cooper.

Bernie Cooper?

BERNIE

Out on the verandah, I watch the way Mitchell's shoulder kicks up with the shot, nothing out here to stop me seeing it over a hundred yards, or a hundred miles. I can watch the desert creeping out from the Centre here, a shimmering beige disease. I could stay inside and listen to the cracks of the rifle ripping through the stillness at a steady pace, or watch, from here. Be with him somehow, from here.

He's not alone out there. The dogs are with him: Tilly and Rex sit patiently, waiting for him to finish. And the dingo trapper, Ned Preston, is out there too. He goes over to Mitch now, asking him something; Ned has stopped by today to help dig the trenches for the sheep. It's so sad. This is the last of them on the station that haven't been sold or sent on agistment to Yass. Mitch couldn't sell these ewes, or justify feeding them when they're so sick it's a cruelty to keep them alive. Their lambs were born too weak and they all died as well; little ragdolls in the dust, eighteen of them. Didn't allow me to indulge in any bottle-feeding. I couldn't do anything for them. There's been no reason for me to be here at all these past four months, apart from not being able to leave Mitch.

Everyone else has left, his two stockmen and the cook; and the shearers didn't have to bother coming at all. Even the rabbits have left the district apparently. Despite knowing all this was happening, I had no idea how hard things could be out here. Mitch will be all right; the Lockharts have got plenty of assets to sell before they have to hock the Tom Roberts. Money's no comfort against having to shoot your stock, though. It makes Mr Paterson's silly Hay and Hell poem shameful, and it's making me a vegetarian. Or at least it's doubtful I'll ever eat lamb again after this. The worst drought in living memory, so it's been declared.

Mitch and Ned start swinging the sheep into the trench; sixty-three of them altogether today. Where there were once twenty thousand. All gone. As the sun starts to sink they shovel the grey dirt back over them, and that's that. The close of Hell Station, for the time being.

He waves to Ned as they part ways, and Ned waves his hat towards me as he gets up on his horse and rides off, back to the pub, the One Tree Hotel that's named for the one tree that exists between here and Booligal. It's half a mile from the pub and it's dead too. Where's our poem about that? Mitch starts walking back up to the homestead, rifle in one hand, shovels in the other, dog either side of white moleskins that are spattered in blood.

He gives me that crooked smile as he nears and asks me: 'You going to tell this story too, Dette?' His fortitude is breathtaking.

I say: 'Quite likely.' I've written a fair bit already about this quiet, forgotten war on the land, which never ceases. We cling round the edges of a continent that doesn't want us; no wonder we hold peace so dear. Perhaps that's why the Japs seem to have changed their minds about invading too: they came, they saw and said to themselves, these people are all mental, we can't possibly take them on. Mr Jacobs says it's sounding good, the inference being: hurry it along. *Too Much To Lose* is doing so well, he thinks he's going to have to reprint it. People seem to like it. Well, the thirty-seven people who turned up to his Ginger Jar soiree do, he said *Such a shame you couldn't join us*. Abe Jacobs must have some very loyal friends, mustn't he. But I'll finish this next one for the weary defeat in Mitchell's eyes alone. Someone's got to tell this tale, don't they.

'We'll head off in a couple of days,' he says, tapping my arm with the brim of his hat as he passes me. Kicking off his boots as he goes into the house. It's made of rammed earth, a squatter's cottage, a piece of wild west history. Part of me doesn't want to leave.

I can imagine myself living here, with the pedal wireless, and the kerosene lamps, and the old wood stove, and writing every day in between looking after Mitch. No telephone ringing; a timelessness in that. I love this quiet, and I do love Mitch. Our differences and needs are so complementary. A grazier's wife needs an inner life, or some kind of interest, or she'd be a real madwoman real quickly; and I have that life. I have a lot to give Mitch. It's time for me to make a decision.

'It'll be so good to see your mum,' I follow him in.

He shrugs and tosses a broody cluck over his shoulder, mocking her, as he pours himself a glass of water, but I'm sure he's looking forward to seeing her too. Mrs Lockhart has only been home herself for a few weeks, back from Wilcannia. Her sister Ivy had a stroke, not a bad one, and she's all right now. And I would love to be able to call Mrs Lockhart by her name, Bess. She's been like a mother to me, and I do want her to be my mother, really. It makes so much sense all round. It'll stop bush telegraph tongues from wagging, too, as they must be by now. *Ooo, what's that Bernadette Cooper doing out there with Mitch Lockhart? Living in sin?* We might as well be if desire can be counted as action. But no, I'm not going to let history repeat in that respect: Mrs Lockhart won't be getting a shotgun with this romance.

He raises his glass to me. 'Don't know what I might've done without you here, Dette. Thanks, for everything.' Scrubbing his Scotch twill and his moleskins and enduring the daily torment of his washing at the trough under the kitchen window. Service to the nation, don't need to thank me. But he just has, and I could let him have me here on the kitchen floor for it. What's it going to be like when I finally do let him have me? Then I will finally be in love with him, won't I?

That almost makes my mind up. Makes me *want* to be his wife. Even more surprisingly, makes me want for a child of my own. Against all this death, I suppose, I want a new life. I want a family of my own. I'm ready beyond a shred of doubt for that now.

But still, something is not letting go. Silly, it's as if I want a note from Hughie telling me it's all right. It's probably just proof what they say about first loves is true: you'll never have another like it.

It'll always niggle that I never heard from Gordon again; that's life. Tough. Can't wind back the clock.

I should consult the Sicilian oracle. Truly: I should tell Mrs Zoc now what I'm planning anyway, before anything's official. She's not going to be overjoyed, I don't imagine, but that's life too. I'll take Odds over to One Tree in the morning, call her from the pub. I've got to go over and settle the account for the groceries anyway.

Me and Mitchell: we're just like Odds and Pete. A little chestnut pony and a great white stallion. I hand him his clean clothes and fall into a little standing dream, of the day we rode the horses out here from Hay over Christmas, Mitchell Lockhart and me, thirty miles to Hell. Magical. It was some sort of gift after the loss of all the lambs, and he spent the next two days laughing before I could walk upright again. I can hear Gordon laughing too.

GORDON

'Oh, I *see*.' Glyn grabs my hand. 'You *know* Bernie Cooper? You were *engaged*?' she repeats what I've just told her, just as whacked, and she tells me: '*You're G.*'

'I'm what?'

'G. In the novel.' Glyn's eyes wide with it. 'The boy, in the book – he's the reason I'm reading it now for a third time. The way she's drawn him, so poetic, so tender, and she strings you along and along – is he a real boy or is he only in her dreams? Well, now I know. She's very clever. A real original. I've never read anything quite like it. How on earth did you let her get away from you? And *why*?'

'That's a long story.' And even then I'm not sure it would give an answer. I can't get past the idea that Bernie's written a novel. A novel? She can tell a story like there's no tomorrow, she can make my head spin with her words, but I can't think of a novel we've ever discussed, not a proper one. I don't read novels. I read science fiction magazines and she reads romances on the tram. I once tried to impress her with a quote from some writer – what was it? Some bullshit. Like *Wuthering Heights* is a film starring Merle Oberon and Laurence Olivier. But that was a million years ago ... Bernie? What's happened to you? I don't know this girl.

'Gordon? Gordon, are you all right?'

'Yeah,' I say. No: I am quilted. Flattened. Steamrolled into the granite beneath us. 'I'm sorry, I ...'

'Don't be sorry.' Glyn squeezes my hand. 'You're still in love with her, aren't you?' She whistles out across the ranges. 'I can hardly blame you.'

I can blame me. And her. She can write a novel, but she never wrote to me? Bernie Cooper: she's a flip. She always has been. Unpredictable. Unreadable. Chaotic. This is just like her. I tell Glyn: 'No, I'm not in love with her. Not any more.'

Glyn gives me the eyebrow arch. 'I think you'd better read the book then, my sweet G – because it sounds like *she's* in love with *you*.'

She picks the book up from where it's sitting between us on her swag and holds it in front of my face. It's small and white. It's got a flower in the middle, between the title and her name. Something about the flower seems familiar, and Glyn is telling me: 'This is too wild a coincidence. You know, I only picked this up because one of my girlfriends in Sydney dragged me along to one of her book club things in a cafe at the Cross. This new author, Bernie Cooper, this fearless wordsmith of a girl, rah rah rah, was supposed to be there, but had to send her apologies because of some Land Army commitment. I thought, well, a girl who can't come to her own party because she's driving a tractor, that's a girl whose story I'll bother to read. But there aren't any tractors in it. Her descriptions of the land, her longing for you ... It's beautiful, Gordon. That's not a word I overuse, and I don't believe in coincidences. Read it.'

That's what I'm doing when Tim comes back, to find me and Glyn with our backs to each other on our separate swags. I'm reading and she's writing in her notebook. 'Weird mob, you whitefellas,' he says. 'You drink that Akurra water?'

I can't answer him. I can't put this book down. But I don't know if it's about me. I don't know what it's about. These trees she keeps talking about, the love trees: *vanilla-limbs entwined, as our roots cling to the banks, as the river falls and falls away. Leaving us, thirsty, hungry. The corellas stripping our branching bare as crows feeding on a corpse. I shout them away! No! Go away! Leave us be.* Is this us? Where is she? I don't know, but then she's describing Coogee, the house in Arcadia Street, and she is describing us, in her bedroom. I recognise the wallpaper and the curtains – and me, kissing her. My words: *Only in my dreams. I only ever dream of you. I only ever will.*

The house is strange, though. Every time she goes back there, she flies there and she's always alone, dreaming and kissing G inside a blanket box that's full of little glass pearls and yards of silk that becomes a road. That all makes me wish I'd paid attention in English at school. Everything is confusing. Why's she alone? I flick back to the beginning, to page five, where she says: *My father died in the war and my mother after him of the heart she dropped on the kitchen tiles at the news.* That can't be true. This is fiction. She says so: *I was made by them of a fine, strong blarney thread, any finer and you wouldn't see me.* And the war she's talking about isn't this war in particular. It seems like any war, any time, this *blood-sucking creature that drags men away.* Go back to where I was at page seventy-four and: *You haven't been taken by the creature, have you, my darling G. That bunyip didn't catch you. You will come back to me. If I stay in this dream, you will come back to me.*

Turn the page: *Hughie, you wouldn't take Mum and Dad, and G too, would you?*

Jesus. She starts smashing Mrs Cooper's good china against the laundry steps. Another fifty pages of this and I'd like to do that too.

They stole all my words, all my letters to you, and they think they're so clever, that they've stolen you too, but they didn't count on what dreams can do. I steal you back from the Department of Cruelty. I take you back. If I scream across the water loud enough and long enough, you will hear me.

Come home, G. Tea's ready. Your Ricky Triumph is waiting for you round the side path. She'll rust to death if you don't come home soon. There'll be nothing left but a dirty red smudge on the bricks to say she was ever here at all. What's the red stuff made of? Iron something ending in -ite or -ide, I can't remember what you told me now. You have to come home to tell me again, G. Come home and lean me against the wall and tell me again and again.

But still you don't come. And still the tap of my steps up Heartbreak quickens with the pulse of the sea upon

*the cliffs, as I decide just for us, just for once or just
forever, not to doubt, not to slip or fall away, just in case,
beyond my dreams, the breeze decides that you will come
home today.*
THE END

The end?

No.

My pulse is fairly quick.

No. This is not the end.

I am coming home, wherever that might be. I have to find her.
What happened to her letters? What's happened to the Coopers? I
have to know. What happened to us, Bernie?

I say: 'I have to get back to Adelaide.' As if I might run
there today.

*

I almost do. I get to Leigh Creek in two days, do the drive in
under seven hours. Flying. Please, I want to be on a plane today,
to wherever she is. That might be a bit unlikely but that's what
I'm after anyway. I go round to the dark side of the Chemistry
Department first. A quarter to one Friday afternoon, I just catch
Major Gibbons before he leaves the office for lunch. 'Please, could
I use the phone? I've got to make an urgent call. To Sydney. It's a –
family emergency.'

He gives me an eyebrow, as if that's anything for him to be
bothered about. He says: 'Are the excavations underway?'

No, they're all sitting on their arses waiting for the pits to deliver
themselves. I say: 'Yes. The blasting is underway. Can I please use
the phone?'

'Shouldn't you be overseeing the quality of the ore?'

'Yes. I should. I will. When there's enough of it turned out for
me to look at. In a few days. Not long. It's all good. Can I please
use the phone? It's an emergency.'

'All right. But you'll have to pay for the call.'

'Fair enough.' I point to the phone. 'Please?'

He lifts it around on his desk to face me, but makes no attempt to leave. I lift the receiver and ask for the Coopers' number in Coogee. And then it rings. And rings.

'I'm sorry, sir, there is no answer at that number.'

I'm about to ask her to try again but then I think, no, try Mrs Zoc. She must be home. Please. And on the third ring, she is. 'Hello Zoccoli?'

'Mrs Zoc? It's Gordon.'

She screams: '*GORDON?*'

Gibbons gives me another eyebrow, glances at his watch.

'Yes, it's me.' I can hardly hear over the blasting underway in my head, and over Mrs Zoc's crying: 'You nearly kill me! My boy! Where have you been? What are you doing to me? You are worse than my sons!'

'I need to speak with Bernie – urgently.'

'Ah!' Mrs Zoc makes a sound like she's about to start slamming pots. 'Gordon! Bernadetta! She wants to marry another boy!'

'She what? Who?'

'This boy Mitchell Lockhart. He is a sheep farmer. She must not marry him. He is a good boy, but they are not good for a marriage. He loves his horse more than a woman. She telephones me only the morning before yesterday to say she wants to marry him. She wants a family, he is a good man, she is going to talk to his mother. I say you will not! But she won't listen to me. Gordon, she must not marry this Mitchell Lockhart. This is the worst mistake of her life.'

I don't know how to begin to respond to this. Mitchell Lockhart? I know the name well enough. I went to school with him. His mother is friends with Mrs Wells. Bernie wants to marry him? He's a grazier. For all that I've been convinced she's with someone else, this doesn't make any sense at all.

'Where is Bernie?'

'She telephones me from a place called One Tree, near the sheep farm. This farm is called Hell! She buys the groceries at the public house! Mama mia!'

Mama mia, all right. She's *living* with him? At Hell. I've never stopped there, but I know it: it's the Lockharts' run.

'You have to go and stop her, Gordon, stop her from this mistake. She says she will talk to Mrs Lockhart on the weekend when she goes back to Hay – this is *tomorrow*, Gordon. Please.'

Somehow I manage to say: 'But she's living with the bloke … ?'

'No! It is not like this, she keeps the house for him, don't you listen to anything else from anyone. She is a good girl. My girl! Gordon, you must go. Please!'

Go and do what? Tell Mitchell Lockhart I want my girl back off him? The last time I saw him he was at least a foot taller than me. School prefect, rugby captain, throwing a second-former up against the dormitory lockers for looking sideways at me. And who am I to step in on him anyway? He was here and I wasn't. But he's a grazier. Bernie can't marry a grazier. Flaming hell. Who am I to say what bloke she can marry? I'm not Gordon to her any more. I'm G. I'm a character in a novel.

I don't know what to do.

Yes I do. Have the guts. Life can be too short.

Tell Mrs Zoc: 'I'll do my best. I'm leaving now.'

Get back in the ute. I can't hang around here to wait for a plane. Start driving. What's it to Hay from here, three-fifty, four hundred miles? Straight along the Sturt Highway.

If I don't break an axle, I'll be there tonight.

*

I break more than an axle. I break approximately a hundred percent of the essential end of the ute. I don't think I've even made it out of the State. I don't actually know where I am, apart from somewhere near the Victorian border. I've just passed a one-pub, about five miles back along a battling stretch of irrigation fields. I didn't take note of the name. I've hit my head on the wheel.

I've hit a bull.

It's standing there looking at me, saying: *Go on, do that again and I'll be unhappy.*

Bastard. Big one.

Can't credit how I didn't see it sooner. I veered to the left when I did. It veered left too. I veered right. I even slowed down.

So did it. Giving me a choice: it or the only three trees in its territory. I've hit both.

I've punched the dash when I did. This is not good. I look at my hand. This is a bit worse than the last time I punched something. This is not good at all. I have to get to Hay and back and I've only got the weekend to do it. I have to stop Bernie from marrying Mitchell Lockhart. I have to be back picking through pitchblende by Wednesday: I told Errol I would. I'm going to hold up delivery of uranium to California. This is not good at all.

I get out of the car. I've got my wallet and my compass. I've got my water bottle. I look up the highway. At least five miles to the one-pub. I'll get there by sunset.

I have to get the vehicle off the road first, not that it's much of a road. It's a stock track with a bit of gravel on it. But I should get the ute past the trees so no one hits it travelling after dark. I buggerise around with the brake but the vehicle won't move. I can't push it. I can't take in a full breath. This is not good at all. Look at the wreck. It's fortunate that this is not a government vehicle. Sorry, Dad.

I look at the bull: fucking shit, go on, have a go.

He ignores me, dumps a load and walks away.

I start walking too. Sort of. A wagtail hops up the track ahead of me, then flies off. Yeah, good on you. I watch a cloud forming on the horizon to the south. It's green-bellied, carrying a storm. Probably hail. From Antarctica. It fills up the sky. It starts to rain.

Now, it starts to rain.

It starts to hail.

A lot.

SIX

FEBRUARY 1944 – AUGUST 1945

BERNIE

'Well, look who's come down the Paddock with the rain.' Mrs Lockhart sweeps down the hall, arms outstretched to receive her guests. Mrs Verity Fitzgerald and her daughter Jenny, from Yarranbulla Station via Coolabah. Getting out of Hay's taxicab, from the airstrip.

Mitch and I haven't been here half an hour, and Mrs Lockhart has been in some kind of a fluster since we arrived, as if the King might be coming. Mrs Lockhart doesn't fluster: the King would get yesterday's cake if he dared set foot. But these Fitzgeralds are obviously important to her. She's never mentioned them before, though, I don't think; nor has she said why they're here today. Mitch asked her just now and she told him, with a warning in her voice, to be especially kind to Jenny: the boy she was waiting for, Lindsay Someone, was killed in the Kokoda fighting last year, and soon afterwards she had a fall off her horse that put her in bed for several months, only just back on her feet.

She doesn't look too delicate to me stepping up onto the verandah: wholesome AWLA peachy poster-girl smile, even if she's gone a wee bit over with her peroxide and pluck.

'Look at you,' Mrs Lockhart coos over her. 'Haven't you grown since I last saw you, and haven't you grown prettily. Of course you have.'

Next second I'm shaking hands with this Jenny girl and saying: 'Pleased to meet you.' Be especially kind, make chat: 'Isn't the rain wonderful?'

'If it lasts,' the mother says, marking me down as irrelevant. 'Terribly dry at home,' she tisks to Mrs Lockhart. 'Nyngan's shocking.'

That was pointed; as if I'm deliberately being shut out of the conversation. Or perhaps I'm only a bit flustery myself. That storm last night; welcome, but fierce. It frightened me, brief as it was, and gave me a bad dream of being lost out on the plain, in the black mud. Remember that this Mrs Fitzgerald has had her own troubles lately too: possibly frightened that she might lose her only child to a bad fall, and whatever else the drought might have brought her.

Continue to be kind to Jenny; I ask her: 'Good trip? I've never been in a plane.'

'Oh, it was all right,' she smiles; quite a lovely smile really. 'It was my first time and I'm not in too much of a hurry to do it again.' Then she presses my hand and lowers her voice as we head inside: 'I'm so pleased to meet you. Our Gordon's Bernadette.'

Our Gordon's Bernadette? What an awful thing to say. Surely she knows that things didn't work out there. Would you like me to ask you how irrelevant *your* fiancé is these days? I say: 'Oh? Have you seen him lately?'

But Jenny Fitzgerald's platinum smile dims. 'No. We're all a bit worried about him. I thought you might have heard–'

'Oh, I'm sure he's all right.' I let out a little hideosity of a laugh, tinny, hollow, surprising me with its bitterness. My bitterness.

Mrs Fitzgerald and Mrs Lockhart disappear into the chintz tea roses as Jenny leans in to me and whispers: 'I *loved* your book – don't let on to Mum I've read it.'

Right. 'Thanks.' That's how it is on the bush telegraph, I see. I'm not a nice girl: I've written a dirty little book, with kissing in it. Kissing *your* Gordon.

'Mitch!' Jenny suddenly calls over my shoulder down the hall as she sees him.

And his face lights up with a bright and generous smile. 'Jen.'

Not a smile for a distant acquaintance. They know each other? Of course they do.

'How you going, Jen?' He is positively radiating goldness all over at the sight of her. 'You're not a kid any more, are you? Last time I saw you you were flying off the back of a horse at that gymkhana at Wagga.' They have history. Jenny flies off her horse regularly.

'Don't remind me,' she laughs. 'Please.'

'What did you do to yourself this time?' Mitch asks her.

'Will you be a darling, Bernadette, and bring in the tea?' Mrs Lockhart calls from the teal velveteen, and a bolt of resentment shoots up my spine: don't you Cinderella me. What's going on here? But I go and get the tea tray.

Come back to see Jenny has Mitch captivated with her story: '… so Dad says, *I told you so, no place for a woman. You're not coming mustering again.* I said: *Not with you, I'm not.*'

Mitch's laughter is the warmest sound; sharing it with her. I might as well not be in the room. And nothing could make me feel dirtier than I feel right now. All the things I've lately written about my want of Mitch. Smouldering in the bottom of my suitcase.

I hear Mrs Lockhart say: 'So you've still got five thousand on the run at Yarranbulla?

'Oh yes, Phil's confident we'll see it through,' Mrs Fitzgerald nods, sucking in her cheeks, arch and wry. 'But as you know, he's always had his eye out for a Riverina run. Waiting for a bargain.'

'Might have found yourself one, Verity dear, you just never know,' Mrs Lockhart chinkles.

And I see. How absolutely irrelevant I am. This is a squattocratic business transaction I'm witnessing. No such thing as romance when the farm is on the line. Mrs Lockhart is not going to sell one teacup's worth of assets. She's going to expand. Sell her son to finance it.

He doesn't mind. Stretches his legs out, making himself comfortable, in spotless moleskins I laundered and pressed. 'Yeah, they're still up at Yass, going all right. I'll head over that way in a week or two. Hey, you don't want come and have a look, do you? The ewes are …'

Ow. Ow. Ow.

You mean, rotten, selfish user. You bas–

Saved by the bell. The telephone rings. 'I'll get it,' and I leap out of the room to take it from the hall extension, down towards the kitchen.

'Ah Bernadetta?'

'Mrs Zoc?' No: go away. Had enough of an earbashing from you Wednesday morning. Ringing up now to tell me I told you so, because she is in fact a fortune teller.

She says: 'Is Gordon there yet?'

'What?' Isn't there a pill you can take against this?

'Gordon. I speak to him yesterday. Is he there yet?'

'No.' But I give her the benefit of the doubt. 'You actually spoke to him?'

'Yes, he called me, on the telephone.'

'Oh?' This is not real. I'm hearing voices. 'Where was he calling from?'

'I don't know, he didn't say where he was. I will check with the telephone people. I didn't ask him at the time. I was busy – I tell him your stupido plan. He said, *I'm leaving now*. He is not there?'

'No.' And I make a very firm decision with this: 'He's got till Tuesday to get here. I'll be on the next train back to Sydney. I'm coming home.'

*

Mrs Lockhart hugs me on the platform. 'Don't leave it too long. I don't want you to go at all, my darling.'

I'm stiff as a board in her arms. All my self-control twisted around not spluttering out at her what a humiliation this departure is. Don't have to tell her, though; she's dealt it to me. Still, it's Mitch I'd like to slap. Just one slap of the lion jaw, for leading me on. Letting me go on living in his house for all that time, doing Hughie knows what to my reputation. Ha! Leading myself on. And anyway, whatever the Lockharts have done to slight me, it's nothing personal; it's business. Hard people. Hard life. One the likes of Jenny Fitzgerald is more suited to. They can fly off the back of horses together, and perhaps I've only got the kick in the pants I deserved, and needed. I was going to settle for a man because, out of the corner of my eye, he reminded me of someone else.

'I'll telephone when I'm in.'

'Please.' Mrs Lockhart's tear is squeezed out of guilt as much as love. She says: 'It's about time you went and enjoyed being an authoress, though, isn't it?'

'Oh yes,' I laugh: tinny, hollow, bitter. I'll go and burn all those pages I wrote in Hell. I won't, there's a story somewhere in there I do want to tell. Oh, but Hughie, there won't be a bloke called M in it, will there. I'll be spending a bit of time imaginatively incinerating him, and wondering how I'm ever going to escape Gordon.

Why say *I'm leaving now* from Adelaide, as Mrs Zoc discovered easily enough, and not turn up at all? It doesn't take four days to get from Adelaide, unless you're going equestrian class. Or not coming.

No phone call. No nothing.

I think I know why.

He's made his decision too.

As I have made mine, more firmly with each day that's passed. I'm going back to Sydney, telling myself I told you so the whole way: should have stayed a spinster all along, shouldn't I.

GORDON

'Of all the irresponsible, reckless things that you could do – what did you think you were playing at, Brock?' Major Gibbons is doing his block. With every reason.

I am supposed to be in charge. I am supposed to be in the field inspecting pitchblende for death rays. It'll be all right. It's going to take a few weeks to get the ore out at any quantity by camel train anyway, and the road grading won't start for another month or so to speed it up. By which time I should have been released from the Royal Adelaide. But I don't say that. Major Gibbons is expecting an answer, for everyone to hear, across the general ward.

'Were you drunk?'

'No. I ...'

'Who's this Bernie character? Some mate of yours? Some *mate*.'

'No. I ...' It doesn't matter what the story is. I've stuffed up. I've failed in every conceivable way. I've destroyed my father's ute. I've lost Bernie for good. And almost killed another farmer's wife turning up on her doorstep at dusk and vomiting blood all over her front verandah. The Aerial Medical Service had to come from Broken Hill to get me and fly me back to Adelaide. I am suffering more embarrassment than I know what to do with, and it's worse than my ribs and my hand put together.

'Was that your mother yelling at you on the phone the other day?'

'No. I ...' I can't believe I've destroyed the ute. The only thing of value Dad ever owned. He bought it for a hundred and seventy-five pounds second-hand in '37. Cash, harder earned than I'll ever know. And I've destroyed it. Left it for scrap on the Sturt Highway. Dead dog up a hill backwards, and I am the dog.

'You don't have much to say for yourself, do you, Brock? Are you the right man for this job?'

That makes me sit up. 'Yes I am.' And not let him see that hurts quite a bit. 'I made a mistake, over a girl. It won't happen again. It's over.'

It's definitely over. I've seen the X-rays, thrown up again. It's over.

Ask him: 'Did someone pick up my rifle and my swag?'

'Least of your problems, Brock,' he says, walking away.

Stuff you too.

'Poor sweetheart.' Glyn comes in five minutes later to bring me down some more: 'Well, this'll hold things up a bit.'

'Not holding anything up. Not now.'

'What do you mean?' She touches my face.

'I'm not doing that again.' Please, get your hand off me.

She leaves it there. 'Oh. I see. But Gordon, don't be like that. Won't help things, you know. Flesh and bone heals, but hearts don't tend to fare as well – are you sure you'd want to give up that easily? I'd be rather flattered if a man crashed a car into a sturdy farm animal for me.' She's trying not to laugh.

'I'm not giving up,' I tell her, not finding this entertaining at all. 'I'm giving in.' And sensibly. Bernie's nearly killed me. Twice, if you think about it. It's becoming scientific law.

'If you say so.' Glyn kisses me, just long enough to get one extra embarrassment from the situation. 'I've got to go, flight to catch,' she says. 'Look me up in Sydney sometime?'

'Yeah.'

'Too right you will,' the old bloke in the bed next to me winks.

But I won't do any such thing. I look at my hand, black and blue, not resembling much of one. I busted it the first time over Jenny Fitzgerald, and this time ... The doctor's going to have another go at getting the jigsaw back together this afternoon. Fix it with some silver wire. Doctor Wilson, it is. Doctor Marjorie Wilson. Christ, and then I'm never going within cooee of a woman ever again.

BERNIE

'**B**ut he *did* say he was going to come to you, Bernadetta. Bernadetta, please. He said, *I do my best*. Something has happened. Don't look at me as if I am a stupido old woman.'

I've barely got my bags in the door and she's chasing me with a tin of almond shortbread.

I say: 'You are not a stupid old woman, Mrs Zoc. I love you, but you are a study of unfounded hope in denial of cold fact. There won't be a happy ending for us just because you happen to want one.'

'You!' Mrs Zoc whacks the biscuit tin down on the hall table. 'You are a bad girl!'

That's me.

There's a letter sticking out from under the biscuit tin, which she'd have brought in too. Handwritten address, quality envelope, looks personal. I whip it out and start to open it, but stop to shake out the cramp in my hand that's been annoying me all the way here; must've cricked a nerve, holding too much in my fist.

'You are a rude girl!' Mrs Zoc slams the door on her way out.

I kick Good Companion across the boards and into my room. Look at this old forget-me-not wallpaper. *Blawch*. It has to go. Years of fragrance of lamb fat ingrained in every room, no comfort any more. It's all got to go. Tomorrow. Mum'd be wanting to spruce the place by now at any rate, and I'm going to spruce it all right. Take to it with Dad's paint scraper, viciously, and swear a lot.

Go back to opening the letter. It's a card, elegant ivory, embossed with a butterfly in the top right corner.

Dear Miss Cooper
Just a brief note of congratulation and appreciation. Too
Much to Lose *is by far the most exciting novel I've read in*
ages, and I read a lot. I'm a devotee of Mrs Ellie Jacobs's book
club at the Ginger Jar. I hope to run into you there one day.
*   All the best*
*   Nerida Wesley*

Isn't that a timely slip of niceness. Thank you, Nerida Wesley. Funny it's found me here, though; she must have looked me up in the phone book. Knew there was a reason I kept that subscription going. To receive this sweet note, telling me: Bernie Cooper, it's time for you to face the music.

I've written a novel. One that people truly do seem to like. That is truly exciting. It's time to start promising myself that I will believe it is exciting. Soon.

*

Five weeks later, I've barely set foot out of the house, apart from to go down to the shops under the Aquarium for sustenance, and up to the Spot to buy five pounds' worth of paint I can't really afford with my now dwindling finances. Attacking the walls of Arcadia with the scraper has felt therapeutic, while I'm avoiding everyone and everything, including apologising to Mrs Zoc. I'll do that when she gets back from Townsville and I can swallow the idea that her Tony and Arthur have been returned to her, merrily poisoning the neighbour's mangoes and awaiting Manny's imminent release, while it remains that I have no one. And nothing but painting a house that should have my parents in it, and cursing Hughie for a mean and miserable Scot. Put a cork in it, Bernie, see if it floats. I'm going to start sprucing in the kitchen and work my way up to the front of the house. I've chosen cream with bottle-green trims for the cupboards; Mum would love it: crisp and smart.

I've just got the lid off the cream when the phone starts up. It'll be Mrs Lockhart to pester me about eating properly or some blither. 'Hello?'

'Bernie, is that you?' Man's voice: urgent.

'Yes, who's that?'

'Abe Jacobs,' he growls. 'You didn't tell me you'd come back to Sydney.'

'Oh, well, I've, ahhh, been flabbering about with this next story.' Lying my pants off.

'Oh, well, ahhh, that's good,' he teases. 'I've been arranging another reprint of that other one – you know, that old thing? That's six thousand copies now. Don't you think it's about time we met in person so that I can shake your hand?'

'Wowee. Six thousand copies?' Six thousand little paper birds flutter out of my chest with some sort of thrill at that figure.

'Six thousand copies, yes, and that's without a review, not even a mention in any of the women's magazines,' he says. 'You understand that?'

'Yes.' Six thousand copies word of mouth. I worked in advertising long enough to know what that means. I can probably stop worrying about the price of paint.

'Why don't you come down to the Ginger Jar, this evening – no occasion, just dinner. Come and meet my wife Ellie and a couple of friends. Seven o'clock. Please.'

'All right.' I've got six hours to find an excuse. I don't want to face this music at all, put my hand up to six thousand and say, yep, that's me, the girl who lost her G. Lost everything. Can't my story just be, without me? It's not a novel; it's my life. My heart. Part of me wishes I'd never written it. Substantial part. 'Mr Jacobs, I'm sorry, I–'

'Don't you think it's about time you started calling me Abe? We'll see you at seven. No excuses accepted.'

I'll find one.

Three kitchen cupboards later I find a letter in the post box when I go out to check, to get away from the paint fumes. Handwritten one, on cheap, lined paper.

Dear Miss Cooper
I have never written a letter to an author before and so I hope you don't find it presumptuous my writing to you. Your book, Too Much To Lose, *has made a profound impression upon me these past weeks that it has taken me to read it. I lost my boy, my son, Steven, in October last year, and although I'm sure your book is about a lost lover, the way you have worded things put me very much in the mind of the way I felt about my boy when he was a little fellow. I loved him with such a great ferocity, and I always will. You have reminded me that these emotions will never have an end and nor should they. In this way, I believe your words have helped save my sanity in my grief, perhaps given me a rope to hold on to in this lonely sea, to know that someone else feels as I do. Thank you, Miss Cooper.*
I hope the future treats you kindly and that your life is filled with as much love as you have so given outwards of yourself to the world.
Yours sincerely
Mrs FA Barry

Well.

There's what you'd call a gentle shove: pull yourself together, Missy. Piccoli meows around my ankles: that's correct. Little blobs of paint on my nails concur.

When I can move again, I go back inside. Open my wardrobe. My rainbow trove of pretty dresses I haven't worn for years. Close your eyes and pick one. Get out of here.

*

Into Kings Cross. I've never been to the Cross. It's only two minutes from Taylor Square, but I was never allowed to come here, Mum and Dad both terrorising me off any curiosity with tales of the cutthroat sly-grog razor gangs doing the bidding of brothel madams with guns. Now it's overrun with Americans, as I step off the tram.

'Hey cutie.' With a real Yankie drawl. Hundreds of American servicemen. Saxophones bellowing all up the road. Why did I come on the tram? I should have got a cab. It's dark now, quarter to seven, and 'Hey, wanna come dancing, baby doll,' translates into wanna be assaulted and thrown naked into a ditch? The atmosphere, the massed drunkenness, is panicking me. This isn't Sydney. But then I haven't been out of an evening in Sydney, anywhere, for about five years. I quicken my steps, almost running: look like I know where I'm going, in heels that no longer seem to belong to my feet.

But now I see it, the Ginger Jar: a sunburst leadlight over the name, windows either side filled with cakes, and I can smell the coffee beans from here. How long has it been since I've had a proper cup of coffee? Last time I had lunch with Yoohoo, I'd guess. A million years ago. A friendship that got away, too long ago. I just about fall through the door of this cafe, and I find I've fallen into the safety of plush, cosy calm. Nothing for the soldier in here. It's just a nice Continental cafe, people chatting over their meals.

'Is this Bernie?' I hear the growl and I turn to my left to see a man that matches the voice. He's a great big bearded bear.

'Abe?'

'It is!' He laughs like a bear. 'Wowee.'

The bear is shaking my hand in both of his, and I'm being introduced to Ellie, his wife, who's as tiny as he is huge, and then there's Ray Someone, the typesetter, and Rose Someone, about a dozen of their friends, all friendly faces, but this is not what I would call *just dinner*. I'm wondering how I'm going to keep my hands from shaking at the table as we all start sitting down.

'Miss Cooper, I'm Nerida,' says the voice next to me. 'Nerida Wesley. You might have got my note … ?' She's about my age, but there's something both distracted and accomplished about her, unruly auburn curls pushed back by a headband, and I just know she's been to university.

Nerves creep up my throat. 'Pleased to meet you, Nerida. Do call me Bernie.' Who do I sound like? Princess Primula of Primland.

But Nerida smiles, then blushes. 'Silly, I'm so wound up meeting you, though it feels as if I know you.'

'Yes, it's a bit odd, isn't it?' Please don't talk about the book, please don't talk about the book.

Her hand shakes as she picks up her napkin: good. She's not going to say any more; but then she does; she says: 'Oddly enough, a friend of a friend, Glyn Kay, knows your G too. Small world, and how glad of it I am, that I can meet you. I was shocked to hear about the car accident, though.'

Did she just say car accident? 'Car accident?'

Nerida Wesley goes fuchsia with it. 'You don't know?'

'No.'

'Oh, I'm terribly sorry. I just assumed–'

'Tell me, please, what accident?'

'He had a crash, driving out of Adelaide, I think she said.'

'Is he all right?'

'Well, I can't say I know. Glyn said he was in a bad way, with the Flying Doctor having to go out to pick him up. Quite the drama by the sounds of it. She'd just been to see him in the hospital when I spoke to her and–'

'When was this?'

'Oh ... four or five weeks ago.'

'Oh.' That would explain why he didn't make it to Hay.

He's had a car accident. And it's my fault.

I stand up at the table.

The universe spins, and then disappears altogether.

*

Ellie Jacobs brings me a bowl of soup. 'Here darling, just have some of the broth if you don't want to eat.'

I don't want to eat. I don't know where I am. Down the road at the Jacobs's apartment in Elizabeth Bay, wherever that is. I don't want to breathe until Abe Jacobs gets off the phone, first from this Glynis Kay, and then Adelaide Hospital, to tell me: 'Well, he was discharged last Thursday as fit to leave. This is good.'

If you can call a month in hospital good. A month to contemplate how much he despises me for hurting him – quite comprehensively, by the sounds of it. Why else didn't he call? Why didn't he let Mrs Zoc know? Too hurt to call … was he? I don't know. The gulf between us seems to stretch and stretch and stretch our tracks apart.

'Writers,' Abe growls, but not unkindly. 'I should have known there'd be a real boy somewhere.'

'Don't Abe,' Ellie chides him and reassures me, rubbing my hand: 'We'll find out where he is in the morning. I know someone at the university down there and Glyn said that's who he's working for, the Geology Department, it'll be easy.'

But it's not.

Adelaide University has no record of him as ever having worked there.

Gordon Brock. Not a real boy but a phantom in this six-penny gone wrong.

And I've had enough of this merry-go-round. I'm getting off. I've got the message. We're not meant to be together. Never were. The end.

GORDON

'This must be real special medicine.' Tim's looking at my hand, asking me why I would drive up from Adelaide looking like I should be on the cover of a pamphlet for war-industry safety. I've asked for him to come up and meet me here, beyond the yard of the pub at Hawker. A place he can't come to without police permission. That's just not right.

I've come here to tell Tim the truth, that's all, since I can't give him anything else of any worth. 'It's not medicine.'

'No bull,' he says. He knew that. 'What you getting them rocks for then?'

'For a weapon, against the Japs. It's a secret. Not even the miners know why we're mining it and they're under contract to keep quiet.'

'Bullshit.' Tim's interested now. 'What sort of weapon?'

'I don't know. There's a lot of scientists in America trying to work it out.'

He shakes his head, at all of us. 'That rock have Akurra in him. You won't know what he'll do. That why you were in such a hurry to get out of here before?'

'No.' I shake my head. 'That's a different story.'

'Well, go on then.' He wants to hear it.

Tell him the truth. 'I was chasing a girl. Didn't catch her. I hit a bull on the Sturt Highway instead.'

'No bull!' When he stops laughing he says: 'How'd the ute come out of it?'

'She didn't make it.'

When he stops laughing again, he says: 'What you come here today for then, ay? You want me to drive you up to Leigh?' He looks over at the jeep I've come up in, the government vehicle that I'm driving very responsibly.

I say: 'No. No reason. Just to say hello.'

'No bull.'

'No. No bull. I want to ask you something, though.'

'Go on.'

It's a question I already know the answer to, but I want to hear it from Tim. 'What do you think of all the mining and that? What does it mean to you?'

'Whitefella business,' he shrugs, as if we could put the rocks back in the ground now anyway. 'You wouldn't understand what I reckon.'

'Tell me anyway.'

'Them rocks, that land. It's our mother. What would you think if your mother got cut up and sent away?'

I tell him: 'I don't know. I haven't got a mother.'

'That's no good,' he says. He looks at me for a few seconds, with something like sympathy or pity, I can't tell. Then he smiles. 'Don't worry, Dozy. I've got five of them. Mum and four aunties, always giving me shit. They'd all be happy if you got rid of the Japs, but.'

'Why's that?'

'My little brother, Frank, he's over in New Guinea getting shot at. He's got to come home so they can get him with the frypan.'

I can't say anything to that. That's the worst bullshit I've ever heard.

He says, 'You come by here and say hello whenever you are round this way, ay?'

'Yeah, I will,' I tell him. And I will do that. I want to come back and go bush with Tim Gottlieb. One day. When the war is over.

*

The war ends on the nineteenth of October for me, with a memo come up with one of the truckies. *Brock, cease operations – effective immediately. Secure the sites as appropriate. Gibbons.*

Pack up, go home, see you later. Is our uranium the shit that's going to end it for the Japs? Who would know? We don't even know what happens to it once it gets to Adelaide, what hands it passes through. But I do know I've never been less angry or bothered about any of it. The war is ending for the Japs soon, however it comes. They'll be running out of iron ore now, as well as fuel, with the British taking back the Burma Road. It's not going to take much to knock them over. Death rays. I'm only curious about them now. What exactly are the Yanks going to do with them? End the war. Tomorrow would be good. Beyond that I don't care. So long as they get what's coming to them. On their mongrel knees begging for mercy would be good.

Errol rubs his hands together, walking up from fixing the grate over Little Gem. He says: 'Doze, my mate, my scholar, my gentleman, by geez I need a root.'

I say: 'I could probably do with one too.'

'What? You coming with me?'

'No thanks. Just checking to see if you're listening.' I tell him: 'I'm going home.'

I'm going to buy a vehicle and then I'm going home to Nyngan to put the property up for sale with the stock and station, tidy up my affairs. Then I'm going bush. I'll have a spell back out here with Tim and then I don't know what. Maybe I'll go into the Centre, go and look at a lot of haematite. See what it reckons. See what happens.

BERNIE

There's a poster up on the Aquarium noticeboard saying, *AMERICAN SERVICEMEN'S BALL*, for this coming Saturday. Someone's written *Thanks for coming* underneath it, a polite way of expressing the general the sentiment of the day: now buzz off. Hurry it up so we can roll up the barbed wire for another time and go back to being allowed to eat our own pork. Let's return to a gentler day when Saturday nights were reserved for biff between boaties and surfies. I won't be going to the ball, either way.

I pop into Cobber's, the tackle shop, for a box of worms, then head back up the bluff, round to Forget-Me-Not Bay, as I call it these days, to avoid thinking his name. Going to catch my tea. Not altogether recreational fishing: I'm going broke. Unfortunately second novels don't write themselves. *Too Much To Lose* has sold almost ten thousand copies, but the five percent royalty is so tiny I can't live off it. I need a job, or inspiration. Abe says give it time, and he's good for a loan if I need one – he'd blooping well want to be since I've provided him with a nice little earner.

Throw my line in and wonder if I should just go and get skunked for inspiration, like a proper writer. Loosen up the imagination. Hm. That poor Bernie Cooper, only wrote one book and then became an alco. Or I could have a steamy love affair with a tortured artist. Nerida did, sort of: she slept with her English professor and he minced up her heart so badly she's been trying to write about that for the last five years. We've already decided that if all else fails we'll just be penniless spinsters together. That wouldn't be so bad: Nerida is lovely. Funny and clever and she doesn't care at all that I'm not as educated as she is – that I thought the Angry Penguins might have been a new line of grim paperbacks, rather than a modern poetry magazine, from Melbourne. She thought that was hilarious; showed me a couple of issues and we flapped around the Ginger Jar connipting for hours over the nonsense in them. I could write about that, couldn't I? The good things that come from fainting at dinner parties. New friends. New ideas. None of which are settling into –

'Bernadetta! Bernadetta!' Mrs Zoc calls down from the top of the boat ramps.

Oh, here we go.

'I get a letter from the solicitor!' she shouts, takes it out of her apron pocket, waving it in the air.

I pull up my line and walk up to her.

'Mr Duncan writes to me,' she's so happy. Stuart Duncan, Mrs Lockhart's solicitor and the man who rescued my Arcadia from the wolves, he's been dealing with Mrs Zoc's application for naturalisation, which had been rejected, the Department of Complete Rubbish said, because the suspicions against her and her sons' *unlawful activities* had not been disproved. Not proved either, but there's no accounting for institutional stupidity, is there. Only lawyers win there.

I ask her: 'Well? What does it say?'

'He says he has sent the application back to the Department. We will prove we are Australian this time. He has a letter from Mrs Lockhart, and from the assistant superintendent of the camp at Hay, for my good character, and all of the receipts of all of the taxes we pay back to 1925. They put us in prison but we still pay our taxes!' She puts her hands on her hips, proud of it. 'We will win this time.'

She does a little compass dance on the grass. Thoroughly certifiable. Should she need more proof she's Australian?

I tell her: 'You will win.' Or die trying.

'But that is not all.' She keeps dancing her compass dance. 'Armando has telephoned me ...' A pause till she's turned the full circle, and then with a clap: 'He is getting married!'

She holds my hands and shouts: 'Aha!' Manny is getting married. The surf is crashing on Wedding Cake behind me, with that little ache that will never go away. But it's all right. Hundreds of people get married every day. I squeeze Mrs Zoc's hands in return. 'That's marvellous news.'

She says: 'Pick up your fishing things, you have dinner with me tonight, bella.' I gather my gear and all the way back down to Arcadia she fills me in with the details of Manny's triumph, finally getting permission from his Palermo girl's father, with the proviso that they settle in Coleambally now, where the girl, Gabriella, has some relatives on her mother's side. 'I understand this condition,' says Mrs Zoc, so overjoyed: 'Who with all their right marbles would live in Townsville with the cyclones and that bad wet air? It's not good for the health. And Coleambally, it is five hundred miles closer. Manny complains, *But Mama, I already build her the house in Shirbourne*, and I say, *So? You build the girl another house.*' She wants grandchildren. She's going to get them.

I'm wondering if they've yet got permission from the Department of Cruelty for Gabriella to come out from Sicily at all, when Mrs Zoc says: 'You will be next to be married, Bernadetta.'

I say: 'Shush.'

Shut my ears before she can get going with one of her theories about Gordon. Her present favourites are that I should remain in a state of suspended apprehension because it can take a man four times as long to heal as a woman, and I should be patient because everything will be resolved shortly now that Mount Vesuvius has erupted outside Napoli. I'm not listening to whatever she's going on about now we round the crest of Arcadia. I can see someone sitting on the brick fence out the front. A man. A uniformed one.

It's Colin, with a bunch of flowers.

Standing up, saying: 'Hey Bernie, I've come back for what's owing.'

For a moment I can't think what he's referring to, partly because of the burst of happiness I'm feeling at seeing he's home, and partly because he looks not much at all like my old boatie boy: he looks wonderful. Never thought I'd put the words *Colin Quinn* and *wonderful* together but here they are. He's grown into himself somehow.

I say: 'Hello Colin.'

Mrs Zoc mutters to me: 'Don't you dare.' Leaving me to despatch him.

I'm not sure if I want to.

He says: 'I'm home permanently, back at the Marrickville workshops.'

A man who's not going to go anywhere now. That's an attraction in itself.

He's defensive at my silence. 'I got promoted, that's all. There's nothing wrong with me.'

'No,' I tell him. 'There's nothing wrong with you at all, Colin Quinn. You're a picture. You're magnificent.'

I let him kiss me, here by the front fence, in full daylight. I give him what I promised him. But I don't put my rod or my tackle box down. He notices, and stops, and I tell him: 'I'm sorry, Colin, I'm not up for it, and I never will be. Go and find a girl who loves you. You deserve someone to love you.'

'You kill me, Bernie, you always have,' he says, and I can't bear the look on his face a second longer. I've known him since we were six, mandarin pips down the back of my blouse. He's survived Nazis in Greece, he's a decorated escapee, just come back from New Guinea, and I kill him.

I run into the house and shut the door on him, on all of it.

I shut myself in my room. My room that I painted the palest oyster-shell pink because it's my favourite of the colours that swirl in my jasper B.

Jasper B that worked its way under my pillow again sometime between wanting the merry-go-round to stop and starting on the skirting boards, because I thought it might help him heal, and me too, from all the hurts inflicted by cold hard circumstance. Because I can't let him go.

I've tried and I've tried. And I can't. I can't have Gordon, though. Not even Mrs Lockhart has been able to find him with all her connections, prime ministerial and countrywide. But I can have the next best thing: no one. And it's all right. I'm twenty-five years old. I don't need a man. I need a job.

GORDON

'They reckon ten million gone,' Jim Fletcher tells the head of his beer on the bar of the Court House.

'As many as that?' I say. You can mention the death of ten million sheep, but not one of your mates.

'That's only here, across New South Wales,' he says, letting out a big sigh.

'That's a lot of sheep,' I nod. A lot of sheep giving the topsoil a spell off cloven hooves, too. There's a lot of pasture gone. It's hard to imagine the grasses and the scrub coming back even if it started raining tomorrow.

'It'll have to break next year or it'll be the end of this town.' Jim shakes his head, as if he's down on his luck. He's got a new hat, and his boots look new too. Tough times suit him: when labour is scarce, contractors always do well. Contractors always do well anyway. *Maggots*, Dad would say under his hat in a bad mood. I look into the head of my beer as if I might find him there. I suppose I do.

I say: 'What pushed Dad to it? And don't give me any bullshit this time.'

That shocks Jim out of his hard luck. He puts down his glass. 'I never gave you any bullshit, Gunner. Never. I thought he was in Brewarrina – we all did – because that's what he said.'

'Where did you find him?'

'Jesus, kid.'

I'm upsetting Jim and he can be flaming well upset.

He says: 'Gunningbar Creek.'

So Dad didn't get much further than the back fence.

'No one thought anything of it till afterwards.' Jim is still wearing the guilt of it. I can see that plainly on his face. 'We were all round here, the wireless was going, and that Menzies is saying he regrets we're at war, and next minute your father's gone off. We thought he'd show up when you come home that November. He didn't. I don't know, Gunner. I suppose he didn't want to know about it, for a second time.'

Fair enough. It's what I've supposed myself. I just wanted to hear it.

Jim turns it on me: 'Where the bloody hell have you been yourself? You've had the women worried, thinking the worst for you. Bolting off the way you did, leaving my mare out there to wander.'

Thinking I might have followed Dad. I might have, for a minute or two. I didn't, though, because I'm not Dad.

I say: 'I've been around.' And then laugh at how that sounds. Exactly like Dad. So I tell him: 'I've been doing government work, but I can't talk about it.'

Jim's not interested in it anyway. He's never been interested much in the world outside his patch on the Paddock. He tells me: 'Jenny Fitzgerald give up waiting for you to show up – she's got herself married, a few months back now.'

I laugh again. 'Lucky escape for Jen – and lucky she wasn't waiting for me.'

'Don't bet on it, Gunner. Anyway, she's gone now, down to Hay it was.'

'Where all the good women go,' I tell no one in particular.

But Jim says: 'What do you mean by that?'

After all this time, I'm surprisingly still sore about the woman issue as I tell him: 'The girl I bolted out of here for when I went to work for that oil company. Bernadette Cooper. She married a bloke from Hay way too.'

'Rough country for a city girl,' Jim says, as if Nyngan isn't. 'Who'd she marry?'

'Bloke I went to school with. Mitchell Lockhart.'

Jim pushes his hat back off his forehead with a start. 'You sure about that?'

'Yeah, pretty sure. Why?'

'That's who Jenny Fitzgerald married.'

*

I don't tear off like a halfwit this time. It's been nearly a year since I did that. It's been almost five years since I've seen her. If she's not met someone else by now, she's a famous author, she's someone else. Doing her own thing. With a life that doesn't include me. There's so much gone on, for the both of us. I'm not sure if I want to see her myself anyway. Bullshit. I only have to think of those words of hers, from her novel. Her voice. Her face. The shape of her fingertips. I'm as stuck on her as I was when I was seventeen. I've loved Bernie Cooper for a long time. Nearly a decade. I'm going carefully about it now.

I'm driving up to Mrs Wells at Kyra for a cup of tea first, to apologise for my behaviour last time I came home. I have to apologise to Mrs Zoc as well. I'm ashamed of myself for not ringing her back. I don't know why I didn't. Too caught up with having the shits and not wanting to know, and then I just forgot about it. Forgot she'd be worried about me, more than she already was. I might have to build up a bit of courage for that apology.

Not for this one, though. Mrs Well comes out onto her verandah to see who's this turned up in a filthy second-hand army-surplus jeep down her drive. When she sees it's me she jumps and waves her hankie. 'Gordie!'

I could just stay here for the rest of my life and be treated like a five year old.

She says: 'Look at you. Darling heart. Aren't you a sight! Where on earth have you been?'

'Working,' I say: 'And not much shearing. I'm sorry about–'

'Don't bother with sorrys, Gordie. I know where you've been, even if I don't know the first thing. I saw it in your eyes. But look at you now! Oh you're marvellous, aren't you.'

In two seconds I'm being stuffed full of her fruitcake. It's good being five. Always room for another grandkid with Mrs Wells. There's twice as many photos of them all over the top of the piano as there was the last time I sat here.

She says: 'What brings you back today?'

'I'm going to sell Still Waiting,' I tell her, though I'm already having second thoughts. 'It's about time, don't you think?' And that's as close as I'll go to upsetting her about Dad.

'No!' She just about jumps off her seat with the upset. 'Don't do that.' I think she's wanting me to hold on to it for the same sentimental reasons already working on me, but then she says: 'Just wait till this drought breaks, see if you don't get a better price.'

I laugh. The floodwaters won't reach Still Waiting. They never do. But I say: 'All right, I'll wait.'

She says: 'It will break next Christmas – you mark my words. Hughie will arrive with trumpets. Then sell the year after.'

Righto. Mrs Wells has arranged it with the man in the sky. As if she might arrange the rest of my future, she says: 'It's about time you settled down. Have you got in touch with that Bernadette Cooper again yet? I've heard she's back in Sydney, poor girl. All on her own. You know you broke her heart. She's still holding a candle for you.'

I'm not happy I broke her heart. I know that feeling. And the only thing more incredible than the idea that she might still be waiting for me is the extent of the CWA telegraph. I would bet Mrs Wells has never even met Bernie, but she knows her. Knows what she had for breakfast. I'm resisting the urge now to bolt to her. Thank you for the information, ladies, I'll be on my way. But Mrs Wells has me fixed in my seat. She says: 'A hardworking girl, that one. Done a lot with the CWA and setting up with the Women's Land Army. Bess Lockhart has a lot of time for her. She's had a lot to contend with, too. And she wrote a book in amongst it all – did you know that?'

'Yeah.'

'Have you read it?' Mrs Wells looks like she has.

'Yeah.' That's embarrassing.

'Do you think it might be time to go and end the story well for her?'

'Yeah.' I go to get up from the table.

But Mrs Wells says: 'Stay right where you are and I'll get the clippers. You're not going anywhere with a daggy head like that.'

I submit to the shearing and put the essential pieces together. Slowly. Bernie's not married. She's had a lot to contend with. She's on her own, in Sydney, without her Mum and Dad. Everything she wrote in that novel is true. Except she left out the part that says I'm an idiot.

Mrs Wells says: 'And don't you go tearing off without a nap. You know you shouldn't drive for long stretches without resting your eyes – you might hit a bull or something.' She laughs. She knows all about that too.

She says: 'Mrs Morrison, up at Bourke, her nephew Harry was the AMS pilot that got you back to Adelaide. You were carrying on delirious about someone called Bernie, to the extent that Harry phoned the police to go and check the wreck for another boy. No one could work out who this Bernie might have been, till Mrs Morrison mentioned it as a curiosity to me when she came down for the Nyngan race day.'

Which means the entire country knows what an idiot I am.

'Isn't that funny?'

'Too funny.' I look at the telephone out in Mrs Wells's hallway. I could call Bernie right now. Tell her I love her right now. Tell her I'm sorry. But I'm not going to do that. I don't know how I could begin to tell her everything that needs to be said. Not going be worrying about the cost of a call while I'm saying it, either. No. I'm going to have a good night's sleep and drive to Sydney in the morning. After I've been to the bank. I've kept meaning to make a donation to the Flying Doctor and keep forgetting. Not forgetting any more. I'm pretty glad I'm alive.

BERNIE

For the umpteenth time I've walked past this sign in the window of Niagara: *WAITRESS WANTED*. And kept walking. Mum would be horrified: waitressing, in a milk bar. She did too much Cinderellering herself to want any daughter of hers to serve and clean up after others for a handful of coins. But I need the coins; and I don't want a proper job where I'd actually have to think. And there's not much choice at the moment. Ellie suggested Abe get me some proofreading work with Ray, the typesetter, and Abe roared, there's no other word for it: *When we need someone with expertise in creative grammar, I'll let you know.* I'm barely literate. I'd go back to school and learn some grammar but I haven't any blooping money for a course.

Still, I keep walking right past the sign at Niagara again, on my way down to the south end, for a surf. A few hundred others are of the same mind. The weather is perfect, Christmas holidays perfect, four o'clock in the afternoon and plenty have knocked off early to enjoy it at Coogee, and if I ignore the barbed wire I can almost believe the peace has been won. That Japan is not hanging on to this stupid war like a mad dog with a bone. No one really believes they're coming here any more, except for real estate agents who can't sell anything because no one's quite prepared to gamble on their surrender yet. It's only a matter of time before they're chased out of the islands. Hurry up and lose, I tell them, squinting out over the Pacific before I duck in under a wave. Give up, go home.

I imagine I'm a torpedo heading for Tokio. I want to blow them all to smithereens. I'll show them a new world order: where they have nothing left. *Whoomp.*

Stop it, Missy. Push out through the wash, push these black-cloud thoughts away. Try to. Out the back of the wave, I turn and look at the beach. The sand, the people, the prom, the sheds, all the Heartbreaks around the bay. My home, but somehow I am disconnected again. Treading water, that's all I seem to do, under a storm that never eventuates. Sometimes it seems as if I've cursed myself into believing that I won't write the end of *The Ending* until the war actually ends. At least it has a title now, I suppose.

Maybe I should go back to Hay for Christmas, see if it doesn't change my view and get things going. Just move. Mrs Lockhart's invited me for the holidays, and I would love to see her. I've missed her, I've missed Odds too, but I don't want to see Mitch. That still scrapes at me.

I get dumped on a wave coming back in now and that scrapes more, scraped half the skin off my knee, so I get out of the surf and lie on the sand to take the last of the sun and pretend that Gordon's lying next to me, his skin gone the colour of the red earth I am yet to see in reality. He's asking me if it's time to go up to Niagara for a malt. Another curse. Waiting for the war to end so that I can end things with him too.

So that I can actually cross the threshold of Niagara one day without crunching through the million irreparable pieces that my world has smashed into. There's a nicely overblown, overwrought proper-writerly metaphor. I let some tears fall into my towel, of frustration more than grief. I want this endless ache to end. I lie on the sand till my arms are numb under my head and my head is a blank.

Pages and pages and pages of blank.

'Hey Bernie!'

Look up and see Colin.

Oh no. Not today. Please.

But I see he's with a girl, a nice one, Beverley Someone, went to Sacred Heart. Bev … Reilly, yes. They wave, going for a walk after work, khaki cuffs rolled. Something good.

It's getting late, though, and the breeze is cooling. Teatime. Time to go home.

What for?

If I could turn myself into a damp smudge of sea and disappear into the sand I would.

GORDON

In the time it takes me to pull on the handbrake and get out of the jeep, Mrs Zoc is out her front door, across the lawn and screaming: 'Gordon! Where have you been? Gordon! What are you doing to me?' Slapping me hard across my face. Screaming the whole time: 'You didn't call. I thought you were dead. You are bad. Look at what you have done! I love you like my best son. And you – *you* – ' She gives me a mouthful of Italian I might not understand but take the meaning from anyway. I have a lot to answer for.

'I'm sorry.'

She raises her hand. I think she's going to hit me again but her eyes do the job instead. She says: 'Stupido.'

'I'm sorry.'

'And what you do to Bernadetta. You are–'

'Is she here?' If she is she's hiding. Half the street is looking out their front doors and someone's opened a window up the top of the flats on the corner.

'No.' Mrs Zoc sniffs. 'She went to the beach, to swim.'

'I'll wait here then.' Go and sit on her front fence. My face is still stinging. I thought Mrs Zoc would be upset but I wasn't expecting that. It's not as though I've been off having a party. I've also been driving all day, since dawn.

She comes over and puts her hand on my shoulder, and I almost flinch again, but she says: 'I love you, my boy. Don't you ever do that again.' Then she turns around and goes back in her house.

I look at the road, and wait.

BERNIE

The breeze has turned chilly coming off the water, blustering me up the steps, and I hold my parcel of hot chips against my chest to keep warm. I've eaten half of them already. Half of one thing less I've got to do this evening when I get in. Might go round and play gin rummy with Mrs Zoc.

Round the corner I see there's a great ugly army jeep sitting outside our Arcadia. There's something else to do, while we're playing gin rummy: I can complain about that eyesore. It's a dirty thing too, covered in dust.

Red dust.

And then I see the moleskins sitting on the fence. I see blue Scotch twill.

No. No, it's not him. Don't be ridiculous. I am the primary agent of cruelty to myself.

'Bernie?'

But it sounds like him.

He stands up.

It is him.

I can't move. I can't speak. I can't even say his name.

GORDON

She stares at me. Not just shocked. She's wary.

I should have called, or sent a note. You can't just turn up on the doorstep after five years. She looks sad. Holding it in. Her big brown eyes are so sad I'm ashamed she has to look at me.

I tell her: 'I'm sorry. Tell me to go and I'll go now.'

She shakes her head and says: 'Do you want a chip?'

'No. Thanks.'

She drops the chips. She says: 'Rock.'

Her arms are around me, and I'm home. Never leaving home again.

BERNIE

There couldn't be a more perfect ending for our second beginning. At the first touch of his lips on the top of my head, five years fall away with the ache and we start gathering and mending what's precious together. In my parents' bed. That's our bed from today. Somewhere inside it, inside his arms, I hear him say: 'Does this mean we're still engaged, or should I ask you again?' And I say, right into his heart: 'No. Definitely not. It's a jinx. Every time marriage comes into anything, terrible things happen. I don't want a wedding. I only want you.' He says: 'It's good to know you're still a flip.' Mental. And he gives me all I want again.

We tell each other our stories through the night, but we keep our secrets close. I'm not ever going to tell him all of what I've learned of grief, just as I'm sure he'll never tell me all of what happened in Rabaul. It's enough to know for now that a man called Errol Flynn saved his life rowing him almost back to Queensland. You couldn't make that story up, could you, and some stories can't be shared. I can't avoid telling him what happened to Mum, though, and when I do, it hurts him.

'I'm sorry, Bernie, I'm so sorry I wasn't here, with you.'

I tell him: 'Not your fault, and you're here now. And I want to make my family with you.' I hope it's already begun. I hope for as many children as Hughie will allow us.

My Rock says: 'We should get married. I want to marry you. We can just go to the registry if you want.'

I say: 'No. If we do that you'll get hit by a tram the next day.'

He laughs: 'You're beautiful.'

Oh I am, much more than beautiful, when he looks at me that way, those cool-warm grey eyes promising …

… So much that I get out of bed, put my dressing-gown on and tell him: 'I've got some work to do and you're a time-waster. Why don't you go outside and play.'

I go out to the kitchen table to Good Companion and I start writing the ending for *The Ending*. He goes and plays with the motorbike, then rides it into the university and he comes back with a job of his own. Course he does. Six months' research in chemical mineralogy, whatever that is. 'Looking at dirt under a microscope,' he says. 'See what this drought is doing to soil fertility.'

'Hm.' I push him back into bed, and I'm glad he's got somewhere to go in the morning, or I'd never get out of it again.

*

The Ending just happens. Like breathing. A little under three months it takes, but it feels like about three days. Fancy that. I'd wonder if I've dreamed this too, but for the dire state of my fingernails. I give the pages to Gordon first and he stays up all night reading the whole thing. It's thrilling to watch him read. I know it's good. I just know it this time. There's three parts to it: The Peace, set in the camp; The War, set out at Hell; and The Price, set here, in our bed. It's a story about what peace means and costs, from the end of the line and back, to here at the beginning. A compass circle dance. I knew exactly what I was doing this time. I could write my own catalogue copy on it. When he's finished, my Rock looks up at me and he says: 'You're amazing.'

I say: 'You are.'

Abe says he'll give me a hundred pounds for it, and then he phones back again to add: 'Could have wider appeal, this one. I'm thinking of sending it off to an old friend in New York. Don't get your hopes up, but let's see, eh?'

I do a cartwheel up the hall.

Then I drag Gordon up to the Ginger Jar, to get out of the kitchen as much as to celebrate. Not just finishing *The Ending*, but to celebrate us. Look at us. Three months he's been home. Three months in my bed. He's real. Nerida keeps making faces at me behind his back and mouthing: *No! Gorgeous!* Isn't he what? He's so wonderful to watch, meeting my friends, the way he has about him, genuinely interested in interesting people. Listening all the time, clearly. He's the thoroughly good article. He has more laugh lines on his face than frown lines. How did that happen? Miracles, each one of them, and I'm more in love with him than ever.

On the way home, walking up to Taylor Square for the tram, he squeezes my hand: 'Bernie, I really want to marry you. Before the obvious happens, you know. Please?'

'Oh all right.'

And at the tram stop at Taylor Square we kiss, dizzy with the wine and the trams and the buses and the crowds spinning round us. In the centre of the universe, we kiss.

An American calls out: 'Hey, baby doll, you're breaking my heart.'

Let it break. We deserve our peace. Every last caramel-tasting second of it.

*

Poor Mr Curtin, our Prime Minister, doesn't get to enjoy his. He's died, of heart failure, on the wireless just now: *Dead from a coronary occlusion brought on by the stress and worry of the war.* It wasn't quick like it was for Mum, but it's got him in the end and I doubt there's a dry eye in the country, from either side of the political fence. We're just about to win – for real. Rolling up the wire, the Nazis have surrendered, just waiting for the Japs to give it up and sign the papers too when they get tired of being bombed to smithereens in Tokio. And Mr Curtin, so responsible for this peace, for us men and women of Australia, has died. On the fifth of July. It seems too great a cost. With the death of the American President a couple of months ago now too, it seems a curse of peace.

The phone rings, and it's Mrs Lockhart, you could set your watch by her: 'Oh Bernadette dear, did you hear the news about

John Curtin? Oh yes, well that's what smoking and drinking will do to you, I don't care what anyone says. But poor Elsie, she loved him so. They had a cup of tea together around midnight, he said, *It's time you went to bed, Mother*, and she did, and then he left her around four. Terribly sad, but not wholly unexpected. Tell me, though, how are your wedding plans going?'

'Still for August, the eighteenth,' I say.

Disappointing her: 'But you know that's the weekend of the christening.' Mitch and Jen's little Elizabeth. 'You haven't been able to change it?'

'No.' And I lie again: 'It's the best date to fit in with Gordon's work.' The date doesn't matter. Gordon is beholden to no one but some bits of crystal something -ide to do with bauxite on some other research thing he's got and I just don't want to make a deal of our wedding. If we invite Mrs Lockhart, I have to invite Mitch and Jenny, which will mean all the Fitzgeralds will come, and then half of Nyngan, plus Dad's Aunty Ena from Gilgandra, and then the Quinns would have to come too, and then Mrs Cronin, and on and on it will go. I want to marry Gordon, not half the nation, and I want to do it without worrying about which church will horrify the least people. We're just going to pop round to the registry with Mrs Zoc and the Jacobs and have a party at the Ginger Jar afterwards. Full stop. I'm going to get to meet Errol Flynn. That's enough for me.

'Oh well darling, you two know what you're up to these days, don't you.'

Yes, I suppose we do. But when I hang up from Mrs Lockhart I go to Mum's blanket box and unfold the magnolia shantung of my wedding dress, run my hands across her thousand glass pearl beads, and I shiver as I hold it. Silly, winter and the silk is cold, and no doubt only a cloud rolled into my mind with Mr Curtin's leaving us, but I'm asking the pearls: is getting married the right thing to do at all?

Of course it is. I'm only having difficulty seeing myself in this dress because the obvious is happening right now, isn't it. Yes, Missy, it is. Curse is a month overdue, this magnolia shantung is bias cut across the hips, and wedding is six weeks away. Cutting it fine.

My smile curls around the vast warm ball of this idea as I look over at the package sitting on my dressing-table: the pages of *The Ending*, with Abe's red pencil scribbled all over them. He wants me to do a bit of rewriting, and I don't want to do that either. I just want to have a baby. Can't everything be perfect just as it is? Not quite. There's no such thing as a perfect manuscript. There's no such thing as curses that say something dreadful will happen to Gordon, to us, if we marry either. My emotions are all over the place because I'm going to have a baby.

I'm just thrilled out of my mind. Won't tell him yet, though. Not till I'm sure it's taken to me. Please baby, be ours this time.

GORDON

'You've never been much of a desk man, have you,' Professor Richardson says at the door to my desk on the lonely side of the Geology Department. It's no secret to him that I'm bored stupid here. Indoors, specks of aluminium hydroxide crystals floating before my eyes. If I didn't hate chemistry before, I do now.

'Have you given any more thought to your own research?' he asks me. He'd do anything he could to help me with it too. He still feels bad about recommending me to Southern Star. Not his fault; he didn't sign the contract. And I shake my head. I know what type of research I'd like to do. I want to study soils, strangely enough. I don't know what for yet, though. I want to go back to the Flinders Ranges. I want to go into the Centre too. I have to go bush to find out what I want to do. But I can't, can I. Can't take any kind of field work now. That would take me away from Bernie. I don't know what's wrong with me that I think I can't live without her for five minutes. The eight hours a day I spend here is hard enough. I'm amazed she doesn't find me annoying. Yet. I can't leave her alone.

Professor Richardson smiles, to himself as much as me. 'You'll probably make up your mind a bit more quickly once you're married and the children start to come along. They're always more expensive than you think.' I think he means that teaching will look attractive then. Doubtful. He asks me: 'When's the big day again?'

'Eighteenth of August,' I say and then, 'Shit,' as I remember, it's the sixth today. 'I'm supposed to be at the tailor for four o'clock – what's the time?' I look at my watch: it's five to.

Professor Richardson laughs as I run down the hall: 'All fun and games, young Brock – enjoy yourself.'

I bolt out onto Parramatta Road for the tram into town, but there's been an accident, a cart tipped over across the tracks. The traffic is banked up for miles. So I keep running, up Broadway, up George Street. At the cross of Goulburn the footpath is blocked with blokes, though. Uniforms spilling out of the pub there. Throwing their hats in the air. Falling over each other, celebrating. Someone's won big on a race, I think, when I hear one of them shout: 'It's over now. Oh yes, it's over now.'

'What's over?' I ask one of them as I push through the crowd. Is this finally it? I'm hopeful as I ask: 'The Japs have surrendered?'

'Not yet, mate,' he says: 'But they will now. The Yanks just dropped a twenty-thousand-ton bomb on them.'

That's a big bomb. And that's impossible. Nevertheless, the suit will have to wait for another minute. I go inside the pub, where there's a couple of dozen more uniforms but all of them quiet, around the wireless.

'*... early reports say that the city of Hiroshima has been wiped out by an atomic bomb dropped by the United States Strategic Air Force at eight am this morning Tokio time. The smoke and cloud of dust from the attack was said to have been visible one hundred and sixty miles out to sea.*'

Someone shouts: 'Big fucking bomb – *ooowee.*'

'Shut up or get out,' someone else shouts back.

'*... surrender or be annihilated is the message sent to the people of Japan by this new bomb. Early estimates are that the heart of the city of Hiroshima was completely burnt out by such an intense conflagration it could not be compared with a normal fire. The crew of a heavy bomber ten miles away felt the concussion like a close explosion of flak and could not believe what they saw. Mountains of smoke mushroomed up with the stem pointing downwards, some three thousand feet of boiling dust.*

'Exactly how such a fiercely destructive force was created remains secret, but it is understood that Washington military circles have been working closely on the project with top scientists for at least the last two years.

'We repeat, United States Strategic Air Force have dropped an atomic bomb on the city of Hiroshima, at eight am this morning Tokio time. Tens of thousands of Japanese will have been incinerated immediately by ...'

By one bomb. A super-incendiary. Charlie was right. A bit more super than I ever imagined.

It's too big.

Why have they dropped it now? They didn't have to do that, not now. The Japs were going to surrender anyway. No one has wanted to show them some rough vengeance more than me, but now ... ? They've destroyed a whole city with one bomb? The people there, they would have been cremated as they ran. Women and children and public servants just going into work. They would have had nowhere to run with that force.

One bomb? One.

I can't understand it but I do.

A new type of chaos has been let out into the world and I don't feel good about that. Not good at all. *That rock have Akurra in him. You won't know what he'll do.* This is your E=mc², whitefella.

My head fills with the screams of the marys and the kids and the chooks at the market, the shells falling all around us on Rabaul. To-An is shaking me: *You enemy, you fella enemy,* and I start to run again.

BERNIE

It's six-fifteen and I start to worry. Half an hour late is not even late. He's been delayed at the tailor, that's all. Just because he's always home by five forty-five doesn't mean he's been hit by a tram tonight. I'm becoming – I'm becoming a spud-watching housewife is what.

I put the wireless on, something not the ABC news. Find the soothing tones of 'The Wonderful World Of Plants' as I go and put one of Gordon's jumpers on over mine. It's damp and cold tonight and the wind is finding its way through the bricks. Not helping. He's been hit by a tram, and we'll know who and what to blame, won't we, Dad: petrol rations. He'd take the bike but it's so expensive to run and petrol is so precious. Do the patriotic thing and take the tram. And listen to yourself: you've just suggested it'd be safer to ride a motorbike than catch the tram. Does every woman go completely mental when they're pregnant or is it just me? And I'm only two months gone.

Six-thirty and the phone rings, and I pounce on it. 'Hello, Bernadette Cooper?'

'Oh hello, darling, it's only me.' It's Mrs Lockhart: 'I just wanted to check that you're all right.'

'I'm all right,' I say. Why wouldn't I be all right? Fear screams up the back of my neck again: Gordon's been hit by a tram on the Sturt Highway and the CWA has found out before me. I ask her: 'Why do you ask?'

'No reason, really. Just calling for a chat ...' Not *now*, I'm wailing inside: what if Gordon's trying to ring? She blithers on about this atomic bomb thing for several interminable minutes, '... you know, dear, I don't think John Curtin would have liked this at all. Always had a respect for that Jap tenacity ...'

'Did he?' I hope the Americans drop ten bombs on them, surrender or not.

'I can hear you're not with me, dear – did I catch you at dinner?'

'Hm yes,' I say. 'I'd better go.'

'All right. Bye bye, dear. Love to Gordon, bye bye.'

I go back to 'The Wonderful World Of Plants'. Did you know that aphids and lace bugs can be deterred from your roses by – another blooping bulletin on this bomb thing:

'Ladies and gentlemen, we are suspending our normal programming this evening for a special bulletin on what is expected to be the imminent surrender of the Japanese, followed by discussion of the topic from the physicist Doctor–'

I switch it off. I don't care what happens to the Japs. I only want to hear that it's finished and never think about them again.

I hear now, coming up the front path: 'You put your hands on me again and I'll–'

Gordon. Angry. Swearing. Very foul language. I open the door and he storms straight past me without a word. And Colin is behind him. Paying the cab fare, apologising to the driver and to me: 'Bernie, I'm sorry. He's drunk.'

Mrs Zoc is standing at the fence between our houses. 'Bernadetta, what is it?'

'I'll tell you later – don't worry,' I say, and push Colin down the hall. 'What's gone on?'

'I don't know,' Colin says. 'He was putting them away down at the Bay, one after the other. Not talking to anyone. I thought maybe you'd had a barney or something. Then this other bloke, behind him, he says something, and your bloke turns around and decks him. Knocks him flat. Don't worry, it was no one local.'

Oh good: so we won't have a mob of enraged surfies banging on the door in a minute.

'Stuff you.' Gordon's in the bedroom banging things around. I have a look through the doorway: he's packing.

'Gordon, what are you doing?'

He ignores me.

Colin says: 'I'm sorry. I thought bringing him here might calm him down. Don't worry, I'm not leaving you alone with him. There's something wrong in his head. The way he decked that bloke – it's not normal.'

'Gordon,' I ask him as if I might calm him down yet, 'what's happened?'

He's buckling the straps round his swag, ignoring me as if I don't exist at all.

'Gordon,' I raise my voice. 'You're frightening me.'

'Frightening you?' he says, but he doesn't look at me. 'There's plenty to be frightened of. Nothing's going to be the same from today. Can't put it back in the ground now.'

He walks straight past me, gets in the jeep and starts it up.

Colin yells after him: 'You'll kill someone.'

But he drives off, like a maniac.

Colin says: 'You didn't have a fight, did you.'

I shake my head: 'No.' Our ending was perfect. Almost.

'Do you want me to stay, in case he comes back?'

'No thanks, Colin.' I want to hide in the back of my wardrobe from whatever that thing was.

Mrs Zoc comes round to stay with me. To wonder what on earth we should do.

'Bella,' she says and she is frightened too, 'that boy has seen the Devil.'

SEVEN

AUGUST 1945 – JANUARY 1946

GORDON

I don't get further than the Spot. A dog runs out across the road and I nearly go through the window of a shop to avoid hitting it. I start to sober up, sitting here, looking in this shoe-shop window. My hand starts to hurt. I don't regret hitting that bloke. I heard: *What do you call an Abo with a stutter?* I didn't wait for the punchline. I had to hit him. Wrong time, wrong place, wrong psychopath. I should turn around, go home and explain that to Bernie. Right now.

But I sit here a while longer. The more I sit here, the quicker I sober up, and the more my hand hurts. I know what I've done. So I get out and go across the road to the Repat. I should turn myself in as a psychiatric patient. But I call Bernie from the public phone there instead.

She says: 'Bernadette Cooper?' Sad and wary.

I say: 'Bernie, it's me. I'm sorry, I ...'

She says: 'Hm?'

I say: 'I might be a while getting back. I think I've busted my hand.'

She says: 'Well, that's less than you deserve, isn't it. Don't expect me to come running up to get you, because I won't. I never will. I'll never throw myself after you. Do you understand that? Never.'

And she hangs up. Less than I deserve.

'Weren't you ever told to be careful with this hand?' the doctor says to me when he's had a look. He's a military doctor, used to talking to drunken halfwits, so he doesn't expect an answer. I think he's going to tell me I've done the worst job on it yet, but he says, 'It's not too bad. You're lucky. This time.'

Tell that to the rest of me. Stone cold, I drive back home just after midnight. I don't know how I do that. I've never been this tired. When I pull up I don't look at Mrs Zoc giving me the evil eye at her window. I don't need to.

Bernie's in bed, pretending to be asleep. I get in beside her.

She says with her back to me: 'You tell me exactly what went on tonight and why, or the whole thing's off. And I don't say that lightly – I'm pregnant, you know, and I'd rather raise a child alone than married to a violent alcoholic.'

Fair enough. I tell her everything I can think of to explain myself. Why I got so angry. I tell her about Johno and Rabaul. I tell her about the uranium and that it feels like I just incinerated twenty thousand kids. You'd never know if any of our ore was used. It's just ... it's all the chaos in my head. I've never said so much to anyone about anything and I've got no idea if I've made any sense. She doesn't say anything. Doesn't turn around. She doesn't move at all. I'm sick of the sound of my voice now too, so I say: 'I'm not making excuses, but that's why I went off. I hate myself more than anyone else. I'm not going to do this again.'

'No.' She says something finally. 'No, you won't do this again.'

BERNIE

'It's just on dawn and a currawong starts calling outside the window, *getup-getup getup-getup* ringing round the tiles under the gumdrop gable of our Californian verandah. Rock doesn't hear it; he's asleep now. I watch the sun light his face as it makes its way up the bluff and through the curtains. I knew that whatever he'd endured was awful beyond my understanding, but it's personal now ... *Ernie, he was a vulcanologist, he wouldn't hurt anyone. He didn't have a gun. They killed him first.* It's going to take me a long time to understand how he can have any compassion for the Japanese at all. How he could say, *I hate myself more than anyone else.*

But I look at his hand, all bandaged up there by his side, and I'm still cross too. Blockhead thug, whacking people in pubs. Never mind that: you will never walk past me like that again, as if I don't exist. Ever. You will *never* do that again.

No, he won't, that's a fact. There'll be no repetition of these events. How could there be? Man goes to pub for a drink to try to calm himself down because of a bomb in Japan, and whacks a complete stranger for making a joke about Aborigines. Why? Because his friend Johno had a theory about thermodynamics. Much of what Gordon said last night is beyond me, but this is a one-off.

Isn't it?

The war ruined them both. Mrs Lockhart's words keep coming back to me, corellas shredding a rivergum. Ross and Caroline Brock. That's what's kept me from sleeping at all. Bill and Peggy

Cooper. Our parents, all ruined by this. How can I ensure that this history will never repeat? What can I do differently? What can we do differently?

Not marry. That's the only sure thing. I touch my belly: you poor little lamb. Both parents mental. Hughie, do you listen in to this channel for a laugh?

My Rock groans into the pillow now: 'What's the time?'

I say: 'It doesn't matter. How are you feeling?'

'Shi– headache.'

'I bet you've got a cracker.'

GORDON

She phones the uni and tells Admin I slipped in the bath. No one's going to miss me, are they. I don't get out of bed. I can't, I'm that tired. She says: 'You stay there, sleep it off.' I sleep for three days. But then Professor Richardson calls on Friday, to talk to me, so I get up.

He says: 'A second bomb, yes, on another city, Nagasaki. But this one is a plutonium bomb.' He asks me: 'What's the difference between the plutonium and the uranium? Can you shed some light?'

Not really. I can't get past my own questions. Why didn't the Japs surrender on Tuesday? Why have the Americans dropped this second bomb? Because they wanted to see the difference between the crude uranium and the more unstable synthetic themselves. I tell Professor Richardson: 'Two protons. I don't know.'

'You don't sound well. When will we see you?'

'Monday.' I don't know. I'm not well.

I go and turn on the wireless. Bernie says: 'Don't.'

But I want to know: *Estimates of fifty to eighty thousand perished in each of the cities.*

She turns it off. She says: 'It's got nothing to do with you – it's not your fault.'

No, it's not. But I'm not rational. Nothing is. I turn the wireless back on. The Japs are arguing the terms of the ultimatum. That's almost admirable. Life goes on. The Japanese are flaming cracked as.

Monday morning, I get up. Face the day. Tell Bernie: 'Don't worry if I'm late. I will be with the tailor this time.'

She says: 'No, don't do that.' She's getting up too, putting on her dressing-gown, yawning. 'There's not going to be a wedding now.'

'What?' Don't do this to me. 'No. Please, Bernie, I–'

'Don't be silly, it's nothing like that. I just don't want to get married now.' She walks off, waving it away. I'm a pest.

'But you're pregnant,' I say, following her down the hall. 'We have to get married.'

'No. Not now. Maybe afterwards,' she says.

'After what?'

'Just no – shush, will you.' She closes the bathroom door on me. There's rational for you.

I walk down to the tram under some new weight of gravity. I can't believe nothing's changed. People going to work, schoolkids mucking up at the back of the tram, being told off. Don't they know how much has changed? America has just ransomed the whole planet. Until someone steals the science off them or works it out themselves. Then what? That's too cracked to contemplate. What are we doing bringing a baby into this?

I go into work, but I care about aluminium hydroxide about as much as I care for tinea, and it's annoying that I have to get a student in to write for me. I get the shits when I see he's started putting all the $Al(OH)3$ results in the $a\text{-}AlO(OH)$ column and mixed up my slides. I yell at him: 'Are you a fucking idiot?'

He's not. He goes and complains about me to Professor Richardson, who comes in to tell me to pull my head in. 'Why don't you go home, Gordon. The sun's not going to refuse to shine if you have another week or two off. You're obviously in pain.'

Not that kind of pain. It's just in my head. Splitting apart.

Bernie sees it at the door when I get in. She says: 'Unfortunately the universe doesn't stop expanding just so you can take a breath, does it. You need to rest.'

She is so much smarter than me. I love her so much. But I've got a chemical resistance going on here. I say: 'I don't want to rest.'

She says, not taking any bullshit: 'Go back to bed. Now.'

I go and sit on the edge of the bed. She sits next to me, and she holds me as she says: 'Grief, it's like sinking down into the bottom of a gluepot some days, isn't it.'

It is: that's exactly what it's like. How am I ever going to get out of here?

Errol turns up on the Wednesday, for the wedding we're not having this weekend. He says to Bernie as he belts in from Broken Hill: 'Well, hello there Mrs Not Brock. That was a good call – I wouldn't marry him either. He's too odd.'

I can't even smile, never mind shake his hand. He knows what's going on. He says to me as soon as we're alone: 'Brockie, mate, it's not the end of civilisation as we know it, crying shame that is. Trust me. It was going to be discovered eventually, wasn't it? It just happens to be now, and you and me, we just happen to be lucky, don't we. Could even be a good thing, you know, and I don't just mean for cheap electricity. Keep the bastards peaceful.'

'Yeah. I know,' I tell him. But I only want to listen to the wireless. The reports about the radiation poisoning coming in now. People who were otherwise unharmed by the bombing, several miles outside the field of destruction, are dying of some type of anaemia caused by the gamma rays. Doctors and nurses that have gone there to help, and those just gone for a look, they're dying too. Blood transfusions won't stop it. It's destroying their bone marrow and their skin. They're dying at a rate of a hundred a day.

How can I understand this as a reasonable result? I can't. I keep thinking: my rifle is out in the back shed. That could be a good thing. Some type of equilibrium. Fine line between guts and suicide.

Bernie turns it off. 'Go to bed. Now.'

Yes. That's probably a good idea.

BERNIE

'Come on, Gordon, get up.' I throw the blankets off him in the morning. 'I'm not cancelling life for your nervous breakdown.'

There's no light, no light at all in his eyes as he says: 'No. I'm not coming. I can't play tennis.'

True, he can't hold a racquet at the moment, but that's irrelevant. I say: 'You can play left-handed. It's not a competition match. It's a picnic. Get up, Rock. Abe's expecting us, and Errol didn't travel across the breadth of the State to watch you unravel, fascinating as that has been.'

'I'll look after her when you're gone, mate,' Errol calls out from the kitchen.

In your dreams, *mate*. Errol Flynn is exactly as his moniker suggests: a moustachioed, rum-swilling chaser of adventure and skirts. Who'd do anything for Gordon, and has done.

I tell him: 'That's right, Dozy, I'll have to marry Errol – you don't really want to condemn me to that life, do you?'

He says, seriously: 'My racquet needs restringing.'

'You don't need your racquet, darling, I was only joking about the tennis.'

He grunts. But he gets up. So defeated he's breaking my heart all over again and more. I promise his back: you're not going to die of this. I'm not going to let it happen. Not without a fight. This is the work of the Devil and there's only one way to deal with him, according to Mrs Zoc: stare him down. Give him a few hard truths.

I say: 'There's someone Abe wants us to meet, someone from New York.'

'Oh?' That gets his interest, thinking this is all about my stories. But it's not. He's up for some much harder truth than that today.

*

'Geez, I wouldn't have thought there was that much money in books,' Errol says, pulling the eyesore up outside the Jacobs's new Bellevue Hill pile.

I say: 'There's not – unless you're a publisher. A good one.' Abe and Ellie have done well for themselves, had a *good* war. Wonder Publications six-pennies grace every newsstand across the nation, and Angus & Robertson have just made them an offer for their nice little literary list. A clever pair, getting in before British Best Penguins flood the market again. Even this house was a post-Jap-invasion steal.

Ellie makes a dash for Gordon, dragging him inside with Errol, as Abe kisses me hello and whispers: 'The editor loves it – he's only waiting on the publisher to give the go-ahead.' In New York. My heart skips a beat, or thirty-seven. The Americans, this Fantail Paperback Company, are really going take *The Ending*? But Abe adds: 'They're going to take both books.'

'Don't say that.' My hand flies to my belly with the surprise, and I start to cry, wild crashing dump of emotions.

Abe hides me in his big bear arms and growls: 'Rough week, eh?'

'Yes. And you're horrible to ambush me like that with this news.' I look up at him and smile, and marvel, not only at Abe, but at whatever made Hughie decide to send us such good friends.

'Couldn't keep the burden of it to myself,' he smiles back. 'Come on,' he takes my hand: 'Come and meet Clara.'

By the time we've got through the house and out onto the lawn, Gordon's already met her. Clara Jacobowitz. She's fifteen, tall and skinny, with a smile so wide it'll take a few years for the rest of her to catch up with it. She's Abe's niece, from New York, via Poland and London and a chain of good friends. She's missed a lot of school the last few years and before the Nazis took her books and her school and most of her family away from her she loved mathematics.

Ellie's wasted no time getting onto the business end of it, instructing Gordon now: 'The exams for Sydney Girls are in October – you can tutor Clara for it, can't you?' Does our Gordon have a choice? No.

He laughs, as if the world has just returned to technicolour; he knows he's been had, and he turns to Clara: 'Sure. Where were you up to before?'

'Some calculus ...' she says, uncertain and awkward and then quickly talking about things with him that will never make a dot of sense to me. Such as nuclear physics.

But I do know one thing: when it comes to new world orders, I prefer the one where America has a big bomb, to the one where children of a particular religion are forced into hard labour in prison camps, or gassed to death. That's what the Nazis did, apparently. Murdered little girls with chestnut plaits and little boys with big blue eyes. Abe thinks it could be several million killed that way, all the Jews of Poland, including his eldest brother, Clara's grandfather, a story that will come out one day. Just as one day Gordon will see he did the right thing, the only thing. Everything's just as it should be because it can't be any other way.

While Gordon and Clara talk about mathematics, Errol Flynn is chasing Nerida Wesley around a tennis court in this back yard in Bellevue Hill, and I'm mouthing: 'No! Dangerous!' at her, to no avail. Nerida's gone for him after five minutes: she can write about him. Someone should.

GORDON

It's January and her bathers are straining around her belly. She's six months gone, but she still won't marry me. She says: *Who cares and who's going to know but us?* No one, if you don't include most of the country. It's embarrassing.

It's beautiful. She is. More beautiful every day. In her white sandshoes and her white bathers, she's walking across the rocks of her Forget-Me-Not Gordon Bay and she's caught a bream for her tea. Holding it up. 'Ha!' Showing me. She is a different species of human.

The shapes of her that say I'm going to be a father make me that happy sometimes I don't know what to do with the feeling. She wants as many kids as we can have: it's going to be expensive. Probably not financed by her writing. But who would know? The Americans want a third one from her. *And Afterwards*, she's thinking of calling it. Realistically, though, I'm going to be the primary financial contributor, and I have to make a decision, about work. I have a choice, between two desks. Get back into soil analysis at the CSIR in Canberra, or continue with chemical mineralogy in Sydney. Not much of a choice, but I can't take on any field work now, can I. I can't make Bernie live in Canberra, either. So I suppose it'll be Sydney. If I buckle down and get a doctorate, in Christ knows what, I'll get on permanent staff, teaching, job for life, good holidays. As many kids as Bernie wants. That's a plan.

Something else might come up, anyway. There's plenty of work around. A lot of rock and metal needed to rebuild the world. There's a lot of money going into industrial research. It's a good time to be in science, of any type. Unless you're into haematite. We do have a continent full of iron ore; I've seen the survey data. It's strange that it's not being dug up like there's no tomorrow. There'll be a racket behind that decision somewhere. Not my problem, though. It can stay in the ground forever for all I care. I've got nothing against mining: we've got nothing without it. I just don't want to be a part of it myself. I want to give more than –

'I'm hungry now, darling, can you … ?' Bernie hands me her fish. Wanting me to scale and gut it. She won't do anything like that any more; and she won't eat any meat other than fish. I want to give her everything but she only wants cake, ice cream, peaches and fish, often on the same plate.

I'm just about to ask her if she'll share some of it with me, it's a good-looking bream, when I hear what I think is a tremor. The rock groans. It's coming from the cliff face above us.

Bernie didn't hear it, though. I must've imagined it. She says: 'What's that funny look for?'

But then I hear it again. She does too. She turns around. 'What was that?'

'That's rock moving,' I say and I drop the fish as I pick her up and run for it, fully prepared to be embarrassed if I'm wrong. I'm moving fairly quickly, across the rocks with her over my shoulder. I don't stop until we're on the sand, almost up to the dinghy ramps at the back of the bay.

I've just put her down when it groans again, louder, and then it cracks. I look across the rocks: no one else fishing this side of the bay this arvo. That's good. And then it comes down. A slice of the cliff comes away from the face and smashes into the sea. Right where Bernie was sitting not two minutes ago. The spray of dust and water shoots higher than the cliff top. That's not something you see every day.

Bernie's fingernails are digging into my ankle at the sight, and I've come to my decision.

I'm not taking any job in a box. Life can be too short. There's too much else I want to see. Things I have to do. To know.

I look down at Bernie. She's still staring at the fresh-cut sandstone face and she's saying: 'Oh my God.'

Then she laughs. She sees it too: the power of it. This earth wasn't made for us: it makes itself. It just said so. Everything creates as much as it destroys.

That's it. I help her up and I have to say: 'What would you reckon if we went bush, the pair of us?'

She says: 'What, now?' squinting at me. I think she's going to tell me that's a new type of mental. She's going to have a baby sometime in April. She's not in any state to be going bush, not anywhere much at all.

But then she smiles. She presses her belly against me and puts her arms around my neck. And then she says: 'I thought you'd never ask.'

BERNIE

Monday, the twenty-first of January and the jeep is packed, the bills are paid up, and we set off, stopping first at Taylor Square for a formality at Darlinghurst Court of Petty Sessions on the way.

I seem to need a bit of a shove getting back out of the jeep for it, though. Somehow over the past fortnight I've gone from manageably plump to the size of a small planet. Baby is as excited as I am about it, kicking and tumbling inside, and I grab Rock's hand so he can feel it too: 'There it goes.'

'Yeah, good, Bernie.' He can't wait to push me indoors. I have far too much fun teasing him with it.

'Darling, I don't know what you get in a knot about – everyone's having a baby. Look.' Two, no three, getting on a Bondi tram right now. There have never been more pregnant women in a bunch at any one time. Can't open a newspaper or a magazine without a free pinny pattern. Every woman in the country is going to give birth in the next three to six months, and we no longer wear trousers because we can't fit into them.

He says: 'Yes, and they're all married, aren't they.'

'Oh don't–'

'Bernadetta! Gordon!' Mrs Zoc waves as we come through the doors of the court, and she rushes over to kiss us, as though we didn't just see each other half an hour ago in Arcadia.

She's lit up from the inside, so excited but trying hard to contain herself in these sombre surrounds. She's a little girl waiting for

Christmas for a present she mightily deserves. Mrs Zoc is becoming an Australiana today.

Once she's had a good public go at our belly herself, and called her soon-to-be daughter-in-law Gabriella over for go too, and they've both agreed it's a girl, again. While Manny and Gordon, hands in their pockets, pretend they don't know us.

'What names are you thinking of, Bernadetta?' Mrs Zoc asks the baby.

'I don't know,' I say.

As a man calls out from a door in the vault: 'Zoccoli – female. Z-O-C-C-O-L-I.'

Won't be that name. But Mrs Zoc jumps at it, her hand in the air: 'This is me!'

She darts across the foyer; this is her moment, her naturalisation ceremony is about to begin. She's so proud about all this she's even kept the notice the solicitor had to place in the paper, put it in a tiny frame on her mantelpiece: *I, Emilia Maria Giovanna Zoccoli, of Italian nationality, born at Palermo ... intend to apply for Naturalisation under the Nationality Act 1920.* Any objections, speak now, Australia, or forever hold your peace.

'Come,' says this court-clerkish man, directs her towards the door, and I've already started to cry. Hopeless: I'd cry at two flies walking up a wall these days.

Rock holds my hand as we follow her, our Mrs Zoc. Her back is as straight as an iron rod as she steps towards the desk, proud and elegant, black crepe and white hair. But she looks so small against all the imposing oak around her, my hand goes to my throat with a last moment fear: I'm sure the clerk is going to say the forms have been filled in incorrectly, or they've brought in the blasted English test they've been threatening to introduce to keep out the Continental Hordes and all the Italian POWs that want to stay, and she'll have to start the application all over again.

But he says, in his bored and harassed clerk's voice: 'Are you prepared to take the Oath of Allegiance?'

'I am,' she replies: just try to stop this train.

'After me: *I swear by Almighty God.*'

'*I swear by Almighty God.*' I swear she's even been working on flattening her vowels.

'*That I Emilia*' et cetera.

'*That I Emilia Maria Giovanna Zoccoli ...*' Will forever have a name that is music itself. Maybe Emilia would be a good name for baby ... Emily ... Emma? It is a girl, isn't it ... '*Will be faithful and bear true allegiance to His Majesty King George the Sixth, his heirs and successors, according to law. And that I will faithfully observe the laws of Australia and fulfil my duties as an Australian citizen.*'

'Sign here please, madam. You are now a naturalised Australian of the British Commonwealth.'

That's it? Sign the paper, on your way. For King George who? I don't like that. We're not British anything, not these days. But Mrs Zoc doesn't care. She turns from the desk, beaming, waving her certificate in the air.

And she stamps her foot: 'Bravo!'

'Come on, Mum.' Manny ushers her out before she starts dancing.

And Rock says: 'Come on, Bernie, we'd better get going, too, if we're going.' Already loosening his tie.

Oh, we're going all right.

'Bella,' Mrs Zoc holds my face in her hands, 'you telephone me every Sunday or I will die.'

'I'll call, don't worry.' If there's a phone, wherever we find ourselves on Sundays.

'Ah well,' she sighs, letting go, 'it could be worse, I suppose. At least you are not going to New York.'

No, we're not. At least not yet.

'Bella fortuna, bella,' she cries as she waves us some beautiful luck. 'Bella fortuna.'

*

As beautiful luck would have it, it starts raining as soon as we turn on to Parramatta Road. It rains all the way up the Great Western Highway and through the mountains to Blackheath, where Gordon frowns as if he might see into the Western Plains through solid cloud. 'Flaming trumpets, Bernie. You'd better phone Mrs Lockhart and check on the roads that way.'

'Oh my darling,' she says, 'you just caught me packing up. The levee's been breached at Wagga and we'll be next. The road's underwater at Narrandera,' and she couldn't be more thrilled about it either: Hughie's in town. The flood has finally come and there'll be pasture again over Hell this year. 'How are you carrying?' she says.

'I couldn't be better or rounder,' I tell her.

'Good girl,' she tells me. 'Come to us on your way back through, my darling, and please be married when you get here.'

'Hm.'

She says: 'I'd better rush, I've got Mitch lugging the settee into the attic.'

Of course you do.

'Bye bye, darling.'

'Bye bye.'

Rock says: 'What did she say?'

I say: 'She said no-go that way.'

Setting our course: we'll go northwest from here instead. To Nyngan. Tomorrow. Where the word is Gunningbar Creek breached all over Still Waiting last Wednesday, for the first time in living memory. And no one could be happier. Than me. At last I'm going to see the red earth that made the man I love.

*

Red mud after Narromine and he pulls the jeep up at the pub. 'It's going to be rough from here – how you travelling, really?'

'Good, really.'

He goes into the pub to ring Mrs Wells to check on the floodwaters there, and I walk up to the edge of the road, where the bitumen ends, red muddy puddle as far as I can see under a huge cobalt sky. I step into it and look down at my boots over my belly, my feet in this red earth, all my dreams coming true, the length and the breadth of the land we'll be travelling, the two of us, then three. I'm going to see Albert Namatjira's love trees for real. Somewhere.

I'm going to meet a man called Tim Gottlieb one day at any rate. We'll go up to Townsville at some point too, for Zoccoli mangoes off the tree, and for Rock to meet up with his friend Johno's dad. And when we get into the desert, he's going to teach me how to drive. A girl can't not know how to, not out there.

I look up again and there's an emu watching me from behind a fence, from a field beginning to sprout bright green paddock. He's looking doubtful about the prospect of the fat lady taking the wheel, looking to bolt. But I'm not worried. Not a dot. We'll all survive my learning to drive. My man can survive anything: he has a camp oven with bullet holes for vents to prove it, and I'll get that story out of him one day too.

'Bernie, look,' he says now, and I turn around and look at him, walking towards me, holding out something in his hand. It's a little flower, a tiny purple daisy, just like the ones in my hair comb. He says: 'I haven't seen one of these for a while.'

He puts it in my hand and tells me: 'This is home.'

I pick it up and look at it, look into its centre, and in its sunburst of pollen I see it: the fragile and the indestructible. The little specks of stardust we truly are.

But enough, I love you, and that is all there is to say.
John Curtin, to Elsie, January 1942

AUTHOR NOTE

This Red Earth, like *Black Diamonds* before it, is a work of fiction, inspired by history and a fascination for my beautiful and sometimes baffling country, its rich veins of colour, contradiction and character.

Here, at the end of the ending, I would like to remember for a moment the real men and women abandoned by circumstance and bad planning on New Britain in 1942. Lark Force, as it was called, was the military garrison of around fourteen hundred men stationed on the island, comprised of both AIF of the 2/22nd battalion and Volunteer New Guinea Rifles militia. Attached to this garrison were six nurses. There was also an unknown number of civilian men on the island at the time of the Japanese invasion. Of the men, some were killed in initial attempts to defend Rabaul, and at least one hundred and thirty were tortured and massacred at Tol, on Wide Bay, for no apparent military purpose. Those taken prisoner – eight hundred and forty-five AIF and two hundred and eight civilians – were unwittingly torpedoed by an American submarine en route to Japan, and all were lost. The casualty rate for Lark Force was the highest of any of the Allied forces during the war: ninety four percent of them were killed. Miraculously, though, all six nurses spent the duration of the war as prisoners in Tokyo and were returned to Australia at its conclusion.

On the home front, the Australian Women's Land Army was never fully recognised with official honours for their contribution to the war effort. Without them, Australia, as well as about a million American GIs, wouldn't have eaten too well.

Personally, I couldn't have done without the women who had a hand in the original publication of this novel: editors Cate Paterson, Julia Stiles and Emma Rafferty; cherished friends Jody Lee, Selwa Anthony and Narelle Woodberry; as well as Lou Johnson for her enthusiasm in respect of this new edition. Thank you, one and all. I'm also forever grateful to the National Library of Australia for their incredible database of archive materials, Trove; I could not have written this novel, or happily lost time procrastinating, without this resource. And I wouldn't have dreamed this dream at all without my wonderful, amazing real-life rock, Dean Brownlee.

Take a journey through time with Kim Kelly. You've never seen Australia like this before...

JEWEL SEA

Based on the true story of the loss of the luxury steamship *Koombana* to a vicious cyclone off the coast of North-Western Australia in 1912, **Jewel Sea** is a tale of fatal desire, theft and greed – of kindred spirits searching for each other, and for redemption.

WILD CHICORY

A journey from Ireland to Australia in the early 1900s, along threads of love, family, war and peace, *Wild Chicory* is a slice of ordinary life rich in history, folklore and fairy tale, and a portrait of the precious bond between a granddaughter, Brigid, and her grandmother, Nell.

PAPER DAISIES

A haunting tale of love, murder and misogyny. Unfolding at the dawn of 1901, as Australia at last becomes a nation and her women rally for the right to vote, **Paper Daisies** tells of the dangerous path one woman must tread to see justice done – and the man who lights her way.

THE BLUE MILE

Against the glittering backdrop of Sydney Harbour, **The Blue Mile** is a story of the cruelties of Great Depression poverty, the wild gamble a city took to build a bridge – a wonder of the world – and the risks only the brave will take for a chance to truly live and love.

BLACK DIAMONDS

From the foothills of the Blue Mountains to the battlefields of France, comes a story of war and coal. Told with freshness, verve and wit, **Black Diamonds** is the tale of a fierce young nation – Australia – and two fierce hearts who dare to discover what courage really means.

For links to all major retailers, please visit: kimkellyauthor.com/books/

KIM KELLY

Kim Kelly is the author of six novels exploring Australia and its history. Her stories shine a bright light on some forgotten corners of the past and tell the tales of ordinary people living through extraordinary times.

An editor and literary consultant by trade, stories fill her everyday – most nights, too – and it's love that fuels her intellectual engine. In fact, she takes love so seriously she once donated a kidney to her husband to prove it, and also to save his life.

Originally from Sydney, today Kim lives on a small rural property in central New South Wales just outside the tiny gold-rush village of Millthorpe, where the ghosts are mostly friendly and her grown sons regularly come home to graze.